AN OFFER HE CAN'T REFUSE

JOHN SALZONE

AN OFFER HE CAN'T REFUSE

ISBN: 978-1-963705-29-4

Published in the United States of America by Harbor Lane Books, LLC.

www.harborlanebooks.com

For Kevin, who asked me to write him a book.

xoxo

PROLOGUE

He had a hangover. A wickedly bad hangover. But that didn't make sense because he wasn't much of a drinker. So, why was his head pounding this way?

He had a vague memory of bottles of champagne being popped open last night. Flutes of fizzy amber liquid being drained one after another. They went down so smoothly!

He must have been celebrating. But what was the occasion?

He looked around the room for answers. He wasn't in his Upper East Side apartment.

It looked like he was in a hotel room.

In a king-size bed.

With black satin sheets.

And were those red rose petals scattered on the carpet and on top of the bedspread?

Rose petals?

He began to massage the sides of his head, trying to remember the night before, when he realized there was a ring on his left hand.

He waved it in front of his eyes and took a closer look. He wasn't wearing just any ring. He was wearing a gold wedding band.

What?

Before he could figure out why the band was on his finger, he heard a sound. A light snore.

He wasn't alone.

His eyes shifted to the right. There was a figure next to him, hidden under the bedspread.

It moved. The bedspread shifted and an arm stretched out.

With a hand wearing a gold wedding band—a wedding band that was identical to the one on his own finger.

But there was even a bigger problem.

It wasn't his fiancée, Vivianna Confetta, rumored Mafia princess from Bensonhurst, Brooklyn, in bed next to him.

It wasn't even a woman.

It was a man.

Apparently, his husband.

And then, it all came rushing back to him, right from the very beginning when this whole mess started...

CHAPTER
ONE

June 2022

"I think I might be pregnant."

Sebastian Fontana choked on his first sip of iced coffee and started to cough as he stared at his best friend. "What did you say?" he gasped, once he was able to catch his breath.

Vivianna Confetta took off her oversized Chanel sunglasses, folded them on the table, and gave Sebastian a knowing look. "You heard me."

"Say it again."

"I think I might be pregnant."

"Think or know?"

"I think." She shrugged. "Maybe?"

"Have you taken a pregnancy test yet?"

"No."

"Then, how do you know you're pregnant?"

"Because I'm late. I'm never late. Plus, my stomach has been queasy the last couple of days."

"Maybe you're coming down with something."

"In early June?" Vivianna shook her head. "No one gets sick in early June."

Sebastian chewed on his straw, then took another sip of his iced coffee. "I'm assuming this is a souvenir from your recent girls trip to Cancun? Or was it from the Florida pit stop you made on the way home when you visited your cousins?"

"Stop! You're making me sound like a tramp!"

Sebastian held up his hands. "No judgment. Everyone needs to get their groove on."

Vivianna nibbled on her lower lip. "There was a guy in Cancun."

"Didn't you use protection?"

Vivianna rolled her blue eyes, eyes that were close to the same bluish purple color of those of Sebastian's favorite movie star, Elizabeth Taylor. "Of course we used protection! But nothing is one hundred percent guaranteed to work."

Now, Sebastian was the one to give Vivianna a knowing look. "There's only one way to find out."

An expression of fear washed over Vivianna's face. "I know, I know! Don't pressure me."

But pressuring Vivi was what Sebastian was good at, ever since they'd become best friends in high school during their freshman year and were assigned to be lab partners in Basic Anatomy class and Vivi refused to dissect the pig they had to work on.

"If you don't do some cutting, you're going to get a failing grade," he had argued.

"I don't care. I can't do it."

"Yes, you can and you will," he had insisted, putting the scalpel in her hand and guiding it along the belly of the pig.

At first Vivi had shut her eyes, but eventually she'd popped them open and done some of the work when she realized the pig really was dead and wasn't going to squeal in pain.

There was the time she was afraid to go back for her driver's test after she failed it the first time.

"Who needs a driver's license," she had argued. "I'll just take public transit. Or walk. Or have someone drive me."

"Sure, you can do that. But what if you ever leave New York? You need a car in other parts of the country. Besides, think how cute you'd look in a red convertible. You know your mother would buy you one. All the other girls would be so jealous."

If there was one thing Vivi loved, it was making all the other girls jealous. She was definitely the alpha of her clique at St. Peter, Mary and Joseph Catholic High School and all the girls wanted to be her best friend. She wore the best clothes from the hottest designers—with all the latest accessories—had a hefty allowance, threw the best parties, and had every guy in school wanting to date her.

But Vivi only had eyes for one guy.

The one who constantly broke her heart. The one she kept going back to. Thankfully, he had been out of the picture for the last few years. Sebastian never offered advice when it came to Nico. He just listened. There were two levels to Vivi's relationship with Nico Morelli when things weren't good with him: either rant and rave in anger, or sob her heart out.

Even though Nico would never be his favorite person because of the way he had treated Sebastian when they were kids—and he wasn't going to dwell on that today—he wasn't going to judge him as a boyfriend.

Vivi and Nico's relationship was complicated. So complicated.

And Sebastian wasn't in the mood for complicated today. He was in the mood for brunch. But before ordering, he still felt like he had to give Vivi a bit of a nudge. He gazed at her over the top of his menu. They were sitting outdoors at Cafeteria, a restaurant in the heart of Chelsea with the most adorable waiters. It was a perfect Sunday morning, hinting at a perfect summer to come. He didn't want to ruin the mood, but he couldn't allow Vivi to pretend a problem didn't exist when there might actually be one.

"Have you thought about, you know, if you are—"

Vivi cut him off. "Don't say it!"

"But you did!"

"I said I *might* be pregnant. If you say it, it makes it sound more real. Like it could actually happen. Bash, what would I do with a baby?"

A baby would definitely turn Vivi's life upside down. Could he see her doing the single mother thing? Maybe, if she threw herself into it one hundred percent. But did she want to be a mother? She was thirty and a baby hadn't been in her plan, although there were certainly people in her life who could help her, including him.

But until they knew for sure... "Do you want me to be there when you take a pregnancy test?"

"You're sweet, but I'm a big girl. I can do this myself."

"Okay. But if you need me, you know I'll be there."

Vivi picked up her menu. "Enough about me. Tell me about your love life. Meet anyone new while I was away?"

Sebastian sighed. "What's there to tell? It's exactly the same as before you went on your travels. No prospects on the horizon. I've stopped going to those speed dating events at the Gay & Lesbian Center, and none of my gay friends have anyone to fix me up with. Maybe I should start asking my straight friends. How about you, Vivi? Got a man for me?"

"I wish I did, but I don't. I've told you, you should try some of those dating apps."

Sebastian stubbornly shook his head. "I've told you this many times. I'm an old-fashioned guy. I like doing things the old-fashioned way. I want to meet a guy in person. I want to make eye contact."

Vivi smirked. "You mean you want to cruise him."

Sebastian stuck his tongue out. "Make eye

contact and see if he responds. Make a connection. Then, start to talk, see if we have anything in common other than just a physical attraction and take it from there. You know it's more than just looks for me. You've always known that. It could be the way a guy walks into a room. Or the way he dresses. A colorful pocket swatch on his jacket or a tie with a crazy pattern that shouts, 'Look at me!' A book that he's reading; although these days, with Kindles and Nooks, you never know what anyone is reading anymore. Or the scent of his cologne as he walks by. Connecting in person is so much more fun than connecting online."

Sebastian tried to sound upbeat and confident, but sometimes he felt like Charlotte on that episode of *Sex and the City* where she had a meltdown during brunch, wailing, "I've been dating since I was fifteen. Where is he? I'm exhausted!"

That's how Sebastian felt. Exhausted, and wondering if he would ever find his Mr. Right. He met these guys, went on a handful of dates, thought something was building, and then, for whatever reason, things came to an end.

Among his most recent adventures in dating:

The guy who told him after three months of seeing each other that he reminded him too much of his verbally abusive ex-boyfriend. Uh, it took him three months to figure that out?

The guy who ghosted him, also after three months of dating, only to resurface six weeks later when he wanted Sebastian to join him in attending personal development classes that would get his acting career back on track. Sebastian did a little online research and discovered that the "classes" were actually a smoke screen for a cult. Next!

The guy he met at a gay mixer for singles thirty and over who said they had a lot in common because they were both wearing J. Crew jeans. And although the lighting at the event was dim, Sebastian could have sworn the guy had used liquid White-Out on two of his teeth. There was no exchange of contact info at the end of that night.

Like Charlotte said, exhausting.

Vivi placed her hand over Sebastian's. "Oh, Bash. Always the romantic. That's what I love about you. He's out there, I know he is. You're a catch. You just have to be patient. He's going to find you."

"I hope so." Sebastian closed his menu. "Okay, change of subject. No more talk about relationships. Let's talk about something else."

"How are things going at the bakery?"

Sebastian tried not to visibly flinch. It was like Vivi had pressed a hot poker against his flesh.

The bakery. Not exactly what he wanted to talk about. In fact, when he wasn't at the bakery, he tried to forget it even existed.

Sebastian had been a theater major in college. From the time he was a small boy, he loved to perform. Put him in front of an audience and he was ready to go. Singing. Dancing. Acting. He always got cast in school plays. He always got the lead in his high school and college musicals. He even had the chance to audition for a spot in a boy band, although he didn't get it.

He was good. But not good enough.

The first sign he should have paid attention to was when he applied to LaGuardia, the High School of Performing Arts in Manhattan, and didn't make the cut. Granted, famous alumni included Oscar nominee Timothee Chamalet and Oscar winner Adrien Brody, so the bar was set pretty high.

He should have realized all the way back then that not getting into LaGuardia meant he wasn't going to make it as an actor.

Yet, he ignored it. Maybe that's why he and Vivi were such close friends. They had so much in common. Like burying their heads in the sand when they didn't want to face a problem.

It wasn't like he didn't work after he graduated from college. Yes, there were some off, off, off, off-Broadway plays, but those hardly paid anything. There was also some dinner theatre, some work on cruise ships, a few chorus roles in actual Broadway shows, as well as being an extra on an episode of *Law & Order: SVU* and every other TV show filming in New York City.

But Sebastian's acting career was going nowhere. He could sing and dance and act, but he didn't seem to have the *it* factor that made him stand out in front of a casting director and made them want to hire him.

Jesse Tyler Ferguson had it when he was starting out. Michael Urie had it. Andrew Rannells, too. And let's not forget Jerry Mitchell. He'd gone from chorus boy to Tony-award winning director, complete with a house on Fire Island.

All these successful gays!

And then, there was him. Was he ever going to be successful? Was he ever going to get his big break? And if he didn't, what was he going to do with the rest of his life?

Like Vivi, he was already thirty. He'd been at

this for eight years. How much longer was he supposed to try before giving up? It was a question he was constantly asking himself.

If there was one thing Sebastian was, it was practical. No struggling actor was able to make it just by performing. They needed to have other sources of income. And like most actors and actresses, he did the cater-waiter thing, and any other part-time work he could find. Plus, he lived with a roommate, Liam, also an actor, to keep costs down.

He also did some baking on the side. It was just something he fell into. He had always liked experimenting in the kitchen, mixing different ingredients and flavors together and seeing what the end result would be. Sometimes it would be tasty. Other times, not so much.

One time after a show closed that he was in, he brought some of his baked goods to a cast party. His lemon zinger cookies were such a hit that some of his former castmates asked if he would take orders from them. Word of mouth spread and the next thing he knew, he was baking desserts for private parties. It wasn't a full-time business, but it supplemented what he made from performing and waitering.

Then, two years ago, during the busy holiday season, Vivi had told him her mother needed some part-time help at her Brooklyn bakery. Would he be interested in some hours? Never one to turn down work and extra cash, Sebastian said yes.

He worked at the bakery for a couple of weeks in December, making sure it was well stocked with panettone, struffoli, and mostaccioli. Then came some hours in the spring during the bakery's Easter rush where he made ricotta pies, canestrelli, and torta di Agnello, as well as Italian Easter egg cookies. Having made all those desserts with his Italian grandmothers when he was a child, it was a piece of cake, so to speak.

Then, last summer, when the bakery needed a new baker, Vivi's mother offered the job to Sebastian. Full-time with benefits.

Sebastian made a decision. It was time to be a grown-up. It was time to forget about being an actor and try to become something else.

A baker.

So, he accepted the offer. Because he had an idea of his own.

Eventually, he would open his own bakery. One in Manhattan's theatre district. The rent would probably be sky-high crazy, but he *knew* he was excellent at baking and that once people had a taste of his desserts, he'd have a line out his door every day.

His cookies, cakes, and pies were already in high demand.

He had thought he could use Vivi's mother's bakery as a launching pad for some of his desserts. Give them a trial run. See what was popular and what wasn't. People were always asking him when he was going to open up a bakery of his own, so why not?

But what did they say about the best laid plans?

No! He wasn't going to think about his job or baking. Not today. Today was his day off and he was having lunch with his best friend.

"What are you going to order?"

"I can't make up my mind." Vivi took another look at the menu. "It's a choice between the eggs Benedict and—" As soon as she said the words, Vivi started to gag. Then, she bolted from the table and ran for the ladies room.

Sebastian sighed. He didn't think Vivi was going to need that pregnancy test.

CHAPTER
TWO

"Sebastian!"

At the tone of his boss's voice, Sebastian cringed. He knew that tone. He knew what it meant.

His boss was not happy.

When it came to Big Viv, there were different tones of voice. There was the happy tone. The annoyed tone. The too soft tone.

And then, there was the dangerous tone. That's what he was hearing right now.

"Yes, Viv?" he called out.

"Can you come out here?"

Sebastian sighed and put down the bowl of vanilla cream he was making for cream puffs, wiping his hands on a dish towel as he left the kitchen and headed out to the main part of the bakery.

Viv's had been a Bensonhurst, Brooklyn mainstay for twenty-seven years. If one wanted the best in Italian desserts, they came to Viv's. Cheesecakes, cannolis, biscotti, cookies, as well as wedding cakes, birthday cakes, and custom cakes for every special occasion. It was located in an ideal location, right on a corner by a subway station and two bus stops, as well as six blocks away from the local high school.

So, there was always plenty of foot traffic in the bakery. In the mornings when commuters were heading off to the city for their jobs and kids were on their way to school, they stopped off for a quick sweet, not to mention after school when said students were on their way home and the commuters returned from Manhattan.

The bakery definitely had items that sold well, but times were changing. The neighborhood wasn't as Italian as it used to be, and palates were different. Not everyone wanted a biscotti. Not everyone wanted a sfogliatelle—or as non-Italians called them, lobster tails. They wanted cupcakes or brownies or cronuts. Not even donuts... cronuts!

Sebastian wanted to make sure the bakery didn't lose business, so sometimes he experimented and tried his hand at a baked good that Viv's didn't usually sell, just to see what would happen.

But Big Viv wasn't a fan of change, as evidenced by her hair, make-up, and wardrobe. If something worked for Big Viv, she stuck with it. Her ash blonde hair was a mixture of Farrah Fawcett's flip during the height of her *Charlie's Angels* fame and the big hair era of the eighties. It was just past her shoulders, but there was a lot of teasing and hairspray on top.

Speaking of the eighties, Big Viv loved her shoulder pads. She added them to all her tops. Plus, there was her gold jewelry, tight skirts, and high heels. Not to mention her generous bosom—thus, the nickname Big Viv, supposedly given to her in eighth grade when she developed at a pace much faster than her other female classmates, according to Vivi.

Put it all together and Big Viv always looked like she was ready for a night on the town. Which the older gentlemen in the neighborhood loved. Not to mention some of the younger ones. Because if there was one thing Big Viv knew how to do, it was flirt and wrap a guy around her little finger.

Well, straight guys, anyway. And Sebastian wasn't straight.

But, of course, no one ever made a romantic move on Big Viv. Rumor in the neighborhood was that she had started her bakery with Mafia money twenty-seven years ago after the death of her husband, Gino. Supposedly, she had caught the attention of a local foot soldier working for the Gambino crime family. Maybe she did. Maybe she didn't. No one in the neighborhood really knew because no one had ever seen Big Viv out and about with another man since her husband's death. There were always rumors and whispers—supposed sightings of her and her man in local restaurants or Little Italy or Atlantic City—but never any solid proof. And Sebastian had never brought the topic up with Vivi.

So, the fact that she might be in business—and in bed—with someone Mafia connected kept the men a respectable distance away.

And allowed Big Viv to rule with an iron fist. Not just at the bakery, but in all aspects of her life. Wherever Big Viv went in the neighborhood, she commanded respect and attention. No one was going to disagree or double cross her. Not if they knew what was good for them. No one really knew if she was Mafia connected, so why take the risk?

"What's up, Viv?" Sebastian asked, trying to sound innocent. "You look nice today."

And she did. Today's outfit was a wrap dress in a

bold pattern accessorized with gold hoop earrings and slave bracelets. Very Halston and Elsa Perrini. Sebastian had just finished binge-watching *Halston* on Netflix, so he was up on his seventies designers.

Big Viv jerked a thumb over her shoulder. "What does that sign say outside?

"Bakery?"

"It doesn't say bakery."

"It doesn't?" Sebastian had played this game before with Big Viv and he found it worked to his advantage to play dumb.

"It says *pasticerria*."

"Um, isn't that the Italian word for bakery?"

Big Viv ignored him. "That means we give our customers an authentic Italian experience." She pointed a French manicured finger at a display case and curled her red-coated lips. "What are those?"

"Cheesecake brownies."

Big Viv stared at Sebastian in horror. "Cheesecake brownies?"

Sebastian pulled out the almost empty tray. "Want to try one before they're sold out?"

"No! And why are you wasting my cream cheese on cheesecake brownies when you're supposed to be using it to make cheesecakes!"

"Everyone loves chocolate so I thought I would

try something a little more sophisticated. What's wrong with trying some new things? We can rotate them and see what sells and what doesn't."

"And what are we supposed to do with what doesn't sell?"

"Bring it to a homeless shelter?"

Big Viv waved a finger at Sebastian's face. "People from all over Brooklyn come to Viv's because of our desserts. Italian desserts! Cheesecake brownies aren't Italian! At Christmas and Easter and all the other holidays, we have lines out the door. I ain't messing with that! No more cheesecake brownies."

"But Viv..."

"No. You know the desserts that you're supposed to make, and that's what you're gonna make. I don't want to see any other desserts in these cases unless I've approved them. *Capisce?*"

"*Capisce.*"

Sebastian's Italian was rusty. Growing up, he had two sets of Italian grandparents living nearby, both sets fluent in English and Italian. When he was little, he could understand them and follow their conversations, but as he grew older, he spoke Italian less and less until finally he was only able to retain a handful of words and phrases. *Capisce* was one.

Pazienza was another, which he kept reminding himself to have. Eventually, Big Viv had to listen to him, right?

She peeked at the time on her diamond encrusted wristwatch. If there was one thing Big Viv also loved, it was her jewelry. "Where's Little Viv? She's late. She was supposed to have been here an hour ago. What could she possibly be doing?"

Sebastian shrugged, although he had a pretty good idea where Vivi was and what she was up to. But he wasn't going to tell Big Viv that her daughter was probably in a bathroom peeing on a stick.

CHAPTER
THREE

The stick was pink. A bright vivid pink.

Pink meant pregnant.

She could not be pregnant.

Vivi had lost count of how many pregnancy tests she had taken. First Response. E.P.T. Accu-Clear. Each and every time, the result was the same: Positive.

And positive meant pregnant.

Which meant, in bakery lingo, she had a bun in the oven.

Big Viv would go through the roof.

Granted, her mother was always nagging her for grandchildren, but if she knew her mother, she would want everything in the proper order: the engagement party, the bridal shower, and then the wedding.

How could this have happened?

Well, Vivi had a pretty clear idea of how. The only question was when. And with who?

Although, deep down in her gut, she had a pretty good idea who her baby's daddy was.

Nico Morelli. The nephew of her mother's nemesis, Deena DiGregorio.

For as long as Vivi could remember, her mother had been feuding with Deena. It had something to do with when the movie *Saturday Night Fever* was filming in Brooklyn. The two had once been best friends and had hatched up some sort of scheme to meet John Travolta. Seducing him had been the plan, although, how they didn't figure out their scheme was doomed to fail since there were two of them and only one John, she didn't know. Unless, of course, they had been imagining a three-way—and Vivi's mind did *not* want to go there—which wound up being a bust. But Deena had caught the eye of one of the movie's producers on location in Bay Ridge and it was goodbye Brooklyn, hello Hollywood! After that, their friendship was over and they became sworn enemies.

Because of that, Vivi and Nico couldn't have

anything to do with each other. Deena's younger sister, Angie, Nico's mother, made sure the feud lived on by being her sister's proxy in Brooklyn.

Vivi could still remember the first time she laid eyes on Nico. It was summer 2007 and it had been a scorcher. She was hanging out on the corner of Bay 25th and Benson with two girlfriends, licking an Italian lemon ice, although the heat was melting most of it away. She was sucking up the last bits of juice, the white paper cup all wet and squishy since she was almost done, when Nico and some of his friends walked by.

Actually, the better word would be *strutted* by. They were definitely showing off and trying to get their attention, having just finished a workout, because underneath their shorts and tank tops, their recently toned muscles were nicely on display, glistening with sweat from the gym and the summer heat.

"Like what you see?" Nico asked with what only could be described as Italian swagger.

Ordinarily, Vivi would have shut him down. Guys like Nico were all over Bensonhurst, showing off and thinking the world revolved around them.

"Like what *you* see?" Vivi tossed back. She didn't know why she said it. She just did.

"Your mother owns that bakery, right? The one on the corner of 25th?"

Vivi nodded. If he knew who her mother was, then he knew who she was. Her stomach did an excited little flutter. "How come I've never seen you in there?"

"Not allowed."

Vivi laughed. "Not allowed. Why not?"

He shrugged. "My ma told me to steer clear."

"Too bad. Sometimes, I work the counter."

"Where are you going to high school?"

"St. Peter, Mary, and Joseph."

"I go there, too. I'm going to be a sophomore."

"So am I."

"How come I've never seen you around?"

"Guess you weren't looking."

"I wouldn't forget someone as foxy as you."

Okay, the line was cheesy, but Vivi's stomach fluttered again. Even though he was in high school, Nico looked like a man. The guys in her class still looked like boys. He had that dark Italian look that she loved and his eyes were a piercing ice blue. Like a wolf. The Big Bad Wolf.

"Those uniforms aren't exactly flattering," she said.

"If you came to school looking like this, I'd definitely remember you."

Vivi threw her finished lemon ice wrapper into a trash can. "Maybe I'll see you in the fall." And she walked away, her two girlfriends following, knowing that Nico was watching the sway of her hips and the wiggle of her ass in her hot pink short shorts.

That September, on her first day of school as a sophomore, Vivi took extra care with her appearance. She went for the sexy Catholic school girl look with her uniform—skirt hiked a little bit higher than usual, white shirt unbuttoned as much as possible so a little bit of the lace of her bra was exposed, her blonde hair pulled back in a high, sleek ponytail, plus some extra mascara, blush, and lipstick to make her features pop.

Nico caught a glimpse of her as she walked into the school—she made sure to wear a pair of heels instead of flats—and you would have thought he was a cartoon wolf from the way his eyes nearly popped out of his head when he saw her.

She stopped to glance at him over her shoulder, slowly looking him over from head to toe before giving him a *slight* smile and turning away.

Mission accomplished.

For only five minutes. Because as soon as Sister

Mary Ingnacious manning the front desk caught sight of her, she was dragged by the ear into the main office and handed a jar of cold cream and a box of tissues.

"Off!" Sister Mary ordered. "All of it, off your face. And button up that shirt!"

That first year, Vivi and Nico didn't date. They saw each other in the halls at school and around the neighborhood, but Vivi was too busy with her advanced placement classes. The workload was insane, not to mention her extracurricular activities after school and helping out in the bakery.

And then, there was the Deena factor.

Vivi knew her mother was no fan of Deena DiGregorio. She'd been hearing about her mother's "backstabbing ex-best friend" all her life. Usually when they were channel surfing and Deena's face filled the TV screen. But what she didn't know was Nico's connection to Deena until he started telling her about his famous aunt who lived out in Hollywood. And then, once she started asking questions and all the pieces fell into place, she realized that Nico's Aunt Deena was the same Deena her mother loathed and despised. And she knew, without a doubt, that when Big Viv learned

Nico was Deena's nephew, he wouldn't be welcomed with open arms.

So, she chose to bide her time. Eventually, Nico would ask her out. And when he did, she'd worry about the consequences.

Until then, there were other guys. It was never anything serious. A few dates over a couple of weeks and then things would fizzle out. The guys were all perfectly nice. Sweet.

But nice and sweet wasn't what Vivi wanted.

She wanted a bad boy.

And while Nico wasn't exactly bad, he wasn't an angel, either. He was barely passing his classes, and more often than not he was in detention for cutting classes, arriving late, or just not following the rules. How he managed not to get expelled, she didn't know. She suspected his aunt might have had something to do with it since the new school library was named after her. The rumor was she'd given the school a hefty donation.

So, they kept circling each other until it was time for her Sweet Sixteen party in April 2008. Her mother pulled out all the stops, having the party at the best catering hall in Brooklyn, making sure there was a cocktail hour as well as a Viennese hour. It was like a mini-wedding and Vivi did *not* want to imagine how out of control her mother was going to be when it came to planning that day in the future. Maybe she'd elope. Ha! She could just imagine the meltdown her mother would have if she did that.

One day at school, she met Nico at his locker and handed him a pink envelope.

"What's this?" he asked.

"An invitation. To my Sweet Sixteen. I thought you could come."

Nico turned the envelope around in his hands. "Yeah?"

"Yeah."

And then, he gave her a smile. A smile that showed off his two dimples and made Vivi tingle from head to toe because she knew Nico didn't smile often. That smile was for her. Only for her.

"I think I can make it."

And he did.

He was there when the party started, and when it was time for the first dance, Vivi chose him to be her partner.

She knew her mother wasn't happy. She could see her glowering from the side of the dance floor. Obviously someone had already told her who Nico's aunt was.

But she didn't care. It was *her* party. Her Sweet

Sixteen. Tonight was her night. Anything she wanted was hers.

"You look like you stepped out of a fairytale," Nico told her as they danced. "Like a princess."

"Does that make you my prince?" Vivi asked.

Nico lowered his lips to hers and gave her a kiss. Their first. "You bet it does, Princess."

The kiss was like nothing Vivi had ever experienced before. It was soft and sweet, but as her party guests began to cheer them on, the kiss became something more. Deeper. More intimate.

And Vivi was in heaven.

Surprisingly, Big Viv didn't explode. In fact, at the end of the night, she didn't say anything to Vivi about Nico being at the party.

Maybe her mother was finally getting over her feud with Deena.

For the rest of the spring, Viv and Nico dated. Movies. Concerts. Hanging out with friends. There were car rides, too, in the back of Nico's Mustang (a gift from Aunt Deena for his sixteenth birthday) and explorations in the backseat. But nothing ever went too far.

Vivi should have known it was all too good to be true.

She should never have underestimated Big Viv. No one ever pulled a fast one on her.

During the last week of school, Big Viv made her announcement over breakfast. Vivi would be spending the summer in Italy with relatives.

Vivi blew up at her mother, telling her she knew what she was doing. She was trying to keep her away from Nico.

Big Vivi stared calmly at Vivi while she sipped her espresso. "Okay, don't go. Stay in Brooklyn and suffer in the heat."

"You mean it?"

"Would I say it if I didn't mean it?"

Vivi eyed her mother with suspicion. She never gave in without a fight.

Something was up.

Later that day, she found out exactly what when Nico told her his summer plans.

He would be spending the summer in California at his Aunt Deena's.

Apparently, Nico's mother was following the same game plan as Big Viv: Separate them in the hopes they would forget about each other.

Vivi expected Nico to be just as upset as she was at the thought of being sent away from Brooklyn. But much to her annoyance, he wasn't. *At all.* He was excited about going out to California and spending time with his aunt, visiting film sets and meeting celebrities. Driving out to Malibu and hitting the beaches to do some surfing. Vivi was an afterthought, which made her even angrier.

And resulted in their first break-up.

The most frustrating thing was that Nico didn't seem to get it. He was absolutely clueless.

"I'd be crazy to pass up this trip," he had said. "We'll be back together in September. What's the big deal about spending the summer apart?"

Vivi couldn't put it into words because then it would make her look shallow and insecure. It *was* a big deal because Deena was an actress who lived in Hollywood. It was a whole other world from Bensonhurst, Brooklyn, filled with beautiful people, especially beautiful young actresses.

How could she compete with that?

She couldn't. She was a bakery owner's daughter from Brooklyn who was called a Mafia princess behind her back. Because of rumors connected to her mother. Everyone in Bensonhurst said her mother had a secret boyfriend who was in the mob. There was no boyfriend. Sure, her mother was friends with Mafia wives who frequented the bakery, but that didn't make her mother Mafia related.

Since Nico wouldn't be in Brooklyn, Vivi decided to go to Italy, although she didn't tell her mother why she had changed her mind. She wasn't going to give her the satisfaction since she was sure Angie Morelli and Big Viv had been working together to sabotage Vivi and Nico's romance.

Well, mission accomplished.

The big surprise came when Vivi returned home for her junior year. All summer, she'd been imagining that she and Nico would get back together.

But Nico wasn't in Brooklyn. He had decided to stay in California with his aunt and finish high school there.

Vivi was devastated. It was like she was going through their break-up all over again.

In those days, the only way to keep in touch was either by phone call or mail. There was no social media. No Facebook. No Twitter. No Instagram. She had absolutely no idea what was going on in Nico's life.

Well, correction. Some customers who came into the bakery—those who loved to gossip—gave Big Viv updates. Things that Deena had relayed to Angie and others from the neighborhood whom she was still in touch with. Sometimes, Vivi was working in the bakery when these little tidbits were dropped. Other times, she heard them through the neighborhood grapevine herself.

There were so many different stories, but the end result was always the same. Nico was having a blast out in California. His grades had improved. He had new friends. He was trying his hand at acting. He even had a new girlfriend.

The news snuffed out whatever hope Vivi had that she and Nico would ever get back together.

The next time they saw each other was four years later when they were in college. It was during Christmas break and Vivi was working the counter at the bakery. At first, she wasn't sure it was him. How often had she imagined Nico coming back to Brooklyn for her?

But then, he gave her that smile. As soon as she saw those dimples, she knew it was him, and all those old feelings came rushing back.

"I thought your ma told you to steer clear of this bakery," she said, teasing him with the words he'd said the first time they met.

"Hello, Princess," he said. "You're just as beautiful as I remembered."

During the Christmas break, they picked up right where they left off. Only this time around, there was sex added into the intoxicating mix. Vivi certainly hadn't been a virgin at this point, but she'd often imagined what making love to Nico would be like.

She finally knew. It was everything and more.

The holiday break eventually came to an end, and they both went back to college with promises to keep in touch.

They didn't.

Over the years, there would be other reunions—secret trips to California she didn't tell her mother about—with promises of making things work between them. But they never did. Often their reunions ended with harsh words and tears and vows to never see each other again.

Until the next time.

Like this past spring. Nico was back in New York. They'd crossed paths again. Picked up where they left off.

And now, Vivi might be pregnant with his baby.

There was only one person who could help her. Her best friend.

CHAPTER
FOUR

Sebastian was experimenting with a cookie recipe.

He wanted to try and create a Reese's peanut butter cup in cookie form. Not a cookie necessarily filled with peanut butter, but a cookie with the taste combination of chocolate and peanut butter.

He thought he had finally figured it out. What he did was create two kinds of dough: peanut butter and chocolate. Then, he took a scoop of each and rolled them together into a neat ball before using the flat bottom of a glass and pressing each ball into a circle.

He had debated between using semisweet or bittersweet chocolate before deciding to go with bittersweet. It would give the cookie a smoother taste and balance out the sweetness of the peanut butter.

Now, all he had to do was bake them for fifteen minutes and sample the results.

By that time, however, his cooling cookies were forgotten when a panicked Vivi came rushing into the bakery's kitchen.

"Where's my mother?"

"Not here. I don't know where she went or when she'll be back." He held out a spatula with a cookie on it. "Want to try one? It's a new recipe."

Vivi shook her head.

"What's wrong? You never turn down one of my cookies." And then, Sebastian remembered. "You took the test," he said, putting down the spatula.

Vivi slowly nodded as she reached into her shoulder bag and pulled out a stick.

"And..."

Vivi handed it to him, and he saw the pink plus sign. "Pregnant?"

"Pregnant," she confirmed.

Sebastian closed the gap between him and Vivi and hugged her. She looked about ready to fall to pieces and he needed to stop that from happening. Vivi was never good when it came to stress. "Congratulations! This isn't a bad thing. You know that, right? You're going to have a baby! A little version of you!"

"Or Nico."

Hearing those words, Sebastian jerked back and Vivi clasped a hand over her mouth.

"Wait. Wait, wait, WAIT!" Sebastian exclaimed. "What do you mean 'or Nico?' I thought you had a one-night stand in Cancun."

"I did."

"Was that one-night stand with Nico?"

"No."

"Then, please fill in the blanks for me. What aren't you telling me?"

"Nico and I hooked up," Vivi admitted with a sigh. "A couple of times. Before I went away."

"What? When? Where?"

"Here. In New York City. This past spring."

"And you didn't tell me?" Sebastian tried not to sound hurt. He and Vivi told each other everything. If they weren't on the phone four or five times a day, they were constantly texting.

"There was nothing to tell. It ended before it even started."

"But how did it start? Or, rather, restart?"

Vivi sighed again. "How does it always restart? He came to the bakery one weekend while I was helping out behind the counter, we started talking, decided to go out to dinner—you know, for old times

—and the next thing I knew, we were in bed and back to being a couple."

"Not for very long," Sebastian pointed out.

"I don't want to get into it." Vivi's tone made it clear she would *not* be discussing it.

"Why didn't you tell me?"

"I know Nico's not your favorite person."

"For a number of reasons. The current one being he didn't bother to use a condom."

"This isn't his fault," Vivi said in his defense. "He offered to. And I'm on the pill, which obviously didn't work. We were caught up in the heat of the moment and it had been so long. You can figure out the rest."

Sebastian knew he had to tread carefully with his next words. He'd once tried to talk with Vivi about her relationship with Nico and she had shut him down with, "You've never been in love! Don't tell me what I should or shouldn't feel about him! You don't know what it's like."

The words had hurt. Deeply. Because Vivi had been right. He never had been in love. And he still wasn't. So, who was he to judge?

But he didn't want to see his best friend get hurt. Again.

And now there was a baby added to the mix.

"Why do you keep going back to him?"

Vivi sighed. "He was my first love," she said softly. "A part of me is always going to love him. Maybe I keep hoping it will work if we try again."

Sebastian's heart turned to mush. "Oh, Vivi." He gave her a tight hug. How could he scold her for something he wanted for himself? Who didn't want their own special someone?

But Nico? Nico Morelli? Vivi deserved so much better than him.

Sebastian and Nico had a history that went all the way back to their grammar school days when Nico used to bully him. Okay, maybe bully was the wrong word, but Nico had called the shots on the playground where he ruled when it came to sports and Sebastian didn't. So, when it came to picking teams, Sebastian was always chosen last. Or Nico told him to go hang out with the girls. And woe to Sebastian if he and Nico ever were on the same team together.

He could vividly remember eighth grade gym class.

Volleyball.

The one sport where you couldn't pretend you

were playing and run away from the ball in a rush of bodies the way you could when you played basketball or football. With volleyball you were stuck in one position and had to defend your turf, making sure the ball went back over the net.

He was on the same team as Nico and missed the ball that had come his way. Nico, who hated to lose, went ballistic, screaming, "Hit the ball, you fucking faggot!"

At the time, Sebastian didn't know if he was or wasn't gay. He'd started to wonder, but he didn't need his classmates wondering, too.

The rest of it was relentless teasing. Calling him teacher's pet. Poindexter. Shooting spitballs at his back or flicking his earlobes if he was sitting behind him in class. Elbowing him in the hallway as they went from one class to another so his books would fall to the floor. Messing his hair if he walked by in the cafeteria.

All silly juvenile stuff. Some might call it boys being boys, but deep down, Sebastian always wondered if the reason Nico picked on him, if the reason he made fun of him, was because he knew Sebastian was gay.

He never failed to make Sebastian feel less than.

And someone like that wasn't good enough for his best friend.

He remembered when Vivi first started dating Nico. Sebastian had been horrified. He was expected to share his best friend with the person who made his life torture? Whom he went out of his way to avoid?

But Nico seemed to get that a bond existed between Sebastian and Vivi, and there wasn't going to be anything he could do about it.

So, they learned to co-exist.

Whenever Vivi was around Sebastian, Nico was always on his best behavior. There was never any teasing or name calling. But when she wasn't around, it was the same as always. Sometimes even worse.

Sebastian put the past behind him and refocused his attention on Vivi. "If you're not sure who the father is, then you're going to have to take a paternity test."

"I know, I know." Vivi reached for a cookie and began munching on it.

"And then, once you know? If it *is* Nico's baby?"

"I can't think about that right now," Vivi said, finishing the cookie in two bites and reaching for another. "These are good. New recipe?"

Sebastian ignored the compliment. He knew what she was trying to do. Avoid the topic.

"Here's something else to think about. Or should I say worry about? What's your mother's reaction going to be when she finds out?"

Vivi didn't answer. Instead, she closed her eyes, finished her second cookie and reached for a third.

CHAPTER
FIVE

"Viv!"

Big Viv kept walking, pretending she hadn't heard Carla D'Bruzzi call out her name. She was only a few feet away from Vivi's front door. All she had to do was get the key in the lock, open the door, and she'd be home free.

But wouldn't you know it? The key was somewhere at the bottom of her shoulder bag. As she desperately searched for the key that would bring her sweet escape, Carla caught up with her, poking her in the arm.

"Hey, Viv! Didn't you hear me?"

Big Viv plastered a smile on her face as she turned. After all, Carla was someone she had known since high school, and also a customer at the bakery.

Poor Carla. She'd always been an outsider, desperately trying to fit in with the other girls who, sensing she wanted to belong, purposely kept her out. They hadn't been close friends back then, but Big Viv had never been unkind to her. Not even now, when she sometimes got on her nerves.

Carla came from a huge family—eight siblings who were all married with batches of kids—so she always bought her desserts at the bakery for family gatherings. Carla had never gotten married. For whatever reason, she had never found the right guy. Compared to her two older sisters, she wasn't a knockout, but she was nice looking with pretty green eyes and a slight overbite that two years of braces hadn't been able to fix. Her shoulder-length brown curls were gray streaked, making her head look like a dusty mop. Okay, maybe Carla didn't want to spend the money on a professional dye job, but hadn't she heard of Nice 'N Easy? The shapeless track suits that she wore 24/7 didn't help either. If anyone was ever looking for someone to do a makeover on, Carla would be perfect. She still lived in the house she had grown up in and had recently retired from her job at the post office as a mail carrier. Most of the day she was perched by her living room window, watching the comings and goings of 25th Avenue, while smoking Marlboro Lights. She must have spotted her when she walked by her house and figured this was where she was heading.

Vivi lived only six blocks from the bakery, and once a week Big Viv stopped by to stock up Vivi's fridge. There was nothing better than a home cooked meal, and Big Viv always had plenty of leftovers. Today, she had a shopping bag filled with chicken cutlet parmigiana, eggplant rollatini, baked ziti, and seafood salad in individual Tupperware containers, ready for the freezer. When it was time for dinner, all Vivi would have to do was pop a container in the microwave.

"Did you hear the news?" Carla asked.

"What news?"

Carla looked like the cat who had swallowed the canary. Instantly, Big Viv got a bad feeling in the pit of her stomach. A very bad feeling.

"They're doing a big celebration for the 45th anniversary of *Saturday Night Fever*. There's going to be an entire weekend devoted to the movie. A walking tour. Dance contests. A screening of the movie at King's Theater. There's even going to be original cast members signing autographs and posing for pictures. Maybe even John Travolta!"

"Oh!" Big Viv was pleasantly surprised.

The 1970s was when she came of age, and disco had been all the rage. There was no movie that captured the era better than *Saturday Night Fever*. Starring her all-time favorite actor, John Travolta. She had been a fan of his since his debut on *Welcome Back Kotter*—set in Bensonhurst, Brooklyn, and modeled after her alma mater, New Utrecht High School!—as Vinny Barbarino, leader of the Sweathogs, a group of students placed in remedial classes.

That thick brown hair. Those blue eyes. That cleft in his chin. Those luscious, kissable lips.

She fell in lust with him the first time she saw him.

And he was pure animal magnetism in *Fever*. The scene where he was blow drying his hair in his black bikini underwear? Those tight polyester shirts buttoned almost down to his waist, showing off his furred chest? The dance scene where he kept bouncing up and down on his knees as he moved across the brightly lit disco floor? It was like he was playing peekaboo with his crotch. She was starting to get flushed just thinking about it.

"I hadn't heard," she told Carla, making a mental note to have Sebastian do extra baking that weekend once she knew the date. There were sure to be crowds. And crowds got hungry.

"That's not all."

"There's more?"

Carla nodded slyly. The bad feeling started to return. This wasn't going to be good.

And then, Carla dropped her bombshell. "Rumor is Deena's coming back for it."

Big Viv made sure not to show any emotion on her face. She knew Carla was looking for a reaction, and she wasn't going to give her one. If she did, it would be all over the neighborhood. The latest piece of juicy gossip.

Gossip that would also make its way back to Deena.

Big Viv knew Deena was still plugged into the old neighborhood. Even though she lived all the way out in California, churning out her B movies and cheesy TV shows that never lasted more than one season, she knew Deena still had eyes and ears reporting back to her.

Let them. Deena might have turned her back on the neighborhood and their friendship, but Big Viv had become somebody. She was a success.

As big a success as Deena.

Everyone in the neighborhood knew about her

feud with Deena DiGregorio. No one held a grudge like an Italian.

They used to be best friends. Their families had immigrated to New York from Italy at the same time in the 1960s and their friendship started in grammar school and continued all the way through high school. They had so much in common: Italian girls wanting to Americanize while their mothers wanted them to remain old school, waiting hand and foot on the men in their lives—grandfathers, fathers, brothers, uncles, cousins—never expecting them to want to do more than get married and start having babies of their own.

Uh uh. No way.

Sure, they wanted to one day get married. But before that, they wanted to explore the world. Have some fun!

After graduating from high school, they both got jobs in the city as secretaries. They worked 9 to 5, Monday to Friday, and went out on the weekends. When they had vacation time or if there were long weekends, they would go on trips together with their clique from high school: Francesca "Foxy" Gallo, Charlotte "Chunky" Umberto, and Patricia Pallamente. San Francisco. Seattle. Boston. New Orleans. They would go out. Dance. Flirt—okay, sometimes more than flirt—but they always had each other's backs.

Because they were more than best friends. They were sisters.

At least, that's what Big Viv had always thought.

The origin of their falling out started when she and Deena wanted to be extras in *Saturday Night Fever*. The entire filming took place in Brooklyn and they had been there the day John filmed his two slices from Lenny's Pizzeria scene on 86th Street and 20th Avenue. Someone who had gotten their hands on the script said there was a scene in the movie where a girl at the disco would ask John if he was as good in bed as he was on the dance floor. Big Viv and Deena both wanted to be that girl, so they dressed in their finest disco wear and staked out 2001 Odyssey in Bay Ridge where the dancing scenes took place, all in the hopes of catching John Travolta's eye. Unfortunately, neither one was chosen—not that they even had a chance. The role was already cast to future *Nanny* star, Fran Drescher, but somehow, in the massive crowd that had shown up, Deena caught the eye of one of the associate producers. He'd invited her back to his hotel room in Manhattan.

Deena, who'd been looking to ditch Brooklyn from the day she first saw Susan Lucci debut as Erica

Kane on *All My Children,* eagerly hopped into his limo, telling Viv she'd give her a call the next day.

She didn't.

Instead, the following morning Big Viv found a note in her mailbox, saying: *I'm going to give the West Coast a shot!*

And that was it. Big Viv was taken totally by surprise. Sure, Deena had been in a couple of plays and musicals back when they were in high school, but it wasn't like she talked about *wanting* to be an actress.

For Big Viv, it was the ultimate betrayal. How could her best friend have left her like that? With only a note? She couldn't have called? Asked for her advice?

Yes, she was hurt. But also...

Although she would never admit it to anyone, deep down she had been the one hoping for that big break. For the chance to escape Brooklyn and make something of herself.

Deena didn't even ask her if she wanted to come along! She'd just abandoned her without a thought. That hurt most of all. Like a knife in the back.

But life went on. Big Viv kept working as a secretary until she met her Gino, got married, got pregnant, had Vivi, and then became a widow after

Gino was hit by a car when Vivi was two. She grieved for a year, then opened the bakery in 1995, making it into the success it was today. It certainly didn't hurt that a number of Mafia wives frequented it, wanting to show their support for a widow who was raising a child on her own. They told their friends, and those friends told their friends, and soon word of mouth spread, giving her more business than she ever could have imagined. Not only did she sell through the bakery, she also catered desserts for family events, always giving those Mafia wives an extra discount for their support.

Meanwhile, Deena showed up in a couple of low budget horror movies, some guest spots in sitcoms, and even a year-long run on a daytime soap opera.

Was Deena a good actress? Meh. Her style of acting consisted of lots of vamping, purring, buggy eyes, and slinky body movements.

If there was one thing Deena didn't have, it was star quality. Yet, somehow, she kept chugging along from project to project.

And then, there were the husbands. Each one richer than the other. At last count, there were five exes.

It wasn't like Big Viv was *following* Deena's career. What was she supposed to do if she turned on the TV and Deena was on the screen, change the channel? She had to hate-watch for a bit. Plus, everyone was always talking about her or passing around clippings from *US Weekly* and the *National Enquirer*—Deena was not *People* magazine material—so that's how she was kept in the loop.

Everyone made sure she stayed in the loop. Because everyone still saw her as Deena DiGregorio's best friend. It didn't matter that she never heard from Deena. There were no phone calls or letters. No congratulations when she got married or had her baby. No sympathy card when Gino died. It was like once Deena left Brooklyn, their friendship ceased to exist.

But once a friend, always a friend. That's what the neighborhood believed.

Twenty years went by without a word exchanged between them. And then, one day Deena showed up at the bakery during a visit home, acting like no time had gone by as she threw her arms around her former BFF in a hug.

It pissed Big Viv off.

And maybe it was her imagination, but there was something very smug about Deena's visit that day as she walked around the bakery, asking questions, nibbling on the samples Big Viv had out on the counter.

Almost condescending. Like she was looking down on Big Viv. Like she was saying: I got out and you didn't!

Big Viv didn't have it out with Deena that day. So much time had gone by. Why bother? But by her frosty tone and body language, she made it clear to Queen Deena that they wouldn't be picking up their friendship where it had left off in 1977.

Deena got the message. Loud and clear. She bought a pound of pignoli cookies and left the bakery.

The next day, everyone in the neighborhood was talking about what happened at the bakery, and word of the feud spread. How could it not? Big Viv was sure Deena was doing as much as she could to come across as the one who had been wronged. After all, she was an actress and she was giving a performance to the residents of 25th Avenue. Naturally, everyone said—behind her back, never to her face—that Big Viv was jealous of Deena. How ridiculous! What was there to be jealous of? She had a successful business, a healthy bank account, and a beautiful daughter.

But she wouldn't be honest if she didn't admit

that the gossip did piss her off. She hated anyone making a fool of her behind her back.

So, while not exactly bad-mouthing Deena, whenever an opportunity presented itself to get in a little dig, she took it, especially when asked if she had caught one of Deena's performances. She always pretended she had, praising Deena's lackluster acting, while at the same time saying things like: HD TV wasn't Deena's friend, magnifying her wrinkles and age lines. The camera really did add fifteen extra pounds. At least, it seemed that way when Deena was on screen. And now that Deena was a woman of a certain age, she heard Lifetime was going to remake *Whatever Happened to Baby Jane?* and Deena was being considered for the role of Jane, not Blanche, since the network wanted an actress whose looks had started to fade.

She knew these little tidbits always made their way back to Deena, because whenever she returned to Brooklyn and came by the bakery, she addressed them. Never directly. Always indirectly, and with her own insults aimed at the bakery.

And then, there was the Nico situation.

She knew Deena's younger sister, Angie, had gotten married and had a son the same year she'd given birth to Vivi. What she hadn't known at that time was that Deena's nephew went to the same high school as Vivi and that they had started flirting with each other. She only found out when a customer filled her in. Vivi had been at that sullen teenage girl stage where she never told Big Viv anything, so trying to find out about her social life was a losing battle.

As soon as Big Viv confirmed it was true, she made a decision. There was no way she was letting her daughter get involved with Deena's nephew. The apple didn't fall far from the tree, and if Deena could turn her back on their friendship, she could only imagine what Nico would do to her sweet Vivi.

He was handsome, she would admit that. She could see why Vivi was attracted to him. But the more handsome the guy, the harder the heartache. And she didn't want her Vivi experiencing any heartache.

Angie, brainwashed by her sister into believing Big Viv was the enemy, didn't think Vivi was good enough for her baby boy. She never came out and said it, but that was the sense Big Viv got when Angie came around all those years ago. She'd never set foot in the bakery before that day. After looking around at the display cases and waiting until there were no other customers around, she got right to the point. "Your daughter and my son are sniffing around each other. We gotta put a stop to it before it's too late. If you know what I mean?"

Big Viv knew what she meant.

Virginity didn't last very long in Bensonhurst. Not when there were so many Sylvester Stallone wannabes roaming the streets of Brooklyn.

"What are we gonna do?" Angie asked.

Big Viv thought about it. The problem with Vivi was that nobody could tell her *not* to do something. Because if they did, even if she was originally planning on doing what they asked of her, she now would do it because they had told her not to.

Stubborn. Just like her father.

So, Big Viv and Angie put their heads together and decided a little time apart would cool things down.

The plan worked better than they thought it would. Not only was Vivi upset that Nico didn't mind being sent to California—resulting in a break-up that came much earlier than expected—but he decided to stay out there when the summer was over, preventing them from getting back together.

There were other boyfriends that came after Nico, but they never lasted very long. Sometimes, Big Viv wondered if she had made a mistake by trying to protect her daughter. But then she remembered the way Deena had treated her, the pain she had felt, and realized she had made the right decision.

She did wish, though, that her daughter would settle down. Vivi had just turned thirty. When was she going to get married and start a family? She wasn't getting any younger. Well, she'd worry about that another day. Right now, she had to deal with Carla.

"If Deena's coming back to Brooklyn, then I'm sure she'll drop into the bakery," Big Viv said. "She always does so she can buy some pastries to binge on."

Carla's rheumy blue eyes widened in shock. "Binge on?"

"Didn't you know? Deena binges and purges. It's so sad, not to mention unhealthy. Well, when you get older your metabolism slows down and it gets harder to keep the weight off. But what other choice does she have if she doesn't have any willpower to stop herself from eating more than she should?" Big Viv shrugged. "Getting her stomach stapled hasn't seemed to work."

"She got her stomach stapled?" Carla gasped. "Who told you that?"

"I read it online. One of those gossip websites," Big Viv lied, pressing a heavily jeweled hand against her ample bosom. She did this often. Created a rumor about Deena and then pretended to be relieved that it wasn't true. "You mean, it's fake news? She doesn't binge and purge? Oh, I'm so glad. That makes me feel so much better. Now, I won't feel at all guilty the next time I take her order, although I hope I'll be able to recognize her this time."

"Recognize her?" Carla gave Big Viv a puzzled look. "Why would you say that?"

Big Viv leaned in close, trying not to recoil from the scent of cigarette smoke and garlic on Carla's breath, as if confiding a secret. "Didn't you see her on that talk show a few weeks ago? The one in the morning on channel 11? Deena's eyes were looking a little bit...cat-like."

"Cat-like?"

Big Viv nodded knowingly. "That only happens when the skin is pulled too tight. You know, plastic surgery."

"Deena's had plastic surgery?" Carla gasped in disbelief.

"Well, I think she has no choice. There's only so much fillers and Botox can do."

"Fillers and Botox?"

Big Viv was getting tired of Carla repeating her words. It was time to wrap this up. "Come on, Carla. Don't be so naïve. I'm sure you noticed in her last Lifetime movie she could barely move her face. Botox. It takes away the ability to move your face and make expressions. What actress in her right mind would do that, I don't know." Big Viv paused. "Well, we do know. Deena." Big Viv finally found the keys she was looking for and opened the front door, escaping into Vivi's house. "Bye, Carla!"

———

Big Viv sighed as she stared into Vivi's nearly empty refrigerator.

Didn't her daughter ever eat?

If it wasn't for her weekly deliveries, her daughter would starve. There were a few cans of Diet Coke, two eggs, some lettuce, and a couple containers of yogurt. She opened the kitchen cabinets, finding them bare, too. She found a pen and paper and started to make a grocery list. Then, she began emptying her shopping bag, opening the freezer and rearranging the Tupperware dishes she had brought over last week to make room for the new ones. Once she was finished, she emptied the dishwasher and then refilled it with the dishes and glasses that were in the sink.

Why her daughter wanted to live on her own, she didn't know, since Big Viv was still the one who cooked and cleaned for her. But Vivi had insisted. She wanted to be on her own. How was she ever going to take care of a husband and kids if she could barely take care of herself?

After doing a little dusting in the living room, Big Viv made her way upstairs to the bedroom. Surprisingly, the bed was made, so she didn't have to do anything there.

Then, she made her way to the bathroom, where she found wet towels on the floor and an overflowing wastebasket. She threw the towels into the hamper, replaced them with fresh ones from the linen closet, and picked up the wastebasket to empty downstairs.

As she headed down the stairs, a word from one of the cardboard boxes in the wastebasket jumped out at her.

PREGNANT.

Big Viv stopped. She reached for the box and took a closer look. It was a home pregnancy test.

A feeling of excitement began fluttering in her stomach.

She took another look at the wastebasket. It was overflowing with home pregnancy tests. She gasped. That must mean...

No! It couldn't be. Could it?

Was Vivi pregnant?

If she was pregnant...

Then, that meant Big Viv was going to be a grandmother! At last!

Big Viv tried to keep her growing excitement under control. She didn't want to set herself up for disappointment. Just because Vivi had taken a couple of tests, it didn't mean she was pregnant.

She had to know for sure. And the only way to do that was to track down Vivi.

CHAPTER
SIX

Sebastian repeated his question. "What's your mother's reaction going to be when she finds out you're pregnant?"

Suddenly, there was an ear-piercing shriek.

"So, it's true. You *are* pregnant! I really am going to be a grandmother!"

Sebastian turned around in shock. Barreling toward them with a huge grin on her face was Big Viv. How she could even run in those high heels, he had no idea. But she was. And her arms were wide open.

"I'm going to be a grandmother!" she exclaimed again, scooping a startled Vivi up in a hug.

Well, okay. This was good. Really good. Big Viv

wasn't having a meltdown. She seemed genuinely happy.

For the moment.

She still hadn't found out who the baby's daddy might be. And Sebastian did not want to be around for that.

"I think I'm going to take my lunch hour. I've got some errands to run," Sebastian said, backtracking toward the door. "I'm sure you two have lots to talk about."

"No!" Vivi shouted in a panic-filled voice. "Stay!"

"I should really go."

Big Viv clamped a jeweled hand around Sebastian's wrist. "You can't leave. We have to celebrate. With champagne! Well, champagne for us, ginger ale for Vivi."

Big Viv began rummaging through the industrial size refrigerator in the bakery's kitchen. "I know I have a bottle of Dom somewhere in here."

"How did you know?" Vivi asked, her voice hoarse and a shocked expression on her face. Vivi had obviously *not* been expecting this, and he could see the wheels in her mind churning as she tried to stay one step ahead of her mother.

"I swung by your place with some Tupperware to leave in your freezer. I was doing a little bit of cleaning up and found these in your bathroom." Big Viv reached into her shoulder bag and pulled out a bunch of pregnancy test boxes, happily waving them. "Why didn't you tell me?"

"Uh, I just found out. Literally. This morning. That's why I'm here. I was looking for you so I could tell you."

That was a good save, Sebastian thought.

"Who's the father?" Big Viv eagerly asked, unwrapping the foil from the bottle of champagne she had found. "I didn't even know you were dating someone." Big Viv turned to Sebastian as she started to loosen the cork in the champagne bottle. "She's always so secretive with her dating life. Ever since she was a teenager and dating Deena's nephew, Nico." Big Viv made an expression of distaste. "What she ever saw in him, I never knew. He ran off to California the first chance he had and never looked back. He abandoned my Vivi."

"Aren't you being a little hypocritical?" Vivi pointed out. "You were never a fan of Nico's. You and his mother hatched up that little scheme to keep us apart that summer. Don't you think you should be shouldering some of the blame?"

"He's just like his aunt," Big Viv said, ignoring Viv's words. "Cold and unfeeling."

"That's not true!" Vivi exclaimed, coming to Nico's defense. "It's not fair to say something like that. You don't know anything about him."

Big Viv shrugged. "Why are we even talking about him? He's ancient history."

The words slipped out before Sebastian could stop them. "Sometimes, history repeats itself."

Vivi glared at him while Big Viv gave him a puzzled look.

"I'm glad he's out of your life," Big Viv continued. "He never would have made you happy. But I bet the new man in your life is making you very happy. She never tells me anything, but I bet she tells you everything, Sebastian." She locked her eyes on him. "Do you know who the father is? I bet you do."

Sebastian bit down on his lower lip. There was no way he wanted to get in the middle of this. He shrugged. "You know Vivi. She loves her secrets."

"Don't keep me in suspense! Who is he? When am I going to meet him?"

Sebastian waited for the bomb to drop. How was Vivi going to handle this? She wasn't even sure if Nico was the baby's father. But if he was, he did not want to be around for that announcement.

"Sebastian," Vivi said. "Sebastian is the father of my baby."

"What?" Big Viv exclaimed in shock as the cork flew out of the champagne bottle and white foam began to bubble out.

"What?" Sebastian exclaimed simultaneously.

"That's right. Sebastian is the father," Vivi confidently stated, rushing to his side and slipping her arm through his. "Surprise!"

"Wait," Big Viv said, her voice thick with disbelief, the bottle of champagne abandoned. "This doesn't make sense. I thought Sebastian was gay. I heard—"

Vivi cut her off. "Don't tell me you listen to neighborhood gossip?" She gave an exasperated sigh. "Just because Sebastian likes to cook and bake, the *stunads* in the neighborhood have always said he was gay. But he's not!"

"But I've never seen him with a girl. Ever."

"Have you ever seen him with a guy?" Vivi countered.

"Well, no," Big Viv admitted.

"So, then why would you think he was gay?"

Big Viv shrugged. "I just assumed. I mean, I could have sworn..."

Big Viv stared at Sebastian, looking him over from head to toe as if seeing him for the first time. He could see the shock on her face. All these years, she had thought he was gay and now Vivi was telling her he was straight and she was trying to figure out how she could have been so wrong. She was looking for an answer. But he didn't have one to give. What was he supposed to say? Vivi had totally blindsided him. He didn't know what she was up to, but he was afraid of doing or saying anything that would ruin whatever plan she might have up her sleeve.

And if he knew Vivi, there was a plan.

"Sebastian dresses well, looks good, and always smells nice," Vivi said. "Another reason for those goons to be jealous and spread their lies. Maybe if they used a little deodorant from time to time, they'd have women in their bed, too."

"Women?" Big Viv did a double take. "Sebastian has *women* in his bed?"

Sebastian laughed nervously. "Let's not exaggerate, Vivi." He gave her a pointed look. "You'll give your mother the wrong idea about me."

"So, when's the big day?" Big Viv asked.

"Big day?" Vivi asked.

"Big day?" Sebastian repeated. "What big day?"

Big Viv stared at the two of them in exasperation. "You know, the wedding?"

"Wedding?" Vivi gasped.

Big Viv laughed. "Oh, Vivi, I remember when I was pregnant with you. My mind would get so foggy. I'd have the hardest time following the simplest conversation. Yes, the wedding. Your wedding. We've got to start planning it! There's so much that needs to be done, but not enough time to do it in. We want a slim bride walking down the aisle. No baby bump! Don't worry, I'll handle everything and loop you both in on the important decisions. This is going to be so much fun. We're having a wedding. And a baby! This is so going to trump Deena's return to Bensonhurst for the 45th anniversary of *Saturday Night Fever*. I can't wait to tell everyone!"

With those final words, Big Viv kissed them both on their cheeks and left the bakery, off to spread the good news and make plans.

At first, Sebastian and Viv stood in shocked silence. Then, Sebastian walked over and began to chug champagne straight from the bottle.

"Couldn't you have at least said I was gender fluid?" he asked. "That would have been a bit more believable."

"I'm sorry! I panicked."

"I'll say. This morning, I was a single gay male and now I'm a straight white male about to be married with a baby on the way." Sebastian took another chug of champagne. "What are we going to do?"

"What do you mean?"

Sebastian did a double take. "Your mother is getting ready to throw the biggest wedding Bensonhurst has ever seen. With us as the bride and groom. Tell me what's wrong with this picture, Vivi!"

Viv paced the kitchen. "We'll pretend."

"Aren't we already doing that?"

"We'll keep pretending. Go through with the wedding."

"Go through with it? Are you nuts? Your mom has been awfully good to me, Vivi. Yes, she drives me crazy most days, but I don't like lying to her this way."

"Do you think I like lying to her, too? I can see how excited she is. About the baby. About planning a wedding. But until I can find out if Nico is or isn't the father of this baby, you have to go along with this. There's no telling what she might do. She could cut me off without a cent!"

Sebastian knew Big Viv had a short temper. He'd seen her lose it with some of their distributors when an order was late or they were shorted on supplies, especially during their busy times of the year. She could be ruthless, taking her business elsewhere. And when it came to holding a grudge...well, just look at her and Deena DiGregorio to see how well that worked out. That grudge was the whole reason they were in this mess!

Big Viv owned a number of buildings in Brooklyn, and Vivi worked as her mother's property manager when she wasn't helping out at the bakery. It was a job that gave her a good salary and a lot of freedom. It was no secret in the neighborhood that Big Viv was grooming Vivi to one day take over everything. But if her mother felt hurt or betrayed, she could lash out. She could fire Vivi. Even worse, she could disinherit her.

And if Big Viv found out *he* had been lying to her...

If she thought he was trying to make her look like a fool...

He shuddered. He didn't want to think of the consequences, especially if those Mafia rumors were true.

"Please Sebastian," Vivi begged. "I'll make it up to you."

"How?"

"I'll put up the money for your bakery."

Sebastian blinked in disbelief. "Are you serious?"

"Would I say it if I didn't mean it?"

"Why are you making the offer now? Why didn't you make it before this?"

"Because you wouldn't have taken it. You're stubborn. You would have said you wanted to earn the money yourself."

She was right. Sebastian's pride would have made him say no.

But this was different. It wouldn't be like Vivi was just giving him the money. He'd be earning it.

Hazard pay.

The offer was tempting. Very tempting. Why not accept it? What did he have to lose? It wasn't like he was dating anyone at the moment. His love life had been dormant for the last year.

And it wasn't like the marriage was going to be real. They would go through with the ceremony, then get the marriage annulled once Vivi figured out who the father of her baby was. Besides, how could he not do it? This was Vivi, his best friend. She needed him.

"So?" Viv asked, a hopeful tone in her voice.

Sebastian sighed. "Yes. Against my better judgment, yes. I'll do it."

"Yay!" Vivi threw her arms around Sebastian in a hug. "We're getting married!"

Sebastian hugged her back. "I just hope I don't regret this."

The following morning, he did.

CHAPTER
SEVEN

"Your mother did what?" Sebastian wasn't sure if he'd heard Vivi correctly.

"She hired a wedding planner."

"Why would she do that?"

Viv stuck a finger in the bowl of chocolate frosting that Sebastian was using to frost a birthday cake and popped it in her mouth. "Why do you think? Because she's a control freak. When we walk down the aisle in a couple of weeks, it's going to be her vision of the perfect wedding, not ours."

Sebastian put down the spatula he was using to frost the cake.

Suddenly this was becoming real.

Yesterday, he'd gone along with Vivi, not giving

the situation enough thought, thinking that everything would eventually work itself out.

But it hadn't.

They were meeting with a wedding planner. Today. To discuss their wedding. He was marrying Vivi. Suddenly, the room started to spin.

"What's the matter?" Vivi's voice was panicked. "You look like you're going to faint. Here, sit down." She pulled a stool over and pushed Sebastian down on it. Then, she handed him a paper bag. "Take deep breaths. Pull yourself together. She's going to be arriving with him any minute."

"We don't need a wedding planner," Sebastian said as he breathed in and out of the bag. "Do you know how much that will cost? And then, when we have the marriage annulled? She'll go ballistic! You know how your mother hates to spend money."

"You don't have to tell me. She's got her living room furniture set from 1990 covered in plastic like all old school Italians. But what are we going to do? Her mind is made up. She called me last night to tell me that she found this guy who got a rave review from *New York* magazine. He just went out on his own, so maybe he's not that expensive."

"That's not the point." Sebastian put down the

bag. "Don't you see? The deeper we get into this, the harder it's going to be to get out of it."

Vivi waved a hand dismissively. "Don't worry. I know how to handle my mother. And we'll figure out a way to handle this wedding planner."

"You handle your mother," Sebastian said, picking up his spatula. "I'll handle the wedding planner. How hard could it be?"

———

Dominick Campinello dressed for success.

If you didn't look successful, people weren't going to think you were successful. Plus, as a wedding planner, he had to project a certain image to his clients. Sleek. Polished. Attractive. Otherwise, they would never trust him with the most important day of their lives.

Since it was summer, he decided he would wear light, tropical colors today. Buttery yellow pants, a white cotton shirt, red Gucci loafers—without socks! —and a yellow and red plaid jacket with a complimentary pocket square. He usually wore his black hair longer in fall and winter, but during the warmer months, he preferred a buzz cut. Less fuss and muss.

He inspected himself in his bedroom's full-length mirror while giving himself a spritz of his favorite cologne, Blue de Chanel.

Perfection!

Now, who were today's clients?

He opened up his iPad and began to scroll. Ah! There it was. The happy couple. Sebastian Fontana and Vivianna Confetta.

Judging by their last names, they were Italian. Italian weddings were always a blast. He knew from planning them as well as attending them. So much unrestrained joy and fun. No one knew how to celebrate like an Italian.

He closed his iPad and headed for the front door. He had a nine o'clock appointment to meet the mother of the bride, Viv Confetta, at her bakery in Brooklyn before meeting the future Mr. and Mrs. Fontana.

He had a good feeling about this. He couldn't wait to meet the happy couple.

———

This was the happy couple?

Usually when Dominick met a couple for the

first time, they were bubbling over with excitement, barely able to contain themselves as they bombarded him with thoughts and ideas. And why not? They were getting ready to discuss and plan one of the most important days of their lives.

But these two weren't talking about their big day and how they envisioned it.

In fact, they both looked like they would rather be anywhere else instead of the back office of the bakery where this meeting was taking place.

He had met Ms. Confetta outside the bakery promptly at nine and she had instantly insisted he call her Big Viv. "Everyone does," she said.

Glancing at her chest, he could see why.

"Why don't we head inside?" Big Viv suggested, opening the door for him.

The bakery was cute. There were two long display cases that formed an L, full of baked goods. Behind them, there were shelves filled with all sorts of luscious cakes, cookies, and pies. There were also the two front window displays on both sides of the entrance for those walking by to gaze at. One window was filled with plastic samples of birthday and wedding cakes that could be made to order. The other was filled with more freshly baked desserts.

The floor was Italian tile and the walls were mirrored, so everywhere customers looked, they were tempted by something sweet.

As Dominick walked in, he couldn't help but inhale the delicious scent of chocolate, cinnamon, and vanilla.

"Everything is baked fresh daily. By the end of the day, we're always sold out. What we don't sell, I send home with my staff. I don't sell anything that's a day old," Big Viv proudly stated.

There were two white-haired Italian grandmotherly types with teased white bouffants behind the counters, waiting on customers.

"Can I get you something?" Big Viv offered. "Some seven layer cookies? A biscotti?"

"Thanks, but I don't have much of a sweet tooth."

"Smart man. Probably what keeps you so thin." She gazed at him appreciatively from head to toe. "Your clothes look good on you. Stylish. I like that."

Dominick thanked her for the compliment. Then, he asked, "Is this a family business?" He always found it useful to learn a little bit about his clients. It made working together easier.

"It's just me, but my daughter helps out on occasion during the busy times of the year."

"What does your future son-in-law do?"

"He works here." She jerked her thumb in the direction of the kitchen. "He's my head baker. I guess you're right. It's going to be a family business."

"Does that make you happy?"

Big Viv shrugged. "I like doing things my way. Sebastian always wants to make changes."

"Change is good."

"Sometimes. Not always. And not when it comes to my bakery."

Dominick could hear the tone of steel in her voice. Poor Sebastian. Well, not his problem. His problem was keeping the client happy.

"I've been thinking about the wedding," Big Viv said. "I want roses. Lots and lots of red roses. Everywhere you look, nothing but red roses."

"Is that what Sebastian and Vivianna want?"

Big Viv stared at him like he had just asked the dumbest question.

"Huh?"

"Do Vivianna and Sebastian want red roses?"

"What does it matter what they want? I'm the one who's paying, right?"

Dominick tread carefully. He didn't want to piss Big Viv off, especially since she hadn't signed his contract yet and it was a nice fat one. His bank account was badly in need of an influx of cash. He'd only just gone out on his own, and when a steady paycheck wasn't coming in every two weeks, every job mattered.

"Yes, you're paying," he said in a soothing tone of voice. "And I'm sure your daughter is going to want your input when it comes to everything. But have you asked her how she envisions her wedding?"

"Vivi trusts me. I've got good taste."

Dominick bit his tongue as he took inventory of Big Viv's outfit. She wore a low cut neon green cheetah print wrap dress. Around her neck was a solid gold lion's head pendant. It was a bit...much.

"Why don't we all talk together?" he suggested. "That way, everyone is on the same page and there's no miscommunication. We want everyone to be happy."

"I guess," Big Viv reluctantly agreed, leading the way into the kitchen. "Vivi! Sebastian! We're here!"

As they entered the kitchen, the future bride and groom spun around with guilty expressions on their faces. Like they had been caught doing something they shouldn't. Then again, they were rushing to get this wedding planned since the bride was expecting a baby as her mother confided when she hired him yesterday afternoon and didn't want a baby bump at the ceremony.

He couldn't put his finger on what it was that was off, but they didn't seem like a happy couple. Dominick always went with his first impressions. Maybe the baby was stressing them out, especially since it had been unplanned (again TMI courtesy of Big Viv). Still, he'd been doing this for a while. Most couples were a team. There was an energy between them. It was like they could read each other's minds. Finish each other's sentences. Anticipate what the other was going to say or do.

He wasn't getting that vibe. At all.

Well, he was going to be working closely with them over the next couple of weeks. Hopefully he'd be able to figure it out and give them their dream wedding.

"Hi. I'm Dominick Campinello." He held out a hand, giving them both a smile. "Or Dom, if you prefer. Your wedding planner. I'm not here to take over. I'm here to make planning your special day as smooth and easy as possible. I'm here to work for you. Assist you."

"I'm the bride, Vivianna." She took his hand and gave it a brief shake. "But you can call me Vivi." She pointed to her groom. "This is Sebastian. Sometimes, we call him Bash."

Dominick released Viv's hand, offering it to Sebastian.

At first, Sebastian didn't take it. He just looked at it, confused. Like he wasn't sure what he was supposed to do. Maybe he was a germaphobe?

But then, he did take his hand, giving it a hearty shake. And he didn't let go.

———

Sebastian didn't want to let go of his hand.

He wanted to hold on to it. For as long as possible. Dominick was adorable. Sooo adorable.

Sebastian was trying not to openly stare, but he couldn't take his eyes off him. He sort of resembled the actor, Matt Bomer. He found everything about him attractive. It had been a long time since Sebastian had experienced such a physical reaction to another guy.

Or maybe he'd simply gone too long without getting laid. That could be it, too.

Whatever it was, he couldn't tear his eyes away. Or let go of his hand. But he had to.

He wasn't supposed to be ogling the wedding

planner! He was a "straight" guy who was getting married and his bride-to-be was pregnant with "his" baby.

"What are you looking at?" Big Viv asked, cutting into his thoughts.

"Huh? What?"

She narrowed her eyes. "You're staring."

He quickly released Dominick's hand. "Was I?" Sebastian's mind scrambled for an excuse. "I was just admiring Dom's pocket square. I've never seen one so elaborate."

Dominick came to the rescue before Big Viv could say anything.

"Isn't it cool?" He pulled it out of the front of his jacket and held it out to Sebastian. "They're handmade by this woman named Barbara Campbell. Saks Fifth Avenue used to carry them, but now I buy them off her website. She picks all sorts of unique fabrics and designs."

"It definitely livens up your jacket."

"I know, right?" He returned it to his pocket. "It's my statement piece. Always wear one thing that will grab attention. More than one and it's overkill."

He was gay.

He was gay!

He had to be gay.

How could he not be? No straight guy would wear such an elaborate pocket square. Straight guys always had boring white pocket squares and Dominick's was yellow with a ruffled red edge so that it looked like a flower when it stuck out of his pocket.

Not to mention the red Gucci loafers. They weren't a muted red, or even a burgundy red. No, they were a bright fire engine red. They were shoes that were meant to be seen, so one's eyes would travel up and notice everything about the man wearing them.

Plus, Sebastian's gaydar was going off BIG TIME.

Why did that make him so happy? It wasn't like he could do anything about it. Not if he wanted to help Vivi. Not if he wanted to open his own bakery. Not if they wanted to fool Big Viv into believing they were a couple with a baby on the way.

Why, today of all days, did he have to meet the perfect guy? Okay, he might be exaggerating things a bit by calling him perfect. After all, they'd just met and Sebastian didn't know anything about him.

But so far, things were looking good. The packaging was very nice.

But he'd been down this path before. Pretty on

the outside. Shallow, empty, ugly—take your pick of words—on the inside.

He'd told Vivi that he would handle the wedding planner, but now he was second guessing himself. Contrary to what he'd told Vivi earlier, this was going to be hard.

Very hard.

CHAPTER
EIGHT

"I'm getting married."

It was the first time Sebastian had said the words out loud. And to another person. He hadn't even said the words to himself until his panic attack that morning.

Sure, he had always wondered if he'd one day get married. And now he was.

But he'd imagined a groom standing next to him. Not a bride.

His roommate, Liam, paused his chopsticks over the container of chicken chow mein he was eating in their kitchen. "Wait! What?"

Liam abandoned his food and rushed over to Sebastian, lifting him off the floor as he gave him a huge hug.

Like Sebastian, he was also an actor. But he had far more success finding jobs. And why wouldn't he? He was over six feet tall, muscular, with a face that rivaled Brad Pitt's and the most amazing green eyes. When he wasn't touring with shows—he had just returned home after six months on the road playing the Beast in Disney's *Beauty and the Beast*—he also did some modeling, including a number of historical romance book covers. Who wouldn't love Liam as a Regency rake or in a kilt as a Scottish Highlander? Sebastian knew it was only a matter of time before Liam got his big break. Little by little, he kept climbing up the acting ladder.

"Who's the lucky guy? I've only been gone six months. That must have been some whirlwind courtship. And you haven't posted anything on social media. You didn't even mention him when we were on the phone or texting. Keeping him all to yourself, huh? I want details, man! Details! Pics, too! And how's the sex? Hot?"

Leave it to Liam to ask about the sex. If there was one thing he loved, it was sex. And looking the way he did, he had plenty of it. Guys were always throwing themselves at him, and Liam was more than happy to indulge. Maybe that was why Sebastian had never been attracted to his roommate.

He knew Liam didn't want an emotional connection. The physical side of things was enough for him.

Until the next hot guy came along. Then, it was usually up to Sebastian to clean up the mess that Liam left behind as guys called the apartment or tried to come up, begging to see Liam one last time in the hopes of salvaging things with him. It never worked. When Liam was done with a guy, he was done.

He was sort of like Dean Cain's character in the Greg Berlanti movie, *The Broken Hearts Club*.

So, Sebastian was the one who got the tears, who had to listen, who gave the pep talks, who told the guys they'd eventually find someone else.

It was exhausting.

Thankfully, no one had gone full-on Alex "I'm not going to be ignored, Dan" Forrest from *Fatal Attraction* on Liam. Yet.

Sebastian suspected there was a reason why Liam slept around so much. It might be Liam's way of shielding himself. Maybe from getting a broken heart. His gut told him there had to be some sort of backstory, but today wasn't the day to play therapist. He figured one of these days Liam would tell him why he'd never really gotten close to anyone. When he did, he'd be ready to listen. Because Liam was a catch. He could be kind and thoughtful. He gave encouraging pep talks and always remembered birthdays and special occasions. And whenever Sebastian was in a show—well, when he still used to be a performer—Liam always had tickets in the front row and was always the first to lead the audience in a standing ovation, clapping and whistling and hooting for Sebastian. For now, he ignored Liam's question and focused on cleaning up the mess in the kitchen. He and Liam shared a two-bedroom apartment on the Upper East Side of Manhattan. Sebastian was the neat freak and Liam was the slob, as evidenced by the empty Chinese take-out containers on the kitchen counter and the half-empty packets of soy sauce and hot mustard. He wasn't even going to think about the piles of dirty laundry scattered throughout the apartment.

"My mess can wait," Liam said, dragging Sebastian back out into the living room and collapsing on the couch. "I want to hear all about your guy."

"It's not a guy."

Liam gave him a blank look.

"Huh?"

I'm not marrying a guy."

"What do you mean you're not marrying a guy?"

"You heard me the first time."

"If you're not marrying a guy, then who are you marrying?"

Sebastian gave a heavy sigh. "If I'm not marrying a guy, then I must be marrying a woman, right?"

"You're marrying a woman." Liam said it slowly.

"Yes."

"A woman woman."

"Yes."

"Not a drag queen. Or a transgender woman."

"Yes," Sebastian said for the third time, trying not to lose his patience.

"An actual *female*. A real woman with breasts and a uterus and who can have babies?"

"Yes!"

"Is this a joke? Are you punking me?" Liam's head swiveled up, down, and sideways. "Are there cameras hidden in the apartment?" Liam got off the couch and began looking around, behind the drapes and inside closets, as if he expected a camera crew to suddenly jump out.

"It's no joke. I'm getting married. To Vivi."

"You can't do this!" Liam exclaimed in a burst of anger.

Sebastian was taken aback by Liam's tone. "I can't?"

"No, you can't!"

"Why not?"

"Why not? Why not? Because it doesn't make any sense." Liam threw his arms up in the air. "You're a gay man! You like men! That's what turns you on! You like everything about us. The way we walk, talk, look, smell, taste! For as long as I've known you, you've been gay. Sure, you're going to get a nice party and lots of gifts, but when you head off on your honeymoon the only thing you're going to have on your wedding night is a case of blue balls!"

Leave it to Liam to offer up a reality check. Everything he said was true. So true.

"Are you shitting me? You're really marrying Vivi?"

"Why are you having a hard time wrapping your head around this?"

"Oh, I don't know. Because when I left six months ago, you were a complete and utter homo. You were downloading porn from Gay Tube, listening to Kylie Minogue, watching *RuPaul's Drag Race,* and spearheading a NYC Free Britney campaign. Why would you even want to marry Vivi? Don't get me wrong. She's great. But I've never seen you as her type."

Sebastian blinked at Liam. "Vivi has a type? What's her type?"

Liam waved his hands in the air. "One of those Italian thug types."

"Italian thug types?" Sebastian exclaimed, shocked.

"A mafioso! That's what I meant. Don't they like to keep it all in the family? I mean, her mother's connected to the mob, right?"

Sebastian didn't answer. Because he honestly didn't know. Growing up, there had always been rumors and stories about Big Viv. And there had always been a line of black limos outside the bakery. Men in dark suits and sunglasses going in and out. Big Viv sometimes following after them when they were leaving, giving them huge hugs and kisses on the cheek before they stepped back into their cars.

He'd never discussed the subject with Vivi. Why would he? How did he ask his best friend if her mother was the mistress of a mafia foot soldier and tell her people in the neighborhood were saying the bakery was sometimes used to launder dirty money?

He didn't.

Sebastian had a decision to make.

Did he tell Liam the truth about why he was marrying Vivi, or did he make him think he'd suddenly developed a taste for breasts and cunnilingus?

He loved Liam like a brother. They'd been roommates for five years after they had done a season of summer stock together in Williamstown. He could trust him.

"Okay, look. I'm going to tell you something but you have to promise me you're not going to tell anyone else. Promise?"

"Bash, who would I tell?"

"Maybe one of your one-night stands?"

"I'm not into pillow talk."

"Swear!" Sebastian demanded.

"Okay, okay." Liam held up a palm, then crossed his heart. "I promise not to say anything to anybody. Ever."

And so Sebastian told him the entire story from beginning to end. There were breaks in the narrative whenever Liam asked a question. The only part Sebastian didn't tell him about was Dominick, the wedding planner. Why, he didn't know. Maybe because he was still processing that himself. Finally, when Sebastian was done, Liam was silent.

"You don't have anything to say now that you know the truth?" Sebastian asked. "You had plenty to say before."

Liam gave a low whistle. "I've met Vivi's mother. Many times. She kind of scares me. You don't want to get on her bad side. She seems like the type who could make someone disappear, if you know what I mean."

Sebastian buried his face in a couch pillow and screamed. "Enough with the Mafia stereotypes! Big Viv isn't going to rub me out when the truth comes out."

Liam gave him a skeptical look. "Are you sure?"

"I grew up around the woman! Of course, I'm sure."

"If you say so," Liam said, getting off the couch. "I'm going to go take a shower. I feel grimy from all the traveling I did today. Maybe we can watch something on Netflix when I'm done."

Sebastian didn't answer. He was still thinking of Liam's question and his answer. And what he didn't say. Because he *was* sure. He was.

But maybe not one hundred percent.

———

Something was definitely off about the engaged couple, but Dominick couldn't put his finger on exactly what it was. He'd been thinking about it ever since he'd met them earlier that day, but so far he'd come up with nothing.

After the initial awkward moment when he first met them, Dominick had slid into wedding planner mode, bombarding Vivi and Sebastian with all sorts of suggestions for their wedding, showing them images from other weddings he had planned and asking them questions so he could form some sort of game plan for their big day.

But he hadn't gotten much of a reaction out of either of them.

The future groom had seemed especially zombie-esque. Granted, he was a guy, and most guys weren't all that into wedding planning. They usually allowed their brides to handle everything.

But Vivi hadn't been as excited as other brides-to-be that he had worked with, either.

Something was definitely going on with them.

Maybe they were still processing not only the fact that they were going to be married sooner than they'd expected, but they were also going to be parents. Maybe they'd been caught off guard by Big Viv hiring him. Of course, Big Viv was in a class by herself. He was definitely going to have to figure out a way to handle her, otherwise she was going to take over this wedding and steamroll over all of them.

Whenever he'd asked Vivi and Sebastian a question or opinion, Big Viv would answer before they could. Until finally, he had gently suggested she let the engaged couple talk for themselves so he could get a sense of what they wanted for their big day. Big Viv had bristled at first, but then excused herself to go out into the bakery and help wait on customers.

Her absence hadn't changed anything. Vivi and Sebastian had still either remained mute or given the most lackluster answers to his questions.

The only other thought he had was maybe they'd planned to do everything themselves and they weren't sure how to work with him. Hopefully that would change in the days ahead.

In the meantime, he had other weddings to plan, with more excited brides and grooms. And their excitement was infectious, allowing him to come up with as many fun and creative ideas as possible that he was eager to share with them.

But before he could do that, he had to make a stop.

———

Someone was knocking on their apartment door.

Sebastian abandoned the latest John Grisham

thriller he was trying to read and got off the couch. As he approached the apartment door, he hoped it wasn't another one of Liam's jilted boyfriends. He was getting tired of cleaning up his messes. And after the day he'd had, he wasn't in the mood.

He pressed his eye to the peephole. When he saw who was on the other side, he quickly undid all the locks and flung the door open.

"Dom! What are you doing here?"

"Sorry to drop in unannounced. Did you know your front door is broken? I was able to walk right into the building. You should tell your superintendent about it."

"We have. Many times. And it still stays broken."

Dom reached into his shoulder bag and pulled out a pile of papers, handing them to Sebastian. "As I was sorting through my folders on my subway ride back into the city, I realized I had picked up a bunch of invoices when I was at the bakery today. Somehow, they got mixed up with my paperwork. I wasn't sure when we'd be seeing each other again, so I thought it would be easier if I just dropped them off. I wasn't sure if you needed them right away. Plus, it's less of a trek to here than back out to Brooklyn."

"How did you know where I lived?" Sebastian asked in confusion.

"Vivi gave me your address. I called her."

"Why don't you come in?" Sebastian held the door open wider. "Would you like something to drink? Beer? Wine? I have both."

Dom stepped inside the apartment, gazing around. "Nice place. You and Vivi don't live together?"

"No. I have a roommate."

And speaking of said roommate, Liam chose that moment to waltz into the living room, wearing nothing but a bath towel wrapped around his waist.

Talk about timing!

Sebastian was hoping for a little time alone with Dom. Today at the bakery had been awkward. Between Vivi and Big Viv, he felt like he'd had to keep his guard up so neither one would know how attracted he was to this man. And now this!

"Well, hello," Liam purred, turning on the charm as soon as he became aware there was another male in the room. "Who are you? Bash, aren't you going to introduce me to your friend?"

Sebastian gnashed his teeth. With no other choice, he made the introductions. "Dom, this is my roommate, Liam West. Liam, this is Dominick Campinello. He's the wedding planner."

"Whose wedding planner?" Liam asked.

"Sebastian and Vivi's," Dom said.

"Bash! Keeping secrets! You didn't tell me you had a wedding planner."

"Didn't I?"

Liam shook his head. "No, you didn't. You left out the best part of your story." He turned his attention back to Dom. "I've been out of town touring with a show. I'm an actor and today's my first day back. Just before you got here, Sebastian was filling me in on his whirlwind romance with Vivi. But he didn't mention you."

"He must have forgotten."

"Maybe he did. But I wouldn't forget someone as cute as you."

Dom blushed.

No, no, no! Sebastian started to panic. He had witnessed this before. Operation Seduction. In other words, when Liam turned on the charm and got whatever guy he was interested in to fall into bed with him.

He couldn't let that happen. He wouldn't.

He knew if he told Liam he was interested in Dom, he would instantly back off. In all their years of friendship, they had never gone after the same guy. But Liam didn't know he was interested. Otherwise, he wouldn't be making his usual moves.

"I'm sure you want to get into some clothes," Sebastian said.

Liam shrugged. "Why? I'm perfectly comfortable. If you can't lounge on your own couch just wearing a towel," he said as he sat down, "where can you?"

"Maybe you'd be more comfortable in a steam room," Sebastian said, taking off the gloves. "Isn't that where you usually like to go when you just want to have meaningless sex?"

For all he knew, Dom was into meaningless sex, too, and within the hour he'd be writhing against the sheets with Liam. Hopefully not here, though. That would be too much for Sebastian to deal with.

"What's wrong with sex without any strings attached? That sounds much nicer than saying meaningless sex. Sometimes, you just need to have an itch scratched," Liam explained. "Isn't that right, Dom?"

"I guess, if that's what you're into," Dom said in a way that gave Sebastian hope. He wasn't into meaningless sex!

"A cutie like you is probably going to hit the bars

tonight." Liam rose from the couch. "Give me a couple of minutes to get dressed and I'll join you."

Dom shook his head. "No bars for me tonight. I'm heading home. I've got a lot of work to do."

Liam gave Dom a disappointed look. "Maybe another night?" He gave Dom a warm smile. "I'd love to hang out and get to know you better."

Once again, Liam was turning on the charm. Sebastian had seen him in action before, but this was the first time Liam was pursuing a guy Sebastian actually wanted to date.

Stop! He couldn't think about dating Dom. He was engaged to marry Vivi.

"Are you absolutely sure?" Liam pleaded, batting his green eyes. "One drink? My treat."

"This is my busy time of the year," Dom explained. "Summer. Lots of weddings to plan. Long hours. I become a complete workaholic. None of my friends ever see me until Labor Day weekend."

"I get it," Liam said. "Well, if you have an opening in your calendar, you know where to find me. Or I can call you in a couple of weeks. You know what they say, all work and no play makes Jack a dull gay boy. What's your number?"

"You can get it from Sebastian."

"I'll give you a call," Liam promised as Dom left

the apartment and said goodnight to Sebastian. "I'm up for anything," he called out. "Anything!"

I'll just bet you are, Sebastian silently fumed as he closed the door behind Dom.

———

Dominick stood in the hallway outside Sebastian and Liam's apartment, trying to figure out what had just happened.

He wasn't exactly sure what had gone on, but it felt like he'd been caught in a tug of war between Sebastian and Liam. Like they were fighting over him. Which made absolutely no sense.

When Sebastian had opened the door, it was clear he'd been happy to see him. He'd been warm and smiling and much more animated than when Dominick first met him at the bakery.

But then, as soon as Liam showed up, it was like Sebastian totally shut down. He became sullen and angry and, for a straight guy, almost bitchy.

It was clear he didn't like Liam showing an interest in him. Although, why would that bother him?

Well, they were going to be working together. Maybe Sebastian just wanted to keep the wedding stuff and his personal life separate. Maybe he was just looking out for him, trying to avoid any sort of conflict or problems with his roommate. But Sebastian really didn't need to worry. Dominick was a big boy. He knew a player when he met one, and Liam was a player.

He always steered clear of players.

Dominick would never be interested in a guy like Liam. He knew the type very well. Only interested in sex. Nothing else.

Dominick didn't want that.

He had to admit, though, Liam's interest *had* been flattering.

He turned back to the apartment door. Maybe he'd made a mistake. Maybe he should indulge in a one-night stand.

But he wasn't a one-night stand type of guy! If he had a dollar for every guy who'd never called him back because he didn't want to jump right into bed on their first date, he'd have a nice wad of cash.

When he went to bed with a man, he wanted it to mean something. He'd always felt that way. He believed in love and romance.

That's why he did what he did. And every time he planned a wedding, a little part of himself wondered what his own wedding would be like one day. The flowers. The music. The vows. The rings. The first kiss. The location. The guests. The party. The food. The honeymoon.

And, of course, who his groom would be.

No, he'd made the right decision turning down Liam's not so subtle offer. Liam West was definitely *not* the marrying kind.

And that's the only kind he wanted.

As he walked down the stairs to the lobby, Dominick wondered how Sebastian and Liam had wound up being roommates. What could they possibly have in common?

———

"Looks like you left out part of the story," Liam said once Dom was gone.

"What part?" Sebastian asked in a crabby tone. He was bummed that Dom was gone and bummed that he hardly got to spend any time with him thanks to his horndog roommate.

"The wedding planner. The *gay* wedding planner."

"Oh."

"Is that all you have to say?"

"What do you want me to say?"

"You were shooting daggers at me whenever I spoke to him. Why?"

"Maybe I was just looking out for him," Sebastian said. "Ever think of that?"

"Dom's a big boy. I think he knows how to take care of himself."

"Not when it comes to you. I'm the one who always has to put back together the pieces of those hearts you break, remember? I know what you're like."

"What am I like?"

Sebastian gave Liam a look of disbelief.

"Maybe I'm changing my ways," Liam defended himself, settling against the couch cushions. "Ever think of that? Maybe I want to find a nice guy and settle down."

"Uh huh."

"So, how about that number?"

"What number?"

"Dom's number."

Sebastian stubbornly shook his head. "I'm not giving you his number. Forget it."

"Why not? Why does it bother you so much if I give him a call?"

Before Sebastian could answer, Liam's eyes widened in shock. "How could I be so stupid? You're interested in him! That's why you were acting so crazy when he was here, and that's why you won't give me his number."

The words slipped out before Sebastian could help himself. "And what if I am?"

"Bash, are you crazy?" Liam jumped off the couch. "You can't be interested in him. You're engaged. You're getting married. To Vivi. And don't forget who your mother-in-law is going to be. Big Viv! You do NOT want to get on her bad side."

Sebastian stared at Liam, not knowing what to say, until finally he found his voice. "Well, if I can't have him, you can't, either." And with those final words, Sebastian stormed into his bedroom and slammed the door behind him, the way he used to do when he was a kid.

CHAPTER
NINE

Being a wedding planner, it wasn't often that Dominick had a free weekend to himself. After all, Saturday was the most popular day of the week to get married. But between leaving his old job and starting his own business, he had lucked out and didn't have any work obligations for the next two weeks.

There was nothing he loved more than waking up on a Saturday morning when he was off. The lazy feeling of lying in bed, knowing that the entire day was yours. You could do whatever you wanted, whenever you wanted.

And that's exactly what he was doing today.

After flipping through the latest bridal magazines to make sure he was up to date on all the latest wedding trends, he called up his BFF, Lolly, and asked if she wanted to have lunch. They had become friends years ago when they were both working at a Bridal Expo show. After a long day of dealing with bridezillas on the hunt for freebies, the two had left the Jacob Javitz Center and found the nearest gay bar where they each ordered a frozen Cosmo and quickly became friends. Lolly was an aspiring wedding gown designer who worked freelance retail while trying to find someone to back her line. Whenever he could, Dominick suggested her as a possibility to his clients, but they always, always, ALWAYS wanted a "brand name" designer. Vera Wang. Carolina Herrera. Oscar de la Renta. Monique Lhuillier. It didn't matter that Lolly's sketches were better than anything they could find in an upscale boutique, and at half the cost! When asked who they were wearing, his brides wanted to drop a name. In Dominick's opinion, it was insane to spend so much money on a gown that was only going to be worn once, but who was he to judge?

Dominick knew Lolly was going to eventually find an investor for her line. It was only a matter of time.

Currently, she was working as a freelance perfume spritzer on the cosmetics floor at Saks Fifth Avenue. She had a late afternoon shift, so when they met for lunch near Union Square, she was more dressed up than Dominick—who had gone casual in madras shorts, a sky blue Ralph Lauren polo, and Ferragamo loafers—in a black leather mini-skirt, black sleeveless cotton turtleneck, and black gladiator sandals with a five-inch heel. Her cascade of honey blonde corkscrew curls was pulled up on top of her head in a Pebbles Flintstone top knot. As always, Lolly looked effortlessly chic.

They decided to go for Thai, and after lunch was over, they headed in the direction of Union Square, where Lolly would be able to catch the uptown 6 train.

As they walked, Dominick decided to drop a bombshell. It was something he'd been thinking about for a couple of weeks, and who better to bounce his idea off of than Lolly?

"I'm thinking about a dating service."

"A dating service?" She stared at him like he had three heads. "For what?"

"Duh. Dating."

"Isn't that expensive?"

Dominick shrugged. "Probably. I haven't looked into pricing yet."

"Didn't you recently start your own business?"

"Yes. Why does that matter?"

Lolly ignored the question. "Didn't you tell me just the other day that you're on a tight budget? No new clothes. No new shoes. No vacations or weekend getaways this year. You were going to be counting every last penny because you need to build up a nest egg until you feel your business is on solid ground."

"Yes—"

"If you're looking to save money, why would you pay someone to set you up? There's no guarantee you'll find someone."

"But that's what these dating services do. They guarantee results."

Lolly shook her head, her corkscrew curls bouncing from side to side. "You can't guarantee someone will meet their perfect match," she said, her voice filled with skepticism. "It's impossible."

"Why is it impossible?"

"Because falling in love is spontaneous!" Lolly exclaimed, staring at Dominick as if he should already know this. "It just happens. No one can explain it. You meet someone and there's a spark. An attraction. A click."

"I'd be attracted to the person I'm going out with. The agency sends you options to choose from."

"It needs to be more than just physical. Sure,

that gets the ball rolling. But what if you meet for lunch or dinner or a drink or whatever this agency sets up, and you have nothing to talk about?"

"The agency matches you up based on a questionnaire you fill out," Dominick reasoned. "I tell them my likes and dislikes, what I'm attracted to, and they do the rest."

Lolly sighed. "You're missing the point."

"What's the point?"

"You don't need a dating service! Why waste your money? You're the complete package."

"As lovely as that is to hear," Dominick gave Lolly a gentle kiss on the cheek, "this complete package is collecting dust. No one is curious about what's inside the packaging. And they haven't been for the last couple of months."

Lolly waved her hand dismissively. "You're having a dry spell. We all do. You'll get over it."

Dominick sighed. "I'm tired of dry spells. I'm tired of dating. Sure, the first couple of dates are fun at first, when you're just starting to get to know each other. But then, as time goes by and the novelty wears off—or the newness of another hot guy—the guy loses interest. And then I'm back swiping on my phone or buying two-for-one drinks during happy hour."

"But isn't that what's going to happen if you follow through with this dating service? Only you'll be out hundreds, if not thousands, of dollars. The dating service might find you the guy, but they can't guarantee you'll keep him!"

Dominick blinked at Lolly. She was right. Why hadn't he realized that? The dating service made the match, but that didn't mean their matches would stay matched.

"I just had another one of my brilliant ideas," Lolly said, doing an imitation of Blair Warner and her catch-phrase from the 80s sitcom, *The Facts of Life*. "I could do it for free."

"No," Dominick instantly replied before Lolly could go on. "Thank you, but I've had my fill of your blind dates."

"They weren't that bad."

"They were." He shuddered. "Every single one of them."

Lolly wrinkled her nose. "You're too picky."

"I'm not picky. All I ask is that a guy brush his teeth and hair. Is that too much to ask?"

"Kyle is a method actor! He was auditioning to play a hermit. He only ignored his personal hygiene for a month."

"I thought you'd be into this idea," Dominick said.

Lolly slipped her arm through Dominick's and gave it a squeeze. "Dom, sweetie, why the sudden urge to find Mr. Right?"

He shrugged. "I don't know. Maybe it's being surrounded by love and romance 24/7. It's making me realize what I'm missing out on. Don't get me wrong. I love planning weddings. But deep down, I'd like to be planning my own."

Lolly rested her head on Dominick's shoulder. "You will. Someday."

"If only I knew when that day was."

"How about I buy you something sweet to cheer you up?" Lolly said as they approached Union Square. It was filled with the weekend Farmers' Market, along with other vendors selling their goods. "Maybe a cookie?"

Dominick gave her a smile. "Sure. Why not?"

"This looks cute." Lolly approached a purple booth with a pink and white banner that read, SWEETS FOR THE SWEET.

Dominick noticed there was only one guy in the booth, and he was currently helping a customer. From a distance, he was cute. Nice body. Clothes that fit well. Stylish haircut. Maybe he'd get more than just a cookie. Maybe he'd be lucky enough to get a phone number, too. He'd have to dust off the old flirting skills.

But as they got closer to the booth, Dominick realized he knew who the guy was.

And he forgot all about flirting.

It was his newest client, the baker from Brooklyn. With the pregnant fiancé.

Sebastian had just handed a waxed bag filled with cookies to a young Asian woman with pink hair when he looked up and caught sight of Dominick, his eyes widening with surprise.

"Dom?"

"Sebastian."

"What are you doing here?" they both asked at the same time before laughing.

"This is my friend, Lolly," Dominick introduced. "We just had lunch and she's off to work. She's grabbing the 6 train before buying me a cookie."

"Everything looks so yummy!" Lolly exclaimed, gazing at the array of baked goods. "What do you recommend?

"Depends on what you're craving," Sebastian said. "If you're in the mood for a cupcake, I've got a couple of choices. First, there's the maple bacon cupcake. It's vanilla with small pieces of bacon baked inside and a maple syrup frosting. Then, there's the s'more cupcake. This one's vanilla cinnamon with a vanilla fluff center, chocolate frosting, and bits of marshmallow on top. If you want something citrusy, I've got two choices: lemon cupcakes with lavender frosting or orange crème cupcakes. They taste like orange creamsicles."

"I love creamsicles. I want one of those!"

"But then, there are the cookies," Sebastian added. "On top of the traditional chocolate chip and oatmeal, I've also got peanut butter cookie sandwiches and dark chocolate Mounds bar cookies drizzled with dark chocolate. Or, if you prefer brownies, I've got red velvet Oreo brownies, Nutella brownies, and fudgy chocolate brownies."

"Why are you making this so hard?" Lolly whined.

Sebastian smiled. "Last but not least, there are the bars. I've got oatmeal fig bars, chocolate peanut butter cheesecake bars, and lemon strawberry crumb bars."

Lolly stared at all the cookies, brownies, and cupcakes, nibbling on a long fingernail painted hot pink and decorated with yellow polka dots. "I can't make up my mind. They all look so yummy!"

"Why don't I make this easy for you?" Sebastian

filled up a box with a little bit of everything. "On the house."

"Oh, I couldn't let you do that!"

"Any friend of Dom's is a friend of mine."

"But if I eat all these, I'll get as big as a house!"

"You said you were on your way to work, right? Share with your co-workers and tell them where they can find me. We'll consider it free advertising."

"That is so sweet of you."

"Now, how about you?" Sebastian asked, turning to Dominick and giving him a wide smile. "What would you like? Same as Lolly?"

"No!"

Sebastian laughed. "I think you can indulge in a few sweets. You look like you keep yourself in pretty good shape."

"I get to the gym when I can, but I try to stay in shape by running. With so much to do, it helps me clear my head and keep myself on track."

"I can tell it works. Very nice legs."

Dominick blushed. "Thanks." He pulled his gaze away from Sebastian and back to the baked goods. "These all look amazing. How come I didn't see any of this stuff when I was out at the bakery earlier this week? Did it all sell out?"

Sebastian sighed. "I wish. As I'm sure you've

figured out by now, Big Viv is very opinionated as to what I can and can't bake at the bakery." Sebastian waved a hand at all his confections. "None of these fit the bill."

"You work at a bakery?" Lolly asked as she delicately nibbled on a creamsicle cupcake.

"In Brooklyn. During the week," Sebastian explained. "It's an Italian bakery and the owner has very clear ideas on what she wants to sell. But on the weekends, to make some extra cash, I sell my own stuff here. It also allows me to be a little bit more creative."

"Well, keep doing what you're doing," Lolly said as she took a bigger bite out of her cupcake. "You know how to bake!"

Dominick, never one to refuse anything made of Nutella, took a bite of the Nutella brownie Sebastian offered him. As the liquid chocolate burst into his mouth, he closed his eyes in ecstasy. "This is amazing. I haven't had anything this good in my mouth in a long time."

"I'm sure that's not true," Sebastian said.

"Trust him, it is," Lolly said, a sudden wicked gleam in her eyes. "But I'm sure you could change that. Don't you think, Dominick?"

He ignored her question. "You know, if you're

looking to make some extra money, I could probably swing some work your way. That is, if you're interested."

"I'm interested," Sebastian instantly answered. "Very interested."

"I could probably use you at some of my party events. My primary focus is weddings, but I'm also branching out into bridal showers and Sweet Sixteen parties and whatever else might come my way."

"Maybe we could get together and talk about it?" Sebastian suggested.

Dominick nodded. "Sure. I'll definitely be in touch."

"You know where to find me," he said. "Just call the bakery."

"Sorry to break this up, but I've got to run," Lolly interjected. "Saks Fifth Avenue calls." She held up the box. "Thank you again, Sebastian."

"My pleasure," he said, although his eyes remained locked on Dominick.

———

"He likes you," Lolly whispered excitedly as they walked away from the booth.

"Who?"

"That guy."

"What guy?" Dominick asked, his head swiveling around, looking to see who might be checking him out.

"The one who gave us all the free goodies. The baker!"

"Sebastian?" Dominick shook his head. "No. You're wrong."

"Why am I wrong?"

"Because he's getting married to a woman—a *pregnant* woman—and I'm planning their wedding."

"No!" Lolly gasped, her green eyes widening.

"Yes!"

Lolly peeked over her shoulder at Sebastian. "Maybe he's bi-curious?"

"Stop looking at him! I don't want him to think I'm interested."

"Aren't you?"

"I'm not coming between this guy and his baby mama."

"He must have been drunk," Lolly deduced.

"Drunk?"

"To have slept with her." Lolly stole a peek over her shoulder again. "He's literally undressing you with his eyes!"

"What?" Dominick suddenly found himself

tingling from head to toe. "No!" As nice as it was to hear the words, they couldn't be true. He could not tingle. Sebastian was engaged!

"Yes!"

Dominick glanced over his shoulder. Lolly was right. Sebastian *was* staring at him. Although, as soon as he noticed Dominick looking back, he tore his eyes away.

Dominick was totally confused. What was going on?

After dropping Lolly off at the subway entrance, Dominick made his way home. As he walked, he thought about all his encounters with Sebastian, and the pieces of the other day started falling into place.

Had his first instinct been right? Had Sebastian been jealous of Liam hitting on him because Sebastian was also interested?

But that didn't make any sense. Sebastian was getting married. To a woman!

Sure, there were plenty of gay men who married women. Either it was a marriage of convenience, or the guy hadn't yet realized he was gay. It happened all the time.

But this time, the equation was different. There was a baby involved. Vivi was pregnant and Sebastian was the father.

They could have slept together by accident, like Lolly said. Anything was possible. But still, why get married if he was gay? There were plenty of gay and straight parents out there who raised children together without getting married. So, why would Sebastian and Vivi be tying the knot? It didn't make sense.

Did he want it to make sense? Did he want to try and figure out what was going on?

They were his clients. He couldn't disrupt their wedding. It would be unethical. Immoral! Seducing the groom away from his bride.

Wait, who said anything about seducing?

Well, Sebastian was cute. He sort of reminded him of Chris Pratt. What guy wouldn't want to lock lips with him? And for a baker, he looked like he was in pretty good shape. He'd instantly noticed that, even from a distance, as they approached his booth. His clothes clung to his body in all the right places, showing off clearly defined muscles.

Muscles that Dominick wanted to touch.

Stop, stop, stop! He could not go there!

This was a nice, juicy contract with lots of zeroes. Maybe the bride and groom were lukewarm about their big day, but the mother of the bride was not. And he had a feeling if he pulled this wedding off, more work would be coming his way, courtesy of Big Viv. And more work was what he needed.

Love and sex and all that other good stuff would just have to wait for another day.

After all, if Sebastian was gay, he would say something, right? Why keep it a secret?

CHAPTER
TEN

Sebastian had never been good at keeping secrets.

All his life, whenever anyone said to him, 'It's a secret, you can't tell anyone else...' he immediately wondered who he could tell. Not that he ever did. On purpose. With a little gentle prodding it was never hard for him to spill what he knew.

And now, he had a secret he wanted to share with Dom. About Vivi and the baby.

He didn't know why he wanted to tell Dom the truth. He barely knew the guy.

Okay, that was a lie. He did know why. He liked Dom. A lot.

And if he didn't tell him how he felt, he was afraid someone else would come along before he was free of this wedding sham, and by then, Dom would be that someone else's boyfriend.

Knowing Vivi, she probably had a plan as to when their marriage would end, but right now, he was in the dark. Three months? Six months? How long did they need to be married for everyone to believe it was real? He couldn't leave his life in limbo without knowing when he would be back in control of it. And right now, he wasn't. Vivi was calling the shots. As much as he loved her, as much as she was his dearest friend, it really upset him because even being married to her for one day could mean losing a chance at real happiness.

He wanted to be Dom's boyfriend. Or at least be given a chance to audition for the part. For all he knew, Dom wouldn't be interested. But maybe he would.

Yet, he couldn't expect Dom to sit around waiting for him. Especially since he didn't even know how Sebastian felt.

But if he did know, would he wait?

Sebastian's gaze wandered around Union Square. Every weekend, he felt like he was trapped between heaven and hell. The heavenly part was all the money he made from his baked goods. He always sold out. The hellish part was watching all the couples—gay and straight—who came to Union Square on the weekend, holding hands, doing their weekly shopping after having brunch, searching for the perfect fruits and vegetables, breads, meats, and cheeses, then heading back to their apartments to snuggle up together with the weekend *Times* before getting ready to throw a dinner party or order take-out and settle on the couch with Netflix or go out to dinner and a movie.

He wanted that, too.

Okay, so maybe he was going overboard with the fantasy he was spinning. Not every couple had the perfect life. But he wanted to find out. He wanted to be part of a couple. He wanted to settle down.

His mother was one of six siblings and his father was one of eight. So, he had lots of cousins. And for the last few years, he had been going to one family wedding after another, watching his cousins say 'I do' before starting new lives with their spouses.

When was that going to happen for him?

"Got any more of those maple bacon cupcakes?"

The sound of Dom's voice pulled Sebastian out of his thoughts. "You're back!" Sebastian tried not to sound overeager, but seeing Dom standing before him made him want to do the Snoopy happy dance.

Dom nodded. "I'm back."

"I thought you had the Nutella brownie," Sebastian said.

"Good memory. A man who pays attention to details. I like that."

The words slipped out before Sebastian could stop them. "What else do you like about me?"

Dom looked taken aback by the question. But then, he gazed at Sebastian, staring at him so intently that Sebastian started to squirm. "I like how you bake," he finally said.

That's it? Sebastian thought to himself. *You like how I bake? You don't want to rip my clothes off and have sex with me right this minute? Because I want to have sex with you.*

Dom leaned over the table, whispering in Sebastian's ear, although Sebastian wouldn't mind if he started to nibble on it. "Can you keep a secret?"

Of course I can keep a secret. I'm keeping a big secret from you. I'm not straight. I'm gay!

"I have a sweet tooth. But don't tell Big Viv. She might get offended. The other day when I was at the bakery I told her I didn't when she offered me some goodies. But if I'd known how talented her baker was, I would have said yes."

"Your secret is safe with me. So, what brings you

back? Unfortunately, I'm sold out of everything, including the maple bacon cupcakes."

"I thought maybe we could get a drink and talk about the wedding. Maybe you could give me some insight into Vivianna and what we can do to make her wedding day perfect. We could go now if you're finished up here."

Sebastian tried not to groan. The last thing he wanted to do was talk about the wedding. At the same time, talking about the wedding meant spending more time with Dom, which he wanted to do.

"But if now isn't a good time..." Dom said, sensing his hesitancy.

Sebastian was torn. He wanted to say yes. But why torture himself? He was marrying Vivi!

Yet, against his better judgement, Sebastian said, "Why don't you come back to my apartment? I'm working the booth tomorrow and I have to do some baking. You could be my official taste tester. And I can whip you up a batch of maple bacon cupcakes. We can talk about the wedding, too," he rushed to add. "What do you say?"

What did he say?

Dominick didn't know how to answer. He wanted to say yes. There was something about Sebastian that intrigued him. And then, there was that question: *What else do you like about me?* It had taken him by surprise.

It was almost as if Sebastian had been fishing for a compliment. But why would he want a compliment from him?

He really hadn't come back for a maple bacon cupcake. He had come back to learn more about the man who made them. To find out if Lolly had been right.

As much as he wanted to go back to Sebastian's apartment, he couldn't. Not until he gave this whole situation some more thought.

So, he made a decision. The responsible one. He pulled out his phone and stared at the screen, pretending there was a text. "I'm so sorry. As tempting as the offer is to be your taste tester, I forgot I was supposed to meet a friend for drinks. He's wondering where I am. I've got to run."

"Raincheck?" Sebastian asked hopefully.

Dominick said the words before he could stop himself. "Absolutely. I'll give you a call."

"Let me give you my cell number," Sebastian

said, reciting the number. "In case you can't reach me at the bakery. As you can see, I'm not there every day. Big Viv has another baker who works on the weekends."

Dominick punched the numbers into his phone, then sent Sebastian a text with a smiley face. "Did you get it?"

Sebastian checked and nodded before going back to cleaning up his booth. "Have fun with your friend."

As Dominick walked away, he wondered if it was only his imagination that Sebastian had seemed a bit disappointed he had to leave. He resisted the urge to look over his shoulder. He didn't know what he would do if he found Sebastian staring after him.

———

Vivi was stuffing her face. She had a craving. Again.

For Funyuns. She had been inhaling bag after bag for the last two days.

This was not good. At this rate, if she kept eating them, she wasn't going to be able to fit into her wedding dress. Not because of a baby bump, but because she was pigging out!

She was in her kitchen, checking to see what she

could pair the Funyuns with when her phone rang. She checked it and groaned. Her mother.

She ignored the call as she licked her fingers and wiped them around the bottom of the empty Funyuns bag, wanting every last salty bit of onion ring deliciousness.

Her mother was driving her crazy. Her latest obsession was wedding dresses. She was constantly calling and texting with suggestions. They were supposed to go shopping next week. Vivi was dreading it. She had always hated shopping for clothes with her mother. They did *not* have the same taste. While her mother preferred bright colors and bold patterns, Vivi was the complete opposite. While she liked her clothes to be form fitting, she preferred muted colors and attention to detail. Designer labels. She went for quality over quantity, building her wardrobe with a number of pieces that would stand the test of time.

Her phone rang again as she was rummaging through her freezer, looking for a pint of Ben & Jerry's Vanilla Caramel Fudge. She glanced at the phone, expecting it to be her mother again, only this time it was Sebastian. She instantly answered. "Hey, what's up!"

"We need to talk."

Uh oh. This didn't sound good. Sebastian's voice was serious. "About what?" she cautiously asked.

"The wedding."

"What about the wedding?"

"I'm getting cold feet."

"Sebastian! Nooo!" Vivi wailed, trying not to panic, all thoughts of ice cream forgotten. She knew him. When he made up his mind about something, there was no changing it. "You can't back out now. You promised you'd help me."

"I know, but—"

"But what?"

"I've met someone."

"You've met someone?" Okay, this was a curveball she hadn't been expecting, but she could find a way to deal with it. "That's great. But what does that have to do with you changing your mind?"

Sebastian sighed. "Vivi, I can't start dating a guy when I'm supposed to be marrying you."

"Then, don't tell him you're getting married."

There was silence at the other end of the line.

"Don't tell him we're getting married," she repeated. "It's not like the marriage is going to last very long. We get married, live together for a couple of weeks, and then we get the marriage annulled.

After that, you can spend as much time as you want with this guy. Problem solved."

"Problem *not* solved. I can't not tell him."

"Why not?"

There was silence again.

"Bash, are you still there?"

"It's complicated," he said.

"How is it complicated?"

"It just is."

Vivi felt like there was a piece missing to this puzzle, something Sebastian wasn't telling her. She just didn't know what it was.

"What about your bakery?" she asked.

"What about it?"

"You agreed to go through with this so you could have the money to open your own bakery. Not to sound harsh or bitchy, but do you really want to throw away your dream of owning a bakery all on some random guy who might not stick around?"

Sebastian's voice got heated. "What makes you think he might not stick around?"

Oops! That didn't come out the way she meant. Obviously, this guy was special to Sebastian. She wanted to point out that Sebastian's track record when it came to relationships wasn't very good, but hers wasn't any better, so who was she to talk?

Besides, she knew those weren't the words he wanted to hear.

"What aren't you saying, Vivi? That I'm lousy at relationships?"

"Of course not! You're never the problem. They are."

"So, now you're saying I have lousy taste in men?"

"No! Why are you putting words in my mouth? That's not what I meant at all. Why are you jumping down my throat?"

"Because I've met a guy I really like," Sebastian stated. "And I want to pursue things with him, but I can't. Because I'm marrying you."

"Tell me about him," Vivi said, thinking that talking about this guy might calm Sebastian down. "Where did you meet?"

"What does it matter where we met?" Sebastian sounded like a pouting child. "I don't want to talk about him."

"Why not?" Vivi tried not to sound hurt, although she knew how Sebastian was when he first met someone new. He was always super secretive. He usually didn't share any personal info until after the third or fourth date. And she didn't get to meet Mr. Right until they were dating for at least a month, sometimes two. Sebastian was always afraid of jinxing things if he told her too much too soon. This wasn't unusual.

But still, he was usually more forthcoming than this. "What's going on? What aren't you telling me?"

"Why would I be on the phone with you if I wasn't telling you everything? All you need to know is that I think this guy is special, Vivi. I don't want to lose him. I don't want to lose my chance to see if maybe we could have something together."

There was such longing in Sebastian's voice, and it was breaking her heart. But she needed his help. Just for a little bit.

"Bash, please. Please, please, please give me a little more time. I haven't even taken the paternity test yet. I'm begging you. Please don't back out on me. I need you to go through with this."

There was silence on the line for a third time before Sebastian spoke again. "Okay. Fine. I'm still in."

Vivi sighed with relief. "Thank you, Sebastian. You don't know how much this means to me."

"I'm sorry. I didn't mean to dump this all on you. The last thing I want to do is stress you out. I can't imagine it's good for the baby. I guess I panicked. I'm just feeling a bit trapped. This whole thing seems to be snowballing."

"Tell me about it. My mother wants to go shopping for wedding dresses next week. And she's already started talking about tuxes. And the wedding party. Start thinking about who you want to have as your groomsmen."

"Vivi..." Sebastian croaked. "You're not helping."

"You're not going to have another panic attack, are you?"

"No, but I don't feel like I'm in control of my life."

"Bash, it's only for a few weeks. A month or two tops. Then, it will all be over. And this guy? The one that you like so much? If he likes you as much as you like him, he'll still be waiting."

"I hope you're right, Vivi. I hope you're right."

And then, Sebastian ended the call.

CHAPTER
ELEVEN

Bloody Mary Brunch was never a good idea, especially when you were thinking about a guy.

And Dominick was thinking about a guy. One specific guy. A lot.

He took a sip of his second Bloody Mary and typed out a text to Sebastian. *Remember when you offered to bake for me? How about you show me what you've got tonight?*

That sounded vague enough. Obviously, he was talking about desserts. He was! But it could be interpreted to mean other things. It all depended on Sebastian, and what he really wanted.

If Sebastian wanted something more, he would let Dominick know, right? But why would he? Sebastian wasn't interested in him. He was marrying

Vivi. A *pregnant* Vivi. He had to stop this. He was going to drive himself crazy.

Dominick began erasing the text.

Why couldn't Lolly have kept her mouth shut? Yes, he had sensed *something* when he'd first shook hands with Sebastian. And it had made him wonder. But he'd dismissed it. Now that he knew *something* might exist, he couldn't help but want to find out more.

He stopped erasing the text and began to retype it. It couldn't hurt to know for sure. Before he could stop himself, Dominick sent the text, wondering how long it would take Sebastian to text back.

A second later, his phone pinged.

Apparently, not very long.

Sounds great. Why don't you swing by my place around seven?

Dominick finished his Bloody Mary in one gulp and waved his empty glass at the waiter, signaling for another.

"Who are you texting?" Lolly asked, returning to the table after a trip to the ladies room. "You looked so intense."

"Who do you think?" Dominick asked somewhat testily, crunching on a celery stalk.

Her eyes lit up. "The baker?"

Dominick sighed. "The baker."

Lolly clapped her hands together, the gold bangle bracelets on both her wrists happily jangling. "Yay! Romance!"

Dominick pointed his celery stalk at her. "It's *not* romance," he emphasized. "It's work. I'm thinking of using him for some events and he's going to show me how good he is in the kitchen."

Lolly arched an eyebrow. "I bet he's good in other rooms, too. Like the bedroom."

The waiter arrived with Dominick's third Bloody Mary and he took a long sip. "This is all your fault. You're the one who planted the idea that he might be interested in me. Now, ever since you said it, I can't get it out of my mind."

"Not might. Is. He *is* interested in you."

Dominick took another sip of his Bloody Mary. "We'll see."

What am I doing? Dominick wondered as he prepared to knock on Sebastian's apartment door at seven. Why was he on this fishing expedition? There was nothing to find out. Sebastian and Vivi were getting married. That was it. End of story. Lolly was wrong.

Then, why was there this niggling feeling that maybe she might be right?

And if she was?

It wasn't like he had a plan. It wasn't like he was planning on seducing Sebastian. So, why had he dressed in one of his "night out at the gay bars with his friends" outfits?

His tightest pair of jeans. His ass looked fantastic in them. No underwear, to show off his package. And yes, he did have a *very* nice package. Or so he had been told more than once. A shrunken T-shirt that showed his muscles off. He was nicely built and went to the gym regularly, but he wasn't a steroid monster with popping veins.

The merchandise was on display, although what was the point? Sebastian was engaged. Dominick sighed. Well, he could always go to a bar after he left.

He knocked on the door and when it opened, it was all he could do to stop his mouth from dropping open.

Sebastian had trumped him.

There was no way this was not a message. Like Liam the night before, Sebastian wore a towel wrapped around his waist. Only a towel.

Didn't these guys believe in robes?

"Sorry, you're earlier than I expected." Sebastian ran a hand through his sweaty hair. "I just got back from the gym. With all the taste-testing I do, I need to stay on top of my weight. Otherwise, I'd be as big as a house."

There wasn't one extra ounce of fat or flab anywhere on Sebastian. The guy must live at the gym.

Dominick pulled his gaze away from the towel and back up to Sebastian's face. "I thought we said seven o'clock."

"Did we? I thought it was eight."

Dominick always liked giving people the benefit of the doubt. Could Sebastian have forgotten the time they agreed on? Maybe. Or perhaps, he hadn't. Perhaps, he answered the door this way on purpose. But why would he do that?

He heard Lolly whispering in his ear. "Because he wants to turn you on!" Dominick ignored her voice. Whatever the reason, he certainly wasn't going to complain. He liked what he saw. For a baker, Sebastian kept himself in mighty fine shape.

Why was he realizing this now?

Well, duh. Because he was only wearing a towel.

"I was just getting ready to hop in the shower."

The words were on the tip of Dominick's tongue, "Want some company?" He clasped a hand over his mouth. Those words didn't slip out, did they? Sebastian was still calmly staring at him. There was no shock on his face. He hadn't said them aloud. Phew!

"Why don't you come in? I won't be very long. Make yourself at home. There's stuff to drink in the fridge. Just help yourself."

Dominick could sense Sebastian's eyes looking him over from head to toe as he walked into the apartment, and he couldn't help but give his butt a little wiggle. Why not? If Sebastian was going to tempt him, then he was going to tempt Sebastian.

"Take your time. I'm sure I can keep myself busy."

While he was in the shower, Dominick explored the living room and kitchen. Both rooms were a mix of flea market finds and Ikea furniture. But everything looked comfortable and lived-in. It felt like a home. There were also lots of photos of Vivi, which he had expected, some of them going all the way back to high school, making him wonder if they'd been a couple since then. There were also photos of Sebastian and his family—faces he assumed were his mom, dad, siblings, and grandparents. He was taking a closer look at a high school graduation photo of Sebastian and Vivi when he heard the click of the apartment door's lock.

That could only mean one thing. Liam.

"Hellooo," Liam said, looking especially hot in a pair of white Adidas booty shorts and a navy blue tank top. "What did I do to deserve this? Are you changing your mind and taking me up on my offer?"

Dominick's first reaction was to say no. But then, he started thinking. This guy was 110% gay. Hot. Correction. Very hot. And interested in him.

So, why not sleep with him? At the very least, it would help him to forget about Sebastian.

Maybe that's what he needed. A mindless fling. He'd clear his head and be able to focus on work. Why not lose himself in sex for once, with no strings attached?

Dominick was about to say yes when Sebastian came out of his bedroom, pulling a Schitt's Creek T-shirt over his head. It was an illustrated image of David and Moira in the kitchen that said, *You just fold in the cheese.*

"Liam! What are you doing here? I thought you had rehearsal for your new show. You weren't supposed to be home until midnight."

"Rehearsal got canceled."

Why does Sebastian sound so panicked? Dominick wondered. It was Liam's apartment, too. He had every right to be here whenever he wanted. But Sebastian had expected to have the place to himself tonight.

Hmm... Maybe it was time to put things to the test.

"Liam was asking me if I wanted to take him up on his offer from the other night," Dominick said, watching as a grin broke out across Liam's face. Sebastian looked like he was about to pass out.

"Are you thinking of saying yes?" Sebastian's voice was barely a croak.

"I might. If Liam can convince me." He turned back to the roommate. "Are you up to the challenge?"

Liam raced to Dominick's side, wrapping an arm around his shoulders. "Why don't we take this into my bedroom?"

Sebastian lifted Liam's arm off Dominick's shoulder and dropped it to his side. "Why don't we not? Dom is *my* guest. I invited him over tonight to sample some of my baked goods. Once that's over with, the two of you can go off and do whatever it is you want to do. Business first, then pleasure. Deal?"

Was that a tone of possessiveness in Sebastian's

voice? Dominick hated to admit it, but he loved hearing it.

Liam sighed. "Fine." He made a shooing motion with his hands. "Why don't you run along into the kitchen, Bash. Make like Mildred Pierce with your cookies and cakes. You don't need Dom for that. After all, you're the baker. We're the taste-testers. Go whip up a few treats and then bring them out. In the meantime..." Liam plopped himself down on the couch and patted the spot next to him, locking eyes with Dominick. "Why don't you come sit next to me and we'll watch some TV. Or do some of the other things people do when they're on the couch..."

"Yes, Veda," Sebastian said through gritted teeth, storming off into the kitchen.

"Actually, I see myself as more of an Ida," Liam called back. "You ever seen *Mildred Pierce*?" Liam asked Dominick. "Great old movie. Won Joan Crawford her one and only Oscar for Best Actress. Veda was her bitchy daughter and Ida was her wisecracking BFF."

"Of course I've seen *Mildred Pierce*. All the gay bars show that clip of Veda slapping Mildred across the face."

Liam chuckled. "I bet Christina would have loved to have done that to Mommie Dearest, although I'm sure Joan would have bashed her with her Oscar if she'd tried."

As he approached the couch, Dominick wished he had an Oscar to fend off Liam. He had a hungry look in his eyes that made Dominick feel a little bit like Little Red Riding Hood crossing paths with the Big Bad Wolf.

But he had to. Because flirting with Liam was getting under Sebastian's skin. Which, he had to perversely admit, he kind of liked.

It definitely bothered Sebastian that Liam was interested in him. The question again was why?

―――――

Sebastian kept messing up his baking. A tablespoon of baking powder instead of a teaspoon. Using vanilla extract when the recipe called for almond. Pre-heating the oven at the wrong temperature.

He took a deep breath and told himself to focus. Focus!

This could be a great business opportunity. A way to make more money and branch out. Network. He didn't want to work for Big Viv for the rest of his life. He wanted a bakery of his own.

A bakery of his own...

He groaned. By this time next year, he could easily have it. All he had to do was marry Vivi and she would give him the financial stake he needed. He just had to get through the next few weeks.

So, why was it so hard? He knew why. Dom. He didn't want to wait a few weeks to see if there could be anything between them. He wanted to find out now. But he'd promised Vivi he would go through with the wedding.

And a promise was a promise.

She was his oldest friend and he would do anything for her. He could do this. He knew he could.

As he cracked eggs into a bowl, he tilted his head in the direction of the living room, trying to hear what was going on out there, but it was quiet.

Too quiet. Quiet wasn't good.

I will not look in the living room, he chanted to himself silently.

Sebastian ignored the mantra and went to look in the living room, sticking his head out of the kitchen while he cradled a bowl of batter under his arm, stirring it.

Liam and Dom sat on the couch, a little closer than what Sebastian would have liked, peering at Liam's cellphone.

Knowing Liam, he was probably showing Dom nudes of himself. In anticipation of what was to come. The photos had been professionally done for his acting portfolio, so Sebastian knew they looked good. He groaned. Why had he told them business first, pleasure later? It was like he was giving them permission to screw around.

He couldn't let that happen. He needed to get Liam out of the way. Not permanently, just temporarily. At the very least, for tonight.

And then, he had an idea. A deliciously wicked idea.

———

"Who wants some cupcakes?" Sebastian announced an hour later, waltzing out of the kitchen with a platter of beautifully designed treats.

Liam jumped off the couch, abandoning Dominick, making a beeline for the platter.

Sebastian smacked his hand away. "Don't be so grabby!"

Dominick laughed. If there was one word that described Liam, it was grabby. On the couch with him, Liam was like an octopus, his hands roaming everywhere. While Dominick enjoyed a man's touch, he also liked to be part of the process. He'd tried doing a little exploring of his own, a little kissing, too, but Liam was the one who wanted to be in control. Dominick never liked that. It meant the guy was going to be a selfish lover, and so far Liam was checking all the boxes. He was like a great white shark with only one thing on his mind: cock. He'd tried to unzip Dominick's pants more than once to slide his hand inside and seize what was hidden away, but Dominick had been quite adept at keeping his pants zipped by twisting his waist away.

"I get it," Liam had whispered in his ear. "You like privacy. We'll disappear into my bedroom after Bash is done baking. Unless you want to slip away now?"

No, he did *not* want to. If he wanted fast, he could do that himself at home with a video and some lube. When he had sex, he wanted the experience to last for hours, to enjoy every last bit of pleasure. Unlike Liam, he didn't want to rush through it. He was saved from answering when Sebastian re-emerged from the kitchen.

Sebastian held the platter out to Dominick. "Our guest gets first pick. I also have some other desserts that I made earlier in the day out in the kitchen. You can sample those, too, if you want, or take them home."

As he studied the cupcakes, listening while Sebastian explained each flavor combo, he couldn't help but notice there was a difference in his host. He seemed much calmer. Almost happier.

Maybe baking relaxed him. He seemed way less stressed than earlier.

Dominick selected a cupcake, and Sebastian handed a pink one to Liam.

"Don't I get to pick?" Liam pouted.

"You've already tried all these. This is a new recipe," Sebastian said. "Let me know what you think."

Liam unwrapped the cupcake and inhaled it in two bites. "Tasty." He reached for a second one.

"You could at least savor the flavors, you primate!" Sebastian groused.

As Dominick sampled his own cupcake, he noticed something.

Liam's face was turning red. Very red. And very quickly. From the neck up, it looked like he was blushing. And bumps were starting to form all over his face.

"Is everything okay?" Dominick asked him.

"What do you mean?" Liam asked, licking pink frosting off his fingers.

"Your face is turning all red."

Sebastian gasped. "He's right."

Liam dropped his cupcake and ran to a mirror in the hallway. "Holy shit! I'm breaking out! And I've got an audition for a TV commercial tomorrow. Bash, what the hell did you put in those cupcakes?"

"Are you having an allergic reaction to something?" Dominick asked.

"Oh no!" Sebastian wailed. "I totally forgot about your allergy to strawberries. They were in the frosting. And the batter."

Liam shot Sebastian a dark look. "How could you forget?"

"I'm so sorry, Liam. I guess I was trying so hard to impress Dom that it slipped my mind."

"That's not so hard to do when it's empty upstairs!" Liam snapped.

"Do you need to go to the emergency room?" Dominick asked.

"No," Liam said as more bumps appeared on his arms and legs. He began scratching himself. "All I have to do is take an antihistamine and soak in a tub filled with baking soda. That is, unless our master baker has used it all up?"

"There's plenty left. I'll run the tub for you."

"I'll do it myself, "Liam grumbled, heading in the direction of the kitchen. "If I let you do it, the water will probably be scalding."

"I'm sorry, Liam," Sebastian said for a second time.

"Uh huh," he said over the opening and closing of cabinet doors. Baking soda in hand, he stormed into the bathroom, slamming the door behind him.

And then, there were two.

"Poor guy. Is he going to be okay?"

"He'll be fine." Sebastian took Liam's spot on the couch. "Come sit down." He held out the platter. "Try another cupcake."

"Maybe he should go to the emergency room, just to be on the safe side. One of us should take him."

"He can get checked out tomorrow."

"Tomorrow?"

"When he goes to the free clinic."

"Why would he be going to the free clinic?"

Sebastian rolled his eyes. "You can't sleep around as much as Liam does and not pick up a few STDs. Not that I'm saying he has. Although, do crabs count?"

"I heard that!" Liam shouted from behind the

closed bathroom door as water began to run. "I've never had crabs!"

Sebastian shrugged. "Whatcha gonna do? Boys will be boys."

Dominick locked eyes with Sebastian, wondering if he really forgot about Liam's allergy. It seemed like he was trying awfully hard not to break out into a smile. "Like all's fair in love and war?"

Sebastian bit into a strawberry frosted cupcake. "That, too."

"I don't think Liam is going to be in the best mood after he gets out of that tub," Dominick said. "Why don't we head out for a drink? We can talk about baking and wedding plans...and other things."

CHAPTER
TWELVE

Sunday night was Big Viv's beauty night.

It was the one night of the week when she pampered herself. First, she started with a detox bath, soaking in a tub of lavender scented water. Then, she washed her hair and followed up with a leave-in conditioner. After applying a deep cleansing mud mask and Crest white strips to her teeth to brighten her smile, she brushed a nail conditioning oil onto her nail beds and cuticles, then slipped on a pair of gloves enriched with botanical butter to make her hands nice and smooth.

It took a lot of work to keep looking good, but Big Viv put in the time.

The entire process was usually two hours in the privacy of her bedroom, often listening to Frank

Sinatra or watching a movie while lounging in her brass bed.

Of course, there were trips to the salon to maintain her color and keep the gray away—no boxed hair dye for her; she wanted her color to still look natural, not fake!—not to mention her weekly manicures and pedicures. And every couple of months, she treated herself to a weekend away at a health spa where she indulged in massages.

Yes, she really should have an exercise plan, but she watched what she ate and didn't overindulge. A glass of wine once or twice a week, and maybe a dessert. She wasn't as thin as she used to be, but who the hell was? Aging slowed down one's metabolism, and she wasn't going to starve herself. Every time she went to her doctor for her yearly physical, he talked about bone density and calcium supplements, like she was an old lady! She was only sixty-three, for crying out loud. There was plenty of time for walking around the block in velour tracksuits carrying hand weights.

But now that Vivi was getting married, she was going to need to make more of an effort with her beauty regimen. And there wasn't a lot of time. First, they needed to get a wedding date on the calendar. She made a mental note to follow up with the wedding planner tomorrow. Naturally, she wanted everyone's eyes on the bride, not on Vivi's belly!

And, of course, as mother of the bride, she wanted everyone's eyes on her, too.

There were still so many things to do! Find a gown, decide on her hairstyle, figure out the jewelry she was going to wear.

This was going to be her moment in the spotlight, and she was going to relish it.

Next on her agenda was the wedding list. Who to invite? More importantly, who *not* to invite?

Big Viv's lips curled into a smile that would make the Grinch proud. Yes, she held grudges. She always tried to be the better person, but sometimes people treated others like shit. And when that happened, one was supposed to forget and turn the other cheek?

Never. Not her.

That's why she hadn't forgiven Deena after all these years. They had been best friends…

No! She wasn't going to think about Deena. How much time had she wasted over the years wondering how their friendship had gone wrong? What she had done or said? She had been deeply hurt at the time, and while the pain had lessened as the years had gone by, it was still there. But she wasn't going to think about that. It needed to be all about Vivi.

She still couldn't wrap her head around her daughter and Sebastian getting married. They had been friends for a long time. Maybe friendship had turned to love.

But she could have sworn he was gay.

Although, thinking back on the past, she had never seen Sebastian with a guy, so apparently she had been wrong. And she knew first hand how people in this neighborhood could gossip and trash talk behind one's back. They had done it to her too many times to keep count.

Like saying she was the mistress of a low-level Mafioso. Yes, her beloved Gino had done accounting for guys who had worked for some of the families, but it had been their income tax returns! After Gino died, they used to come to the house to see if she and Vivi were okay. If they needed anything fixed or needed a little help with paying the bills. Gino had been good to them, and in return, they wanted to be good to her. Same thing with their wives, who would also visit, bringing extra food and gifts for Vivi.

But somehow the gossipmongers in the neighborhood had twisted it into something ugly and made it sound like the supporting cast of *Goodfellas* was traipsing in and out of her bedroom.

Eventually, rumors became fact, no matter what the truth was.

As Frank Sinatra started singing *My Way*, Big Viv grabbed a pen and piece of paper off her nightstand, burrowed into the mounds of lace-trimmed pillows propped against her back, and began to write down names in two columns: INVITE and DON'T INVITE.

———

"So, did you really forget about your roommate's strawberry allergy?" Dominick asked as he followed Sebastian into HMSX, a gay bar a few blocks away from Sebastian's apartment. Dominick had suggested the place, having been there a few times with friends who lived on the Upper East Side. The interior of the bar had warm lighting and intimate arrangements of square leather cubes around small cocktail tables scattered throughout the space. There were black and white photos framed on the walls of male torsos and couples kissing, and in an alcove on the second floor, where the bar's office and restrooms were, there was a DJ controlling the music. They found a corner and settled themselves in, flagging over a waiter.

"Of course I did!" Sebastian exclaimed. "Why would I purposely feed him something he was allergic to?"

Dominick shrugged. "I don't know. You tell me. Maybe you wanted to keep the two of us apart."

Sebastian laughed. "That's ridiculous."

"Is it? You seemed pretty possessive the other night. Not to mention tonight. It was almost like you were jealous."

"Possessive? Jealous? Me? Of course not!"

Dominick leaned forward and caught the scent of cinnamon and vanilla. He wondered if Sebastian smelled like that all over. Would he taste like cinnamon and vanilla if he kissed him? If he traced his tongue all over his body? He quickly chased away those thoughts. "What aren't you telling me, Sebastian?"

"I was only looking out for you, okay?" Sebastian admitted. "You're a nice guy, Dom. I don't want you getting hurt. Liam's not relationship material. Don't get me wrong, he's got a lot going for him, but he doesn't know how to commit. He's immature. He's broken a lot of hearts and I don't want yours to be one, too."

Dominick picked up the specialty cocktail menu on the table between them and started scanning it. "Thanks for the concern, but I'm a big boy. I can take care of myself. If I decide to pursue anything with Liam, it's my decision. Not yours." *Not that I'm planning to, but you don't have to know that.* "I've tangled with bridezillas, momzillas, and now gayzillas. I can handle Liam."

"Gayzillas?"

Dominick put down the menu. "Now that gay marriage is legal, straight couples don't have a monopoly on being impossible to deal with when they're planning their weddings. Gay and lesbian couples can be just as bad. The stories I could tell you."

"Like?"

Dominick leaned forward with a look of disgust on his face. "I'll never forget this one bride I had. She was straight. One of her bridesmaids got cancer and had to go through chemo. As the wedding date got closer, she became thinner and started wearing a wig. The bride was afraid she would look bad in her pictures, so she replaced her a week before the wedding and wouldn't reimburse her for all the money she'd already spent on her bridesmaid dress and shoes." Dominick shook his head sadly. "Another bride flipped out on her wedding day when she saw her bridesmaids weren't all wearing the same color of nail polish and ordered them to hide their hands behind their bouquets. One bride asked me to make copies of a handwritten thank-you note to send out. She couldn't be bothered to write them out individually."

"Tell me more, tell me more," Sebastian sang, channeling his performance of Kenickie from *Grease*.

"There was the gay couple who were pissed that no one could afford their destination wedding to Tuscany. They invited two hundred people and only nine said they were coming. So, they sent out instructions telling the guests who weren't coming where they were registered and the minimum dollar amount of the gift they wanted to receive." Dominick rolled his eyes. "And there was this lesbian couple who told their guests they didn't want gifts, just cash for their honeymoon. And I'll never forget this one lipstick lesbian bride who gave printed instructions to her bridesmaids. On the day of the wedding, they weren't allowed to talk to her, they all had to dye their hair blonde and wear it in a French braid—and if their hair wasn't long enough for a French braid, they had to get extensions put in—and they couldn't give her a wedding gift less than seven hundred dollars."

"How do you put up with it?"

Dominick shrugged. "You put a smile on your face and do the best you can. You don't want to piss anyone off because what I do is a word-of-mouth business. Brides and grooms usually have lots of single friends who are going to eventually get married and might need a wedding planner."

A waiter came up to their table, looking down at his electronic ordering pad, but his face lit up when he caught sight of them.

"Hey, Sebastian! Your usual?"

"You have a usual?" Dominick asked as he arched a brow.

"Bud Light," the waiter answered, tapping on his screen. "And you?"

"Dirty martini."

The waiter tapped again. "Be right back."

"The waiter knows you," Dominick stated. "You come here often?"

"Sometimes. With Liam."

"Never by yourself?"

"Why would I come to a gay bar by myself?"

Dominick shrugged. "I don't know. You didn't have a problem coming here when I suggested it."

And had me wondering why you knew about the neighborhood gay bar. What straight guy would know that?

"Why would I? Sure, I might have come here on my own in the past. Who can remember? It's a friendly place. Sometimes, you need a place to unwind."

"But someone might get the wrong idea," Dominick said, gazing around the bar at all the guys talking and laughing with each other. Some were even making out. There were a few women, but not many.

"What do you mean?"

"Usually, gay guys go to gay bars. You know, to meet friends and have a few drinks. But also to hook-up."

"Are you asking if I'm gay?"

Was he? Dominick wondered. He liked Sebastian. A lot. And his gaydar, which was usually always reliable when it came to figuring out if a guy played for his team, was telling him Sebastian was gay.

Of course, if he was wrong, it was going to make wedding planning awkward.

But what if he was right? So, Dominick took the plunge, staring deep into Sebastian's eyes. "Are you?"

———

Sebastian was saved from answering when their waiter returned with their drinks. He handed Sebastian a bottle of Bud Light and placed Dom's dirty martini in front of him. "I'll keep an open tab. When you're ready for a second round, let me know."

As soon as the waiter left, Sebastian popped his beer in his mouth to stop himself from talking. What was he doing here? This was wrong. All wrong. And what was with all the questions? Could Dom actually suspect the truth?

Unless...

No. It was too much to hope for.

He looked over at Dom. The bar lighting at HMSX was always good, and it was making Dom look even more handsome. He watched as Dom took a sip of his martini, waiting for his answer.

It wasn't like Dom had put him on the spot. Sebastian had done that all on his own. He had no idea what he was doing or saying today. Ever since Dom had texted him asking if he could come to the apartment, he'd been totally distracted. He'd burned a sheet of cookies earlier in the afternoon and forgotten what time he'd told Dom to come over.

All because he couldn't stop thinking of him.

What if he *did* tell Dom he was gay? Would that be the answer he wanted to hear?

But then there would be so many other questions. About Vivi. About the wedding. About the baby.

But he was going to have to answer them at some point, right? Why not do it now rather than later? The sooner he told the truth, the sooner he could find out if Dom was interested in him.

He stared at him again, watching as he took another sip of his martini, focusing on his lips. Those very kissable lips. What would happen if he decided to kiss Dom right now? It was tempting. Very tempting.

He started to move closer, his knees brushing against Dom's as he closed the distance between them, bringing his head closer, as if he planned to whisper a secret in his ear.

Mere inches away, he quickly pulled back. What was he doing? He couldn't kiss Dom. He was his wedding planner!

Talk about mixed signals.

He grabbed his beer and took a long sip, trying to calm his beating heart.

That was close. Too close.

Okay, what was going on? Had Sebastian been getting ready to kiss him?

He thought he was, but at the last minute, Sebastian changed his mind.

Dominick was disappointed.

He wanted to know if Sebastian's lips tasted like cinnamon and vanilla. It was like that one last cookie you promised yourself you weren't going to eat. You couldn't help yourself. You wanted it. You had to have it. So, you took it.

And then felt incredibly guilty for eating it.

He was probably breaking Rule # 1 in the wedding planner's guidebook: Never become involved with your client. But he wanted to kiss Sebastian. And if Sebastian wasn't going to kiss him...

Then, he was going to kiss Sebastian.

Sebastian was caught by surprise.

Dom was kissing him. His mouth was on his and the sensation shocked him. It thrilled and excited him. It meant Dom was attracted to him and wanted to be with him.

After that Sebastian's natural instinct kicked in and he leaned into the kiss. Savoring it. Prolonging it. It had been a while since a guy had kissed him, and he was going to make the experience last for as long as possible.

———

He was right. Sebastian tasted like cinnamon and vanilla.

But he also tasted like other things. Good things. The tang of beer. The mint of mouthwash.

Desire and passion.

Definitely desire and passion because there was no mistaking that Sebastian was into their kiss. He might have been caught by surprise at first—Dominick had swooped in after Sebastian had put down his beer bottle—but now, he leaned forward and returned the kiss with intensity. There was an underlying hunger there. Like he wanted the kiss to go on and on.

As much as Dominick wanted that, too, it was time to end it. If it went any longer, he was going to want to pull Sebastian into his arms, make their kiss deeper and longer. Their tongues had already found each other and were starting a slow dance.

"You didn't answer my question," he said, pulling away from Sebastian's lips.

"What question?" A flush rose in Sebastian's cheeks.

"You know which one."

Sebastian laughed. "Oh. That question."

"Yes, *that* question. But I suppose it's moot after *that* kiss."

Sebastian gave him a wide smile. "Some kiss."

Dominick nodded. "Definitely some kiss."

"So, what if I said yes? I'm gay. How would you react?"

"What do you mean?"

"Would you be happy? Excited? Intrigued?"

Dominick answered honestly. "I'm not sure. Right now, I'm confused. I'm wondering why you would be messing around with your wedding planner in a gay bar when you have a pregnant fiancée out in Brooklyn."

"Because I'm not straight," Sebastian explained. "I'm gay. Totally and completely." Sebastian put a hand on Dominick's knee and gave it a squeeze. "I like guys. No, wait, that's wrong. I love guys."

Dominick removed Sebastian's hand. "Then,

how do you explain Vivi? Your bride. The mother of your baby," Dominick reminded him. "I know there are plenty of blended families out there. A guy sleeping with a girl isn't the only way to make a baby. They can also be made with turkey basters or at sperm banks. No one has to do anything the traditional way anymore. But that's not what's going on here."

"What do you mean?"

"You and Vivi have been coming across as a *straight* couple. A straight couple who slept together, got pregnant, got engaged, and will soon be getting married."

Sebastian started to squirm, avoiding eye contact.

"What aren't you telling me?"

"Vivi's mother," Sebastian began.

"Big Viv? What about her?"

"She's thrilled that Vivi is pregnant. Thrilled about the baby. But the father, not so much."

"What are you talking about? She loves you. She's throwing this big wedding and sparing no expense."

"Because she thinks *I'm* the father of Vivi's baby. And I'm not."

Dominick wasn't sure if he'd heard Sebastian correctly. "Did you just say you're not the father?"

Sebastian nodded slowly. "Yes."

"Then, why are you marrying her? Help me out here, Sebastian, because now I'm even more confused."

"Big Viv doesn't know I'm gay. Well, she used to think I was gay. Until Vivi told her I wasn't."

"Why would she do that?"

"It's a long story."

Dominick picked up his dirty martini and took a long sip to prepare himself. He had a feeling he was going to need it. "Then, I suggest you start at the very beginning."

———

Thirty minutes later, Dominick sat in stunned silence. There was so much to process.

Sebastian was gay and Vivi had coerced him—tempted, trapped, blackmailed? There were so many verbs he could choose from!—into marriage so that she could stay in her mother's good graces all because the baby's father might be a guy whose aunt Big Viv had been feuding with for the last forty-five years and would probably have a meltdown if she wound up being related to her nemesis. And Sebastian, wanting to open his own bakery, had agreed to go along with Vivi's plan because he'd been put on the spot and hadn't wanted to betray his best friend.

And then, Dominick had entered the picture, complicating things even more.

"You're not saying anything," Sebastian nervously stated. "I don't know if that's good or bad."

"I'm still trying to sort through everything you told me," Dominick said. "It's a lot. You're being a good friend to Vivianna, but is she being a good friend to you? She's putting you in a tough spot, even if she is going to fund your bakery. She's making you put your life on hold for her. And what about this Nico guy? What if he is the father of Vivi's baby? What's he going to do when he finds out the truth? Have you and Vivi thought about that?"

———

Sebastian reached for his beer and finished it.

Nico. He didn't even want to go there. What was Nico going to do if he found out he was going to be a father? Or if he found out Vivi was pregnant? Because it was only a matter of time.

According to Vivi, he was still in New York. He was bound to cross paths with her again. And when that happened, he was going to start asking questions. Because by then, Vivi would probably have a baby bump.

Sebastian didn't want to be around when that happened. They might be able to fool Big Viv into thinking Sebastian was the father of Vivi's baby, but Nico? Not a chance.

CHAPTER
THIRTEEN

Going to a strip club on a Sunday night didn't feel right to Nico Morelli.

It was almost blasphemous.

When he was a boy, he would go to church every Sunday with his grandmother, who dressed from head to toe in black after his grandfather died of a heart attack when she was fifty. She wore her widow uniform every day, almost like a symbol of pride, until she died thirty-five years later. Nonna Morelli had been a tough old bird. There had been no fooling around with her when they went to church. He had to give the priest officiating the mass his full attention or else he'd get a slap on the back of his head when he started daydreaming or nodding off. But he couldn't help it. Those priests were boring! When they weren't accusing you of not putting enough money in your weekly offering envelope, they went on and on telling you about the dangers of sin and temptation and burning in the pits of Hell. He knew he was no angel, but he didn't think he was going to spend the rest of eternity with Lucifer.

Still, when Sundays rolled around, he always thought of Nonna Morelli. Not just about their trips to church, but the massive Sunday dinners she would prepare once mass was over. The antipasto with her stuffed peppers that were so hot, you needed a glass of milk by your side after taking a bite. The meatballs, sausage and braciola, homemade manicotti or lasagna or cavatelli or spaghetti (Nonna Morelli never bought boxed pasta, she always made it from scratch), and veal cutlet parmigiana followed by fresh fruit and her huge cream puffs filled with sweet vanilla cream accompanied with espresso and a shot of demitasse. The whole family would get together in Nonna Morelli's basement. His aunts would be in the kitchen helping with the cooking, his uncles would be in the living room watching something on TV, talking in Italian, and he and his cousins would be out on the street playing stickball until they were called inside.

Those were some of his best memories of growing up in Brooklyn.

Now, Nonna Morelli was gone and most of his relatives had left his home city, now scattered across Staten Island, Long Island, and New Jersey. So, when he came home and went out to Bensonhurst, it was only his parents still living on the old block. His dad was stubborn as a mule and even though he could get twenty times what he had originally paid for their house, he didn't want to move. He was going to be in that house until the day he died.

But tonight, it was like old times.

He was with his old buddies from the neighborhood at Legs, an upscale strip club in Manhattan. Joey Mazzelli, nicknamed Joey Mozz because he used to make fresh mozzarellas in water when he worked at his father's pork store, was getting married and tonight was his bachelor party.

It was a bottle service type of place with plush seating roomy enough for two if you wanted a little company on your lap. The lighting was low but not too low, allowing you to see the strippers from all angles as they walked around the club in high-end lingerie and heels, offering private shows in discreetly draped rooms before the main event happened onstage. The music was loud but not blaring, and there was security in plain sight in case any of the customers got too rowdy or harassed the ladies.

Once the party started and everyone began razzing Joey about his ex-girlfriends, Nico felt himself loosening up. So what if it was Sunday? They were celebrating a happy occasion and he needed a night out with his friends.

He needed to forget his love life.

He needed to forget Vivi.

He had lost count of how many times they had broken up and gotten back together. But this last break-up was it. He was done. How could he be with someone who called him a liar?

Not that she'd given him much of a chance to explain himself. Vivi presented what she believed were the facts and then told him it was over. Again. He'd tried to convince her she was wrong, but she didn't want to believe it. Maybe he hadn't fought hard enough, but she hadn't even wanted to listen, refusing to answer any of his calls or texts.

So, he gave up. Because if there wasn't trust in a relationship, then there was no relationship.

It was time to move on. Yet, he couldn't stop thinking of her.

Maybe he needed a distraction.

His best friend from high school, Aldo Petrocelli, pounded him on the back. "You've got a frown on your face. That only means one thing. You're thinking about a woman."

"Just thinking about the past."

Aldo stared at him with his piercing blue eyes. His family was from Northern Italy, so unlike most Italians, he was light-skinned and blond. Unlike Nico, who was dark and swarthy. "You mean Vivi."

Nico shrugged. "She's in my blood."

"Then you need a transfusion, my friend."

Aldo gazed around the club, his eyes stopping until they came to a lovely redhead. He gripped Nico by the shoulders and pointed him in her direction. "Transfusion time. Doctor's orders."

"Maybe later," Nico promised, knowing Aldo wouldn't give up until he at least spoke to the stripper. "Let's join the guys. Looks like they're getting ready for a toast."

"I'm going to hold you to that," Aldo said as they walked back to the bar.

Maybe in the past he would have lost himself in the arms of another woman. Gone on a binge of drinking and partying. But it was time to grow up. He wasn't a kid anymore. He was thirty. Look at Joey, getting ready to settle down. Most of his friends were married or had serious girlfriends. Pretty soon, they were going to start having kids. He was the odd man out, although all his Brooklyn friends were envious of his life out in California.

He didn't know what they had to be envious about. He knew when they thought of California they envisioned what they saw on TV. Beaches and bikinis and sunshine. Lots of beautiful women. To a certain degree, that was true.

But California was no different than Brooklyn. You still had to make a living.

He had tried acting when he first moved out there and it didn't work out for him. First, because he didn't have any talent. He wasn't ashamed to admit that, although there were plenty of actors and actresses who made it in Hollywood without any talent. Second, the small roles he did get as an extra or with a line or two? He kept getting typecast as Italian thugs.

"You have to be patient," his Aunt Deena had kept telling him. "So what if they keep typecasting you? Everyone has to start somewhere. If John Travolta could make it as an actor, then so can you. You're just as handsome as he is. And just as talented!"

Nico stuck with it for a few years, but in the end,

acting just wasn't for him. Instead, he began working as a bodyguard after going for forty hours of training and background checks. He kept himself in great physical shape and there were always people in Hollywood in need of protection. So, that helped pay the bills.

And it was the reason he had returned to New York this past spring.

One of his ex-girlfriends from Hollywood, Candy Carlson, had a stalker situation. Candy had started her career on the Disney Channel co-starring on a few tween sitcoms, usually as the sassy older sister. Then, after leaving the Disney nest, she released an album that went to number one due to the success of a hit single, *Feral Bitch*, shaking her girl next door image for dark glamor, complete with a racy video where she was sucking away the blood of her male victims, among other things.

That's when all the nuts came crawling out of the woodwork, including one creep who kept sending Candy letters, telling her she was going to be his vampire bride and they were going to spend all eternity together. The letters on their own were unnerving, but when Candy found one in her bedroom, she freaked, instantly calling Nico.

They hadn't spoken since their break-up three

years earlier, but it had been amicable. A nice fling but nothing serious. And Nico always had a soft spot for his exes.

Candy was in New York, getting to film her first romantic comedy for the big screen, and she hired Nico to come to New York as her on-set bodyguard. She would feel much safer knowing he was there, keeping an eye out for anyone who didn't belong.

Naturally, he said yes. And naturally, since he was back in New York, he took a visit out to Brooklyn to see his folks and stopped at Vivi's mother's bakery, where Vivi happened to be working behind the counter that day.

They picked up right where they had left off five years earlier.

The trouble started when Candy's publicists, trying to build up some buzz for her film, played up the stalker angle, telling a number of gossip columnists how Candy's life was in jeopardy. Then, they played up the bodyguard angle, a la the Kevin Costner/Whitney Houston movie, *The Bodyguard*, telling those same gossip columnists that Candy's ex was protecting her.

All day. And all night. Could romance be blooming again? they asked.

That's when Vivi went through the roof.

Because once she started reading about Candy and Nico's supposed rekindled romance, she accused him of cheating on her, which was not only crazy, but an insult. In all his years of dating, he'd never cheated on anyone. When he was with a woman, she was the only woman for him.

Nico had been upfront with Vivi right from the beginning. He had told her why he was in New York, and he had told her that there was nothing going on between him and Candy, even though they had been involved in the past.

But there was no reasoning with Vivi, and then she'd gone off to Cancun with her girlfriends. When she got back, he again tried to explain things to her, but she refused to listen, giving him the deep freeze until finally he gave up and once again found himself single.

When he reached the bar, he was handed a Cuban cigar and a crystal-cut glass. They were all smoking their cigars and tossing back Johnny Walker Red, toasting Joey, when Nico's cellphone rang. He gazed at the screen and saw it was his Aunt Deena.

He answered, stepping away from the bar and the raucous laughter of his friends. "Yo, Aunt Dee! Whassup?"

"When were you going to tell me?" she demanded.

He had no idea what she was talking about. "Tell you what?"

She sounded pissed. If there was one thing Nico knew, no one ever wanted to get on Aunt Deena's bad side. No one held a grudge like she did, and he knew that from first-hand experience courtesy of her feud with Vivi's mother.

"That you're going to be a father. That I'm going to be a great-aunt!"

Nico almost dropped his cellphone. "What did you say?" He couldn't have heard her correctly. Did she say he was going to be a father? "What are you talking about?" he asked again, his voice filled with disbelief. "Have you been drinking?" He knew his aunt liked her Chardonnay at the end of the day.

"No, I have not been drinking!" she hissed. "Are you telling me you *don't* know?"

"Know what? Aunt Dee, you're losing me here. I have no idea what you're talking about. Start from the beginning, please."

"Vivianna Confetta is pregnant!"

"Vivi? Pregnant? How do you know that? Are you sure? I doubt she called you up and told you herself."

"*Stunad*! How do you think I know? I'm still plugged into the old neighborhood. My old friend from high school, Carla D'Bruzzi, told me. Big Viv is rushing the wedding because she doesn't want Vivi to have a baby bump when she walks down the aisle. And you're the father!"

"What do you mean I'm the father?"

"*Managia*! Who else would it be? You've been sleeping with her again, haven't you?" she accused. "Don't try to deny it. You're back in New York and I know how you get when you're anywhere near her."

"Yes," he slowly answered, still trying to wrap his head around the news.

"So, you're the father," she stated. "It's certainly not that gay guy she's always hanging around with."

"Sebastian?"

"Yes, Sebastian. The guy she's going to marry!"

"What? Vivi is marrying Sebastian? Sebastian Fontana. Are you sure?" He was almost going to ask her again if she was dipping into the Chardonnay, but thought better of it. Yet, none of it made any sense. Why would Sebastian and Vivi be getting married? Sebastian was gay!

"Is there another Sebastian Fontana living in Brooklyn? A straight one?"

"Slow down. You're losing me. Let me see if I

understand all this. Vivi might be pregnant, and if she is, Sebastian is the father, and they're getting married?"

"Yes, yes, and yes," Deena triumphantly stated. "We both know none of it is adding up."

"You really think the baby could be mine?"

"Why not? You just told me you've been sleeping with her. It's been a while since I've taken high school biology, but it's still sperm plus egg equals baby."

Nico started massaging his neck. Vivi was pregnant. And she didn't tell him? Why would she do that?

"This is all Big Viv's fault," his aunt's venom-filled voice hissed over the line. "I'd bet money on it."

Nico tried not to groan. Again with the feud. Again with the tirade against Vivi's mother. How many times had he heard his aunt rant and rave about her ex-best friend? Too many. He didn't know what exactly went down between Vivi's mother and his aunt in the seventies, but it all had been nothing but a pain in the ass to him and Vivi ever since. It was why they broke up the first time. Who knew where they might have been today if it hadn't been for that summer when they'd been separated?

"How dare she try to steal my great-niece or

nephew. And now we're going to be related to her! I'll be damned if she stops me from seeing that kid. And trust me, she'll try. You gotta do something, Nico! Right away."

"Like what?"

"I don't know! You're a smart guy. You figure it out. But no way is that baby his. You gotta get close to him and blow this whole thing up."

Get close to Sebastian? That was a laugh. The guy hated him. Why wouldn't he after the way he had treated him when they were kids?

And *he* hated Sebastian. Well, maybe hate was too strong a word. He disliked him. Perfect Sebastian. Everyone loved Sebastian. Teachers, parents, classmates.

Vivi.

All through grammar school and high school, there was Sebastian, held up as an example. Everything always came so easy for him. The teachers loved him because he was smart and aced all his papers and tests. The girls loved him and wanted to hang out with him during recess and after school because he was so much fun and had the same interests they did. Who got invited to every birthday party? Who made the honor roll every year? Who was always voted best dressed? Most popular? Most friendly?

Sebastian.

Unlike Sebastian, Nico always seemed to struggle. School wasn't easy for him and when he had problems in class, the teachers always paired him with Sebastian. When he started to notice girls, he was tongue-tied around them. He never knew what to say! But Sebastian could talk to anyone, especially the girls in their class. Not that it mattered since he was gay!

And it hadn't taken him long to figure out Sebastian was gay. There was just something about him that was *different* from the other guys in their class. The way he walked. The way he talked. The way he tried not to be obvious about it, but was, when his eyes would follow certain guys in their class.

He was gay. All it had taken was one comment for Nico to be sure. And that's when he pounced.

"You want to suck Carmine Romatolla's dick, don't you?" he whispered in Sebastian's ear as they were waiting their turn to climb the rope to the ceiling during eighth grade gym class.

Sebastian, tearing his eyes away from Carmine's butt hovering in the air above them as he climbed up to the ceiling, instantly turned red, not saying a word as he stared at Nico. He didn't have to. It was all in his eyes. The panic. The truth.

He was caught. And he knew it.

Even at fourteen, Nico knew if someone had a weakness, you exploited it. He'd learned it watching the older guys in the neighborhood. The ones with the flashy cars and the pinky rings and the wads of cash.

He wanted Sebastian to know who was boss. So, once he knew the truth, he crushed him.

Usually, it was teasing and name calling. Sometimes, it was a jab to the side or a shove in the hallway to make Sebastian stumble and look less than perfect. A joke made at his expense, resulting in laughter from their classmates.

Some people might have called him a bully. Or a homophobe. But he wasn't. He didn't have a problem with someone being gay. He had lots of gay friends out in California.

At the time, he had been an insecure kid who felt like nothing he did was ever good enough. He was always comparing himself to other people.

Like Sebastian.

Even though he would never say it out loud, he could admit it to himself. He had been jealous of

Sebastian. So, so jealous. And, if he was being honest with himself, he still was. Because Sebastian had the one woman he had always loved still in his life.

And now, he was going to have her baby, too. A baby that might also be Nico's.

He needed to find out. Because something was going on and he was going to get to the bottom of it. And if he had to play dirty like he used to when they were in school, to find out what was going on, then he would.

Because, in the end, all that mattered was Vivi.

And, if Aunt Deena was right, their baby, too.

CHAPTER
FOURTEEN

It was Sunday night and Vivi was feeling sorry for herself. She was home alone. Feeling fat. And she was craving Funyuns and ice cream again. Definitely not what she should be eating if she was feeling fat. But if the baby wanted it...

The baby.

Vivi placed a hand on her stomach. She still couldn't believe she was pregnant. That a tiny life was growing inside her and nine months from now she'd be holding a baby in her arms.

Talk about a curveball.

One month ago, she had been living the single life. And now, she was on her way to becoming a mother.

As hard as she tried to stay on the couch, she

made her way to the kitchen, powerless to the demands of her tummy. Tonight, instead of craving Ben & Jerry's vanilla caramel fudge, she was in the mood for chocolate fudge brownie. After finding a pint, she grabbed a spoon and a bag of Funyuns. But instead of opening the bag, she reached for a meat mallet and started pounding it. Once the Funyuns were the consistency of dust, she opened the bag and sprinkled them over the ice cream before putting a big spoonful in her mouth.

Delicious!

Returning to the living room, she repositioned herself on the couch and started channel surfing while spooning her Funyun flavored chocolate ice cream into her mouth.

She stopped pressing buttons on the remote control when the TV screen filled with an image from *Grease*. Instantly, she was filled with loathing.

Vivi hated John Travolta. And she hated two of his biggest movies from the 1970s: *Grease* and *Saturday Night Fever*. Especially *Saturday Night Fever*.

If it hadn't been for him and that stupid movie, her mother and Nico's aunt never would have stopped being friends. She and Nico would have been allowed to date and found out if they were meant to be together instead of being stuck in this endless loop of dating and breaking up, dating and breaking up. They'd been doing it for fifteen years!

Was it the thrill of sneaking around behind Big Viv and Deena's backs that made them keep going back to each other? Was that why they kept sleeping together?

Well, yes and no. Even though she'd never met Deena, from the bits that Nico had told him about his aunt over the years, she sounded exactly like her mother: a control freak who had to direct the lives of everyone around her.

So, maybe yes, she and Nico wanted to get back a little of their own. Stick it to Big Viv and Deena and show them who was boss. Let them know they were going to do exactly what they wanted in spite of their ultimatums.

As for sleeping together...

Nico was a great lover. He knew exactly where to put his lips and fingers, among other things. He knew all the spots on her body that gave her maximum pleasure. He never rushed, going slow, making sure everything was okay, asking her questions: Does this feel good? Are you okay? Do you want me to go faster? Slower?

He wasn't anything like the no-neck

muscleheads from the neighborhood that some of her girlfriends had slept with. The horror stories she had heard! Some of them hadn't even had an orgasm, which was never an issue with Nico.

But it wasn't just the sex. She liked Nico, too.

When he wasn't being a jerk.

She was no fool. Nico was a handsome guy. And living in Hollywood, she was pretty sure women were throwing themselves at him all the time. Which was fine. He had his life in California; she had hers in New York. She certainly hadn't been living like a nun all these years. There had been other guys, but never for very long. For some reason, either consciously or unconsciously, she always compared them to Nico.

And they never measured up.

When Nico's dating was out of sight, she didn't mind. How could she complain? They weren't together. They weren't a couple. He could see anyone he wanted. But when it was right under her nose...

For some reason, that drove her crazy!

Over the last couple of weeks, she'd been reading about him and that Candy bitch. It was why she'd gone to Cancun with her girlfriends. To get away from it all after she'd broken up with him. Because

Vivianna Confetta did *not* share, and she was certainly not going to share Nico with some Hollywood bimbo!

She knew they had dated in the past, especially after the *Feral Bitch* video came out. It was the first time she'd actually seen Nico with another woman.

And it had hurt. Much more than she had expected. Because he was *her* Nico.

And now, he was someone else's.

But it didn't last. None of Nico's other relationships lasted, either. And neither did any of hers.

What did that say about the two of them? That they were dysfunctional and unable to be with other people? Or that they were meant to be together?

Whenever they reunited, she always hoped this would be the time that it would last. That this time they would stay together.

And then, it all fell to pieces again. There was always some sort of reason. And this time, it was his cheating with Candy.

Her eyes fell back to the TV screen. Ugh. Danny was trying to date-rape Sandy at the drive-in. At least she stood up for herself and managed to get away. But that wasn't enough for Vivi. There was still the movie's overall message. That in order to get the guy you wanted, you had to dress like a slut and stop being who you are. Because bad boys like Danny weren't attracted to good girls. They only wanted bad girls like Rizzo.

And then, there was the way the women were treated in *Saturday Night Fever*. They were insulted, pawed, yelled at, threatened with violence, almost date-raped, and then actually gang-banged! Definitely not a good look for the guys of Brooklyn.

But because Travolta was the star of both movies, looking all handsome in black jeans, a black T-shirt, and a black leather jacket in one and a white suit in the other, everyone swooned.

Hadn't the 1970s been the feminist era? Where were the feminists when these two movies came out?

"Vivi!"

She hit the mute button on her TV. Was someone calling her name? She heard the voice again.

"Vivi!"

She dropped her spoon to the floor, all thoughts of ice cream forgotten. She knew that voice. There was no mistaking it.

Nico.

She left the couch and headed toward the front door.

"Viiivvviii!"

What the hell was he doing? He sounded like Marlon Brando in *A Streetcar Named Desire*, howling for Stella in the French Quarter.

She took a quick look at herself in the hallway mirror. Whenever she left the house, she always checked out her hair and make-up to make sure she looked flawless. Now, she saw there were smears of chocolate ice cream around her mouth, her hair was in a messy bun, and her face was make-up free, having taken it all off when she'd gotten home earlier in the day. She also wasn't dressed for company, having slipped into the oversized sweatshirt and sweatpants she wore when she was lounging around the house.

She took a peek through the drapes in the front window. Damn! Nico looked good. He was wearing a black Hugo Boss suit with a black silk shirt open at the collar, the better to show off his chest hair and the obligatory gold rope chain across his neck. You could take the boy out of Brooklyn, but you couldn't take Brooklyn out of the boy.

She couldn't open the door to him looking like this. His precious Candy probably always looked like a *Playboy* centerfold when she opened her apartment door.

She ran up to her bedroom and pulled off her clothes, rummaging through her closet and slipping into a violet lace-trimmed negligee with matching cover-up. It had always been one of Nico's favorites. She pulled the clips out of her bun, threw her head down, ran a brush through her hair before tossing her head back up and running it through again and giving herself a quick spray of Dior's Sauvage. She dashed into the bathroom to rub a washcloth across her mouth, wiping away all remaining traces of chocolate ice cream and giving herself a quick gargle with mouthwash.

"Viviii!" he howled for the third time. "I know you're in there! Open the door! We need to talk!"

Vivi hurried toward the first floor, flinging open the front door. "What the hell do you think you're doing?" she asked. "I've got neighbors!"

"I wanna know," he demanded.

"Know what?"

Nico's eyes went directly to Vivi's belly.

Uh-oh. He knew.

She tried not to visibly swallow over the sudden lump of fear in her throat. She tried not to panic. She needed to stay calm. She could handle this.

"Is it mine?"

"Is what yours?" she coolly asked.

"The baby."

"What baby?"

Jesus Christ, how did he know she was pregnant? She hadn't told anyone. And she certainly didn't think Sebastian was blabbing the news.

That only left one person.

She dug her fingernails into the palms of her hands. Her mother. Once again taking control of her life. Didn't she think that Vivi might want to wait a while before letting the rest of the world know she was pregnant? She was probably telling everyone who walked into the bakery.

But how did Nico find out?

He made his way up the front steps and walked into the house.

"Hey, I didn't invite you in!"

"That hasn't stopped you in the past. You used to like it when I dropped in uninvited."

He was close enough she could smell his cologne. But she could also tell he'd been drinking. Scotch. Both scents wafted off him in an irresistible combination. And he had a five o'clock shadow. Nico always looked sexier with his five o'clock shadow. The rough stubble felt so good when he rubbed it across her body...

All thoughts of Funyuns and ice cream were forgotten as Viv's eyes gazed over Nico.

He looked good.

Suddenly, she was hungry for something else. In addition to her recent cravings, she was also finding herself to be extremely horny. Like, all the time. It had to be the additional hormones rushing through her body. She had her vibrator to get the job done when she needed it, but sometimes it wasn't enough. Sometimes, she wanted the real thing.

Suddenly, Vivi was thinking of ex sex.

Nico took a look at what she was wearing, his gaze resting on her chest. "Your boobs look bigger."

His comment snapped Vivi out of her sex haze. "What?"

"Your boobs. Breasts. You want me to call them breasts? I've never seen them so filled out. I hear women's breasts get bigger when they're pregnant." He gave them another appreciative look. "Very nice. Very luscious."

He was about to touch them with a finger, delicately trace their shape as he had done many times in the past—and Vivi was already tingling in anticipation—but she slapped his hand away. She knew if he touched her, she'd be powerless. She'd start to melt. She'd pull him close to her, press her lips against his, and they'd be back in her bedroom, where all this had started.

"I'm wearing a new underwire bra. It gives better support."

"You ain't wearing a bra. That's all you." He moved closer, closing the distance between them, and once again Vivi inhaled his intoxicating scent. "Come on, give me a little taste. You know you want to."

Nico locked eyes with her and she could instantly feel herself blushing. It was like he could read her mind.

No.

She was not getting back into bed with a cheater, and a cheater was what he was. She'd read all about him and his actress girlfriend. If Nico thought he could double dip, he wasn't going to do it with her.

Vivi pushed him away. "If you want a little taste, why don't you head back to the city and pay a visit to Candy? Isn't she sweet enough for you?"

Nico groaned. "How many times do I have to tell you? There's nothing going on between Candy and me. We're just friends. I'm working as her bodyguard. That's it."

"I read the gossip columns. I've seen those mentions online."

"It's all fake. Made up by her publicists."

Vivi folded her arms across her chest. "Uh huh. Sure."

"Vivi, I swear! None of it is true. I haven't cheated on you. You're the only one for me."

"I don't believe you. You're lying. And I think you should go." She held the front door open. "Now."

Nico stubbornly shook his head. "No. I'm not leaving. Not until you answer my question."

Vivi began chewing on her lower lip. "What question?" she asked, even though she knew what it was.

He pointed a finger at her belly. "The baby. Am I the father?"

"Why do you care so much about this baby? If there even is a baby."

"Because if it's mine, I want to do the right thing."

"And what's the right thing?"

Nico didn't answer.

"You don't even know!" Vivi exclaimed in disbelief. "You shouldn't even have to think about it. You should know without even hesitating! Like Sebastian! Yes, I'm pregnant," she confirmed. "Satisfied?"

"No, I'm not satisfied. Because you still haven't told me if it's mine."

Vivi threw her hands up in the air. "*Mio Dio!* Sebastian is the father of my baby and he's marrying me!"

"Oh, really?" Nico sneered. "I don't see an engagement ring on your finger. If Sebastian loves you so much, if he's going to marry you, where's the engagement ring?"

Vivi stared at her ringless finger. Damn! She was going to have to get to work on that. "I don't need a ring."

"You're the queen of bling and you don't have an engagement ring?" Nico asked, his voice filled with skepticism. "Makes me wonder how real this engagement is."

"What gives you the right to even show up on my doorstep and ask me all these questions? In case you've forgotten, it's over between us, Nico. You're out of my life."

"Don't try to pull a fast one on me, Vivi," Nico warned. "I know you're saying Sebastian is the father of that baby, but we both know that's a lie. That baby isn't his."

"It's not?"

"No, it's mine."

"What makes you so sure? You think you're the only guy I've slept with?"

"Vivi, it's me you're talking to. I know you don't sleep around, and I know Sebastian prefers his partners with a little more equipment, if you know what I mean. I don't believe for a second that the two of you slept together and made a baby."

Vivi shrugged. "I don't care what you believe. Sebastian is my baby's father and we're getting married."

Nico laughed. "And you called *me* a liar?" He angrily jabbed a finger at her. "You're the liar, Vivi. You're lying to me right now. I'm the father of that baby. Me. Not him."

"You're wrong," Viv insisted, once again biting on her lower lip. "Now, get out."

"Fine. I'll go. But this isn't over."

Nico gave Vivi a dark look, then stormed out of her house before she slammed the door behind him.

What was she going to do?

There had been no mistaking the look of determination on Nico's face. He hadn't believed a word she said. He wasn't going to let this go. If he started stirring things up, this could turn into a disaster.

She needed to talk to Sebastian now. In person.

She peeked through her front drapes, checking to see if the coast was clear.

But Nico still stood outside, staring at her house, glowering.

She turned off all the lights. Maybe if he thought she had gone to bed, he would leave.

After ten minutes, she cautiously peeked through the front drapes again, not wanting to get caught. The sidewalk was empty. Nico was gone.

But she knew he would be back.

CHAPTER
FIFTEEN

Dominick was back at Sebastian's apartment. He wasn't exactly sure why. Sebastian had suggested they return here to talk some more, where it would be more private, and Dominick had agreed. Although, what was there left to talk about?

"I opened a bottle of wine," Sebastian said, coming back into the living room from the kitchen with two glasses. He handed one to Dominick. "Merlot."

"Thanks."

"I left a glass outside of Liam's bedroom door, too. Sort of as a peace offering. But I don't know if he'll drink it."

"Do you blame him?"

"He probably won't bother us. I'll bet he's

covered head to toe in calamine lotion and he won't want us to see him. Pink isn't his color." Sebastian took a seat next to Dominick on the couch, but he kept enough distance between them, unsure what Dominick would be comfortable with. "So..."

"So?"

"We can figure out a way to make this work. I know we can."

Dominick put down his wine glass. He didn't slam it, but he did put it down forcefully because he wanted to be sure Sebastian was listening. "We can? How? You're getting married. I'm planning the wedding. As much as I like you—"

Sebastian cut him off, his face lighting up. "You like me?"

Dominick rolled his eyes. "You know I do. Otherwise, I never would have kissed you. And as much as I'm intrigued about exploring things between us, facts are facts. You're engaged to be married and I've got a contract with Big Viv to plan your wedding to Vivi."

"What if Vivi says it would be okay?"

"If what would be okay?"

"This." He set his wine glass down, closed the distance between them, and his lips quickly met Dominick's.

Dominick hated to admit it, but the kiss was amazing. Even better than the one at the bar. Maybe because Sebastian was the one giving it. Dominick always loved a guy who knew what he wanted and there was something aggressive—almost possessive— in Sebastian's kiss. Like he was leaving his mark.

So, now they had both kissed each other.

But this was all wrong. Dominick's mind was suddenly flooded with images of Big Viv and Vivi, and he pulled away from Sebastian. "Stop, I can't do this. It feels weird."

"Weird? What do you mean? You liked it. I could tell."

"There was nothing wrong with the kiss. But it feels like we're cheating on Vivi."

"How can we be cheating on her when none of this is real?"

"Exactly," Dominick said. "That's the point. I want it to be real. Or at least see if it has a chance to become real. Whatever this is between us. Don't you want that?"

"Of course I do."

"That can't happen until you're no longer engaged to Vivi."

"Are you asking me to call off the wedding? Because if you want me to, I will. I know I made a promise to Vivi and she'll probably hate me for breaking it, but I don't want to lose you, Dom. I feel like I have to prove myself to you. And if it means choosing between you and Vivi, then I choose you."

Dominick adamantly shook his head. "No way. You're not making me the bad guy. I'm not going to tell you what to do. You have to decide for yourself. I'm not coming between you and Vivi. You said it yourself, you made a promise to her."

"That was before I met you."

"It wouldn't be right. She's counting on you. You can't let her down."

"Can't you help me decide?" Sebastian moved closer, leading Dominick to suspect he was going to kiss him again. Perhaps as a way of tempting him. If that happened, his mind would get all fogged up in a delicious haze and he would want another kiss and another, and then who knew how far things might go? He might do or say something he would later regret.

The last thing Dominick wanted was to come between Sebastian and Vivi. They were best friends. If their friendship ended because Sebastian didn't go through with the wedding, it would all be his fault. Vivi would blame him and eventually Sebastian would, too.

Or there was another scenario. Together, they could decide he was the bad guy, turn against him, and still go through with the wedding after they fired him. Leaving him all alone and with only a fraction of his wedding planning fee.

And then, there was the Big Viv factor. He definitely didn't want to get on her bad side. If she believed her future son-in-law had been lured away from her pregnant daughter by a gay wedding planner, he didn't want to even think of the repercussions. He could easily see her blacklisting him throughout the entire tri-state area.

His business would be finished before he could even get it off the ground. He couldn't be a wedding planner without weddings to plan.

He'd have to leave New York and start over somewhere else. He didn't want to do that. His life was here. What was he going to do? It was a no-win situation. At some point, someone was going to get mad at him. Maybe it was better to walk away from all this before things got too complicated.

But then, there was Sebastian. Sweet, cute, adorable Sebastian. When he looked at him, he wanted to stay right where he was.

"What if I was able to end it all right now?" Sebastian asked, reaching into the back pocket of his jeans and pulling out his cellphone. "I'll call Vivi, tell her I'm backing out."

Before Dominick could do or say anything, there was a loud knock on the apartment door.

"Were you expecting company?" Dominick asked.

"No. Unless Liam hooked up with someone on Grindr, although with the way he looks right now, I can't imagine he would. But he is a horndog, so never say never."

There was another knock. And then, a voice. A female voice.

"Bash! Sebastian! It's Vivi! Are you home? I need to talk to you."

Dominick's eyes widened in horror. "What's she doing here?" he asked, suddenly feeling even more guilty than he already did. Like he had been caught cheating. Which, to a certain degree, he had, hadn't he?

"Calm down," Sebastian said in a soothing voice, much calmer than Dominick expected. "We haven't done anything wrong."

Dominick raised an eyebrow. "We haven't?"

"We haven't," Sebastian insisted, walking over to the apartment door. "You came over to sample my baking because you're giving me some extra work, remember? That's all."

"That's all? It's not exactly how our night unfolded."

"That's all," Sebastian insisted before opening the door to Vivi.

"You would not believe the night I had," she wailed, breezing into the apartment and throwing her Gucci clutch onto a nearby armchair. Dominick held his breath, waiting to see when she would notice him.

She spied the two glasses of red wine on the coffee table. "I could use a glass of that right now, but all booze is off limits until after the baby arrives."

"What are you doing here?" Sebastian asked.

She paced the apartment, throwing her arms up in the air. "You're never going to believe who showed up on my doorstep tonight. Unannounced. Never!"

"Who?"

"Nico!"

Sebastian gasped.

"And he knows about the baby!"

Sebastian gasped again.

"How can he know?"

"How do you think? My mother. She won't shut up about becoming a grandmother. I'm sure she told someone, who told someone, and the news eventually got back to him."

"What was his reaction?"

"Exactly what you would expect. He was pissed. Angry. He thinks the baby is his."

"It might be," Sebastian gently reminded her.

"But it might not," Vivi shot back. "It might be my unexpected souvenir from Cancun."

"What are you going to do?"

"Try to buy some time until I can take that paternity test. I've got to keep him under control. If he makes a scene with my mother, this could all blow up sky high. Especially if Deena gets involved. Can you even imagine? It would be World War III between her and my mother."

"Maybe it's time to get everything out in the open once and for all," Dominick said from his spot on the couch, trying to be helpful despite his ulterior motive. Vivi was the one who had created this entire situation, including roping Sebastian into a sham marriage. She should be the one to clean up this mess, not Sebastian. "Maybe it would be a good thing. You have feelings for Nico. You wouldn't keep getting back together with him if you didn't love him, would you?"

Vivi had been so caught up in herself, she hadn't

noticed Dominick. Now that she had, she zeroed in on him, clearly shocked at seeing her wedding planner at Sebastian's so late on a Sunday night. "What are you doing here?"

Sebastian jumped in before he could answer. "I did some baking for him tonight. He does all sorts of party events and thought he could throw some business my way. He found my booth yesterday in Union Square and liked what he tasted."

"Who told you about Nico?" she asked Dominick, ignoring Sebastian and moving closer to the couch, a dangerous expression on her face. Like she was moving in for the kill. "How do you know so much about him and our past? There's no way you could know unless somebody told you."

Dominick's mind scrambled, trying to come up with an answer. The only way he would know was because Sebastian told him. And he didn't think Vivi would be too happy with Sebastian talking about her love life with him.

Vivi's mind was quicker. Her eyes narrowed and her head whipped back and forth between Dominick and Sebastian. Then, the two glasses of wine on the coffee table.

Dominick could see Vivi putting all the pieces together.

Five, four, three, two...

She exploded. "This is the guy?" she shrieked at the top of her lungs. "Dominick? Dominick is the guy you told me about the other night? He's the guy you're interested in? Our wedding planner? You're cheating on me with our wedding planner?"

"Vivi, calm down," Sebastian croaked. "Please. It's not good for the baby if you get upset. And how can I be cheating on you when there's nothing romantic between us?"

"Calm down? How am I supposed to calm down? First, Nico shows up on my doorstep tonight, totally blindsiding me, and then I get blindsided again when I find out you're romantically involved with our wedding planner! And not only that, you told him all about my past with Nico and how he might be the father of my baby."

"Technically, nothing has happened yet between Sebastian and I, so I don't think you can say we're involved," Dominick pointed out.

Vivi ignored him. "This is why you didn't want to tell me anything about him, isn't it? Because you knew it was wrong and I would tell you you're making a mistake."

Sebastian stared pointedly at Vivi's belly. "Who are you to talk about mistakes? It's your mistake that got us into this mess!" Sebastian clasped a hand over his mouth. "I'm sorry, Vivi. Those words slipped out before I could stop myself. Your baby isn't a mistake. But can't you understand? I had to tell Dominick the truth. He had to know the whole story about why I was doing all this. There's been this attraction building between us and I had to tell him. I had to. It was eating away at me. If I hadn't told him how I felt, it would have gotten weird. What would he have thought of your groom suddenly putting the moves on him without knowing why?"

"So, now that he has context," Vivi said, making quotation marks with her fingers, "that allows you to screw around with him behind my back?"

"Hey!" an outraged Dominick exclaimed. "We're not screwing around. I resent that. I'm not that kind of guy. I'd never insert myself into another couple's relationship."

"News flash!" Vivi shouted. "You already have. As for you," she said, turning back to Sebastian, "do you know what kind of situation you've put us in? We're trying to fool my mother, Bash! We're supposed to be in love. Ready to get married. But not if you're making googly eyes at our wedding planner! My mother's no dummy."

"I never said she was."

"She's a smart woman. Growing up, I could never get anything past her, no matter how hard I tried. She was always one step ahead of me. Eventually, she's going to figure this out."

"Which part?" Dominick asked. "Sebastian being gay? Sebastian not being the father of your baby? Sebastian being interested in me?"

"Take your pick!" Vivi wailed.

"What do you want me to say?" Sebastian demanded. "It just happened! I didn't plan it. I like him. He likes me." He turned to Dominick, sounding suddenly insecure. "Right?"

Dominick gave Sebastian a huge smile. "You have to ask?"

"Listen and listen good," Vivi said sternly. "We're going through with this wedding. You can't do anything to mess this up. Either one of you. You both have to be careful. No sneaking around. No holding hands or kissing. No contact except in the context of the wedding. If my mother finds out the truth, it could blow all our plans sky high." She turned to Dominick. "You have just as much at stake as the two of us. If my mother finds out you've stolen her baby girl's future husband, she will go through the roof. And you don't want to mess with the wrath of Big Viv Confetta. We all have to stick to the plan, got it?"

"Can I ask you a question?" Dominick asked Vivi once he thought she'd finished laying down the law.

"What?"

"Do you love him?"

"Who? Sebastian?"

"Not Sebastian." Dominick knew he was treading into sensitive territory. "Nico."

Vivi's face softened, all the anger draining away. She was silent for a moment, then sighed. "Yes, I love him. I've been in love with him since I was fifteen years old."

"Then he's the one you should be marrying, not Sebastian. Maybe it's a simple matter of miscommunication. Maybe the two of you need to clear the air."

"Yeah, there's some miscommunication," Vivi growled. "And her name is Candy."

"Candy?" Sebastian asked, his voice filled with confusion. "Who's Candy?"

Vivi brought Sebastian and Dominick up to speed. When she was done, Sebastian shook his head. "You're jumping to conclusions. Nico told you nothing's going on between them. Why don't you believe him?"

"Because they have a past! They were involved. Who's to say they're not involved again? Everything I've read online or in magazines and newspapers says they are."

"But what if they're not?" Sebastian asked again. "If you could be with him, would you want to?"

Vivi ignored the question. "He has a pattern," she pointed out. "He falls back into bed with women from his past. He's done it with me, so who's to say he hasn't done it with her?"

"But you don't know that," Sebastian insisted. "You could be the only one."

"And why would that be?" Vivi asked.

"Because you're the one he's always loved?" Sebastian suggested.

"Who would you rather be marrying?" Dominick asked. "Sebastian or Nico?"

Vivi didn't answer immediately. Eventually, she whispered, "Nico."

"Then, why don't you?"

Vivi stared at Dominick in disbelief. "You're really asking me that question after everything you know?" She began counting off on her fingers. "First, there's that stupid feud with my mother and his aunt. They don't want us having anything to do with each other, so I'm sure they would try to stop the wedding.

Secondly, I don't know if Nico is the father of this baby. If he's not, then there's no reason to marry me. Third, there's Candy. What if he'd rather be with her than me?"

"One thing at a time," Sebastian said. "You're going to take a paternity test and once you have the results, you'll know who the father is. And if it's Nico, and if he loves you as much as you love him, then why wouldn't he want to marry you?"

"Candy," Vivi stubbornly repeated. "He's involved with Candy."

Sebastian sighed. "You don't know that. Either you trust him or you don't. What are you so afraid of?"

Vivi looked down at her belly. "What if Nico doesn't want to be with me, even if the baby is his?"

"Oh, Vivi." Sebastian gave her a hug. "Why wouldn't Nico want to be with you?"

"He's never wanted to stay with me before."

"Maybe the timing wasn't right," Dominick said. "Don't forget tonight. As soon as he heard you were pregnant, he showed up. Doesn't that count for something? Doesn't it prove he loves you?

"He said he wanted to do the right thing," Vivi stated flatly. "He didn't say he loved me. And he didn't say he wanted to marry me."

"You didn't give him a chance. You were fighting, right? Maybe now is the time for the two of you to finally be together."

Vivi gave Dominick's words some thought. "Maybe."

"We need to find out," Sebastian said.

"What do you mean?" Vivi asked.

"Don't you see how complicated this whole situation is getting? It's snowballing and we're losing control." He took a deep breath. "Maybe we should call it all off before we get in deeper than we already are. There's still time."

"Call off the wedding?" she repeated, her voice filled with disbelief. "We can't!"

"Why not? You know I'm right, don't you? I know you do."

Dominick held his breath, waiting for Vivi's answer. Would she agree with Sebastian, or was she going to hold him to his promise?

Viv closed her eyes. When she opened them, she gave a resigned nod. "Yes, I know you're right. Deep down, I do. But if we call it off, this isn't going to be pretty. My mother is going to go through the roof. She's told practically everyone in Bensonhurst about this wedding."

"But it won't be her fault. It'll be ours. We'll take

the blame. And you won't have to do it alone. I'll be right by your side. We'll tell her together."

"But we can't tell her the whole truth," Vivi insisted. "Not yet. Not until I know who the baby's father is. For now, it still has to be you, okay?"

Sebastian nodded. "Okay."

Vivi took a deep breath. "Tomorrow, we'll tell my mother the wedding is off. We'll do it at the bakery. Hopefully, she'll cause less of a scene there." She gave Sebastian a kiss on the cheek, then retrieved her Gucci clutch. "Meet me at my place in the morning and we'll go over to the bakery together."

Sebastian walked Vivi down to the street, where she had a car and driver waiting to take her back to Brooklyn. Dominick was sipping his glass of wine when he returned to the apartment.

"That was intense," Dominick said.

"I knew she would do the right thing."

"No regrets? Vivi was going to fund your bakery for going through with the wedding. No wedding means no bakery."

Sebastian snuggled in next to him, resting his head on his shoulder. "How can you even ask that? I'd rather have a chance to explore things with you. I'll get to open my bakery one day."

"Are you sure she's going to go through with it?"

Dominick didn't mean to sound skeptical, but he didn't want to get his hopes up, either. A lot could happen between now and the following morning, although he had no idea what could possibly derail things other than Vivi changing her mind. Hopefully, she wouldn't.

"Vivi and I will tell Big Viv the wedding is off, then tomorrow night you and I are going to have our first official date," Sebastian said, clinking his wine glass against Dominick's. "I'll even cook for you. If you think I can bake, wait until you see what else I can do in the kitchen. It's going to be a feast."

Dominick took another sip of his wine. "If you say so."

"Relax, you're worrying for nothing. What could possibly go wrong?"

CHAPTER
SIXTEEN

"Wake up! Wake UP!"

At first, Nico thought he was dreaming. Then, he thought it was his mother screaming in his ear, but that didn't make much sense. Why would she be in his Manhattan apartment?

He buried his head under his pillow, trying to fall back asleep.

The screaming didn't stop. The voice kept getting louder. And then, he realized the voice didn't belong to his mother. It belonged to someone who sounded a lot like his mother.

Aunt Deena.

But that was impossible, too, because Aunt Deena was all the way out in California. Right?

He opened one eye. Wrong.

She stared down at him from the side of his bed, looking like she had just stepped off the cover of a magazine. Make-up flawless. Dark shoulder-length hair ready for a shampoo ad. A tailored sundress that showed off her glorious California tan. If there was one thing he could say about Aunt Deena, she kept herself in great shape. She was a brunette Michelle Pfeiffer, still as foxy as the day she left Brooklyn all those years ago.

He jerked up, hitting his head on the headboard. "Ouch! Aunt Dee, what the hell are you doing here?"

She crossed the bedroom and pulled back the drapes from the floor to ceiling windows, flooding the room with sunlight. "What do you think? I'm here to help! I took the Red Eye last night."

"Help?" he asked, his eyes squinting in the morning glare. "With what?"

"Stopping that wedding! Come on, get up! We've got work to do."

Nico groaned as he started to rub the back of his head. No, no. Aunt Deena was one complication he didn't need. Things were already complicated. Throwing her into the mix would only make things worse.

Since he slept in the nude, he pulled the sheet

up, making sure his bottom half was covered. He didn't think his aunt had seen anything, but he wanted to keep it that way. It was bad enough she was seeing him bare chested. "How did you get in here?"

"I turned on the Deena charm with your doorman."

The Deena charm. His aunt talked about it all the time. As soon as she gave that mega-watt smile and batted her baby blue eyes, she could get anyone to do what she wanted. Men, especially, were powerless against it. Which was why she was standing in his apartment. He'd have to get the doorman fired.

"Did you see Vivi last night?" she asked.

"Yes."

"And how did it go?"

"She said the baby isn't mine. It's Sebastian's."

Aunt Deena shook her head in disgust. "Like mother, like daughter. *Bugiardi!* Liars. You don't believe her, do you?"

Nico stared at his aunt. "Do I look like an idiot? Of course I don't believe her."

"So, what are you going to do? You can't let her get away with this."

"I'm already one step ahead of you."

Aunt Deena's blue eyes lit up as she sat on the edge of his bed. "You have a plan?"

Nico nodded slowly. "I do." It had come to him last night after he left Vivi's, convinced more than ever that the baby she was carrying was his. For as long as he had known Vivi, whenever she was lying or not telling the entire story, she had a tell that always gave her away. She would bite down on her lower lip. Last night, she had gnawed on her lower lip more than once.

"Don't keep me in suspense," Aunt Deena urged, eagerly leaning forward. "Tell me what it is."

"I'm going to become friends with Sebastian," Nico announced.

Aunt Deena's face deflated. "That's your plan? What good is that going to do? Aren't you already friends with him?"

Nico shook his head. "We've never really been friends. We're more like frenemies who've got Vivi in common."

"Go on."

"My plan is a simple one," Nico explained. "I'm going to tell him I want to put the past behind us. Start over. I made his life miserable when we were kids."

"What good is that going to do?"

"Don't you get it, Aunt Dee? I'm going to stick to this guy like glue. Be his shadow. And make sure he's tempted every chance I get."

"Tempted?"

"Tempted," Nico repeated. "By a guy."

"I'm not following you. What are you talking about?"

"He's gay, Aunt Dee! And I'm pretty sure if the right guy comes along and comes on to him, he'll have a hard time saying no." He gave her a pointed look. "Now do you follow?"

"Oh, you're setting a trap. Like I did in that Lifetime movie, *The Vengeful Mistress,* where I kept following the wife of the married man I was having the affair with so she would catch us in bed together."

Aunt Dee and her Lifetime movies. She never missed a chance to talk about them, although the last one she had made was five years ago. When she was younger, she had usually been cast as the psychotic mistress or girlfriend. Now that she was older, the parts weren't as plentiful as they used to be. Aunt Deena's agent still got offers, but these days it was for grandmas or retirees. And Deena DiGregorio was *not* ready to start playing her age.

"Something like that," he said. "I'm going to put

temptation in his path. Get him to reveal his true colors."

"And then?"

Nico reached for the iPhone on his nightstand and held it up. "Then, I'm going to get the proof I need on video. Once I do, I'll have the upper hand."

"And everything will blow up!" Aunt Deena exclaimed. "I love it."

Nico nodded with determination. "That'll be the end of that wedding."

"I always knew you were smart," Aunt Deena said, pinching his cheek. "I'll let you get started, and I'll get on with my day. We'll reconnect later."

"Where are you going?" He rubbed his cheek. Aunt Deena always pinched too hard.

"To visit an old friend in Brooklyn."

"Aunt Dee," Nico warned, suspecting he knew who the old friend was. "What are you going to do?"

Aunt Deena waved her fingers in the air as she breezed out of his bedroom. "Don't worry, I'm not going to do anything to mess up your plan."

"Don't do anything that's going to make things worse!" he shouted after her, but he didn't think she heard him. And if she had, she was probably going to ignore him.

Nico didn't have a good feeling about this.

Sebastian was nervous. Correction, he was extremely nervous. So nervous that he was starting to sweat, and it wasn't that humid for a June morning.

He needed to pull himself together. Otherwise Big Viv would know something was up the second he and Vivi walked into the bakery.

They were about to tell Big Viv that the wedding was off. He was not looking forward to her reaction. Her temper was legendary. All the blood usually rushed to her head, giving her a tomato red complexion, and her eyes bugged out. Then, she would open her mouth and scream at the top of her lungs.

Man, could she scream.

Sometimes, she would even throw things. He'd seen more than one Capodimonte figurine go flying across a room before smashing to pieces against a wall or floor.

Sebastian witnessed it all first hand when he and Vivi were teenagers. When Vivi constantly broke curfew. When Big Viv found Vivi's birth control. When Vivi "borrowed" Big Viv's credit card and went on a shopping spree at Prada and Gucci during an all sales final clearance. When Vivi took her mother's Porsche for a joy ride and crashed it into a mailbox because she had been too busy checking out some guy's ass instead of keeping her eyes on the road. In Vivi's defense, Sebastian had been in the passenger side, and well, it had been a nice bubble butt. Definitely worth following.

The only time he hadn't seen Big Viv's temper on display was when Vivi was dating Nico. Which was strange since Big Viv hated Deena, and thus, by extension, Nico.

Nico. Sebastian couldn't believe he had been defending the guy last night. He had no idea if any of what he said was true. He had been too focused on trying to make things right with Dom. With trying to get Vivi to see reason and agree to call off their wedding. Did Nico love Vivi? He had no idea what went on in that cold, black heart of his. But what Dom had said last night could be true. Vivi could be the only woman Nico had ever loved.

He just didn't want to see Vivi get hurt. And Nico had the power to hurt her.

Just like he had hurt him all those years ago.

If Nico was the father of her baby, Sebastian knew Vivi would be thrilled. And maybe, just maybe, this might be a way to end the feud between Deena and Big Viv. Instead of making things worse, it could make things better. They could put the past behind them and start over.

One step at a time, Sebastian reminded himself. First, they had to tell Big Viv the wedding was off.

They had walked to the bakery in silence from Vivi's house. Now, standing outside, Sebastian took Vivi's hand in his and gave it a reassuring squeeze. They could do this. Together.

"Are you ready?"

Vivi took a deep breath. "As ready as I'll ever be."

They found Big Viv behind the counter alone. Her two clerks hadn't arrived yet for their shift. The cases were all filled with the baking done the day before while the two assistant bakers were in the back getting started on tomorrow's baking. Sebastian wondered if he'd still have a job after they told Big Viv their news.

"There you are," Big Viv said, eyeing Sebastian. "You're late. You were supposed to be here two hours ago." She wagged a finger in his face. "Don't think you can make your own hours just because you're marrying my daughter."

"Ma, we need to talk," Vivi said. "That's why Sebastian is late."

"About what?"

"The wedding."

Big Viv's face lit up. "I wanted to talk about the wedding, too." She reached under the counter and handed them a tiny wrapped box.

"Open it," she urged. "Please?"

Sebastian gulped. He knew it wasn't very often that Big Viv said please.

Vivi removed the ribbon from the top of the box and unwrapped it. When she lifted the lid, there was a set of keys inside.

"What are these?" Sebastian removed the keys from the box, an uneasy feeling forming in the pit of his stomach.

"Keys to your new house!" Big Viv exclaimed.

Sebastian suddenly became lightheaded. Had Big Viv said what he thought she said?

"I wanted to get the two of you a wedding present, and at first I didn't know what to buy. But then I said to myself, 'Viv, with a baby on the way, they're going to need more space.'"

"You bought us a house?" Vivi shrieked, a look of total amazement on her face, snatching the keys out of Sebastian's hand.

"Yes!" Big Viv reached for the iPad she stored next to the cash register, where she kept a photo gallery of their custom cakes to show customers who special ordered. She typed in her password, then swiped a finger across the screen. "You're going to need a house to raise my grandbaby, aren't you? Sebastian still lives with a roommate, and Vivi, your place is too small. It was only a matter of time before you upgraded, so why not now? It's got four bedrooms and three baths. Lots of room for more grandbabies. Plus, a huge backyard and swimming pool. Perfect for entertaining!" Big Viv shoved the iPad under their noses. "Take a look!"

"Ma, this place is gorgeous." Vivi began scrolling through the photos. "It's really ours?"

"I went to a bunch of open houses this weekend. My intention was only to look and then if I saw something I liked, bring you two along for a second viewing. But as soon as I saw it, I knew you had to have it. I didn't want anyone else buying it, so I made a cash offer and it was accepted. You're not mad, are you?"

"Of course I'm not mad," Vivi gushed. "But it's too expensive!"

"Real estate appreciates in value. It's an investment. Well worth the money. Nothing is too good for my little girl and future grandbaby."

Sebastian noted that he wasn't included in Big Viv's statement. He guessed being the alleged father didn't matter.

Vivi's eyes filled with tears. "Oh, Ma!" She gave her a hug across the counter. "Thank you."

Sebastian poked Vivi in the side. Hard. She was so caught up in new house euphoria, she was getting off track. Way off track. "Vivi, isn't there something you wanted to tell your mother?"

"Tell my mother?" She looked at him in confusion, tearing her eyes away from the iPad. "About what?"

Sebastian gritted his teeth. "The wedding."

One of the bakers stuck his head out of the kitchen. "Big Viv, there's a delivery guy who wants to see you. He's at the back door."

"I'll be right there," Big Viv said.

As soon as she was gone, Sebastian turned on Vivi. "What are you doing?"

"Bash, we can't tell her now. She bought us a house." She held the iPad up in front of his face. "Look!"

Sebastian shook his head. "She can resell it!"

Vivi stared longingly at the photos. "But it's so gorgeous. Did you see the kitchen? Imagine all the baking you could do. You'd have so much space. It even has a double oven!"

Sebastian glared at her. "Not even a double oven

is going to get me to change my mind. We have to do this. We told Dom we would."

"Okay, okay." She reluctantly put the iPad down on the counter. "I know, you're right. We'll tell her."

"Tell me what?" Big Viv said, returning to the front of the bakery. "What's this about the wedding?"

"Sebastian and I have something we need to tell you, don't we, Sebastian?" Vivi began.

But Sebastian was distracted. His attention was no longer focused on Big Viv and Vivi. Because walking into the bakery was a blast from the past.

The one and only Deena DiGregorio.

While she had visited Bensonhurst many times over the years—and come to the bakery during those trips—Sebastian had never seen her in person before. Naturally, like everyone else, he had seen some of her movies: *Killer Love Nurse, Mafia Mistress, Confessions of a Porn Addict* and *Mother of a Teenage Pimp.* They were guilty pleasures where Deena's acting was so over the top, one forgot about the absurdities of the plot and just went along for the ride. In the golden age of Hollywood, Deena would have been known as a B actress and only offered supporting roles in projects turned down by the A list.

But she'd been working non-stop in film, TV, and theatre since the early 1980s.

And then, there was her line of Deena clothing on QVC. Deena by Day, for moms and working women, Deena By Night, for a night out with the girls or your special man, and Deena Deluxxxe, a line of provocative lingerie. Plus, her line of ready-to-eat frozen meals, also available via QVC, Deena's Deelicious Deelights.

The girl from Brooklyn had done well. As well as Big Viv?

Or better?

Was that what this entire feud was about? Oneupmanship? How could they have been friends for so many years and then abandoned that friendship? Did they even remember why they had stopped being friends in the first place? Sebastian couldn't imagine not having Vivi in his life.

He'd asked Vivi about it once when they were in college and she had just shrugged, saying, "It had something to do with John Travolta and *Saturday Night Fever*. That's all I know."

Exactly what that something was, Sebastian never found out, but he had been fascinated for all these years.

"I came to visit an old friend, but I didn't think

I'd be lucky enough to meet her daughter and future son-in-law."

Deena surprised both Sebastian and Vivi by enveloping them in a hug. He could smell the scent of her perfume, Shalimar. It surrounded her like a sweet cloud.

"You're positively glowing, Vivi," she said, taking a step back and gazing at her from head to toe. "I can see why my nephew, Nico, fell for you all those years ago. It's a shame things ended the way they did. Who knows what might have happened? You might have been having his baby!" She glanced over her shoulder at Big Viv. "You would have loved that, huh Viv? We would have been related."

A stone-faced Big Viv made the sign of the cross over her face. Sebastian assumed she was going to try to play it cool and not react to Deena in any way. Smart. Deena was probably hoping to get under her skin, but Big Viv obviously wasn't going to give her the satisfaction.

Deena turned to Sebastian. "And you! The future daddy. So handsome. I'm sure if the baby is a boy, he's going to look just like you. Because all sons look *exactly* like their fathers," she said with a smirk. "Isn't that right, Vivi?"

Sebastian locked eyes with his best friend, and it was like they were reading each other's minds.

Deena knew.

Sebastian didn't know how, but Deena was fully aware Sebastian wasn't the father of Vivi's baby. And she suspected Nico was.

What was she up to with this cat and mouse game she was playing? Had she come here today to blow everything up? To expose them? If Deena did that, it would be game over. Big Viv would be devastated. She'd feel betrayed and hurt by both Vivi and Sebastian. Even worse, the damage would be done by her ex-best friend, who'd get to witness it all and probably gloat.

A queasy-looking Vivi made Sebastian realize she had come to the same conclusion. "I'll be right back." She clutched her stomach. "Morning sickness. I need to find a bathroom."

She raced behind the counter and into the back of the bakery, leaving Sebastian alone with Big Viv and Deena.

"What can I get you?" Big Viv asked, reaching for a pastry box and some wax paper.

"Is that any way to greet an old friend?" Deena held out her arms. "How about a hug?"

"I don't have time for hugs. Hugs don't pay the rent. Do you want to buy something or not?"

Deena perused the display cases. "I chipped a tooth the last time I had some of your biscotti. It was hard as a rock, even after I dipped it in my coffee, so I'll skip those."

"I thought dentures could hold up to anything," Big Viv shot back.

"I still have all my teeth, no thanks to your stale biscotti," Deena said. "Can you say the same?"

Sebastian realized that Big Viv and Deena were no longer aware of his presence. It was like he was invisible. They were focused only on each other, like two predators out in the wild, slowly circling the other before getting ready to strike.

"You're looking good," Big Viv grudgingly admitted. "But I can't say I'm surprised. Where you live, everyone gets a little maintenance, am I right?"

Deena looked up from a display case. "Are you implying I've had work done?"

"Have you?" Big Viv shrugged. "It's not any of my business. If you have, it's nothing to be ashamed of."

"I haven't."

"Hair looks good. Is that from your wig line?"

"Wig line? What wig line?"

"Someone told me you were selling a line of wigs. After you lost all your hair in 2010, you weren't happy with any of the wigs you found so you started your own line. All those harsh chemicals they put in your hair and filming under those hot lights must have taken a toll. Did you lose it gradually, or did it fall out in clumps?"

"I'm not bald!" Deena screeched in outrage. "That's a lie. This is my real hair." She yanked at it. "See?"

Big Viv leaned across the counter, grabbed a handful of hair in her fist and gave it a hard pull.

"Ouch!" Deena shrieked.

"Yep, it's real," Big Viv confirmed, letting go. "I read in some magazine that you're getting ready to make a new movie. I can't remember the name of it, but it's the type of movie that Joan Crawford and Bette Davis made popular in the 1960s." Big Viv pretended to think. "You know, the kind where crazy old ladies go on killing sprees." Big Viv snapped her fingers. "Hag horror! That's the genre. I'm sure the offers are going to come pouring in after you finish this movie. You've finally aged into your niche."

"I'm not making a horror movie. And certainly not a hag horror movie," Deena's words were icy.

"You're mistaken. But it's understandable. The memory starts to go once you get older." Deena's eyes traveled over Big Viv from head to toe. "Not to mention everything else. It must be tough looking in the mirror and seeing your whole body has gone soft and flabby. Not to mention wrinkled! Do you need some beauty creams, Viv? I can get you an insider's discount on some of the products at QVC. They work miracles, but you might be too far gone for them to do much good. Spanx is always a good investment, though. It sucks everything in and gives you back your shape so you don't look like a blob. But you've got a lot to suck in, so I don't know if it will make much of a difference. You do need to breathe when you're wearing it." Deena gazed around the bakery. "I'm sure working here doesn't help, either. I'll bet you're constantly stuffing your face."

Big Viv slammed the empty pastry box down on the counter. Apparently, Sebastian noted, Big Viv could dish it out, but she couldn't take it. Deena was getting in some of her own shots and Big Viv wasn't liking it.

"Why are you back?"

"*Saturday Night Fever*, of course. I was invited to the big forty-fifth anniversary celebration. I'm going to be a judge for one of the contests."

"Which contest?"

"Who's the best Stephanie and who's the best Annette. Sort of like us." Deena leaned across the counter, bringing her face close to Big Viv's. "I'm Stephanie, and you're Annette."

Sebastian visibly flinched from the insult—and it was a huge insult—and watched in horror as Big Viv's eyes expanded to twice their normal size.

Having watched *Saturday Night Fever* many times, Sebastian knew that Stephanie was the girl in the movie who wanted to better herself, desperate to make a new life outside of Brooklyn. While Annette...well, Annette was the somewhat pathetic character always running after John Travolta's Tony Manero, who ultimately gets her heart broken by him (because he wants Stephanie and not her) and gets gang-banged in the back of Tony's car by his buddies.

This was not going to be pretty.

"So, you're Stephanie and I'm Annette," Big Viv said in a deceptively low tone of voice, reaching for a banana cream pie on the counter, showing it off to Deena. "How about something sweet?"

Before Deena could answer, Big Viv smashed the pie in her face.

"If anyone is Annette, it's you!" Big Viv screamed.

Sebastian gasped as he watched whipped cream and chunks of banana cream filling trail all the way down Deena's face and onto her sundress.

"Don't worry, I won't charge you." Big Viv licked whipped cream off her fingers. "It's on the house."

"Well, you can charge me for this." Deena reached for a chocolate blackout cake and smashed it into Big Viv's face.

Seconds later, there was an all-out food fight in the bakery as cakes, cookies, and pies were grabbed by both women and flung in every direction.

Sebastian ducked for cover behind the counter, not knowing what to do. Should he try to break up the fight? Let them get it out of their system? A cherry cheesecake slammed into the wall behind him, slowly sliding to the floor and leaving a trail of cherry juice in its wake. The sight was like a knife to Sebastian's heart. His baked goods were being destroyed! All that deliciousness gone!

And then, in the midst of the screaming and insults and flying desserts, there came the sound of a ringtone.

Dean Martin singing *That's Amore.*

Sebastian knew it was Big Viv's cellphone. For some reason, she answered it.

Seconds later, Sebastian heard her whisper two words, "La Strega."

All went silent in the bakery.

And then, Deena started laughing. Hysterically. Almost maniacally.

He cautiously raised his head from behind the counter, ready to duck if anything came flying his way. The bakery looked like a war zone of slaughtered desserts. Big Viv, covered from head to toe in all kinds of frostings, creams, and fruit juices, was still holding her phone, looking as pale as a ghost.

Deena, who was wiping whipped cream off her face, laughed again. "Good luck with that old witch! You're going to need it." She reached into her Louis Vuitton hobo bag and pulled out her wallet, tossing a few hundred dollar bills on the counter. "This should settle things between us."

Then, she left.

Silence fell over the bakery once Deena was gone. Sebastian didn't know what to do other than start cleaning up. But Big Viv still hadn't moved from where she stood. It was like she was frozen in place.

"Big Viv, are you okay?" His voice was filled with concern. "Who called? Was it bad news?"

Before Big Viv could say anything, Vivi returned from the bathroom, staring around the bakery in disbelief.

"What the hell happened? And what's wrong with my mother? She looks like she's in shock."

"I don't know. There was an all-out cake war between her and Deena. In the middle of it, your mother's cellphone rang and after she answered it, it's like all the life drained right out of her."

"Did someone die?"

"I don't know! All she said were two words. La Strega."

Hearing those words, Viv went as pale as her mother had earlier.

"What is it?" Sebastian asked. "What's going on? You're reacting the same way as your mother. Why are those two words so scary?"

"La Strega is the family nickname for my grandmother, Nonna Julia, who lives in Italy. My mother's mother."

"You know how rusty my Italian is. What does *la strega* mean?"

"Witch," Big Viv answered. "The witch."

Sebastian remembered Deena's words right

before she left. *Good luck with that old witch. You're going to need it.* Apparently, she was familiar with Nonna Julia and didn't think too highly of her, either.

"Wicked witch is more like it," Vivi said. "She's horrible."

"And she's the one who called?" Sebastian asked Big Viv. "What did she want?"

"She's coming to Brooklyn. For the wedding. She must have found out from someone in the neighborhood. She still talks to people." Big Viv faced Vivi. "You know what this means, don't you?" She didn't give Vivi a chance to answer. "We're moving up the date. This wedding will be happening as soon as possible. Even if she knows you're pregnant, I'm not having you walk down the aisle with a baby bump, Vivi. Nonna Julia would never let either one of us live it down."

Vivi waved a dismissive hand. "I don't care what Nonna Julia thinks."

"Well, I do. You're getting married as soon as possible."

With that final decree, Big Viv left the bakery with an impervious, "Clean up this mess!" reminiscent of Faye Dunaway as Joan Crawford in *Mommie Dearest* after beating Christina in her bathroom with a can of Dutch cleanser, which then exploded.

Sebastian and Viv gazed around the bakery. Where to begin?

"We can't tell her today, Bash," Vivi began, her voice firm. "We can't. Not after what just happened with Deena, and now with my grandmother coming for the wedding. She'll look like a fool. I can't do that to my mother. I can't."

Sebastian hated to admit it, but Vivi was right. There was no way they could tell Big Viv the truth today. She was too angry. Too upset. Too everything! It would be a disaster. And he didn't want to make Big Viv look like a fool, either.

Which meant they were still trapped in this fake engagement. And they were still having a fake wedding.

What was Dom's reaction going to be? Tonight was supposed to be their first date. Last night, Sebastian and Vivi had told him they were going to tell Big Viv the truth. And now they weren't.

"Okay, fine." Sebastian gave a resigned sigh. "The wedding is still on. For now. But we've got another problem."

"What?"

"How do we break the news to Dom?"

CHAPTER
SEVENTEEN

Dominick was in his home office. Well, not an actual office. It was a tiny space in the corner of the living room of his one-bedroom apartment. He had one of those old-fashioned roll top desks with cubby holes, and every cubby was filled with some sort of book, catalog, or document related to his business. Mondays were usually Dominick's day for doing his paperwork. He would pay bills, send invoices out to clients, go over contracts from catering halls, florists, and deejays, and plan out his schedule for the rest of the week.

But nothing was getting done today because he couldn't concentrate. He kept checking his silent cellphone. He'd expected it to ring by now, but it hadn't.

What was going on in Brooklyn? Sebastian and Vivi must have talked with Big Viv by now. Why hadn't she called, telling him the wedding was off? It shouldn't be taking this long.

As if he had suddenly willed it, Dominick's phone began to ring. He glanced at the screen and saw Big Viv's name and number. Finally!

"Hello, Mrs. Confetta," he said. "What can I do for you today? Some additional thoughts on the wedding?"

He wasn't supposed to know the wedding was off, so he kept his voice upbeat and cheerful. Smooth as silk. He was ready to be a sympathetic ear in case Big Viv needed one, although he did feel slightly guilty. After all, Sebastian was backing out of the wedding because of him.

"Change of plans," she barked.

"Change of plans?" He hoped he sounded innocent and caught off guard.

"Yeah."

"Well, these things happen. Planning a wedding is never predictable. In fact—"

Big Viv cut him off. "Yeah, yeah. I know. But whatcha gonna do? Listen, we're moving up the date of the wedding, so I'm gonna need you to rev everything up. You gotta focus on this 24/7. I want this wedding to happen ASAP. The sooner, the better. Don't worry, I'll double your fee for all the extra work you're gonna have to do."

Dominick wasn't sure he heard her correctly. "You're moving up the wedding date?"

"Yeah."

The words slipped out before he could stop them. "Don't you mean cancel?"

"Cancel?" she shrieked. "Why would we be canceling the wedding?"

"Sorry, we must have a bad connection," he said. "You're fading in and out. I thought you said to cancel the wedding."

"What's the matter with you? Are you not listening? We have to move the wedding date up."

"Up?" Even though he heard the word, his mind wasn't processing it. What was she talking about? This didn't make any sense. The wedding was supposed to be off.

Unless Sebastian and Vivi hadn't talked to Big Viv. Dominick gave a sigh of relief. Yes, that had to be it. They just hadn't done it yet, and Big Viv was taking control of things the way she always did without consulting them.

Although, Sebastian and Vivi were supposed to

talk with her first thing this morning. It was almost eleven o'clock.

"Have you seen Sebastian and Vivi today?" he casually asked.

"This morning. when I gave them the keys to their new house."

"What?" The words came out harsher than Dominick meant them to. But they hadn't been what Dominick was expecting.

"I gave them keys to the house I bought them. You know any interior decorators or landscapers, Dominick? Because this place is gonna need a complete makeover, inside and out. It's got good bones, but everything needs to be freshened up."

"You bought them a house," Dominick sputtered.

"Four bedrooms, three bathrooms," Big Viv boasted.

None of this made any sense.

"I've got to go, Mrs. Confetta. There's someone at my door with a package."

"Call me back as soon as you can," she ordered. "We've got a lot to do and not much time to do it."

When the call ended, Dominick tossed his cellphone on his desk. His first reaction was to call Sebastian and ask him what the fuck was going on. But he wasn't going to do that. If anyone was owed a phone call, it was him. The plan had been for the wedding to be called off, not moved up. So, what went wrong? Had they changed their minds because of a fucking house?

When a text came through his phone, it was Sebastian. Dom ignored it. He was too angry.

———

After getting off the phone with Dominick, Big Viv was trying not to panic.

She had a wedding to throw and a wedding planner who seemed to think the wedding was off. Talk about the day from Hell. Could it get any worse?

First, there had been that unexpected visit from Deena. Then, the phone call from her mother.

How the hell did she find out about the wedding? She hadn't planned on inviting her. The last thing she wanted to see on the happiest day of her life was her mother's sour puss. The woman never smiled. Never laughed. Never experienced a moment of joy out of life.

Big Viv couldn't remember the last time she had spoken with her mother. Phone calls between them were few and far between. To say that Big Viv and her mother weren't close would be an understatement. Some women weren't meant to be mothers, and Big Viv's mother was one of them. If she went through her memories, she really couldn't remember any moment in her life when her mother made her feel special or loved. She was all about business and making a profit. When they lived in Italy, she ran the family grocery store with an iron fist, and when they came to America she did the same when they opened a new grocery store.

Big Viv was the youngest of four. Her two older brothers, Antonio and Giovanni, and her sister, Sophia, had each been born a year apart after their mother got married at sixteen. But by the time she came along, ten years after Sophia was born, her mother was over having babies and Big Viv had been an unexpected surprise. She was the "oopsie" baby. As a result, all her life, Big Viv had felt like an outsider in her family.

Her siblings were a close knit trio who didn't want anything to do with her, since she was so much younger, and her mother and father were too busy running their business to give her any attention. She was an inconvenience, but also a source of free employment at the grocery store, where Big Viv was put to work, both in Italy and

America, as soon as she was able to count and add numbers.

When she was younger, she tried to make her parents proud. She studied hard and did well in school. She listened and followed the rules. She was a good Italian daughter.

But no matter what she did, none of it mattered. Her parents continued to ignore her, focusing only on their business and how much more money they could make.

So, she asked herself one day, why bother? Why follow the rules?

Instead, she started doing what she wanted to do. She started rebelling.

And her first rebellion was her friendship with Deena.

Her mother had never liked Deena. Big Viv knew it the very first time she brought Deena home after school when they were in the first grade to work on a project together. Her mother didn't say anything negative in front of Deena, but then again, she didn't have to. Actions spoke louder than words. It was the way she looked at Deena's clothes. The way she gazed at her from head to toe—studying her hair, her face, her body, and finding fault with it all— her upper lip curling into a sneer. The passive-aggressive comments she made. And then, the way she criticized Deena after she went home, implying that Deena was too loud. Too messy. Too independent. She could do better than Deena DiGregorio, her mother said. There were other girls she could be friends with.

But Big Viv ignored her mother's words and continued to be friends with Deena all through grammar school and high school until she disappeared from her life.

Deena was fun. Deena was the one who introduced her to make-up. The one who suggested she dye her brown hair blonde. The one who held her hair behind her head the first time she got drunk, and the one she smoked her first cigarette with.

So many firsts with Deena.

And so many fights with her mother. She didn't want her to be friends with Deena and had said that more than once. But there wasn't much she could do about it since she was working at the grocery store 24/7. So, Big Viv did what she wanted, and to hell with what her mother thought.

But when Deena went off to California and didn't bother keeping in touch, her mother took great pleasure in saying, "I always knew she was no good. And now you do, too."

After her father died of a heart attack in the early '80s, her mother decided to return to Italy. By this time, her siblings had all married and started families, returning there as well. Julia expected Big Viv to go back with her.

But she didn't. She told her mother she was staying in New York. She had a job and was able to support herself. She had friends. A life. Why should she give it all up?

That led to an epic meltdown with Julia accusing Big Viv of abandoning her. As the unmarried daughter, she was expected to stay with her mother and take care of her in her old age.

In the end, Big Viv held her ground. She stayed in New York. At first, she tried to keep in touch with her mother, but her letters were never answered and phone calls were always terse and short.

Big Viv didn't know what her mother wanted from her. Did she expect her to grovel? Beg for forgiveness? But for what? Living her own life?

After a year, Big Viv finally gave up. Why make an effort when her efforts clearly didn't matter? She stopped writing letters, remembering only to send cards for birthdays and holidays, and she called less and less.

When it came time to get married to Gino, she

dreamed of a big wedding. The gown. The church. The flowers. The reception. But who would there be to invite? All of her family was in Italy and she doubted they would come back for the wedding. And Gino's family was small, scattered in a couple of different states.

In the end, they went to city hall, got a marriage license, and were married by a city clerk. No muss. No fuss.

But this wedding was going to be different. She wanted Vivi to have what she didn't. A big lush wedding, surrounded by family and friends. A day her daughter would always remember. The more lavish, the better.

Did she want her daughter to know how much she loved her and love her back the same way? Did she want her own mother to see how much she loved her daughter? How she gave Vivi the love Julia had never given to her?

Maybe.

With this wedding, she felt like she had something to prove. To Vivi. To Deena. To her mother.

And to herself.

———

"You have to give him a chance to explain himself. You can't just shut him down." Lolly waved a forkful of salad greens at Dominick. "You like this guy, right?"

They were having lunch at Rockefeller Center, sitting on a marble bench on the plaza across the street from Saks, surrounded by planters filled with red, yellow, orange, and purple tulips. After getting off the phone with Big Viv and receiving Sebastian's text, Dominick had called Lolly asking if she could do an emergency lunch so they could discuss these latest developments. She was working, but she was able to spare an hour.

"Yes," Dominick answered, although he was still mad. Steaming! Lolly wasn't doing a good job calming him down. Instead, she was sticking up for Sebastian.

"Then, you have to give him the benefit of the doubt. I don't think he would be stupid enough to trade you in for a house."

"It's a pretty big house," Dominick said, taking a sip of his lemonade. "Four bedrooms. Three bathrooms. Big Viv sent me the listing link."

"Look, I didn't spend much time talking with him on Saturday, but what little time I spent with him, I liked. He seems like a good guy. You must think so, too, otherwise you wouldn't be interested in him. Aside from his hot body."

"But he lied to me. Do I really want to get involved with a liar?"

Lolly waved her fork at Dominick again. "You don't know if he lied to you."

"He was supposed to tell Big Viv the wedding was off and he didn't. He's also lied to me since I first met him. Both he and Vivi."

"How?"

"Seriously? By pretending to be straight. By pretending to be the father of Vivi's baby. By going through with this wedding."

"But it was a lie to help a friend, wasn't it?"

"I suppose," Dominick reluctantly conceded.

Lolly pinched two fingers together. "More like a little white lie."

"I wouldn't call it a little lie. More like a big fat one."

"Would you do something like that for me if I needed your help?"

"You know I would. But—"

Lolly cut him off. "Then, what's the difference? Why is it so wrong when Sebastian does it for Vivi? You can't have one set of rules for him and another for yourself." Lolly began tossing the remains of her lunch into a paper bag. "Go home. Do some work. Then decide what you're going to wear tonight and make yourself look irresistible. You're a prize, honey!"

"I'll keep an open mind," Dominick promised.

"Sebastian isn't going to want to lose you. I would bet money on that."

"You think?"

"I know. No one ever said the road to love was smooth. At the very least, you're getting a free dinner out of this. Be nice and bring him flowers tonight."

"Flowers? No, I'm too mad to bring him flowers. He's lucky I'm not standing him up."

"He did send you that text," she reminded him.

"Why didn't he call?" Dominick shot back.

"Too scared," Lolly said without hesitation. "I'm sure he knows his text didn't go over too well."

"You're probably right."

"Just keep an open mind tonight. Listen to what he has to say, okay? If you want to call me after you're done, I'll be home."

Dominick knew Lolly was right. He needed to listen to Sebastian. Talking to her helped a little bit. But would he be able to remember her advice later tonight?

The first thing Sebastian had done after Big Viv left the bakery was send a text to Dom rather than call him. He hadn't wanted to take the risk of being overheard by anyone. He'd also been afraid of talking to him. Not because he expected Dom to be angry—he had every right to be—but because he had let him down. He was dreading hearing the disappointment in his voice.

Change of plans. But only temporary! Will explain everything tonight. XO

He had debated including the XO, but bravely decided to. He needed all the help he could get, because he had a feeling Dom wasn't going to be happy with this change of plans.

He had expected Dom to text back within seconds. He hadn't. Complete silence. Sebastian didn't know what it meant. Was Dom too busy to text back, or was he too upset?

He didn't blame him. If anyone had reason to be upset, it was Dom. He and Vivi had just thrown him an unexpected curveball.

As the day went on and there was still no word from Dom, Sebastian continued to worry. Even if he was mad, wouldn't he at least let him know? Was he giving him the silent treatment? Were they even still on for their date tonight?

"Well, this place almost looks back to normal," Vivi said, giving a final spritz of Windex to a display case and wiping it with a paper towel.

After Big Viv had disappeared, Sebastian and Vivi had closed the bakery, spending most of the day cleaning desserts off the floor and walls. Vivi had then called in a painter to come in and paint the place overnight because some of the fruit stains wouldn't come off the walls. The bakery would be as good as new in the morning. Hopefully the next time Deena dropped in for a visit there wouldn't be a repeat of what happened today.

"Tell me more about this grandmother of yours," Sebastian said. "La Strega."

Viv sighed. "Nonna Julia. Where to begin? She's not one of those warm and fuzzy grandmothers. You're not going to find her in the kitchen baking cookies. I don't really know her that well. I only spent one summer in Italy, the year that Nico's mother and mine separated us. She's very cold and distant. Aloof. She never smiles. She's like the Grinch. Her heart is four sizes too small. She's heartless. I don't know what made her that way."

"Your mom went as white as a sheet when she was on the phone with her."

"Growing up, I don't think my mom had the best relationship with her. She doesn't talk about her much. When she was younger, she tried to please her, and then she just gave up."

"Think that's why she overcompensates with you?"

"Is it ever! A shrink could have a field day. Anyway, you'll get to meet Nonna Julia in a few weeks."

"Should I be worried?"

"We should all be worried," Vivi answered. "Still no word from Dom?"

Sebastian shook his head while restocking a display case with cupcakes.

"What are you going to do?"

"I'm going to go home and make dinner. Hopefully our date for tonight is still on. If not, I'm going to have a lot of leftovers this week."

"Bash, I'm sorry."

"It's not your fault."

"Yes, it is. If only I hadn't opened my big mouth when my mother found out I was pregnant."

"I could have said something at the time and I

didn't. We're equally to blame. Eventually, we'll get ourselves out of this."

"And if we don't?"

Sebastian handed her the last cupcake on his tray. "Then, I guess you'd better get used to being Mrs. Sebastian Fontana."

Sebastian was hurrying toward the subway entrance for the D train to Manhattan when he felt a hand descend upon his shoulder.

"Where are you going in such a rush?"

That voice. As soon as he heard it, he was transported back to high school. To the days when he was a theater geek who hated gym class and liked boys and was afraid of anyone ever finding out. Who walked down the halls with trepidation, eyes darting nervously around every corner until he was safely in his next class, because there was always that one person waiting for him, getting ready to pounce, waiting to make his life miserable.

Nico Morelli.

Sebastian turned around, facing his one-time nemesis. He hadn't seen Nico in at least a decade.

Not since they had graduated from high school. He hated to admit it, but he was aging well. He was still handsome. Even more handsome, if that was possible. He could see why Vivi would be attracted to him. He was oozing testosterone and Italian swagger.

Nico lifted his chin toward him. "I hear you're getting married and having a baby." He held out a hand. "Congratulations."

"Uh huh," Sebastian said, not sure where exactly this was going as he shook Nico's hand.

"And my Vivi is the lucky bride. I have to be honest, I always thought you'd wind up with a groom. Guess I was wrong."

"I guess you were." Sebastian yanked away his hand, wondering if Nico was toying with him. But there was no smirk or mocking smile on his face. "And Vivi might have been yours once, but she hasn't been your Vivi in a very long time."

"But she's always been yours, right, Bash?"

What did he mean by that?

"You and Vivi. Two peas in a pod. Always together. Joined at the hip." Nico said it almost sadly. "Best friends forever. Is that what happened? Friendship turned to love?"

"Something like that. What do you want, Nico?" Sebastian asked, staring at him warily. "I feel like you have an agenda. If you have something you want to say, just spit it out. Vivi told me you came by her place last night and didn't believe her when she told you the baby wasn't yours."

Nico sighed as he ran a hand through his hair. Sebastian watched enviously as all the strands fell perfectly back into place. "Last night wasn't a good night," Nico said, shaking his head ruefully. "I had too much to drink. A friend of mine was getting married and there was a bachelor party. Guess I started feeling sorry for myself, thinking about the past and all my missed chances with Vivi. We reconnected this past spring and when I heard about the baby, well, I started wondering if it might be mine."

"Guess you were wrong. Again."

"I guess so. I realized that after I sobered up. Maybe a part of me was hoping it would be true. My one last chance with Vivi. But I blew it. Again."

Sebastian knew Nico had dabbled in acting when he had first moved out to California and he wasn't sure if what he was hearing was true. The words were certainly heartfelt, but could it all be an act?

"I'm happy for you. Both of you," Nico continued. "And that's why I'm here. I want to celebrate your happiness."

"You do?"

"I know we weren't the best of friends in high school."

Sebastian gave a bitter laugh. "That's putting it mildly."

"I was a dick. And I'm sorry. Really sorry."

Sebastian didn't know what to make of Nico's apology, so he said nothing. It could simply be more acting. But for what purpose? What did Nico want?

"How long have we known each other, Sebastian? A really long time. And even though Vivi has been a part of both our lives, we've never really been friends. I want to make up for that."

"How?"

"I want to throw a bachelor party for you. As a way of apologizing for the shitty way I used to treat you."

This didn't make any sense. Nico was being nice. Nico was never nice. At least, not to him.

Sebastian's guard was instantly up. Nico was plotting something.

"Think about the kind of party you want and then we'll pick a date. We can do anything. I'll handle everything once you get me the contact info for your groomsmen."

"Groomsmen?"

"For the wedding," Nico reminded him. "How many are there going to be?"

Sebastian had never given a thought to groomsmen. And he didn't think Vivi was thinking about bridesmaids.

"You are having a bridal party, aren't you? What kind of Italian wedding would it be if you and Vivi didn't have at least twelve bridesmaids and ushers?"

"Vivi and I have been putting lists together but we haven't asked anyone yet," Sebastian lied.

Nico's face lit up. "You haven't asked anyone yet? Really? This might sound crazy, but would you put me on the list? I've known you and Vivi for such a long time. I'd love to share your day with you."

His childhood bully and his bride's ex-lover was asking to stand up at their wedding? If it was anyone else, he'd be inclined to say the person was a moron. But this was Nico Morelli he was dealing with, and he knew how devious Nico could be.

But he didn't have time to deal with this. He had to get back into Manhattan and start cooking for Dom.

"Uh, I'll have to discuss it with Vivi." Sebastian glanced at his watch. "And now, I really have to go." He raced up the subway stairs at the sound of the approaching D train to Manhattan.

"Go," Nico called after him. "I can always reach you at the bakery. I didn't mean to keep you. I'm sure we'll be crossing paths again real soon."

———

Now, where is Sebastian off to in such a hurry? Nico wondered. It was like he was rushing off to meet someone.

Meet someone...

Could it be? He wouldn't be that dumb, to see someone while engaged to Vivi? Could Nico be that lucky?

If Sebastian was seeing a guy while engaged to Vivi, that would make the situation even more explosive. And provide more dynamite for when he exposed this sham wedding to Big Viv.

And it *was* a sham.

First, no engagement ring. Now, no bridal party. Those were the first two things instantly crossed off the list of any Italian bride planning her wedding.

And Vivi hadn't done either.

Something wasn't adding up. Because there was a reason. And there was only one way to find out what it was.

Follow Sebastian.

CHAPTER
EIGHTEEN

Mince and chop. Saute and simmer. Stir, stir, stir.

Sebastian was working like a madman in his kitchen. He'd wanted to prepare an elaborate dinner for Dom, but he didn't have enough time to go shopping and get all the ingredients he needed. He would have had to go to too many stores. So, he'd gone to one supermarket and was sticking with the basics. Dishes that were easy to make, yet bursting with flavor.

He chose to start with stuffed mushrooms. After chopping up the stems, he cooked them with minced onions and garlic, then mixed them with breadcrumbs, filled the mushroom heads, and put them into the oven. While they were cooking, he began work on a pot of tomato orzo, assembling the ingredients of garlic, onion, zucchini, fresh corn, cherry tomatoes (which needed to be halved), red pepper flakes, tomato paste, and balsamic vinegar. The tomatoes would cook for twenty minutes to break down, then he would add the orzo and water and let it all simmer for another fifteen minutes before mixing in shredded mozzarella and parmesan cheese.

Hoping Dom wasn't a vegetarian, he had bought two petite filets for the main course, which he seasoned with salt and pepper, along with fixings for a salad and a homemade honey mustard vinaigrette. As much as he was tempted to make something elaborate for dessert, there wasn't enough time. Instead, he had bought vanilla and chocolate ice cream (next time—*if* there was a next time—he would make the ice cream himself) and assembled homemade ice cream sandwiches with the freshly baked cookies he had on hand.

"Something smells good in here," Liam said from the kitchen doorway.

"What are you doing here?"

"I live here, remember? Although after the stunt you pulled last night, I'm rethinking it."

It was the first time Sebastian had laid eyes on

Liam since Operation Cupcake. He was relieved to see all his welts were gone.

"I'm sorry. I don't know what came over me last night. I saw you flirting with Dom and I instantly became jealous."

"So, you decided to knock out the competition." Liam walked over to the counter where Sebastian stood doing his prep and tossed a cherry tomato into his mouth. "I get it. I don't blame you. You must really like this guy, huh?"

"I do."

"Then, what's the problem?"

Sebastian paused his sauteeing of the onions and garlic for the orzo. "You know what the problem is. Vivi and the wedding."

"Weren't you and Vivi going to explain everything to Big Viv this morning?"

"How do you know that?"

"I might have been hiding in my bedroom last night, but I could hear every word you guys were saying."

"Our plan was temporarily put on hold." Sebastian sighed and quickly brought Liam up to speed.

"This is better than some of the soaps I watch."

Sebastian knew one of Liam's dreams was to

someday be on a daytime soap, playing a villain viewers would love to hate. "On that note, how did your audition go? Were you able to make it?"

"I was. I looked normal when I woke up this morning. They had me read the lines, so that was a good sign. You know, sometimes you show up and they take one look at you and they ask you to leave because they have this image in their mind of what they want. But there were at least a hundred guys waiting to be seen, so who knows?"

Sebastian handed Liam a stack of plates and silverware. "Would you mind setting the table for me while I jump in the shower?"

"Anything for true love," Liam said.

"Let's not jinx things," Sebastian said.

"He didn't call and cancel, did he?"

"No. But maybe he plans on standing me up. I wouldn't blame him."

"He wouldn't do that."

"How do you know?"

"He wouldn't. Now, stop worrying. Go take your shower and let me set the table."

"And then you're going out for the night, right?"

Liam raised an eyebrow. "Is that a suggestion or a threat?"

"A little of both?"

"I'll clear out. No worries."

"Thanks, Liam."

"You owe me. For tonight and last night. Never let it be said that I stood in the way of true love."

"I promise to make it up to you," Sebastian vowed.

Liam gave him a wink as he left the kitchen. "I know you will."

After his shower, Sebastian decided to dress casual. He donned a pair of olive green shorts, a navy blue Ralph Lauren polo, and flip flops. A little bit of gel in his hair, a squirt of cologne, and he was good to go. A perfect summer outfit.

He found the dining room table all set, along with two white candles, already lit, in crystal candlestick holders.

"I figured I'd help set the mood," Liam said, pointing to the candles before heading to his bedroom. "I'll be gone in ten minutes."

Sebastian was taking the mushrooms out of the oven when he heard a knock on the apartment door.

He quickly wiped his hands on a dish towel and hurried from the kitchen. When he opened the door, he found Dom holding a bouquet of sunflowers. Sebastian melted at the sight. If Dom brought him flowers, he couldn't be that angry, could he?

———

Dominick was still angry. And he wanted to hold on to the anger.

But it was hard.

First, there were the delicious scents wafting in the air. Then, there was the candlelit table for two.

Sebastian had put a lot of effort into their first date. Plus, he looked adorable.

But he wasn't ready to forgive him just yet.

Dominick was the kind of person who when he said he was going to do something, he did. He didn't put it off. He didn't make excuses. He got it done. He didn't know why Sebastian and Vivi hadn't gone through with their plan to tell Big Viv the truth. Why had they changed their minds? And what did this mean?

If the wedding was still on—and from all indications, it was—then Sebastian and Vivi were getting married. And Dominick had no intention of being the other woman. Or in this case, the other man.

He walked into the apartment, letting Sebastian close the door behind him. Dominick turned around, wasting no time. He wanted answers.

"Start talking," he said.

How to start the conversation, Sebastian wondered. Slowly ease into it, or tackle it head on?

Dom solved the problem for him, filling up the uncomfortable silence. "My day was a shit show. I lost count of how many texts and phone calls I had today with Big Viv. She was more demanding than ever. But why shouldn't she be? Your wedding date is being moved up. Which was a major surprise when she called to tell me."

Sebastian gulped.

He hadn't known Big Viv called Dom, although he should have figured she would. He could only imagine the phone call with her. He was going to have to do a lot of damage control.

"I still don't know what's going on, Sebastian," Dom began. "The last time I saw you and Vivi, the two of you had agreed to tell Big Viv that the wedding was off. Now, not only is it still on, but it's sooner. Care to fill in the blanks?"

Sebastian dove in, telling Dom about the food fight with Deena and the announcement that Vivi's grandmother would be attending the wedding.

"Don't you see, Dom?" Sebastian said when he

reached the end of his story. "It wouldn't have been right of us to pull the rug out from under Big Viv."

"How about pulling the rug out from under me?"

"We didn't mean to!"

"I don't know how this wedding is going to happen. I was on the phone all afternoon, trying to pull in favors. There isn't an available venue anywhere in Brooklyn because we're at the height of wedding season. Those halls are booked years in advance."

"I'm sorry, Dom. Really, I am. But this will all work out, I promise."

"That's what you promised *last* night," Dom pointed out. "And I'm still planning your wedding."

"Can we forget all about the wedding?" Sebastian asked. "Just for tonight and focus on us? Please?"

"Sure, but this problem isn't going away. You're engaged to marry Vivi. If you only opened your eyes, you'd see there's an easy solution to all this. Do what you were supposed to do this morning," Dom stated. "Tell Big Viv the truth and call off the wedding."

"I can't."

"Can't or won't?" Dom shook his head. "Maybe this wasn't such a good idea. Maybe I should leave."

Those were the last words Sebastian wanted to

hear, but he certainly wasn't going to grovel or beg. What more did Dom want from him? He'd explained what had happened. Why couldn't he be a little more patient?

"If you want to leave, then leave," he said. "I can't make you stay if you don't want to be here."

As he said the words, Sebastian felt like he was standing outside his body, watching a scene from a movie, powerless to change it. How had things gone so wrong? This was supposed to be their first date, and it had ended before it even got started.

Sebastian walked over to the apartment door, opening it for Dom. He got the shock of his life when he saw who was standing on the other side.

Nico Morelli.

"Well, well, well," Nico said with a smug smile as he walked inside. "This is a cozy little picture."

Sebastian watched as Nico's eyes fell upon the candlelit table for two. Then, they flitted toward Sebastian, then to Dom. "Date night?" he asked.

––––––––

This was easier than Nico had thought it would be. The Manhattan bound train had been pulling into the station when he followed Sebastian, jumping into the subway car behind his. From the window between their cars, he'd been able to keep an eye on Sebastian as the train headed into the city while a quick Google search on his phone had given him Sebastian's address. He didn't know where he was heading. Maybe home? He wasn't sure if he was going to find out anything, but he had to start somewhere.

Sebastian got off the train at 34th Street, switching over to the Q line, which meant he was heading back to the Upper East Side where he lived. Nico followed, and when the train pulled onto 86th Street, he kept enough distance between himself and Sebastian as they took the escalator up to the street.

Instead of heading straight for his apartment, however, Sebastian made a stop at Whole Foods, emerging thirty minutes later loaded down with shopping bags. Nico had followed him home and then positioned himself across the street from his apartment building.

He had a feeling Sebastian was expecting company tonight. The question was who?

His feeling was confirmed ninety minutes later when he spotted a good-looking man carrying a bouquet of sunflowers heading into Sebastian's building. He didn't know why, but he suspected the guy was going to visit Sebastian. Of course, he could be wrong. But he could be right, too. There had been only one way to find out.

Nico had waited around ten minutes and then walked into the building, finding Sebastian's apartment number by the buzzer. The lock on the front door of the building was broken, so he was able to waltz right in. He was just getting ready to knock on Sebastian's door when it was flung open. There was no mistaking the look of shock and guilt on Sebastian's face when he saw Nico.

Yes! He had been right! Something was definitely up. Why else would Sebastian look like he had been caught doing something he shouldn't be doing?

He walked inside the apartment and took in the entire scene. The table set for two. The candlelight. And then, he saw the guy from the street with the bouquet of sunflowers.

Sunflowers meant for Sebastian. Because who else could they be for?

Nico slipped a hand into his pocket and pulled out his phone, getting ready to hit the record button.

Sebastian's brain went blank.

What was Nico doing here? He must have followed him home from Brooklyn. But why?

He had to have an agenda of some kind.

He turned to Dom in a panic, trying to relay with his eyes the urgency of the situation. But Dom just stared at him blankly. Of course. Why wouldn't he? He had no idea what was going on.

But then, Sebastian was saved. By the last person he expected to save him, especially after last night.

Dom!" Liam exclaimed, emerging from his bedroom before Sebastian could say anything. "You brought me flowers!"

He took the bouquet and gave Dom a big fat kiss. Then, he turned to Nico while hugging Dom close to his side. "Wasn't it sweet of Sebastian to arrange a romantic dinner for Dom and me?"

"You two are dating?" Nico asked.

"Uh huh. I'm Sebastian's roommate, Liam. And this cutie is my honey, Dom." He handed the flowers to Sebastian. "Could you find a vase for these and put them on the table? I want to look at them when we're having dinner." He gave Dom another kiss. "I can't keep my hands off him. I'm almost tempted to toss him over my shoulder and head back into my bedroom."

"But you're not going to, right?" Sebastian returned from the kitchen, slamming the vase of sunflowers down in the middle of the table. "Not after all the cooking I did."

"It'll reheat," Liam said, starting to nibble on Dom's ear. "What do you say Dom? Should we skip dinner and go right to dessert?"

———

Dominick didn't know what was going on. One minute he was getting ready to leave, the next there was a stranger walking into Sebastian's apartment with a smug expression on his face and Sebastian looked like he was about to pass out. Now, he was being manhandled by Liam.

Dominick could tell that Sebastian was not happy with Liam's ruse. If looks could kill...

Well, two could play at this game. Sebastian wasn't the only one who could pretend to be in a relationship.

"It depends on what you're really hungry for," he told Liam, placing a hand on his crotch and giving it a hard squeeze. "If you really want dessert first..."

Liam's eyes widened, happily shocked.

"We'll be eating later," Liam announced,

grabbing Dominick by the hand and pulling him in the direction of his bedroom. Dominick could feel Sebastian's eyes following after them as they headed into the bedroom and closed the door behind them.

Good. Now he knew what it felt like to want someone when they were attached to someone else.

———

Sebastian stared at the closed bedroom door. How had things gotten so messed up?

"What do you want?" he asked Nico, a hostile tone in his voice. Maybe if Nico hadn't shown up, he might have been able to salvage this evening. But now, he would never know. "And how did you know where I live?"

Nico waved his phone in the air. "Google. I was heading back to my apartment when I remembered I've got a friend who runs a tuxedo shop. I thought I could hook you up. He'll give you a sweet price on the rentals."

"Thanks, but I've got that covered."

"You sure? I don't mind putting in a good word."

Sebastian held open the door. "If you don't mind, I've got a dinner I have to get back to."

Nico raised an eyebrow in the direction of Liam's

bedroom. "I don't think those two care about dinner. Although, I'm sure they'll work up an appetite."

"Goodnight, Nico."

Nico walked out. "Night."

After closing the door behind him, Sebastian collapsed against it. Why did he feel like he had just dodged a bullet?

"Hey! No one likes a cock tease," Liam wailed, following after Dom as he retreated from the bedroom.

Dom turned around to face him. "You didn't think I was really going to sleep with you, did you?"

"Why not? We would have had fun."

"I was playing along with whatever was going on here." Dom turned to face Sebastian. "And now that your uninvited guest is gone, I'd like you to fill in the blanks. What just happened?"

"We did a little bit of impromptu theatre," Liam explained.

Dom ignored him. "Who was that guy, Sebastian? An ex-boyfriend? One night stand?"

"It was Nico."

Dom's eyes widened as he instantly recognized the name. "The potential father of Vivi's baby? Why was he here?"

"I don't know. I saw him in Brooklyn right before

I hopped on the train. He gave me some story about having a friend who could get me a discount on tuxedos for the wedding, but that's not why he showed up."

"It's not?"

Sebastian shook his head. "He was up to something."

"Like what?"

"I don't know. But he seemed thrilled to have thought he caught me in some sort of compromising situation."

"But he didn't," Liam bragged. "Thanks to my quick thinking. Good thing I recognized him from the pictures on Vivi's phone."

"There's a reason this guy followed you from Brooklyn," Dom said. "I bet he still loves Vivi. And he doesn't believe any of this story the two of you have concocted. Maybe he came to talk to you about it."

Sebastian shook his head. "He didn't come here tonight because he loves Vivi. He came here to expose me."

"Because he loves Vivi and wants her back," Dom insisted. "Why can't you give him the benefit of the doubt? Maybe he's changed. Doesn't everyone deserve a second chance?"

"He doesn't deserve it," Sebastian said. "You don't know Nico the way I do. He hated me when we were kids, and he probably still hates me. He apologized to me earlier tonight, but I'm not buying it. He was up to no good."

Dom threw his hands up in the air in exasperation. "You know, I really don't care what his reasons are. It's none of my business. I was hired to plan a wedding and that's what I'm going to do. Because you're getting married, right, Sebastian?"

"But you don't want him to marry Vivi, do you?" Liam asked.

Dom didn't answer.

"Sebastian," Liam urged. "Do something. Say something!"

"Why don't you stay?" Sebastian suggested. "Please? The food's all ready. We can talk about it over dinner."

"I know you went to a lot of trouble, but I can't stay," Dom said. "Tonight was supposed to be about us. Now, it's not. It's about you and Vivi. Again. This situation keeps getting more and more complicated, and it doesn't have to be if only you and Vivi would tell the truth. But neither one of you wants to. Who knows what's going to happen next? I don't want to find out, so I'm done. I'll see you at the wedding."

Sebastian watched as Dom left the apartment. He wanted to chase after him, to grab him by the arm and tug him back inside. But he was frozen in place, powerless to move. He knew whatever he did or said, it wouldn't make a difference because Dom was so angry. Suddenly, he had an ache in his chest, and he knew what it was—his broken heart.

"I'll eat your dinner," Liam offered, taking a seat at the table. "It smells great."

"You're lucky I don't force feed you another strawberry cupcake." Sebastian lashed out. "What were you thinking, mauling Dom the way you were?"

"I wasn't mauling him. I was saving your ass," Liam shot back, his own temper flaring. "Did you really want Nico to know this whole set-up was for you and Dom? I had to make it look real."

"You didn't have to throw yourself into it so convincingly."

"I'm an actor. That's what I do. I act."

Sebastian headed into the kitchen and returned with a tray of stuffed mushrooms.

"I know you're angry and upset," Liam said, popping one into his mouth. "You thought tonight was going to go one way, and instead it went another.

But you don't have anyone to blame but yourself for this mess. Don't take it out on me."

"Okay, okay, you're right," Sebastian admitted. "I'm sorry."

"You wanted to help Vivi and you got in over your head. If you want Dom, you're going to have to fight for him. And he's definitely worth fighting for."

Sebastian was shocked by his words. "What do you mean?"

"He still has feelings for you."

"How do you know?" Sebastian asked, not wanting to get his hopes up.

"It's obvious. I was trying to slip him some tongue when we were kissing and when I did, he bit me. Hard. And not in a fun, sexy way. More like a *get your goddamn tongue out of my mouth now* way. It really hurt, but I didn't allow my pain to show," he bragged.

"I didn't get that sense when he left," Sebastian said. "He's done with me."

Liam shook his head. "He needs to cool off, that's all. But maybe you guys also need some alone time. Some place where the two of you can be all by yourselves with no interruptions."

"Like where?"

"How about you go out to the house I'm renting

on Fire Island? None of my housemates are going to be out there this weekend. You can have the whole place to yourselves."

Sebastian hated to admit it, but the thought was tempting. Fire Island was off the beaten track. It would almost be like being marooned on a desert island. They'd be totally out of sight. Three whole days of being together. No Liam. No Vivi. No Big Viv. No Nico.

Just he and Dom. Alone.

Maybe it was exactly what they needed. Maybe they'd finally be able to get their romance on track. He couldn't wait to invite Dom the following morning.

———

If at first you don't succeed, try, try again. Nico's grandmother used to tell him that all the time.

Tonight hadn't worked out. There hadn't been another name by the apartment buzzer. Just Sebastian's. Maybe if he'd known Sebastian had a roommate, he wouldn't have been so quick to jump to conclusions.

But next time, he'd be ready. Because his gut told

him something was going on. And he always trusted his gut.

Something about the situation wasn't sitting right with him. He just didn't know what it was. Yet.

The roommate was gay, so it could have been a date night.

But they hadn't looked like a couple. Something about them had been off.

Unlike Sebastian and Dom. He could have sworn the date night was for them. The air had been charged between them when Sebastian had opened the door. And Sebastian hadn't seemed happy when his roomie was pawing Dom. He had almost seemed jealous. But why would that be?

Nico stared back at Sebastian's apartment building as he walked away from it.

He sure as hell was going to find out.

CHAPTER
NINETEEN

If there was one thing Dominick loved, it was shopping for wedding dresses.

Taking eager brides to bridal salons where they got to have the full princess experience while they tried on gown after gown until finally finding "the one" was one of his favorite parts of the job. He loved watching as they stared into a full-length mirror in awe, swathed in yards of satin and tulle and lace, like they couldn't believe what they were seeing. And then—then!—the cherry on top: Adding a veil or tiara to complete the picture.

But not today.

Today, he was bridal gown shopping with Big Viv and Vivi, and it was a totally different experience. It was not going well. There were cross words. Shouting. Tears.

He was in wedding gown hell.

Big Viv had definite ideas as to what kind of gown Vivi should be shopping for. She wanted her daughter to only try on empire waist or A-line gowns because they would hide Vivi's soon-to-be expanding waistline. But Vivi wanted to try on gowns that were sexier and more form fitting, like mermaid gowns.

They were at their fourth bridal boutique of the day in Manhattan. This one was in Soho, and the ambience was very minimal. The empty showroom consisted of brick walls and a lounging sofa with a low coffee table holding complimentary glasses of sparkling water, and a saleswoman who wasn't sure who she should be listening to before bringing out the gowns. Big Viv was giving orders, but Vivi kept overriding her.

"We want to see anything you've got with an empire waist," Big Viv said.

"And mermaid gowns, too," Vivi added.

"Why won't you listen to me?" Big Viv demanded. "You can't wear a mermaid gown. If you do, your stomach will be on display for everyone to see!" Big Viv turned to Dominick for some help. She was decked out today in white capris and a baby blue silk top with spaghetti straps, her hair pulled up in a high ponytail and Versace sunglasses perched on her nose, looking every inch the power shopper. "Will you please talk some sense into this girl!"

"Your mother is right," Dominick said in what he hoped was a calm and soothing voice. Vivi had just as short a fuse as her mother and the last thing he wanted was to be caught between the two of them. He didn't want Vivi to think he was taking Big Viv's side over hers. At the same time, he didn't want Big Viv to think he was dismissing her concerns. It was a delicate balance. "If we're trying to distract from the fact that you're pregnant, then we need to do a couple of things. I'd suggest a gown that's off the shoulder or has a sweetheart neckline. It also needs to be loose below the waist. Depending on when the wedding is going to be, we should buy the gown closer to the wedding date. If we buy it now, it might not fit for the wedding and then we won't be able to do alterations, so we should definitely order a size up. It's much easier to make a wedding dress smaller than it is to make it larger."

"I'll be right back with some options." The saleswoman gave Dominick a grateful smile before disappearing into the back of the salon.

"Nothing in satin and no stretchy lace," Dominick called after her. "Only organza, chiffon, and tulle." He turned back to Vivi. "Also, no high heels. I would suggest you wear flats."

"Flats?!" Vivi exclaimed in disbelief.

"Yes, flats," Dominick confirmed. "I always tell my brides to wear flats. You're going to be on your feet all day. And in your case, depending how far along you are when you get married, your feet are probably going to be swollen and you won't be able to stand in heels." Dominick took another look at Vivi. "We can also distract with accessories. Maybe a gorgeous necklace and some earrings. And we can do something with your hair, too. Wear it in an elaborate chignon. We want everyone looking up, not down."

The saleswoman returned with a selection of gowns on a clothes rack, wheeling them in front of the sofa. Vivi took one look and wrinkled her nose.

"What's the matter?" Big Viv asked. "Why are you acting like something stinks?"

"I don't like any of these," Vivi stated. She began to text on her phone.

"You haven't even looked at them, let alone tried one on!" Big Viv exclaimed, her voice filled with exasperation.

"I don't need to. I know what I like and I *don't* like any of those."

Dominick had had enough. He grabbed Vivi by the arm, along with a gown, and headed in the direction of the dressing room.

"We'll be right back," he called over his shoulder.

When they reached the dressing room, he handed her the gown. "Here. Try it on."

"Don't be mad," Vivi hissed, looking up from her phone, making sure to keep her voice low.

"Who says I'm mad?"

"You're mad. I can tell." She rubbed her arm. "And you grabbed me a little too hard."

"Sorry. And if I was mad—and I'm not saying I am—don't I have a right to be? You torpedoed my relationship with Sebastian before it even got started."

"I didn't torpedo it! At least, not intentionally. None of this is Sebastian's fault. Please don't blame him."

"Then who should I blame? You? You're both equally at fault, carrying on with this charade. Do you know how devastated your mother is going to be when this all blows up?"

"It's not going to blow up."

"Really?" Dominick couldn't help but smirk. "When was the last time you spoke to Sebastian?"

Vivi shrugged. "I don't know. Yesterday afternoon at the bakery?"

"He had an unexpected visitor last night. On what was supposed to be our first date at his apartment."

"A visitor."

"Uh huh."

"Who?"

"Who do you think?"

Vivi's violet eyes widened with horror. "Nico?"

"Yup."

She grabbed Dominick by the arm, pulling him closer. "Why was he there?"

"I don't know." He removed Vivi's hand from the sleeve of his seersucker suit, smoothing away the wrinkles. "He claimed he could get Sebastian a deal on tuxedo rentals, but Sebastian didn't believe him."

"Damn!" Vivi's fear was now turning to anger. "I knew he wasn't going to give up. What was he trying to find out?"

Dominick shrugged. "I don't know. But Nico knows something is up. I could tell. It's only a matter of time before he finds out the truth."

"I sent everything off for the DNA test this morning and paid extra for a rush. Nico left a toothbrush and hairbrush at my place. I should know soon if he's my baby's father."

"And if he is?"

"I'll deal with that once I know."

"Are you going to call off the wedding if he's the father?"

"Call it off?" Vivi looked at Dominick as if he was crazy. "Don't you understand? I can't. I have to go through with this."

"You don't have to do anything."

"Look, maybe this started because I panicked when I found out I was pregnant. I knew my mother would go through the roof if she thought Nico might be the father of this baby. And there's still that chance. But now things have gotten more complicated."

"More complicated? How?"

"My grandmother. She's a cold woman. Age is supposed to soften you. Well, if that's true, I don't want to imagine what she was like when my mother was younger. She's coming to the wedding and I can't embarrass my mother in front of her. I won't. She's done so much for me my entire life. It's always been just the two of us. Yes, she drives me crazy, but it's only because she loves me so much. Once my grandmother is back in Italy, I'll explain everything to my mother."

"While you're still married to Sebastian."

"Yes!" Vivi stated. "While I'm married to Sebastian. Eventually, we're going to end the marriage, but I don't know how soon after the wedding that will be. How many times do I have to say I'm sorry?"

"Maybe you should be saying that to Sebastian."

"Maybe I already have!" Vivi snapped back. "And don't forget, Sebastian isn't getting the short end of the stick here. I'm going to fund his bakery for going through with all this. Why can't you be a little bit patient?"

"Because I don't like lying, Vivi. That's what it all comes down to. And both you and Sebastian are liars. How can I be in a relationship with someone who doesn't know how to tell the truth? How can I ever trust him?"

"That's a horrible thing to say. You can trust him," Vivi insisted. "Sebastian is one of the most loyal and honorable people I know. When we decided to do all this, we didn't know you yet. I know, without a doubt, that if Sebastian had already been seeing you, he never would have agreed to this. But he hadn't started seeing you yet."

"And that makes it okay?"

Vivi rolled her eyes. "None of this is okay. I only wish I knew why Deena stopped talking to my mother all those years ago. That's what caused all these problems. She turned her back on her."

"Sebastian told me she came to the bakery yesterday. Any idea why?"

Vivi nodded. "She knows about the baby, and I'm sure she suspects it's Nico's. She came to the bakery to cause trouble. The only question is if she's going to come back to cause more."

"In all these years, neither you or Nico have asked each other about this feud?"

"Sure, we talked about it but we didn't know much. Our stories were pretty identical. Each one says the other stopped talking to her, but there was never a reason why. Deena thinks my mother is jealous of her, and my mother thinks Deena put her career before their friendship, making their friendship collateral damage."

"Maybe if you fixed things between Deena and your mother, you and Nico might have a chance," Dominick suggested, trying not to get his hopes up. It couldn't be that easy, could it? After all, these women hadn't been friends in over forty-five years. Still, it could be worth a shot. "Maybe then, you and Nico would be the ones getting married, especially if the baby winds up being his."

"Nico's a snake. A lying, cheating snake." Vivi adamantly shook her head. "I'm never marrying him."

"What's taking so long?" Big Viv called out. "What are you two whispering about? I want to see Vivi in a wedding gown."

Vivi slapped her phone into Dominick's hand. "Hold this until I come back out."

Dominick returned back to the lounging sofa, placing Vivi's phone down on the coffee table.

"What were you two whispering about?" Big Viv asked.

"Just trying to convince her to try on the gown. You've got a stubborn daughter."

"Tell me about it." Big Viv pulled a notepad out of her purse. "Next on our list is the wedding cake. We have to find a baker."

"Why do we need a baker?" Dominick asked, puzzled.

Big Viv looked at Dominick like he had no brains. "To make the wedding cake."

"Isn't Sebastian going to want to do that?"

"He can't."

"Why not?"

"He's the groom. Who ever heard of the groom making his own wedding cake?"

"I think it's sort of romantic. Can't you see Sebastian putting all his love into his own wedding cake?"

Where did those words come from? Dominick wondered. Maybe he'd watched the movie *Chocolat* one time too many. Or maybe he just wanted Sebastian to make a wedding cake for him. He already knew Sebastian was a terrific baker. He could only imagine what something he made for someone he loved tasted like. And a wedding cake was the ultimate expression of love.

"Besides," Big Viv continued, "it's bad luck."

"Bad luck?" Dominick had never heard that superstition. "Says who?"

"Says me." Big Viv pushed her sunglasses on top of her head, her eyes blazing. "Sebastian ain't baking the cake and that's the end of it. What's the name of that fancy baker in NYC who does all those high society wedding cakes?"

"Sylvia Weinstock?"

"Yeah! Her!" Big Viv's eyes lit up. "You think we could get her?"

"She died last year, so I think not."

Big Viv made the sign of the cross over her face. "May she rest in peace. Well, we'll find someone else. Does Martha Stewart still make cakes?"

At that moment, there was a ping from Vivi's phone. Followed by another. And another.

Big Viv leaned forward, trying to read the screen. "Who's texting her?"

Dominick saw a name pop up. Nico. Uh oh. He made to grab the phone, but Big Viv was faster. And when she saw the name, her face transformed from one of serenity to rage.

"Vivi!" she bellowed. "Get out here. Now!"

Vivi emerged from the dressing room in an empire waist wedding gown. It looked good on her, but Big Viv hardly noticed. No, her attention was fixated on the phone in her hand.

"What?" Vivi sullenly asked.

Big Viv brandished Vivi's cellphone in front of her, waving it in the air. "Why is Nico Morelli texting you?"

Vivi, much to Dominick's surprise, didn't lose her cool. "Because we're friends."

"Since when?"

"Since always." Vivi snatched the phone out of her mother's hand. "Look, Ma, you and Deena might have sabotaged our romance, but it didn't end our friendship. We've stayed in touch over the years."

"Are you planning to invite him to the wedding?"

Vivi shrugged. "Maybe I am. I don't know. I have to discuss it with Sebastian. See if he's okay with it. Why, you have a problem with that?"

"No," Big Viv said. "As long as his plus one isn't his hag of an aunt."

"Chillax," Vivi said as she inspected herself in a full-length mirror, moving from left to right in the gown. "I doubt he would bring Deena. He'd probably bring that skanky pop star, Candy."

"The same Candy who sings *Feral Bitch?*" Big Viv asked.

"Yes," Vivi muttered.

"That would get a lot of press, wouldn't it?" Big Viv said to Dominick, her voice filled with excitement.

"Don't get your hopes up. Candy is not coming to my wedding and I'm not buying this wedding gown," Vivi said, heading back to the dressing room. "I'm done for the day."

Big Viv turned to Dominick in a panic. "What are we gonna do? She has to buy a wedding dress soon. Every day that passes, her belly is gonna get bigger and bigger."

"I heard that!" Vivi shouted through the dressing room curtain. "I'm not even showing yet."

"But you will. Sooner than you think," Big Viv shouted back before returning her attention to Dominick. "We need to get the ball rolling on this wedding. Before it looks like the bride has a beach ball under her dress."

"I'm working as fast as I can, Mrs. Confetta, but planning a wedding takes months, sometimes even years," Dominick said, using his most professional voice. He didn't want to upset her. He could see she was agitated and his gut was telling him Big Viv did *not* do well with agitation. "You're asking me to do the impossible."

"I thought you could handle the impossible," Big Viv hissed, her eyes narrowing to dangerous slits. "Should I have gotten another wedding planner?"

Dominick swallowed over the sudden lump of fear in his throat. Why did this woman put the fear of God into him? Was this why Sebastian and Vivi couldn't tell her the truth? Did they feel the same way? He quickly chased the thought away. He didn't have time to analyze it right now. "Just give me a couple more days. I'm waiting to hear back on some calls."

Big Viv jerked a thumb in the direction of the dressing room. "What about her?"

An idea popped into Dominick's head. "I've got a friend who's a wedding gown designer. Maybe she can design something Vivi might like. A custom gown."

"Get her on the phone," Big Viv ordered. "The sooner she gets started, the better."

———

Luckily, Lolly was free that afternoon and invited Dominick to bring Vivi over to her loft. Even better, Vivi had convinced Big Viv to return to Brooklyn. "I need a little space, Ma. I'll look at sketches and if I see something I like, I'll take a pic and text it to you."

Reluctantly, after making Vivi promise not to buy a gown without running it by her, Big Viv headed to her town car while they jumped into a taxi for Tribeca.

"Your mother is really excited about this wedding," Dominick said. "Like, beyond excited. You would almost think it was her big day, not yours."

"In a way, it is."

"What do you mean?"

"She never had a wedding of her own."

"She didn't?"

Vivi shook her head. "My parents did it Carrie Bradshaw style. She and my dad got married at City Hall. They didn't have much family around and I guess it was easier than having a big, fancy event. At the time, she was okay with it, but I think as the years went by she regretted it. Who doesn't want to be a princess for a day? So, I think she's enjoying all the planning. It's the dream wedding she never got to have."

"But shouldn't it be *your* dream wedding?" Dominick pointed out. "And to the man of your dreams?"

"Lay off, Dom." Vivi stared out the taxi window at the passing city. "I'm not in the mood for a lecture and we've already gone over all this. This wedding means so much to her. That's another reason why I have to go through with it. How can I take it away from her?"

"But you do realize that you're going to, at some point."

"Not necessarily."

"What do you mean?"

"Maybe everything will work out in the end."

Dominick couldn't help but laugh. "Sorry, but

how is that even possible? You're marrying a gay man who isn't the father of your baby."

"I don't know! But I'm an optimist. I have to believe everything is going to work out in the end. Let's talk about something else. This friend of yours, the wedding gown designer. Is she good?"

"Very good."

"How come I've never heard of her?"

"Everyone has to start somewhere, right? She's trying to get some boutiques to carry her line, but you know how it is. Everyone wants the brand name designer. God forbid they wear someone who's new and fresh and original."

The taxi stopped and Vivi handed the driver some bills. "Well, maybe I'll wear something new and fresh and original. I owe you at least that much for breaking up your romance with Bash." Vivi turned to face Dominick. "Although, I'm hoping this is only a temporary break-up."

Dominick didn't answer. What was there to say? They were in an impossible situation. "Let's find you a wedding gown," he said instead.

Lolly lived in a rent-stabilized loft that was divided into a living and work area. There were high ceilings, lots of plants, and overstuffed furniture in leather and brocade fabric that looked like it was from the turn of the last century. The space was fun and whimsical and quirky and reflected Lolly's creative personality.

The work area was filled with dress forms in various stages of undress. There were bodices and trains and veils and sleeves and all sorts of fabrics and adornments pinned and draped across the forms as Lolly sketched and experimented with the flow of different fabrics.

"So, Dom filled me in," Lolly said after letting them in and bolting the sliding steel door behind them. "You're the bitch keeping him from his man."

Vivi's mouth dropped open. "What did you say?"

"You heard me." Lolly placed her hands on her hips. "Did I get it wrong?"

Vivi thought about it for a second. "No, you got it right."

"And you need a wedding gown to pull off this sham wedding. Something stylish that will hide your little bundle of joy."

"Are you up for the challenge?" Vivi asked. "We

went to four bridal boutiques today and found nothing."

"I love a challenge," Lolly said, leading Vivi over to her work area. "Let's get started."

———

It had taken most of the day, but Sebastian finally worked up the nerve to call Dom and invite him out to Fire Island for the weekend. He had waited until he'd gotten home from work. Thankfully, the bakery had been quiet that day, with no Big Viv. He went in, did his baking, then came straight home.

At first, the conversation was a little bit cold, with Dom explaining that he and Vivi were shopping for wedding gowns.

"We haven't found anything yet," Dom said, "but my friend Lolly is a designer. She and Vivi are putting their heads together. Hopefully, Lolly can come up with a sketch that gets the Big Viv seal of approval. Because as I've learned today, it's all about Big Viv."

Sebastian wasn't sure if he was supposed to agree with him. And he really didn't want to spend any more time talking about the wedding. So, instead, he apologized.

"I'm sorry about last night," he said. "It was supposed to be a first step for us. We were going to start to get to know each other. Instead, our night was spoiled."

"Yes, it was," Dom said, his voice still icy. "And you have only yourself to blame."

Sebastian chose not to respond to the comment. "I think I have a way of making it up to you."

"You do? How?" Dom's voice was now filled with curiosity, which Sebastian took as a good sign. "Tell me."

"How would you like to go out to Fire Island for the weekend? Liam's renting a house for the summer and he's going to let us have it. Just you and me, away from the rest of the world. What do you say?"

Sebastian expected Dom to start gushing with glee. After all, who wouldn't love to spend the weekend at the beach? And a gay beach at that! The reaction he got wasn't what he was expecting.

"So, now you're trying to hide me?" Dom shouted. "Keep me out of sight? This isn't some Susan Hayward movie from the 1960s where I'm the other woman and you're the married man."

"*Backstreet*," Sebastian said. "Produced by Ross Hunter. Gay, you know. Starring Susan Hayward,

John Gavin, and Vera Miles. Based on the Fannie Hurst novel."

"I see you know your melodramas," Dom said, his icy tone returning. "Maybe because you're currently living in the middle of one?"

How could this be going so wrong? Sebastian wondered, needing to do damage control. He hurriedly explained, "I just thought it would be nice if we could get away. Be alone. Together. With no distractions. I thought it would be sort of romantic."

"Romantic. Hmm..." Dom's voice was softer. Warmer. It sounded like he was starting to thaw. "Well, I do love anything romantic. And I suppose it would be nice to be alone with you."

"So, is that a yes?" Sebastian held his breath, trying not to get his hopes up. "Will you come?"

"I've never been to Fire Island and I've always wanted to go. Let me think about it." Dom's words were like a punch to the gut. "I'll get back to you."

And then, he ended the call.

———

"Weren't you being a little harsh?" Lolly asked. She had just returned from walking Vivi downstairs for a taxi. They'd come up with a couple of sketches and

Vivi was going to run them by Big Viv. Lolly was hopeful that she'd soon have a wedding gown to create.

"Harsh? I should have been harsher. I took his call, didn't I? I didn't let it go to voicemail."

"You might as well have. You didn't even give the poor guy a chance. You were jumping down his throat the second he started talking. He's making an effort. Don't you think he at least deserves a second chance?"

"Why?"

"Why not? Dom, he likes you. He's not giving up. Can't you see that?"

Dominick shrugged, not wanting to admit that he'd been a tiny bit thrilled when he saw Sebastian's name on the screen. Even after last night, when he told him it was over, he hadn't given up on him. That had to mean something, right? "I guess."

"What are you so afraid of?"

"I'm not afraid."

"Yes, you are."

Was Lolly right? All he knew was that he liked Sebastian and he wanted to explore things with him. But there were too many hurdles. And right now, they seemed insurmountable. Did he want to put in time with Sebastian, get to know him, maybe even fall in love with him, only to find himself all alone in the end?

"Well, maybe I am a little bit afraid. You have to admit, the situation is challenging."

"No one ever said love was easy. You might need to jump through some hoops this time around."

"What if I don't want to jump through hoops?"

"You haven't in the past, and look where that's gotten you. You're alone. Maybe it will be worth it in the end. But you won't know unless you try. Besides, I bet he looks really good in a swimsuit."

"I don't care what he looks like in a swimsuit."

"Yes, you do. I know you want to find out."

"I suppose that would be a perk of the weekend," he grudgingly admitted.

"How often do you get to take time off? Never. Other than planning this fake wedding, you have a window of open time on your calendar. Use it! Go off to Fire Island. No one's saying this has to mean anything. If you want to have a fling, have a fling. At the very least, you'll get a nice tan. Maybe one that's all over if you play your cards right."

———

After returning home from Lolly's, Dominick paced his living room. Should he call Sebastian back? Finally, before he changed his mind, he tapped on Sebastian's name in his contacts.

Despite how rude Dom had been earlier, he instantly picked up.

"If we go to Fire Island—and this is a big *if* because I'm not agreeing to anything—there needs to be some rules."

"Okay," Sebastian said.

"First, it's just you and me for the entire weekend. No outside calls. No texting. Just you and me. If we're going to be alone together, then I want us to be alone."

"Deal."

"Second rule. Separate bedrooms."

"Separate bedrooms?"

Was that a note of disappointment he heard in Sebastian's voice? "Yes. You're still engaged to Vivi."

"But you're going away with me."

"Friends can go away with each other."

"Is that what we are? Friends?"

There was that note of disappointment again. Good. He didn't want Sebastian taking him for granted. He was definitely open to trying things again. But he didn't have to know that just yet.

"At the moment, yes. I think so. But if I'm honest, I really don't know what we are, Sebastian. But I want to find out. I'm willing to try, if you are."

"I am," Sebastian said. "And I swear I'm going to find a way to get us out of this mess. I promise."

"Don't make a promise you can't keep," Dominick warned.

"So, when will you decide?"

"I've already decided. I'd love to spend the weekend with you out on Fire Island."

CHAPTER
TWENTY

Things were awkward between them. The question was how did he fix things?

Sebastian had decided their weekend away was going to be something special right from the start. Rather than taking the train out to Long Island and then the shuttle bus to catch the ferry in Sayville, Sebastian rented a car. And not just any car. He wanted something cute and sporty that would harken back to those old Frankie and Annette beach movies from the 1960s.

Like a cherry red convertible.

Luckily, he was able to rent one, and with the top down, he drove over to Dom's apartment on the West Side and picked him up. He'd been hoping to get an invite up to Dom's apartment, just so he could see the place, but Dom was waiting for him at the curb, dressed in jeans with rolled cuffs, a Marc Jacobs Debbie Harry T-shirt in neon purple, and Fendi sandals, designer luggage by his side. Casual chic.

When he slid into the seat next to him, Sebastian leaned over and gave him a kiss on the cheek. From the way Dom jolted away from him, you would have thought he was the Wicked Witch of the West and Sebastian had sprinkled him with a few drops of water.

"What are you doing?" Dom demanded.

"Saying hello."

"We say hello with our voices, not with our lips." Dom gazed at him from behind his mirrored sunglasses before facing forward. "We should get going if we don't want to hit any traffic."

Okay, the kiss was a mistake. Apparently, he still had to make his way back into Dom's good graces.

As they drove, conversation was forced and stilted. They couldn't agree on anything. If Sebastian said he liked Britney Spears, Dom said Christina Aguilera was the more talented singer. If Sebastian said Glenn Close had been robbed of an Oscar more than once, Dom said it was because the caliber of her work wasn't as good as Meryl Streep's. Sebastian thought *Clueless* was superior to *Legally Blonde*, but

Dom, a die-hard Reese Witherspoon fan, disagreed and wouldn't hear otherwise. "Plus, she has an Oscar for Best Actress, her own book club, and she sold her company for millions. No contest." And on and on it went. They weren't connecting at all. It was just empty chit chat, like one would have with a stranger on a plane or train.

They needed to get things back on track. Because if this was an indication of the mood for the entire weekend, they might as well not bother going out to Fire Island.

"How was your week?" Sebastian asked, trying again. It seemed like a safe, neutral topic. Other than their phone call on Tuesday, they hadn't been in touch except to confirm the plans for this morning.

Dom raised his sunglasses and stared at Sebastian in disbelief. "Did you really ask that question?"

"Uh, yes," Sebastian asked, wondering what he'd done wrong.

"How do you think it was?" he snapped. "I was at Big Viv's beck and call 24/7. Planning your wedding, in case you've forgotten."

"I haven't," Sebastian said. *You won't let me forget,* he wanted to say, but he didn't.

Dom's sunglasses fell back into place. "In case

you were wondering, I've nailed down the band, booked a photographer, and dealt with the florist. Wedding favors still need to be chosen, but that will be next week's crisis. Of course, the major headache, which still hasn't been resolved, is where this wedding is going to take place. I'm still trying to find a venue, and I keep hitting a wall. Nothing is available. We also have to decide on the color of the bridesmaids' dresses, which according to Big Viv, needs to complement the flowers. There are going to be four bridesmaids, by the way, so you'd better start deciding on your ushers. After that, the only thing left is the wedding invitations. Big Viv has narrowed it down to two designs. One is a linen finish with foil stamping, the other is a pearlescent paper with embossing. Naturally, Vivi hates both. Once we have a date, which means we'll have a venue, the invitations will be printed and mailed out, the RSVPs will come back, the wedding will happen, it'll all be official, and you'll be a happily married man."

"I might be married but it won't be happily."

"That's nobody's fault but your own," Dom pointed out.

That was it. The final straw. Sebastian wanted to slam on the brakes. He wanted to tell Dom to get out of the car and find his way back to Manhattan. He was so over this little temper tantrum. Did he deserve it? Yes. But enough was enough. He didn't need to be constantly reminded of his mistake.

He took a look over at Dom, ready to lash out, and as much as he wanted to, his anger melted away.

Just the sight of him reminded Sebastian of how much he wanted this weekend to work. So, he took a deep breath, said nothing, and kept driving.

—————

Dominick was trying hard not to be a sourpuss. It was so obvious that Sebastian was trying. And Dominick was being a prick.

A big prick.

Maybe if he hadn't been run ragged by Big Viv all week, he might have been in a better mood. The woman was impossible! Did he resent her because she was so demanding? He'd had clients just as demanding in the past. Or was it because her daughter was marrying the guy he was interested in?

Correction. Very interested.

Dominick peeked at Sebastian out of the corner of his eye.

He liked that Sebastian carried himself with a

lazy confidence. He always looked put together but he wasn't as coordinated as Dominick. Dominick was definitely a clothes horse. He liked shopping, he liked designer labels, and he liked looking like he had just stepped out of the pages of a fashion magazine.

Sebastian, on the other hand, had a vibe that was calm and relaxed. His style was simple and effortless. A little bit messy, too.

He probably woke up in the morning and threw on whatever he found in his closet. He didn't angst over which shirt went with which tie and wonder if he should go sockless or if his jeans should be cuffed or uncuffed (that had been Dominick's dilemma this morning). He probably didn't wonder how much ankle he needed to show when he rolled up his cuffs or ask himself if Thom Browne suits really were a wise investment? Because once you bought one, you could never put on an extra ounce of weight since the fit was so tight.

And then, the light bulb went on over Dominick's head. He was driving out to the beach in a convertible. With a cute guy sitting next to him. A cute guy who wanted to be alone with him.

Maybe he needed to forget about Big Viv. Forget about everything and just pretend that he had just met Sebastian and they were going off together for the weekend. There would be food, wine, sun, and sand. Good books, music, and relaxing.

And maybe sex. Dominick was still waffling about that.

It wasn't that he didn't want to have sex with Sebastian. He did. Very much. But if he did, it would feel like they were cheating on Vivi. Which was ridiculous because there was nothing romantic between her and Sebastian. So, why did he feel so guilty at the thought of it?

He took Sebastian's free hand in his and started tracing his fingers. "Sorry for being such a brat. It was a long, stressful week. I guess I'm still decompressing."

Sebastian squeezed his hand. "You don't have to apologize. I know this situation isn't easy for you. And trust me, I know what Big Viv is like. She's my boss. I deal with her every day. She can be a lot."

When they stopped at a red light, Sebastian reached into the backseat. "These are for you," he said shyly, handing Dominick a plastic wrapped bouquet.

"Sunflowers?" Dominick's face lit up. "For me?"

"They reminded me of you." Sebastian blushed. "All bright and sunny. Happy."

Dominick was touched by the gesture. "That's

why I bought *you* sunflowers the other night. I felt the same way about you. I'm sorry I was a prick all morning. Can we start over? I really am looking forward to this weekend."

"Are you?"

"Uh huh." Dominick leaned forward. "And I was wrong before."

"About what?"

"This." Dominick pressed his lips against Sebastian's and gave him a kiss. "Lips *are* for saying hello." He gave Sebastian another kiss. And then another. "Hello. Hello. Hello."

Sebastian smiled and gave him a kiss of his own. "Hello."

———

After parking the convertible in the ferry's parking lot, they went off in search of lunch, finding a little café by the water. Once they were seated at a cozy corner table for two, they each ordered a glass of Chardonnay and perused the menu. Sebastian decided on the crab cakes and Dom went with oysters on the half shelf.

"How can you eat those?" Sebastian watched as

Dom squeezed a little bit of lemon over them, then sprinkled some Tabasco sauce. "They're so slimy."

Dom raised his eyebrows. "Don't be so judgy. I put lots of other things in my mouth, too, you know. And they've tasted just as good."

Sebastian took a bite of his crab cakes and didn't say another word.

Their ferry wasn't for another hour, so after lunch they went exploring, popping into little antique and thrift shops they found along the way.

"I love antiquing," Dom told Sebastian as he examined a piece of cherry blossom McCoy pottery, pointing out the raised brand on the bottom of the piece that identified it. "It's sort of like going on a treasure hunt. You never know what you're going to find. It could be something you collect or it could be something that just grabs your eye and you have to have it. Plus, there's also the fun of haggling when you try to get the seller to agree to a lower price. Sometimes it works, sometimes it doesn't."

"You can do that on eBay, can't you?"

Dom made a face. "When you're doing it by yourself it's more fun. On eBay, you're competing with other people. The thrill isn't the same."

"Sort of like meeting a guy you like and

wondering if he's just as attracted to you as you are to him?"

"Uh huh," Dom said, abandoning the McCoy pottery and closing the distance between them. He gave Sebastian a kiss. "Your heart starts to race and your stomach does flip flops."

"Is your heart racing?" Sebastian asked. "Is your stomach doing flip flops?"

"Ever since the day I met you," Dom admitted, wrapping his arms around Sebastian's neck and giving him another kiss.

———

The ferry ride to the Pines, the section of Fire Island that catered to gay men, took twenty minutes. The other part, Cherry Grove, which could be reached by a different ferry, catered to lesbians. Once the ferry pulled into the harbor and they stepped onto the dock, they were in a land of hot guys. At least it felt that way to Dominick. Most of them were shirtless, wearing either Speedos, booty shorts, or teeny tiny bathing suits, showing off buff bodies with sculpted abs and chiseled muscles.

"Good Lord! Do these guys live at the gym

24/7?" he exclaimed. "I feel like a ninety-eight pound weakling compared to them."

Sebastian laughed. "Don't worry. A lot of regular guys come out here, too. Not just the beauty queens."

"It's enough to give a guy an inferiority complex," Dominick said, gazing around. "I don't know if I'm going to take my T-shirt off this weekend."

"But I wanna see what's underneath," Sebastian said, tugging at Dominick's shirt.

Dominick swatted at his hand. "Maybe if you're good I'll give you a private strip tease."

"Promise?"

"We'll see."

After stopping at The Pantry, which was the only grocery store in the Pines, they stocked up on supplies and walked to the house. There were no sidewalks or streets, only wooden boardwalks intersecting through the trees in parallel lines. Every so often they saw a few deer in the woods or nibbling on foliage in front of a house.

"How cute!" Dominick stopped to admire them. "Will they let us get close enough to pet them?"

"You don't want to do that. They might look cute

and sweet, but they carry ticks and you don't want to risk getting bit. Lyme disease."

"Yikes!" Dominick shouted, putting as much distance as he could between himself and the deer, as if suddenly afraid that a tick was going to jump onto him.

Sebastian laughed. "Don't worry. They keep their distance."

They kept walking until finally they arrived at their destination.

"From the outside, it looks gorgeous," Dominick said, staring at the two-story cedar shingled house.

"Let's take a look at what's inside." Sebastian unlocked the front door.

The house was two floors with oceanfront views. There was a cathedral ceiling, a wood burning fireplace, built-in bookshelves, and oak floors. There were four bedrooms and four and a half baths. The living room opened up onto the pool deck, where there was a heated pool, hot tub, and outdoor shower, surrounded by a lush landscape of bushes and flowers. The kitchen was filled with stainless steel appliances, stone countertops, and a sub-zero fridge. Not to mention a fully stocked wine cellar right off the dining room with a mission oak table big enough for twelve guests.

"This place is insane!" Dominick exclaimed as they toured the house, staring out through the glass walls at the beach outside, listening to the crashing waves. "How can Liam and his friends afford this? It must easily go for a hundred thousand a season, if not more."

"Well, I think they've had a little bit of help."

"Help?"

"An old boyfriend of his—and well, actually, the rest of the house—makes up the difference."

"How many guys share this house?"

"Four? Five?"

"And they've all dated the same guy? What makes him so irresistible?"

"He's rich. Successful." Sebastian paused. "Older."

"So, he's some sort of sugar daddy?"

"They call him the Silver Fox."

"Silver Fox?"

"On account of his gray hair. He's an investment banker. He likes helping handsome young things who are starting their careers. I guess if you have the money..."

"You can buy what you want?"

"No, Liam's not an escort." Sebastian said, coming to his friend's defense. "He used to date the guy, but eventually Liam reached his expiration date. Someone younger and hotter came along. But it was an amicable break-up and the Silver Fox told him he wanted to stay friends. I guess you could call the house a fringe benefit. The Silver Fox picks up most of the bills for the summer and the guys who stay out here are on standby. Sort of like his harem. You know, in case he wants to hook up."

"If it works for them, I'm not judging."

"I don't think any of them ever believed they were in a relationship with him. They each had something that the other one wanted, so I suppose it was a trade-off. The Silver Fox got a nice piece of arm candy when he needed a date for business events, and Liam enjoyed all the perks of having a rich boyfriend. The Silver Fox picked up a big part of the tab for Liam's share of the summer rental. It wasn't like he was leaving money for him on the nightstand."

Dominick sank into the oversized couch, clutching a Life's A Beach pillow against his chest. "Have you ever wanted a sugar daddy? You could probably get one if you wanted. Just saying."

"Is that a compliment? Well, thank you. But no. I've never wanted one. I'm quite capable of taking care of myself. Liam's a talented actor, much more successful than I ever was, but he's still waiting for his big break. He's going to make it. I know it. He just needs a little help right now."

"I didn't know you were an actor."

"Former actor."

"Why'd you give it up?"

"At some point, you have to grow up and start paying the bills. Face reality. It just wasn't happening for me."

"That must have been tough. Giving up your dream. But you found a new one with your baking."

"And you?" Sebastian joined Dominick on the couch, his fingers feathering the hair falling across Dominick's forehead. "Is this what you always wanted to do? Plan weddings?"

Dominick shrugged. "I sort of fell into it. I graduated from college with a liberal arts degree and really didn't know what I wanted to do. I had a couple of entry level jobs. Publishing. Advertising. None of them really excited me. Then, I saw an ad for a company that did party planning and I decided to apply. I thought it might be fun. And it was. People trust you with their special days and you help them to pull it off. It also allows me to be creative. At first, I was just doing birthday parties. Then, I started working on bridal and baby showers until eventually I started doing weddings."

"How come you went out on your own?"

"Why not? If you do all the work, why not make all the money? Isn't that why you want to open your own bakery?"

"Yes. But I'd also like a little more creative control over what I bake. As I'm sure you're aware, Big Viv has a one-track mind."

"I hope you'll do some baking for me this weekend."

Sebastian pressed Dominick into the couch cushions, placing his body on top of his as he started nibbling on his neck, making his way up to his mouth. "Oh, I hope to heat things up this weekend in a lot of rooms, not just the kitchen." He pressed his lips against Dominick's.

Dominick surrendered to Sebastian's passion. How could he not? Even though he'd been trying to resist it, he couldn't. Not anymore. It had been building since they first met and Dominick wanted to enjoy it.

Sebastian kissed him again. And again. There was a savage hunger in each one. They were raging with desire and the message was clear: Sebastian wanted him.

Dominick found himself becoming hard. His cock throbbed against his jeans, wanting to break free, and he wanted nothing more than to wrap Sebastian's hand around it, holding it captive, controlling him, making him powerless as he surrendered to waves of intensifying pleasure.

So, why not? Why deny himself a little bit of a sneak peek?

He took Sebastian's hand, drew back the waistband of his jeans, and plunged Sebastian's hand down into his groin.

Sebastian instantly knew what to do. His fingers circled Dominick's throbbing cock, slowly moving up and down. Sebastian pulled his hand away for a second, licked his fingers, and then returned to massaging him with an added bit of wetness.

It felt good. So good.

At first, Sebastian moved his hand up and down slowly. It was delicious torture. But as Dominick's cock thrust against the prison of Sebastian's fingers, he tightened his grip, taking a firm hold before he began to move his fist up and down at an accelerated pace.

Dominick could feel the rising excitement. It was like riding a rollercoaster, getting closer and closer to the top before plunging straight down and letting out a scream. And Dominick could feel the scream growing inside his throat, demanding release.

"Like what I'm doing?" Sebastian asked.

Dominick nodded, too caught up in the moment and the exquisite sensations to say a word.

"I think I know something you might like better," Sebastian whispered.

Before Dominick could ask what he meant, Sebastian pulled his hand away.

Dom whimpered, reaching out to pull it back, but before he could, Sebastian yanked down Dominick's jeans and underwear, freeing his erection.

"I've been waiting a long time for this," Sebastian said with a wicked gleam in his eye. His mouth descended upon Dominick's cock, closing around it as he began to suck.

Dominick clutched the sides of the cushion he sat on. Sebastian's warm mouth around his aching cock felt so good. He moaned softly.

At the sound, Sebastian gazed up at him with a look of total control, a hand pressing down hard on

Dominick's chest to keep him in place. "Lay back and enjoy it," Sebastian whispered, then he began sucking even harder.

Dominick could feel his climax fast approaching, but he didn't want to come. Not yet. He wanted to make this moment last for as long as possible. He hadn't felt this good in such a long time.

Sebastian was a master with his mouth and tongue, licking the head of Dominick's cock with just enough pressure to bring him to the edge before finally pulling back. It was a game Sebastian was quite good at. Every time Dominick thought he was going to come, Sebastian gave him a breather.

Until, finally, there was no chance for a moment's reprieve. Sebastian kept sucking, harder and harder, unrelenting in his actions, until Dominick couldn't hold himself back any longer and allowed himself to come in long, thick spurts.

Sebastian nestled himself against him. "Guess we heated things up, huh?"

Vivi's cellphone was ringing. Again. She didn't want to answer it.

But Nico kept calling. And calling. What did he want? Well, that was a stupid question.

He wanted her to admit he was the father of her baby.

Ha! That wasn't going to happen.

But what if the baby was his? In a couple of days, she would finally have an answer.

If he was the father, was she really going to keep him away from his child? That wouldn't be right.

She thought back to her own childhood. Growing up, everyone had a father but her. She'd only been a baby when her father died, so she had no memories of him. When she looked at photos of the two of them together and saw the way he looked at her with so much love, it hurt. It made her realize how much she had missed out on, especially when she saw her friends with their own fathers.

She couldn't do that to her baby. And if she was honest with herself, she couldn't do it to Nico, either.

Didn't a child deserve to know their father?

Of course, if Nico was her baby's father, there was no guarantee that he would be there.

But maybe he would. Did she want his help raising their baby?

A little Nico or Nica. She instinctively knew if he was the father, that their baby would look just like him. Same dark hair. Same sparkling eyes. Same irresistible smile. This baby was going to wrap her around its little finger. She wasn't even going to try to resist.

Why couldn't they finally be together? They'd spent so many years apart.

All because of that stupid feud.

Maybe Dominick was right.

Maybe it was up to her and Nico to fix things between Deena and her mother.

Before she could change her mind, she answered her phone. "Yeah?" No need to make Nico think she was softening. She needed to sound hard. Tough. "What is it?"

"You finally picked up. I've been calling all week."

"You gonna give me grief or are you gonna tell me why you're calling?"

"You doing anything this weekend?"

"Why?" she asked.

"My friend, Joey, is getting married tomorrow. There's a wedding and reception. I thought you might want to come with me."

Vivi snorted. "A little short notice, don't you think?"

"Do you wanna come or not? How much

advance notice do you need to paint your face, fix your hair, and put on a dress? And I've been calling all week. You just haven't returned any of my calls."

"What about Candy?"

Nico gave an exasperated sigh. "What about her?"

"Why don't you ask her?"

"Because she's my boss. I work for her. Besides, I don't wanna go with her. I wanna go with you. So, you in?"

She had to admit, he was relentless. This entire week, he'd been sending her flowers. Big, blooming bouquets. Boxes of candy. Macaroons from Laduree on the Upper East Side. Cupcakes from Magnolia Bakery. Gifts from high-end shops like Prada (a tote bag), Gucci (sunglasses from their summer line), and Tiffany's (a diamond tennis bracelet).

But she was holding firm. All of it went back. She wasn't going down this path again. Something always went wrong when she and Nico tried to be together. Her heart had been broken one time too many. If it broke again, she didn't know if she'd be able to put it back together.

If only Sebastian wasn't gay. As soon as the thought popped into her head, she chased it away. Sebastian *was* gay. He would always be gay. She'd never had any thoughts of being together with him before. Nico had always been the guy she wanted.

But maybe she wanted him to be just a little bit more like Sebastian. Kind. Considerate. Thoughtful. Although, if she was honest with herself, he could sometimes be all those things.

Just not all the time.

Maybe this time they could get things right. All she had to do was give him a chance.

Before she could change her mind, she said the words. "Fine. I'll go with you to Joey's wedding."

"You will?" He sounded surprised. "Really?"

"Are you deaf? I just said I would. Text me the time you're going to pick me up and I'll be ready."

Vivi ended the call before she could change her mind.

———

Nico stared at his phone, doing a fist pump in the air. Finally, he was making some progress!

Nothing he had done this week had worked. Every gift he sent Vivi, she had sent back. His calls went straight to voicemail. Texts were ignored.

Yet today, for some reason, she had answered

when he called. And she had said yes to going with him to Joey's wedding.

It was a step in the right direction.

All he had to do was spend a little time alone with her, whisper in her ear, brush his lips against hers, and she'd start to trust him again. Maybe even give him a second chance. One date could lead to another, and then another. All he had to do was turn on the charm. There was still time to stop her from marrying Sebastian.

And find out if he was the father of her baby.

"Why do you look so smug?"

Aunt Deena was back from an afternoon of shopping. Somehow, she had become his unofficial house guest, moving into his guest room upon her arrival. He'd assumed she'd be staying at a hotel, but she'd brushed the idea off, saying she wanted to spend more time with him, although he wondered if it was because she didn't want to spend the money. She was loaded down with shopping bags from a number of shops on Madison Avenue. She must have maxed out her credit cards.

"You can afford all that?" he asked, eyeing her bags and trying not to sound skeptical. He knew acting gigs had been drying up for her, although she did have her various lines of merchandise with

QVC. That alone must have been making her a nice piece of change.

"Never mind my expenses. Your aunt can take care of herself. Who were you on the phone with?"

"Vivi."

Aunt Deena's eyes lit up. "Finally!"

"She's going with me to Joey's wedding tomorrow night."

"Now, all you have to do is get her to admit the baby is yours."

Nico shook his head. "That's not going to happen."

"Why not?"

"Because I don't wanna piss her off. I'm not going to ask her about the baby. Not just yet."

"I get it. Reverse psychology. You're going to let her think you don't care and then she's going to wonder why you're not asking her and she'll spill her guts to you."

"Aunt Dee, I've known Vivi a long time. She's not going to spill her guts."

"Then, how are you going to get her to admit the truth?"

Good question. How did he handle this?

Well, he had gotten her to agree to go to the wedding with him, so that was a start. He supposed he could just wing it tomorrow night and see where things went.

"You look like you're thinking. Care to share?"

"Just trying to figure things out." He pointed to her bags. "Why all the shopping? You going somewhere special?"

"Getting together with some old friends tomorrow night." Aunt Deena smiled smugly. "It should be a good time."

Nico's radar was instantly on alert. "Old friends? Like who?"

"Just some girls from high school."

"Is Big Viv going to be one of those friends?"

"She's not my friend," Aunt Deena raged. "She's my enemy."

Nico sighed. "Answer my question. Is Big Viv going to be there?"

Aunt Deena shrugged. "I suppose she might be. I'm not the one hosting, so I'm not in charge of the guest list. But we had a lot of the same friends in high school."

Nico groaned. If Aunt Deena stirred the pot again with Big Viv, there was no telling what might happen. And it could jeopardize whatever progress he might make with Vivi. "Promise me you'll be on your best behavior, Aunt Deena. Please. No more food fights."

"That wasn't my fault. She started it!"

"It takes two to tango," Nico said, remembering the scene from earlier in the week when his aunt had returned to the apartment covered from head to toe in a variety of desserts.

"Does she know you're coming?" he asked.

"Not yet. But she will."

Nico didn't like the sound of that.

———

"We could take this into the bedroom if you want," Sebastian whispered into Dom's ear.

They were still on the couch. Still kissing. Hands exploring. Caressing. Lingering. T-shirts had come off and there was the pleasure of skin pressed against skin as nipples were bitten, tweaked, and licked. There was no question Dom was still aroused. Sebastian could feel his erection pressing against him. As eager as he was for a second round, he didn't want to make the first move again. He wanted Dom to feel in charge and in control. He wanted him to call the shots this weekend when it came to sleeping together. Which was why he kept grinding against him with his own erection, sending a not so subtle message.

"We could," Dom said with a nod.

Sebastian felt his insides lighting up.

"But how about a walk on the beach instead?"

"A walk on the beach?" Sebastian asked, trying not to sound disappointed.

"Uh huh."

Sebastian suppressed a sigh, pulling his T-shirt back on. This weekend was all about spending time with Dom. Alone. If he wanted a walk on the beach, he would get it. "Sure. Let's go for a walk on the beach."

"I bet it was impossible for you to fall asleep on Christmas Eve when you were a kid," Dom said, tossing his shirt over one shoulder. "You couldn't wait to see what Santa brought you, could you?"

"Why are you asking me that?"

"Just answer the question."

Sebastian thought about it for a second. "You're right. It seemed to take hours before my eyes would close. I was constantly running over to the window, looking up at the sky to see if I could spot Santa's sleigh. Or listening for his footsteps on the roof."

"But eventually you fell asleep. And you got your presents the next morning, didn't you?"

"Yes." Sebastian slowly answered, not knowing where he was going with this.

Dom gave him a devilish smile before reaching for Sebastian's still hard erection and giving it a gentle squeeze. Sebastian nearly moaned with pleasure as he felt Dom cup him through the fabric, slowly rubbing his hand up and down, causing the most exquisite friction as his cock throbbed. "Sometimes, you have to be a little patient, Bash. If you are, then you get exactly what you want."

With those words, Dominick fell to his knees.

He pushed Sebastian against the wall before yanking down on his zipper and releasing his rigid erection. "Looks like it's my turn now," Dominick said, the tip of his tongue poking out of his mouth before circling the head of Sebastian's cock and then moving to the underside of his shaft.

Sebastian gasped, both shocked and delighted. It felt like small jolts of electricity were shooting through his body. His shaft was beyond sensitive. But this was an exquisite ache, one he wanted more of.

Dom buried his face in Sebastian's pubic hair, taking a deep breath. "I love the way you smell down here. All hot and moist." He licked Sebastian's cock again, and it twitched against his face. "Not to mention wet. Very wet," he whispered as his tongue swirled around Sebastian's shaft. "But it also needs to be sticky." He gazed up at Sebastian with determination. "I'll have to do something about that."

Sebastian gasped again. He'd had many blow jobs over the years, but Dom was an expert. He could feel his teeth softly nibbling the flesh of his cock before swallowing him deep in his throat. Dom's hands cupped Sebastian's bare ass, pulling him closer, making him thrust harder and harder as Dom's mouth was filled by Sebastian.

He reached for Dom's head, gripping it firmly and holding it in place as his cock continued to thrust in and out of Dom's wet mouth.

And Dom was loving it, sucking with all his might, getting Sebastian harder and harder until finally Sebastian had no choice but to come. As he did, Dom pulled away, grabbing Sebastian's cock and aiming it at his chest, spraying himself with Sebastian's creamy load.

Dom looked up at him with a naughty gleam in his eyes as he rubbed Sebastian's come across his well-defined pecs.

"Warm," Dom whispered, "and sticky."

He traced a finger over his chest and slipped it into Sebastian's mouth. Sebastian instantly sucked, tasting himself, before Dom grabbed him by the head and gave him a forceful kiss.

———

Once they had cleaned up, they walked along the waterfront, barefoot, hand in hand, the waves licking at their feet as the tide came in, filling a silver bucket with seashells whenever they spotted them.

"These colors are so gorgeous." Dom picked up a handful of golden shells. "I can see using them in so many different ways. Shine them up with a little mineral oil to bring out the color some more and then hot glue them to a picture frame or mirror as a border. You could also fill up glass vases and bowls and use them as centerpieces. Or make them into wind chimes. Just drill a tiny hole at the top of each one and string them with twine before hanging them."

"Sometimes, you can find sand dollars on the beach, too," Sebastian said, wiping a sheen of sweat off his forehead with the back of his arm. "It's still so hot. I thought the temperature would have dropped by now."

"How about a dip in the water to cool off?"

"But you don't have your swimsuit on."

Dom arched an eyebrow. "We're on an island of gay men. Do you really think someone is going to mind if I go skinny dipping?"

Within seconds, Dom had shed his jeans and T-shirt and was running into the water. He discarded his clothes so quickly and disappeared into the water so fast, Sebastian barely got a look at him in all his naked glory. He just got a quick glimpse of a perfect bubble butt.

He watched as Dom swam. He was like a seal, diving in and out of the waves before finally making his way back to shore.

"You must love the water," Sebastian said.

"I was on the swim team in high school and college," Dom explained, slicking back his wet hair with two hands. "I still swim to stay in shape."

Sebastian could see that. Dom had the perfect swimmer's build, a broad chest coming down to a V with muscular legs.

Not to mention what hung between them. No shrinkage there.

"Looks like you're into manscaping." Sebastian ran a hand over Dom's neatly trimmed pubic hair.

Dom took hold of Sebastian's hand, placing it over his shaft, which quickly sprang to attention.

"Gotta make it easy for a guy to find what he's looking for," Dom purred.

"I don't think we're supposed to be doing this on the beach," Sebastian said, gently pulling his hand away despite wanting to keep it there.

Dom stuck out his tongue. "Spoilsport. So, are you taking a dip? You got to see the goods in public. Now, it's my turn." He clapped his hands together. "Come on. Time to strip."

Sebastian could see the admiring glances Dom was getting from the men who walked by. And why wouldn't he? He had a great body.

But Dom was oblivious to the attention. His eyes were focused only on Sebastian.

"Don't tell me you're shy?"

"Maybe."

"There's nothing to be shy about. I like you with your clothes on. I'm sure I'm going to like you with them off." Dom paused. "No. That's wrong." He stuck a finger in the band of Sebastian's shorts, pulling him closer. "I'm going to love seeing you with your clothes off," he whispered. "Now, drop your pants."

Sebastian promptly obeyed and tore off his T-shirt, earning an admiring smile as Dom inspected him from head to toe. It was an incredible turn-on as evidenced by the hardening of his shaft.

"Now, why don't you go cool off?" Dom suggested.

Sebastian dove into the water.

———

Back at the house, it was time for the dinner that was supposed to happen on Monday. The first date that never was.

Only tonight, it would be perfect. With no interruptions. No Liam. No Nico. No Vivi or Big Viv.

Just the two of them. Alone.

Tonight, Sebastian had all the time in the world and would be able to take extra care with everything.

"Don't go to a lot of trouble," Dom said, rummaging through the refrigerator for a pitcher of lemonade. "We can barbecue on the grill if that's easier."

"I cooked for you on Monday and our date ended before it could even get started." Sebastian pushed Dom out of the kitchen. "I'm making it up to you."

While Dom lounged by the pool with a glass of lemonade and a magazine, Sebastian got busy in the kitchen. It was going to be a light, simple menu, but bursting with flavors. First, there was going to be a caprese salad, followed by a roasted chicken with mustard and grapes, as well as salt and vinegar mashed potatoes. Dessert would be the ultimate summer delight: key lime pie.

While Sebastian kept himself busy with cooking, he kept wondering about the afternoon. As evidenced by their earlier activities, Dom had certainly signaled an interest in sex. Did it mean that after they had their key lime pie tonight, they would follow it up with another kind of dessert?

Sebastian took a deep breath. Whatever was going to happen, would happen. He couldn't worry about it. He had to focus on the here and now. Everything else would fall into place.

Finally, when all the dishes were ready, Sebastian called Dom into the dining room. He had set the table with candles and managed to put together a bouquet from the flowers out by the pool. Adele's most recent CD played softly in the background.

Dom admired the scene. "You put a lot of effort into all this."

"It's our second first date. I had to."

Dom took a seat at the table. "It all looks wonderful. Thank you for doing this. It means a lot."

Sebastian didn't know why, but finally, as he took the seat next to Dom, he felt like he could breathe. The day might have gotten off to a rocky start, but he felt like things were finally as close to perfect as they could be. Hopefully tomorrow would be more of the same.

Dom uncorked the bottle of white wine on the table and poured a glass for himself and Sebastian.

"To us," Dom said, raising his glass in a toast.

"To us," Sebastian said, clinking his glass against Dom's and taking a sip of the cool, crisp wine.

CHAPTER
TWENTY-ONE

Sebastian woke up alone on Saturday morning.

He'd been hoping to wake up with Dom sleeping next to him, but it was just him in a king-size bed, surrounded by pillows.

Last night after dinner, they had moved out to the deck, gazing at the stars while sipping the last of the wine. They finally gave up sitting outside once the mosquitoes started to dive bomb them. Inside, Dom insisted on cleaning up the kitchen since Sebastian had done all the cooking.

Sitting on a stool, Sebastian watched as Dom made quick work of cleaning things up. Loading the dishwasher, wiping down the sink and counters, putting away anything that needed to go back into cabinets and drawers. Finally, when the kitchen was back to normal, Dom dried his hands on a dish towel, folded it and then took Sebastian by the hand, leading him back out to the living room.

Instantly, Sebastian had visions of the two of them snuggling together on the couch again, perhaps progressing to a point where all their clothes came off this time before moving things upstairs to the bedroom. From the way things had gone today, Sebastian felt Dom was ready to get physical.

But that bubble burst when Dom suddenly yawned, dropping Sebastian's hand to cover his mouth.

"Sorry. I'm pooped. It's been a long day. I think it's time for bed." He gave Sebastian a quick peck on the lips. "Goodnight. See you in the morning."

A dumbfounded Sebastian watched as he climbed the steps to the second floor and disappeared into the bedroom he had chosen earlier.

Well, that was that. Other than running after him, what was he supposed to do? Slip naked into bed with him once he fell asleep?

As tempting as the thought was, he wanted Dom to be the one calling the shots. Dom already felt powerless because of the situation with Vivi. If he could give him back some of that power by deciding when they were going to sleep together, then he would.

So, unless he wanted to stay up by himself, he did the only thing he could do. He went up to bed, too. Surprisingly, he fell asleep the second his head hit the pillow, and despite waking up alone, he felt energized and renewed.

Yesterday had been a good day. Today was going to be even better.

———

After taking a shower and getting dressed, Sebastian decided that breakfast by the pool would be nice.

The first thing he did was make muffins. Two batches, a simple blueberry followed by a batch of cranberry crumb. The crunchy topping made from flour, dark brown sugar, cinnamon, salt, and butter provided a nice contrast to the tartness of the cranberries. Then, he cut up some strawberries, cantaloupe, peaches, plums, kiwis, and grapes for a fruit salad and made a pot of coffee.

He brought everything outdoors, deciding breakfast by the pool would be nice. He sat in a lounge chair and watched the sun, sipping a cup of coffee while enjoying the peace and quiet until Dom joined him thirty minutes later.

"Morning, sleepyhead," Sebastian greeted.

"Morning," Dom mumbled, wearing only a silk robe. He ran a hand over his tousled hair.

"Want a muffin?" Sebastian held out the basket.

"I'd love a muffin," Dom said, reaching for a blueberry one and taking a bite. "Mmm. Good. I bet you made these, didn't you? You didn't have to go to the trouble."

"No trouble at all. How'd you sleep?"

"Like a baby. You?"

"My bed was kind of big. Too big. I was lonely in it all by myself." Was that too much of a hint? Well, too bad. Sometimes one had to be obvious.

"Lonely, huh?" Dom took another bite. "Maybe you won't be by yourself tonight."

"Is that a promise?"

"Let's see how the day goes." Dom poured himself a cup of coffee.

"Anything special you want to do today?"

Raising his face up to the sky, Dom closed his eyes. "Feels like it's going to be another scorcher. I thought I would soak up some rays. Work on my tan. How does a day on the beach sound?"

"Looks like you have some nice color," Sebastian said, admiring the tan he already had.

"A friend of mine has a place in the Hamptons. He invited me out Memorial Day weekend so I could get started on my base."

A platonic friend or a romantic friend? Sebastian wanted to ask, but he didn't. Instead, he said, "I didn't notice a tan line yesterday afternoon."

"I sunbathe in the nude. I don't think that will be a problem here, will it?"

"It's Fire Island. You can sunbathe however you want, wherever you want."

Dom pretended to be scandalized. "And give all the guys on the beach a show?"

"I'm sure you wouldn't get any complaints. You had quite the audience yesterday when you were skinny dipping. Those guys were licking their chops."

"Well, there's one opinion I'd be worried about. Yours."

"I've already seen what's underneath that robe, remember?"

Dom got up from his chair, letting his robe fall to the floor. "Still like what you see?"

Sebastian licked some of the cranberry crumb

topping from the top of his lip and locked eyes with Dom. "Very much."

"Be right back."

A naked Dom headed into the house. When he returned, he tossed Sebastian a bottle of suntan lotion and threw himself face down on a lounge chair.

"How about covering me up so I don't burn?" he asked, gazing over his shoulder.

Sebastian approached the lounge chair, admiring Dom from head to toe. It was like his entire body had been chiseled out of marble. Everywhere he looked, there was definition. He sat on the side of the chair and poured the lotion all over Dom's back, caressing it deeply into skin already warmed by the sun. He started on his shoulders, arms, and legs before moving to his butt. Oh, that perfect butt! Sebastian wanted to bury his face in it and take a nice juicy bite.

That's not all he wanted to do. He also wanted to slip his cock between those two perfect mounds and push as deep and hard as he could.

He was dying to ride Dom's ass. Just the thought was making him hard as he envisioned Dom's legs wrapped around his neck as he popped his cherry for the very first time. He wanted to see Dom writhing beneath him, eyes closed in ecstasy, begging for more as they both came at the same time.

But that wasn't going to happen just yet. So, he controlled himself.

Even after Dom lifted his butt in the air and wiggled it. "Don't forget my tush."

Sebastian took a deep breath and when he did, he inhaled the rich scent of coconut lotion. It smelled heavenly, especially mixed with Dom's musky, unwashed scent. And the feel of Dom's hot, slick skin was like silk.

He poured suntan lotion all over Dom's butt and began to massage it in.

Just the slightest touch or scent of this man and he became aroused.

―――――

Dominick hoped he wasn't coming across as a cock tease. He really did like Sebastian. He was attracted to him and he did want to sleep with him. Soon.

Last night had been nice. They could have slept together. He knew Sebastian had wanted to. But he wanted to be the one who decided when and where. He wanted to be allowed at least that much. The stuff they had done earlier, he considered it foreplay. A little bit of an appetizer before the main course.

Dominick flipped himself onto his back, revealing his full erection. He could ask Sebastian to cover the front of his body with lotion, but that would be too mean. Or he could grab Sebastian by the head, pull him down to his knees, and guide his head to his cock. But then, it would be all about him, wouldn't it? It would be about Sebastian pleasuring him. That would be selfish.

Instead, he held out his arms and pulled Sebastian into his embrace. "I think we need to get you out of these clothes, don't you?" he whispered into his ear before taking him by the hand and leading him back into the house up to his bedroom.

Sebastian didn't have to be told twice.

———

Sebastian, much to his surprise, discovered that Dom was a top.

"I'm not saying I'm not versatile, but I enjoy being the one who gives pleasure rather than receiving it, although there's nothing I love more than plugging a tight hole. Is your hole tight, Sebastian?"

"There's only one way to find out," Sebastian challenged him.

Dom pushed Sebastian face down on the bed and fell on top of him, pinning him to the mattress.

"Do you like games?" Dom whispered in his ear.

"What kind of games?"

"Sex games."

"Like?"

"Nothing too crazy. But I love being in control. Having a man surrender himself to me and letting me have my way. How does that sound?"

It sounded good. Very good. Sebastian found himself loving this dominant side of Dom. He wanted to be powerless to him and whatever he desired.

"I surrender," Sebastian whispered. "I'm up for anything."

Dom reached around and grabbed his throbbing cock. "I can see that you are."

Sebastian turned over onto his back as Dom reached underneath the bed and pulled out some silk scarves. "Where did those come from?" Sebastian asked.

"Just some things I like to travel with. I thought we might wind up here, so I figured I'd have them ready for use."

Dom pulled his arms over his head, tying them with a black scarf. He wrapped a red one over Sebastian's eyes.

"No fair," Sebastian said. "I can't see anything."

"You don't need to see," Dom whispered. "You can feel."

Dom climbed onto the bed and positioned himself on top of Sebastian, rubbing a hand across his chest.

"Nice?"

"Nice."

"I'm going to do something nicer," Dom said.

"Like what?"

Sebastian could hear the sound of something tearing. Then, he felt something cold and wet slathered against his butt hole. It made him twitch.

"Time for the main event," Dom announced as his finger slowly circled around Sebastian's butt hole, moving up and down and around, ratcheting up the slowly building tingling and anticipation while gently slipping his finger in and out as he pressed his lips against Sebastian's. "Are you ready?"

Sebastian mashed his lips against Dom's. The touch of Dom's finger was setting him on fire. He could only imagine how he would feel once his cock was down there. The thought made him throb. He wanted to wrap his arms around Dom and pull him close, but he couldn't. Instead, he was powerless as Dom's lips moved over his body, licking, kissing, sucking, caressing, exploring his erogenous zones as he strained to control himself.

He was at the peak of coming, but he didn't want to come alone. He wanted to come with Dom. Together.

As if reading his mind, Dom pushed the scarf away from Sebastian's eyes.

"I want to look at you while we're fucking."

"Is that what we're doing?" Sebastian asked. "Fucking?"

"What would you call it?"

"Making love."

Dom's face lit up, and Sebastian's heart melted at the sight. Dom brought his mouth close to Sebastian's, plunging his tongue deep into its depths. Sebastian instantly latched onto his tongue, locking their mouths together. At the same time, Dom slid his cock into Sebastian's ass. Slowly at first, then with an urgency that Sebastian was unable to resist.

"Yes," Sebastian whispered. "Oh, yes. Fuck me. Fuck me hard."

"I thought we were making love."

"We are. But riding me hard is the special sauce that shows me how much you care."

"Well, I wouldn't want to disappoint you," Dom said as he increased the pace of his thrusts while Sebastian's butt tightened its hold on Dom's cock.

"Ride me," Sebastian begged. "Ride me as hard as you can."

Dom happily obliged.

———

Maybe it had been the build-up. The waiting. The anticipation.

But once they had done it, they did it again. And again.

They went from one room of the beach house to another. They certainly weren't the first ones to christen a room on Fire Island, but to them, it felt like it.

It was fun. Hot. Sweet. Savage. Fun. Joyous.

Every time they came together, it was a different experience. It was sort of like they were trying to figure out their groove as they enjoyed each other's bodies, relentless in their passion for each other, neither one getting enough until finally, in the early afternoon, they decided to take a break and go for a dip in the pool to wash away the hours of sweat and cool off.

"So much for working on my tan," Dom said as he emerged from under the water.

"Sorry."

"I'm not." Dom swam over to Sebastian and scissor-locked his legs around his waist. "This was much more fun than laying on a beach chair."

"Ever do it in a pool? Sebastian asked, a twinkle in his eye.

"Nope. How about you?"

"Never."

"Then I guess we're going to have to do something about that," Dom said as he pulled Sebastian back under the water with him.

———

This time, it was Sebastian's turn. He was the one in control and Dom was the one having to submit.

He pressed Dom against the side of the pool, slipping a hand between his legs as he grasped his cock and took Dom into his mouth, locking his lips around his erection with an intense ferocity.

But there was more. Sebastian emerged from the water and pressed himself against Dom while biting into the side of his neck with a force that left behind a savage hickey.

"That's so you know you're mine," Sebastian whispered. "I don't care what anyone says or does. We're a couple and we're going to be together. Do you believe me?"

"I want to," Dom said.

"You need to." Sebastian sank back underwater, seeking out Dom's ass. Using his tongue, he explored the crevice, pressing forward with greater force each time he felt Dom react, holding his legs in place so he was powerless to escape and had no choice but to submit to Sebastian.

CHAPTER
TWENTY-TWO

She needed to look drop dead gorgeous. Those three words had been going through Vivi's head ever since she'd gotten off the phone with Nico the day before.

The last time she had felt this way was the night of her Sweet Sixteen. She remembered how excited she'd been. That night, she had been dressing for Nico. She remembered wanting to look beautiful for him. And she remembered when they'd danced together for the first time. The way he had held her in his arms and looked at her. Like she was the most beautiful girl in the world.

She wanted him to look at her like that again.

Vivi knew she was a beautiful woman. She turned heads and got her share of appreciative looks from men. Through a combination of pilates, yoga, and spinning, she kept her body in great shape. But that wouldn't be the case much longer. The clock was ticking and she had a feeling tonight was going to be the last night she had to show off her body before the baby took over.

She went through her bedroom closet, discarding dress after dress after dress until finally she found the one she was looking for. She hadn't worn it in a while, but the last time she had she got a number of admiring glances. It was a Herve Leger gold foil bandage dress with a front cutout, long sleeves, and a high neckline. She held the dress up in front of her as she stood before her full-length mirror. Simple, elegant, sexy.

Yes, this was the dress.

All she needed was a pair of high heels and she would be good to go.

———

Nico was speechless. He'd always known Vivi was gorgeous, but today she was a knockout.

"What are you staring at?" she asked as she locked the front door.

"You."

"What's wrong with me?" She reached into her

purse and pulled out a compact. "I've got lipstick on my teeth?"

"You look beautiful."

"Thank you." She put the compact away. "But why do you sound so surprised?"

He admired her from head to toe. The dress she wore clung to her like a second skin, accentuating her curves. Her dark hair was slicked back into a tight ponytail and her makeup was dramatic, highlighting her violet eyes and lips. But it was something else. Something he couldn't put his finger on.

"Something about you is different, but I don't know what."

"Maybe it's the dress."

Nico shook his head. "No, it's not the dress, although it looks great on you." He snapped his fingers. "I know what it is. You've got that pregnancy glow. It makes all pregnant women look more beautiful."

Vivi blushed. "Thanks."

That was all Nico was going to say about her pregnancy. He didn't want her getting defensive or thinking he had an agenda.

Which, of course, he did.

But Vivi didn't need to know that just yet. For

now, he wanted to enjoy the moment. They were together, not fighting, on the way to a wedding. Hopefully, it would be a good day.

Nico slid an arm around Vivi's waist and led her to his car, holding the door open for her. He watched as she slid inside, admiring her long legs and imagining them wrapped around him. He started getting hard at the thought and slammed the door behind her before heading to the driver's side.

Hopefully, it would be a good night, too.

———

Vivi couldn't remember the last time she had been in a church, other than for a wedding or funeral. She wasn't very good about going to mass every Sunday. Well, neither was her mother, so if she had to blame someone for her lack of attendance, she supposed the person to blame was her. With the exception of Christmas and Easter, those were the only times they ever saw the inside of a church. And only if they were able to get away from the bakery, since those were two of their busiest days of the year.

She and Nico sat on the groom's side of the church. She knew Joey and Nico had been friends back in high school, and she recognized some familiar faces from the neighborhood. The bride, Gigi, was also from Bensonhurst, although she was a few years younger than Joey and Nico.

Vivi gazed at the stained glass windows of the church depicting scenes of Jesus and the Apostles. She saw Mary and Joseph, as well as a few saints and martyrs. It was all so familiar. She'd spent twelve years in this church when she went to grammar school and high school, but when was the last time she'd actually been here on a regular basis? Too long.

The organist started the Wedding March, and everyone in the church rose to their feet. The flower girl walked down the aisle, sprinkling pink rose petals. Then, the ring bearer came with the wedding rings on a lace-trimmed pillow, followed by the bridesmaids and ushers. Finally, there came the bride, veil covering her face, on the arm of her father as she glided toward her waiting groom.

Suddenly, Vivi realized something. This was real. These two people were getting married, taking vows, and declaring their love for each other in front of everyone. In a couple of weeks, she and Sebastian would be doing the exact same thing in this very same church, standing where Joey and Gigi were. She'd be wearing a wedding dress, getting ready to exchange vows with Sebastian. They'd be in front of family and friends.

And God.

Vivi usually wasn't superstitious. Being raised Catholic, she believed in God and Heaven and Hell, but she never wondered if she was being judged by her actions. If someone sinned, they went to confession, the priest forgave them, they said a few Hail Marys as a penance, and they moved on.

But this. This was different. Now, suddenly, she felt like she was going to be judged. She would be telling a lie in a sacred place of worship. A whopper of a lie. To God.

Vivi's eyes went back to the front of the church. There was no mistaking the love between the bride and groom as they exchanged their vows and finally said I do, promising to spend the rest of their lives together. How was she going to be able to go through with this?

It would be wrong. So wrong.

"You okay?" Nico whispered in her ear. "Suddenly, you look sick."

Vivi chased away the image of a devil torturing her for all eternity. "I need some fresh air," she whispered back, making her way out of the pew and racing down the aisle to the outside of the church.

———

"You feeling better?" Nico asked.

It was two hours later and they were at the catering hall for the reception. Vivi had told Nico she had been feeling nauseous because of the baby and that's why she needed some fresh air. She couldn't tell him why she'd fled the church, because if she did, well, duh, he would know everything.

Vivi sipped the glass of ginger ale he had gotten her at the open bar. "Much."

"You feel like eating?"

"Sure."

It was the typical Italian wedding reception, starting with a cocktail hour where there was way too much food. Ham, chicken, turkey, and sides of beef were sliced. There was a seafood bar brimming with lobster, crab, shrimp, clams, and oysters over crushed ice. Three kinds of pasta with seafood, pesto, and tomato sauce. Hot and cold vegetables. A variety of nuts and cheeses.

"This must be costing them a fortune," Nico said as he got two plates and filled them with all of Vivi's favorites. A little antipasto, some rice balls, potato croquettes, eggplant parmigiana, and of course, the obligatory slices of Italian bread.

"You only get married once," Vivi said.

"Yeah, you do," Nico agreed.

Vivi expected him to say more. To make some sort of remark about her upcoming wedding. But he didn't.

"Here's where we're sitting," Nico said as he found their table. An older couple in their late sixties was already there. The woman wore her hair in a chic silver bob, and from the interlocking Cs on her black suit, Vivi could tell it came from Chanel.

"Hello!" the woman said brightly. "Come, join us! I'm Evelyn and this is my hubby, Mario."

Vivi gave them both a warm smile. "Vivi and Nico."

Mario, who was short, bald, and stout, grunted a hello and went back to his seafood pasta.

"Don't you just love weddings?" Evelyn asked as Vivi sat next to her. "Mario and I have been married fifty years."

"That's wonderful." Vivi began to nibble on a rice ball.

"How about you two?" Evelyn asked.

"Oh, we're not married," Vivi said.

"Engaged?"

Vivi expected Nico to say something, but he

didn't. Again. "I'm engaged but my fiancé isn't here tonight."

"Congratulations! You must be so excited. I'm sure you've been taking lots of notes for your big day."

Excited? That was the last thing Vivi was. And she did *not* want to talk about her wedding. But she didn't want to be rude, either.

As if sensing her discomfort, Nico asked, "How about a spin on the dance floor?"

He held out his hand to Vivi and she took it with relief, following him away from the table.

It was a slow dance to Frank Sinatra's 'The Way You Look Tonight.'

"Good old Blue Eyes," Nico said, wrapping his arms around Vivi as she allowed herself to be cradled in his embrace. They fit together perfectly. They always had.

Instantly, Vivi was taken back to the night of her Sweet Sixteen and their first dance when Nico had kissed her for the very first time. When he had called her Princess. The song playing had been Etta James' 'At Last'. It was still one of her favorites. Every time she heard it, it took her back to that night. How she wished she could turn back the clock and have a do-over.

"What's the matter?" Nico gazed down at her, his eyes filled with concern. "Why do you suddenly look so sad?"

Vivi blinked back the tears she could feel forming in the corners of her eyes.

"Just thinking about the past," she said. "All the time we've lost. What could have been if it hadn't been for my mother and Deena."

"The past is the past. You can't look back. Only forward. Sometimes, the timing isn't right between two people."

Vivi sighed, resting her head against his chest. "Our timing has always been off."

"It has," Nico agreed.

She waited for Nico to say more, but he didn't. She wasn't sure what she was waiting to hear. That maybe this time they'd finally get things right?

"You're still a great dancer, Princess."

Viv's heart melted hearing his old endearment. "I don't think we've danced together like this since my Sweet Sixteen."

"That can't be right."

"It is. Fourteen years. Been a long time."

"You'll be dancing like this with Sebastian in a couple of weeks."

Vivi pulled herself out of Nico's arms. "Why did you say that?"

"Why not? It's the truth. Did I say something wrong? You're marrying him. He's the father of your baby, right? What are you getting so sensitive about?"

Vivi didn't know what to say. Instead, she began to gnaw on her lower lip.

"You know all I want is for you to be happy."

It was on the tip of Vivi's tongue to confess everything. To finally come clean.

It had to be her hormones. They were all out of control. She didn't know what she was thinking. She couldn't tell Nico the truth. He didn't love her. He was involved with Candy! If she told him the truth, it would be a disaster once her mother and his aunt became involved.

Wouldn't it?

Or maybe, this time, they could figure it all out and finally be together. Maybe this time she wouldn't allow herself to be manipulated by her mother. This time, she would fight for Nico. But wasn't she already allowing herself to be manipulated by going through with this wedding in the first place?

Oh, she didn't know what to think!

The song ended and Nico brought Vivi back to

their table. "I'm gonna go get a drink. You want anything?"

Vivi shook her head, still trying to sort through her thoughts.

"How long have the two of you been together?" Evelyn asked as Vivi sat back down.

"Sorry?"

"You and your young man."

Vivi laughed. "He's not my young man. I'm engaged to someone else, remember?"

Evelyn looked at her skeptically. "You could have fooled me. I have eyes. The way he looks at you? That boy is in love."

Vivi didn't know why, but the words made her happy. "Really? You think he loves me?"

Evelyn nodded with confidence. "I'm never wrong about these things. The question is, do you love him?"

"Why would you ask me that? I'm marrying another man."

Evelyn raised an eyebrow. "I also don't see an engagement ring on your finger. What Italian girl from Brooklyn gets engaged and doesn't have an engagement ring?"

Damn! This was twice now she'd been tripped

up by not having a ring. She needed to get one soon. "It's at home."

"Let me see a picture of it."

"What?"

"The ring. You girls are always taking selfies. I'm sure as soon as you got engaged you were snapping pictures and posting them on Instagram and Facebook and Tik Tok." Evelyn held out a hand. "So, let me see."

"There is no ring," Vivi blurted out.

"Why?"

"We haven't gotten around to buying it yet."

"What girl gets engaged without an engagement ring?" Evelyn asked. Then, her eyes traveled to Vivi's belly. "Oh." She placed a hand on Vivi's arm and gently said, "Listen, honey, the days when a girl had to get married because she was pregnant are over. You don't have to marry a man you don't love. You've got lots of options."

If only that were true.

Before Vivi could say anything else, Mario asked Evelyn if she wanted to dance. She gave her husband a smile, allowing him to pull her chair back.

"He loves you," Evelyn repeated before heading out to the dance floor. "Trust me. He does."

Vivi smiled, watching as Evelyn and Mario took

to the dance floor, whispering in each other's ears and laughing.

Had she and Nico ever said those words to each other? In all their years of make-ups and break-ups, had they ever said I love you? Vivi didn't think so. But maybe they didn't have to.

Maybe they just knew.

But what if she did tell Nico she loved him? What would he say? Would he say the words back to her? And if he did, would he mean them? Or would he only be saying what he thought she wanted to hear?

———

The rest of the wedding was a blur. Vivi had her main course of Caesar salad, prime rib, and baked potato, danced some more with Nico as well as Mario, who was light on his feet, and joined in with everyone else when it was time for group dances like YMCA and the Electric Slide. When the bride prepared to throw her bouquet, Vivi was urged out onto the dance floor with all the other single ladies by Evelyn, then returned to her table empty-handed after the rest of the ladies went wild trying to catch it. Nico joined all the bachelors when the groom removed the bride's garter, tossing it into the air. They watched as the guy who caught the garter put it on the leg of the lucky bouquet catcher. Finally, it was onto the cutting of the wedding cake, and the bride and groom posed for pictures before shoving slices of cake in each other's faces.

All night, Vivi had been thinking of Evelyn's words. Did Nico love her? There was only one way to find out.

She waited until he returned to the table, carrying a huge slice of wedding cake, along with some mini pastries and chocolate gelato. She knew this was only the preview before the Viennese Hour, where there would be even more food to stuff themselves with.

She touched his arm, pulling his attention away from the dance floor. "Nico, I have to tell you something."

"Yeah, babe?" He took a sip from his cup of espresso.

Before she could ask her question, her phone pinged and her eyes widened as she stared at the screen.

It was a Google alert about Nico and Candy. Vivi clicked on a link that took her to a website with photos of them from the night before in each other's arms. Vivi saw red and all thoughts of love were forgotten. Nico didn't love her. If he did, he wouldn't be messing around with Candy. How could she have been so stupid? She brandished her phone in his face. "Mind explaining this?"

Nico visibly paled. "It's not what it looks like."

"Really?" Vivi's voice was ice cold. "Because it looks like the two of you got up close and personal."

"She was drunk. She had too much to drink and I was trying to get her to the limo. She started pawing me. I couldn't stop her."

At best, Candy was ninety pounds. Maybe one hundred. Nico was a strapping two hundred. He expected her to believe he couldn't control her? Vivi laughed in disbelief. "You couldn't stop her? Because she was so big and strong she overpowered you? You honestly expect me to believe that?"

"Vivi, come on! Candy means nothing to me. I already told you, I'm her bodyguard. I work for her. Whatever I had with her in the past is over."

"Pictures don't lie."

"But they don't always tell the truth, either. You know what those paparazzi are like. They're scum! They take a photo that doesn't mean anything and wrap a story around it. Come up with a salacious headline. It happens all the time. Babe, I swear, I'm telling you the truth."

"Don't call me babe." What a fool she had been. All night long, she had thought she and Nico might be able to get back together. And all along, he'd been stringing her along. Thank God she hadn't told him the truth.

"Just calm down. Let's talk about this. We were having a nice night. Don't go and spoil things."

Those were *not* the words Vivi wanted to hear. This was her fault? *She* was overreacting? Before she could stop herself, Vivi reached for her slice of wedding cake and shoved it into Nico's face.

CHAPTER
TWENTY-THREE

Big Viv's book club consisted of three friends from high school: Francesca "Foxy" Gallo, Charlotte "Chunky" Umberto, and Patricia Pallamente. Foxy, Chunky, and Patricia had been their own separate trinity, while Big Viv and Deena had been their own twosome. Yet, somehow they had clicked as a fivesome when they were put together for a group project in Biology during their freshman year.

When they met for book club, they rotated houses, with each member of the group taking a turn as hostess. Tonight, the club met at Foxy's house. She still lived up to her name, even at the age of sixty-three. She had been the hottest girl in high school, wrapping every guy around her little finger—even those with girlfriends. And she had managed to maintain her looks—with a little help from a face-lift or two—so that she managed to resemble an older Angelina Jolie. Foxy was a bulldozer when it came to getting what she wanted, and she had it all: a husband, three daughters who were all successful and married, grandkids, and a McMansion that was so overdone, even Big Viv questioned Foxy's taste level. Everywhere you turned there was marble and gilt and mirrored walls. For Foxy, too much was never enough. But Big Viv kept her opinion to herself. Nobody ever wanted to get on Foxy's bad side because she'd always had a mean streak. Back in high school, she knew which girls to pick on, what to say to make them feel inferior, and what to do to make them cry. No one stopped her. They were all too afraid.

Chunky, on the other hand, was sweet as sugar. She was the peacemaker, always wanting everyone to get along. She wasn't called Chunky because she was overweight. In high school, her favorite candy had been the cube-shaped Chunky chocolate bars. She would eat them every day, sometimes even for lunch, telling the girls, "It's the perfect snack, chock full of nuts and raisins. So healthy!"

Patricia was a combination of Foxy and Chunky. She could be nice, but if somebody ever said or did something to piss her off, they'd better watch their back. She would have her revenge! Unlike Foxy and Chunky, who both married their high school sweethearts, Patricia had been married and divorced three times with no kids. At the moment, she was happily being a cougar, as she'd told the girls last month. "He's thirty-five and hung like a horse! Some days I can't even get out of bed, he's fucked me so hard. The only problem is he's not circumcised, and I hate sucking him off. I gotta make sure it's clean down there, and with it being uncut, sometimes there are days when I can tell he hasn't gotten into all his nooks and crannies."

It was all a little TMI for Big Viv. She was all for everyone having a healthy sex life, she just didn't want to hear the details.

Big Viv lived for the book club. It was the one day every month when she got to relax and unwind with her girlfriends. There was wine, cheese, and lots of conversation where they caught up on each other's lives. Sometimes, they even discussed the book they were supposed to be reading, although it really wasn't about the book.

Who bothered to read the book? Okay, sure, sometimes Big Viv skimmed it. But she really wasn't a reader. Never had been. She just liked getting together with her girlfriends, and when they had suggested the club, she said to count her in. There was only one book they had read that she really liked: *Gone Girl* by Gillian Flynn. That Amy really knew what she was doing, showing her husband who was boss. Okay, she was a little nuts, but her message was loud and clear: don't fuck with me.

She'd liked the movie, too, especially Ben Affleck as Amy's husband. He had that same down-to-earth sexiness as John Travolta, although why Ben Affleck had two Oscars—they weren't for acting, but still!—and John Travolta didn't even have one, she would never know. She still couldn't believe Richard Dreyfuss had won Best Actor for *The Goodbye Girl* over John in *Saturday Night Fever*. What had the Academy been thinking? John's Tony had *grown* throughout the entire movie, from a self-involved boy to a responsible young man, while Richard Dreyfuss had engaged in witty banter with Marsha Mason. Nothing else! It was a romantic comedy, plain and simple, written by Neil Simon, whom people didn't even remember anymore because most of his plays and movies didn't stand the test of time. She'd seen the movie once, and once was enough. On the other hand, she had watched *Saturday Night Fever* at least forty or fifty times. If she was channel surfing and stumbled upon it, she would watch to the very end. It never got old, especially in the eyes of an Italian.

Big Viv had cursed at her TV when Dreyfuss's name was announced. She had been watching alone, rooting for John. In years past, she and Deena used to watch the Oscars together, but by then, Deena had been long gone, off to her new life in Hollywood. For all Big Viv knew, Deena was *at* the ceremony and would meet John Travolta at one of the after-parties when the Oscars were over. It was the first time she had ever watched the show alone, and it hadn't been as much fun. She kept remembering the past, how she and Deena used to comment throughout the whole show, picking apart what everyone wore, criticizing their hair, make-up, and jewelry, talking about what they liked and didn't like and how they would dress if they were ever lucky enough to attend. That night, after John lost, she wondered if Deena had been as upset as she was.

Years later, John lost a second bid for Best Actor, this time to Tom Hanks. That loss hadn't been as hard to handle because Big Viv thought Tom Hanks was a brilliant actor and she was sure playing Forrest Gump was much more of a challenge than John's role as a hitman in *Pulp Fiction*. Still, it was nice of the Academy to announce with John's second Oscar nomination that he was back after the industry had written him off and said he was washed up. Never underestimate an Italian.

Book club always met on Saturday nights. It was the perfect way to unwind, although with the bakery open seven days a week, Big Viv never really got a full day off. On the mornings after book club, she went in late. With all the wine—Foxy loved giving a heavy pour—and getting home after midnight, it wasn't easy waking up early the following day.

Whenever she went out, no matter the occasion, Big Viv always made sure she was the center of attention. And to be the center of attention, she had to have all eyes focused on her when she made an entrance. Whether it was having the latest must-have bag. What she wore, be it a new dress, shoes, or piece of jewelry. A new hairstyle, a change in hair color, make-up, or perfume. No matter what it was, Big Viv always made a statement.

So, she didn't like being upstaged. And she especially didn't like being upstaged by Deena DiGregorio, whom she found sitting on Foxy's black leather couch, gabbing with the women, when she walked into Foxy's living room. Instantly, the room went silent as all eyes went back and forth between her and Deena, waiting to see what would happen.

She was so shocked seeing her there, she almost dropped the tray of cream puffs she had brought from the bakery.

What the fuck? This was twice in one week she was crossing paths with Deena. Only this time, it was at book club. *Her* book club. This was sacred territory.

Before she could say anything, Foxy was by her side, hustling her into the kitchen. But not before Big Viv caught Deena eyeing her from across the living room, a smug smile on her Botoxed face.

"What's she doing here?" Big Viv hissed once they were alone.

Foxy rolled her heavily mascaraed eyes. "Calm down. You're gonna give yourself a heart attack. I invited her, all right?"

"Why?"

"Why not? We were all friends in high school. She's in town. I haven't seen her in years. Plus, it's my house. I can invite whoever I want, and I wanted to invite Deena."

"We're not friends anymore. You know how I feel about her."

"What can I tell you? I'm friends with her and I'm friends with you. She's not in Brooklyn very long and tonight was the only night she could come by.

I'm sorry if you're uncomfortable. If you want to leave, I'll understand. But I hope you'll stay. Now, if you'll excuse me, I need to see if everyone else is set for drinks."

Big Viv watched Foxy walk away. She knew she couldn't leave. Because if she did, everyone would talk about it. And Deena would love every second of it.

So, she was stuck. She took a deep breath and rejoined the others back in the living room, taking a seat as far away from her nemesis as possible. It was after she was seated that she realized Deena wasn't the only addition that night. Carla D'Abruzzi was also there.

That was a surprise. With the exception of herself and Deena, she didn't think any of the other ladies kept in touch with Carla.

"Carla, what a surprise," she said. "You've never been to our book club. Did Deena invite you?"

"Patricia did."

Big Viv tried to keep the disbelief out of her voice. "Patricia invited you?"

That didn't make any sense. Patricia couldn't stand Carla in high school. Why would she invite her to their book club meeting? Sure, living in the same neighborhood, their paths still crossed, but

Patricia had always gone out of her way to avoid Carla.

"She knew Deena was coming tonight and thought I'd like to see her."

Back in high school, Carla had always wanted to be a part of their group. Hanging around their lockers. Wanting to sit at their lunch table. Following them home after school. Big Viv had never had a problem with her. Maybe it was because she felt sorry for her. Compared to her other friends, who were bright, bubbly, and sexy, Carla was none of those things. In addition to the lazy eye she used to have, there was something sad and pathetic about her, so why not toss her a few crumbs and let her join in every once in a while? But the other girls, even Chunky, hadn't wanted anything to do with her.

"She's a freak," Patricia had declared. "She's always lurking in the shadows, watching our every move like we're bugs under glass. It's creepy. Sometimes, I wonder if she's a lez."

If she remembered right, Patricia had even pulled a nasty joke on Carla. What did the kids call it these days? Catfishing. Yeah, that was it. In the seventies, before websites and dating apps, one could write to people through newspaper and magazine ads if they were looking to find someone to date.

During their senior year, Patricia encouraged Carla to answer an ad in the local Brooklyn paper, even going so far as to help her pick which ad to answer. What the others didn't know, until Patricia told them, was that Patricia had placed the ad that Carla was answering. After Carla's first letter was received, Patricia sent letter after letter to her, pretending to be a guy who had the hots for her. She wrote for weeks, putting off Carla's requests to meet in person, before finally asking her to go to the senior prom. Of course, Carla said yes.

And waited at her house for hours for a guy who never arrived.

Patricia had been in hysterics at the prom, telling the others what she had done. Foxy and Chunky had laughed along with her, but Big Viv and Deena had been silent.

After the prom, Big Viv and Deena stopped by Carla's house to see if she was okay. They didn't let on they knew she had been stood up. They pretended they were wondering why she and her date were no-shows at the prom. Carla answered the door, still in her peach satin prom dress, looking sad and wilted, with red eyes and a swollen nose— clearly, she had been crying—telling them she hadn't felt well and decided to stay home. Before Big Viv and Deena could say anything else, she closed the front door in their faces.

Big Viv had never forgotten what Patricia had done to Carla and kept her at a distance after that. All Carla had wanted was friendship and acceptance. Instead, she had gotten her heart broken.

So, why invite her tonight? Did Patricia feel bad about what she did all those years ago?

Not likely.

During the book club, while they discussed Elin Hilderbrand's latest beach novel, Big Viv tried to ignore Deena, but it was hard, since she kept monopolizing any conversation that was started. At first, Big Viv tried to keep the focus of the group on the book they had read, but after a few glasses of wine, the book was forgotten, as it usually was.

"Do you think he's going to show up?" Chunky asked, getting to the topic that was on everyone's mind.

Big Viv knew who *he* was. John Travolta.

"Why wouldn't he?" Deena asked.

"I know you came back for this event, but doesn't he have a much busier schedule than you?" Big Viv asked, unable to resist getting in a dig. "He probably doesn't have that much free time. I mean, he's constantly working and you're not." Big Viv happily watched Deena's face tighten with anger. So much for being an actress if she couldn't hide that she was upset! "Why would he come back to Brooklyn?"

Deena ignored the comments aimed at her. "Why not? After all, this is the movie that made him a star. And he's come back to Brooklyn before. A couple of years ago, he revisited Lenny's Pizzeria and it was a huge celebration, remember? There was lots of press and TV coverage."

That was true. She had forgotten. Damn, she hated when Deena was right.

"That poor man. He's been through so much," Carla said. "Diana Hyland, his first love, died in the seventies, his oldest son died from a seizure when he was sixteen, and then two years ago, his wife died of breast cancer."

"She was a good actress," Patricia said, reaching for a slice of prosciutto and wrapping it around a breadstick. "I liked her movies."

"I loved him in *Grease* with Olivia Newton John," Foxy said. "It's too bad they couldn't make *Two of a Kind* work."

"Remember when there used to be talk of a sequel to *Grease* with John and Olivia?" Chunky reminded them.

Deena held up her hands in the sign of a cross.

"Let's avoid all talk of sequels. Need I remind you ladies of *Staying Alive*?"

There was an audible gasp.

Foxy shook her head sadly. "What was he thinking?"

"Every now and then, someone makes a misfire," Big Viv said in John's defense, although she did agree with Foxy. They must have thrown a lot of money at him. Why else would he have agreed?

"He never should have made that movie," Deena said. "It ruins the legacy of *Saturday Night Fever*. And don't get me started on that travesty of a musical!"

Big Viv had actually paid money to see the musical version of *Saturday Night Fever*. First row orchestra on opening night. She'd been hoping that maybe John himself might show up, even though he wasn't involved with the production in any way. It was dreadful, having none of the charm or magic of the movie. Of course, most of that was due to John Travolta, which the musical didn't have.

The first thing she had wanted to do after leaving the theater was call Deena. It was the first time she had thought of her in years. Maybe it was the memory of when they'd gone to watch some of the filming of *Saturday Night Fever* that made her miss her and want to reach out. But, of course, she couldn't. She had no way of reaching Deena. Not that she would have.

Sometimes she wondered, simply, why. Not as often as she used to in those early years, but on occasion. Why had Deena walked out of her life all those years ago and never looked back? Had it all been for her career?

She stared across the living room at her. Again, why? It had never made any sense. And in all the years their paths had crossed, she had never had the courage to ask her. Was it because she was afraid of Deena's answer? Because it would destroy those memories she still had left and pulled out every so often?

Deena had been her best friend. And she missed her. Still missed her. Even after all these years.

Okay, enough with the trip down memory lane. Obviously she'd had one glass of wine too many if she was getting melancholy, wondering about Deena and the past.

Thankfully, Chunky's next comment distracted her. "You have to admit, his body was in great shape in *Staying Alive*."

"All muscular and oily!" Carla added.

"Right now, he's focused on his kids," Deena said

knowingly, as if she had just been on the phone with John the other day. "His son is eleven."

"It must be hard being a single parent," Foxy said.

"Well, his daughter is twenty-one," Big Viv pointed out. "Even though I'm sure she has a life of her own, I bet she helps her father as much as she can."

"I know him," Deena purred.

"Who?" Big Viv asked, although she was willing to bet money she knew the answer.

"John."

"Travolta? You know John Travolta?" Big Viv stared directly at Deena. She couldn't pretend she wasn't in the room. Not after that comment. But it was all she could do not to roll her eyes. Still, Deena had been keeping it classy. She could do the same.

"Sort of."

"How?" She couldn't wait to hear this.

"We were at the same party once. Years ago. Late nineties."

"That's it? Did you get to talk with him? Have a conversation?"

"I made my way over to him."

"And?"

"He was very nice. Handsome, of course. Those

eyes! And that dimple on his chin. I wanted to stick my tongue in it."

"So, no exchange of phone numbers?" Carla asked. "I remember back in the day, as soon as you met a guy you liked, Deena, you were giving him your number. You barely gave the other girls a chance."

Big Viv couldn't help but pick up on the attitude in Carla's voice. Well, well, well. Miss Carla wasn't a fan of Deena. This was news. All these years, she had thought Carla was slavishly devoted to her. After all, she was constantly filling her in on Deena's life and career. But maybe not. Hmm, interesting. She was going to file the revelation away for later inspection.

Deena shrugged. "He was married. What would have been the point?"

"That never stopped you before," Carla muttered under her breath as she took a sip of wine, although Big Viv was the only one who could hear it.

Okay, what was going on with Carla and her sudden hostility toward Deena simmering beneath the surface?

"Enough about me and my Hollywood life!" Deena exclaimed. "I want to hear about the rest of you." She gazed at Big Viv. "How's the wedding planning coming?"

"It's coming," Big Viv grudgingly answered. Even though Dominick had tackled a chunk of his list, there was still so much more to do. And he wasn't doing it fast enough.

"You must be racing against the clock."

Big Viv's hackles rose. Was that a dig about Vivi being pregnant? "What's that supposed to mean?"

Deena held up a hand. "Calm down. It wasn't an insult. I know you have a lot to do and not that much time to do it before your mother arrives from Italy."

"Thanks for the reminder," Big Viv said, taking a healthy slug of wine. She had tried to push all thoughts of her mother to the back of her mind. This wedding needed to be perfect. Absolutely perfect. Because she knew the second her mother stepped off the plane, she would be criticizing her.

"Your mother is coming back to Brooklyn?" Carla asked in surprise.

"Yeah," Big Viv said, trying her best not to sound glum. "For Vivi's wedding."

"I haven't seen her since she moved back to Italy. It'll be so nice to see her again."

Big Viv knew she'd had a couple of glasses of wine, so maybe her mind was a little fuzzy, but to the best of her recollection, she didn't recall Carla and her mother being friends. Carla had never even been to her house when they were in high school. So, how had their paths crossed? "You knew my mother?"

"I used to deliver mail to your house when I had my route. Some days we used to chat."

Carla used to *chat* with her mother? Her mother wasn't the chatting type. Why would her mother give Carla the time of day? She never gave *anyone* the time of day.

"How old is she?" Chunky asked. "Late eighties?"

"She's ninety-three."

"God bless," Deena said.

"Age hasn't improved her any?" Foxy asked.

Big Viv threw up her hands. "She's still impossible."

"Welcome to the club," Patricia said. "The older they get, the crabbier they are."

"If you need any help, let me know," Carla said. "Give her my best and let her know I'll stop by for a visit. I assume she's staying at your place?"

"She is," Big Viv said, already counting down the days until her mother would get back on the plane to Italy.

"You should have brought Vivi with you

tonight," Foxy said. "It would have been nice to see her and catch up before the big day."

"She couldn't have come," Deena said before Big Viv could answer.

"Why not?" Foxy asked.

"Because she's with my nephew."

"Vivi is with *Nico*?" Big Viv tried not to screech.

"They went to a wedding together. Although, I'm wondering about something." Deena paused, raising her glass of wine to her lips and taking a long, slow sip. "If Vivi is marrying Sebastian, why is she spending her Saturday night with my nephew? Don't you find that a little bit strange? He must be pretty open-minded to let her go out with another guy. Especially one she was once romantically involved with."

"I'm sure they're only going as friends," Chunky said, always the peacemaker. "He probably needed a date and asked Vivi if she was free."

Big Viv gave an absent-minded nod, her mind too distracted to pay attention to the conversation as it continued. Nico and Vivi had gone to a wedding together. And Vivi hadn't told her.

She didn't know what was going on. But she was planning to find out.

Later, everyone retreated to the kitchen, helping themselves to coffee and the variety of Italian pastries that had been brought. Big Viv was on her way back from the bathroom, so she was in the hallway outside the dining room when she heard her name mentioned. The only voice missing from the conversation was Deena's, who had gone upstairs to use Foxy's other bathroom.

"Did you see the look on Big Viv's face when Deena showed up?" Patricia cackled.

"I thought her head was going to explode," Chunky giggled.

"When was the last time the two of them were in the same room together?" Patricia asked.

"Beats me," Foxy said. "Although, I heard they had a run-in at the bakery a couple of days ago. Huge food fight! Cakes and pies flying everywhere. I wish I could have been there to see it. When it was over, the place was a wreck. Vivi had to hire painters to fix the place up before they could open the next day."

"They used to be so close," Chunky said, her voice a bit sad. "Whatever happened between them?"

"They both thought they were better than the

rest of us," Carla said. "Until someone put them in their place."

"Put them in their place?" Chunky asked. "What are you talking about?"

"Shh," Carla whispered. "It's a secret."

"I think you need some more coffee, Carla," Foxy said. "Come with me. I'll fix you a cup."

"I fixed them," Carla said. "Both of them."

"Fixed them? What are you talking about?" Chunky asked. "What did you do?"

Yes, Big Viv wondered, *what did you do?*

But Carla didn't answer.

What the hell was it with the Confetta women throwing desserts?

Nico reached for a cloth napkin, calmly wiping strawberry filling and fondant off his face. He was not going to lose his cool. That was what Vivi wanted, and he refused to give her the satisfaction. "Feel better?" he asked.

Vivi glared at him.

"I told you before and I'll tell you again," he said slowly and patiently, "There's nothing between me and Candy. We were involved years ago and then it ended. Now, I just work for her. Those photos are a crock of shit."

Vivi took another look at her phone. She studied the photos for a bit. Then, she picked up her water glass and threw the water in Nico's face.

Nico blinked away the water in his eyes, and he wiped off his face for the second time before slamming his napkin down on the table. Now, he was angry.

Luckily, everyone was out on the dance floor, so they didn't have an audience.

"Are you crazy? Look what you did!" he shouted, pointing to his wet shirt and jacket. "This is Armani!"

"I never should have come with you today," Vivi said.

"Why did you?" He didn't give her a chance to answer. "I'll tell you why. Because there's unfinished business between us."

"There's *nothing* between us."

Nico stared into Vivi's face. Slowly, his gaze traveled down to her belly. "Wanna bet?"

"I don't have to listen to this." Vivi turned to walk away from the table.

"What are you going to do, Vivi?" he called after her. "Run away like you always do?"

"I'm not running away!"

"Yes, you are! You ran off to Cancun in May, didn't you?"

Viv whirled around. "You're one to talk. You ran off to California all those years ago."

"I didn't run off. I was sent. And it was the best thing my mother ever did for me. Wanna know why?" He didn't give her a chance to ask. "Because it got me away from you!"

As soon as he said the words, he regretted them. It hadn't been the best thing to happen to him. He'd missed Vivi so much those first few weeks. But he was a kid. He did what he was told and tried to make the best of things. He made new friends. Met other girls. Eventually, he put Vivi behind him, although he'd never forgotten her. And she'd never forgotten him. Why else would they have reconnected all those other times when he'd come back to Brooklyn?

Vivi's lower lip began to tremble. Then, she burst into tears.

And Nico felt awful. "Vivi—" he started to say.

But she didn't stay to listen. Instead, she ran out of the catering hall.

Feeling helpless, Nico watched as she disappeared into the night.

The mail was waiting when Vivi got home. It must have been delivered after she and Nico had left for the wedding.

Evelyn and Mario had insisted on giving her a ride home. Vivi could see Evelyn wanted to ask what had gone wrong with Nico, but she didn't. She was quiet the entire car ride. The only thing she said when they dropped her off was, "Remember what I said. He loves you. Men aren't always so smart. Sometimes, they make mistakes and we have to forgive them." She nodded at Mario. "I had to forgive a lot of his mistakes. If I hadn't, we wouldn't be married fifty years."

Vivi had given Evelyn a smile and a hug, waving once she was safely inside her house before they drove off.

As she absentmindedly sorted through a pile of magazines, bills, and junk mail, she found it. The envelope from the testing facility. For a second, she thought her heart was going to stop. She turned the envelope over and over in her hands. Finally, she'd have her answer. She ripped the envelope open and pulled out the letter inside, her eyes scanning for the words she so badly needed.

And then, she found them.

98% compatibility. It was confirmed. Nico was the father of her baby.

At first, she didn't know how to react. She was numb. In shock. She said the words out loud. "I'm having Nico's baby."

And then, the words sunk in. She was having Nico's baby!

A range of emotions washed over her. She was thrilled. Happy. Excited.

Quickly, the joy started to fade away, replaced by reality. She became worried. Nervous. Queasy.

Nico was the father of her baby. This wasn't good. Especially not after tonight. What was he going to do once he found out? What was *she* going to do once her mother found out?

She wished she could call Sebastian and tell him her news, but he had gone out to Fire Island for the weekend with Dominick. They were finally alone, and Sebastian had asked her not to call or text until Monday.

She stared at the letter again before refolding it and putting it back in its envelope. She'd deal with it later. Out of sight, out of mind.

Hopefully, Sebastian's weekend was going better than hers.

—————

After an exhaustive day of sex, sex and more sex, Sebastian and Dom decided to have a low-key evening. Dom cooked, grilling salmon steaks on the barbeque along with corn on the cob and baked potatoes. Once dinner was finished, they watched a movie. There were a number of DVDs to choose from, but finally they selected the 1989 AIDS drama, *Longtime Companion.*

"You up for this?" Sebastian asked. "It's a pretty heavy movie."

"I know. I've seen it before. It seems fitting, don't you think? Parts of it were filmed out here and it's Gay Pride month. It's part of our history. We shouldn't ever forget. These young guys today, they think they can be as reckless as they want when it comes to sex and all they have to do is pop a pill the next morning. Guys back then weren't so lucky."

"Okay. But don't say I didn't warn you." He handed Dom the DVD case. "You get it ready to go. I'll be right back."

Sebastian disappeared into the kitchen and returned minutes later with a bowl of popcorn. "Freshly popped," he told Dom, positioning the bowl between them. "Can't watch a movie without popcorn."

"Ready?" Dom asked, aiming the remote at the DVD player.

"Ready."

At first, they focused on the movie, losing themselves in the lives of Willy, Fuzzy, Howard, David, Sean, and Lisa. Then, Sebastian reached into the bowl of popcorn and his hand brushed against Dom's, who was reaching in at the same time. He looked over to give him a smile and saw his lips were coated with melted butter.

Even after their antics earlier, he couldn't get enough of Dom. Suddenly, Sebastian wanted to taste that butter. He wanted to taste those lips. So, he did. He leaned over the bowl and planted his lips firmly on Dom's.

The kiss was sweet. Salty. Exactly what he was expecting. What he wasn't expecting was the ferocity with which Dom returned his kiss.

Dom put the bowl of popcorn on the rug and held Sebastian's arms over his head, pushing him deep into the sofa cushions as his lips made their way up the V of Sebastian's shirt to his neck and then his lips, where he proceeded to explore Sebastian's mouth with his tongue, much to Sebastian's delight.

It wasn't too long before he found himself getting hard again.

And once again found himself in Dom's mouth. The man did love sucking him off. Not that Sebastian was complaining.

Dom dipped his fingers into the bowl of popcorn, coated his fingers with melted butter, and rubbed it all over Sebastian's hard cock. The warmth of the butter sliding over his erection made Sebastian want to come apart at the seams, but he resisted.

That is, until Dom added his own warmth with his mouth. Within seconds, Dom was sucking with a speed and ferocity that Sebastian was powerless to resist, no matter how hard he tried. He came as Dom drained him dry, a satisfied smile on his face as he pulled away.

"Tasty," Dom said, reaching for the remote, rewinding so they could watch the scenes they had missed. "You're an adorable distraction, but I think we should focus on the movie, don't you? Give it the attention it deserves. If you want later, we can pick up where we left off this afternoon." He reached for the bowl of popcorn and repositioned it between them while Sebastian reached for a pillow and put it on top of his lap.

When the movie ended, Sebastian was bawling his eyes out.

"I've seen *Longtime Companion* so many times," he sniffed as the credits rolled, "but this time around it really hit me hard, especially when Sean was dying and David kept telling him to let go." He reached for a Kleenex from the box on the coffee table and blew his nose. "Can you imagine watching the person you love most in the world suffer like that and you're powerless to help them?"

"I don't know how guys managed to get through their lives back then," Dom said, turning off the TV and DVD player. "Not knowing. Living in fear. Watching all their friends die. Healthy one day, sick the next. Wondering if they were going to get it before they even knew what caused it. At one point, doctors thought kissing could spread it."

"So many men stopped having sex the way Willy and Fuzzy did. How can you not be intimate with someone? Everyone needs love and affection. Everyone wants to be touched by another person."

"Gay men with AIDS were treated like pariahs back then. At one point, there was talk about rounding up AIDS patients and putting them in camps. For their own good, of course. Thank God for Larry Kramer and ACT-UP and everyone else who fought for us. So many people died way too young. So much talent and promise cut short."

Sebastian gazed at the walls around them. "If only the houses on Fire Island could talk. The stories they could tell us about gay life through the decades. So much has changed."

"When did you first know you were gay?"

Sebastian gave it some thought. "I remember being little and watching repeats of *The Rockford Files* with my grandfather. I don't know what it was about James Garner, but I always liked watching him on screen. I felt sort of tingly whenever I looked at him. Rockford was a P.I., so I'd imagine being rescued by him and having him carry me away in his arms. Just the two of us. And I loved him in *The Thrill of it All* with Doris Day! Have you ever seen it? It's a romantic comedy from the sixties. He was so handsome in that."

"I've seen it," Dom said, giving Sebastian a mischievous smile. "Bonus points if you can figure out the connection between *The Thrill of it All* and *The Sound of Music*."

"Too easy. Kym Karath, who played Garner's daughter Maggie in *The Thrill of it All*, played

Gretl, the youngest Von Trapp in *The Sound of Music*."

"Okay, here's another one. What's the connection between the 1950 movie *Caged* and *The Sound of Music*?"

"Another easy one. Eleanor Parker, who played the Baroness in *The Sound of Music*, was the sweet young thing who spends a year behind bars in *Caged* and comes out a tough dame."

"You know your old movies. I'm impressed. But I'll eventually stump you."

"Now, it's my turn. Who played the prison warden in *Caged*?"

"Only the greatest mother-in-law in TV history," Dom said. "Agnes Moorehead, aka Endora."

"As well as Velma Cruther in *Hush, Hush, Sweet Charlotte*," Sebastian shot back. "Oscar nominated for Best Supporting Actress."

"And Orson Welles' mother in *Citizen Kane*, the murderess in the Bogey and Bacall noir thriller *Dark Passage*, and the best friend in Douglas Sirk's *All That Heaven Allows*," Dom listed. "You got all night? Because I can keep going on and on when it comes to old Hollywood."

"Was that when you knew? When you

discovered your love for old movies? Were you not into sports like other boys?"

Dom shook his head. "Nah, I knew early on. My older cousins used to watch a local music countdown show. It was on Sunday nights. They had dancers, male and female. Naturally, my eyes were always glued to the men, especially this one guy named Tony. I would search for him every week. After that, I was curious."

"Curious? How?" Sebastian gave Dom a knowing look. "Did you play doctor with your male friends?"

"No! But I lingered a bit in the locker room when we had to change for gym class, always careful to not focus on just one guy."

"How about in the showers?"

"Never. I kept my eyes on my bar of soap, lathered up, rinsed off, and got dressed. I didn't want to find myself in a situation I couldn't control, if you know what I mean." Dom stared at Sebastian's crotch, then gazed back up at him. "Sometimes, it has a mind of its own."

"I'm well aware of that," Sebastian said. "Did you ever steal a porn magazine from a newsstand?"

"Sebastian, no! Really? I'm scandalized!" Dom exclaimed, his face lighting up with glee. "You naughty boy." He leaned forward, as if waiting to hear a secret. "Tell me more about your criminal past."

"Hardly criminal. It was only once. It was a copy of *Mandate*. There was a cowboy on the cover, and there was just something about that bare chest under his black leather vest. I had to see what he was hiding under his chaps."

"A cowboy fetish. I'll file that away. So, what was he hiding?"

Sebastian blushed. "What do you think? One of the biggest, hardest dicks I'd ever seen. I kept that magazine under my mattress for years. It provided hours of fantasy when I jerked off in addition to immense amounts of Catholic guilt for stealing it."

"But no guilt for jerking off?"

"None. Back when we were kids, it was harder to have access to gay stuff. Once I had it, I wasn't going to feel guilty about using it. Today's kids can go online and see all the dick pics they want. Not to mention what they can find on Facebook, Tik Tok, and Instagram. There are so many images for them to choose from."

"It feels like we grew up in a more innocent time. But everyone says that when they get older, don't they?"

"Hey, we're not old," Sebastian said, poking Dom in the side. "Only thirty."

"Well, this old guy is ready for bed." Dom rose from the couch, holding out a hand to Sebastian. "How about you?"

Sebastian nodded. "You know what I'd like to do?"

"What?" Dom asked.

"I'd like to fall asleep holding you in my arms. How does that sound?"

Dom gave Sebastian a slow, lingering kiss. "I think it sounds great."

———

That night when they had sex, it was different than it had been earlier in the day. It wasn't as wild, or as savage. Instead, it was sweet. Soft. Gentle. Loving.

Once they were in bed, they turned to each other at the same time. Sebastian turned himself onto his side, pressing his butt against Dom's cock.

At first, they just spooned, listening to each other breathe. Then, Dom reached for Sebastian's cock and held it before softly moving a finger up and down his shaft. Sebastian reached for Dom's hand to cover his entire shaft as Dom's fingers slowly explored his entire groin, softly fingering the coarse hair there as he kissed the side of his neck. Then, gently with his knee, Dom spread open Sebastian's legs, pressing into his back as he began nibbling on his ear.

Sebastian turned and gave Dom a kiss, their tongues locking together as Sebastian reached out to the nightstand beside the bed, finding a condom. He handed it to Dom, who ripped it open with his teeth and slid it onto his erection. Sebastian turned away from him, lifting his butt in the air and offering it to Dom.

After a quick application of lube, Dom slowly entered him, but with a gentleness that had been missing earlier in the day.

It felt just as good, if not better. They rocked together as one. Two halves coming together as a whole. Two hearts in sync.

CHAPTER
TWENTY-FOUR

The sharks were circling. They could smell fresh blood and they all wanted a taste.

It was Sunday morning and Sebastian and Dom were waiting in line for a table for brunch at the Blue Whale, one of only two dining establishments on Fire Island. While they waited for the drag hostess to seat them, Sebastian could see Dom was getting a fair amount of attention. There was no mistaking the head-to-toe inspections he was receiving from the guys around them. Some subtle, some not.

On one hand, Sebastian didn't mind. After all, Dom was with him. Arms wrapped around each other's waists as they waited, bodies leaning in against the other, it was clear they were a couple.

On the other hand, contrary to what the others

were seeing, they weren't really together, were they? There was still the matter of him being engaged to Vivi. And if they weren't together...

Well, there was no stopping Dom if another man caught his attention.

And they were certainly vying for his attention. Could these queens be any more obvious? Two had already asked Dom for the time, another asked him where he got his ANNIE HAYWARD DESERVED BETTER T-shirt, one asked him if he knew him from the city, and yet another asked him what cologne he was wearing.

It was all Sebastian could do to stop himself from throwing himself against him and shouting, "He's mine! All mine! So, back off!"

He was entitled to feeling prickly and possessive. Their weekend was ending today. Later tonight, they'd be back on the ferry and returning to the lives they'd left behind. After their wonderful weekend, how was he going to be able to go back to pretending?

When they reached the front of the brunch line, the drag queen hostess, Lola Divine, a gorgeous Latina beauty, inspected Dom from head to toe. It was all she could do not to lick her glistening red lips, she was so brazenly ogling Dom. "Let's get you a table right up front so all the boys passing by can see how pretty you are," she giggled. "Because who doesn't love pretty things?"

It was all Sebastian could do not to snatch the wig off her head.

Once they were seated with their menus, Sebastian said, "I've made a decision."

"About waffles or pancakes?" Dom asked while still perusing the menu. "Because I was thinking of the French toast. Maybe we could share?" He gazed up and gave Sebastian a smile. "After that workout we had last night, I think we can splurge on some carbs, don't you?"

Sebastian tried not to blush at the mention of the previous night's activities. "I'm not talking about brunch."

"You're not? Then what?"

"Us."

Dom closed his menu. "Okay, this sounds serious."

"I want us to be a couple."

Dom waved a hand back and forth between them. "I thought we were."

"That's sweet of you to say. But we're not. You know we're not. Not for real. Not until..."

Dom finished the sentence for him. "Not until you end your engagement with Vivi."

"Yes."

"I'm going to be honest. Until this weekend, I was ready to throw in the towel."

Sebastian held his breath. "And now?"

Dom reached across the table and took Sebastian's hand in his. "It's been a pretty great weekend. I want to have more great weekends with you. I want to do so many more things with you."

"But..."

"But what?"

"No but? I thought there would be a but. A reason why this isn't going to work. A reason why we can't keep seeing each other."

"I'm willing to wait. I'm still not a fan of the situation with Vivi, but I know she's your friend and you're trying to help her. And I think you want to be with me."

"Of course I want to be with you!" Sebastian exclaimed. "How could you even say that?"

"Then, all we need to do is figure out a way to make it happen. Together."

Sebastian nodded. "Together."

Suddenly he didn't feel so alone. He felt like the weight of the world had been lifted off his shoulders.

Dom wanted to be with him. He just needed to be a little more patient. They were going to figure a way out of this, and he and Dom could be together.

———

"So, did she admit it?" Those were the first words out of Aunt Deena's mouth when she waltzed into his kitchen the following morning. Nico was at the counter, scrambling some eggs in a bowl. Two slices of toast popped up from the toaster. Aunt Deena snagged one and slathered it with grape jelly before taking a seat at the kitchen table.

"You want some eggs?" he asked.

"Forget the eggs and answer my question," she said, pouring herself a cup of coffee from the pot on the table. "Did she admit it?"

"No, she didn't."

Aunt Deena rolled her eyes. "What kind of a ladies man are you?"

Nico poured the eggs into a sizzling frying pan. "Maybe that's the problem. I'm not a ladies man, but everyone seems to think I am. Which is why I'm in this mess!"

Aunt Deena took a bite of toast and a sip of coffee. "Okay, calm down. I meant it as a compliment, not an insult. Maybe we've been going about this the wrong way."

"What do you mean?"

"She won't talk to you, but maybe she'll talk to me."

Nico blurted the words out. "Are you nuts? Her mother hates you. You think Vivi's going to admit something that will get her into hot water with Big Viv?"

As soon as the words were out of his mouth, everything made sense. The reason why Vivi wasn't telling him he was the father. How could he have been so blind? It had to do with the goddamn feud. She probably figured her mother would go through the roof if Nico was the father of her baby. Because it would tie her to Deena, her sworn enemy. But what if Deena and Big Viv weren't enemies anymore? Would that fix things? Would it get Vivi to finally admit the truth? And if she did, could they finally be together?

CHAPTER
TWENTY-FIVE

Sebastian was on cloud nine as he arrived at the bakery on Monday morning. His weekend had been wonderful even though it had been hard to say goodbye to Dom the night before.

"I wish we didn't have to leave each other," he had said while driving Dom back to his apartment.

"Who says we have to? Why don't you spend the night at my place?" Dom suggested with a devilish gleam in his eye.

As tempting as the offer was, Sebastian had turned it down. It was too risky. One night could easily turn into two. Then, three or four. The situation was already complicated enough. Why make it worse? Why torture himself? He couldn't completely be with Dom until he got himself out of his engagement to Vivi. And what if Nico was lurking around somewhere, trying to catch them in a compromising scene? He wouldn't put it past him. All hell would break loose.

And speaking of hell, judging from the loud voices wafting out from the back of the bakery, it sounded like it had already broken loose.

Goodbye cloud nine. Hello reality.

Most mornings, it was pretty quiet. Sebastian did the baking while two assistant bakers worked the ovens in the basement, making all kinds of breads and rolls and muffins that they supplied to other bakeries and restaurants throughout Brooklyn. In the front, Big Viv waited on customers with her two other cashiers. But there were some days when Big Viv went off the deep end, for whatever reason suited her best. She was the boss and the bakery was her kingdom. She often told them she could act however she wanted whenever she wanted. Today sounded like one of those mornings.

Sebastian cautiously opened the back door of the bakery and slipped inside.

Where he found himself face to face with Big Viv. An *angry* Big Viv.

"So, you finally show your face!" she snarled. "Where have you been all weekend?"

"What's with the third degree?" Sebastian calmly asked as he popped his head through the top of a white chef's apron and wrapped it around his chest, tying the strings in a knot at the front of his waist. He took off his sneakers and slipped into a pair of chef's clogs. They made it much easier to stand on his feet for hours. Then, he walked over to the fridge and began to pull out ingredients: eggs, milk, butter. He usually started his day by making butter cookies—some plain, some dipped in chocolate, and others dotted with a raspberry jam center—and then moved on to the more complicated desserts. He tried to keep his voice in a flat monotone. There was no way Big Viv could know what he had been up to this weekend. So, she had to be upset about something else. "I'm on time, and what I did this weekend is none of your business. Last time I checked, I only work for you Monday to Friday."

Oops. Had he really said those words to Big Viv? They had slipped out before he could stop himself. Judging from the blood flowing straight to her now tomato red face, he had. Too much happiness with Dom was making him cocky and reckless. Before he could apologize, Big Viv was screeching again.

"You dare to talk to me that way? After

everything I've done for you! Is this how you're going to talk to me after you marry my daughter?"

"Ma, calm down. I'm the one you're mad at. Not Bash. Stop picking on him. Why are you getting so upset?"

It was then that Sebastian noticed Vivi was also in the kitchen, sitting on a stool and sipping a cup of tea. He could smell peppermint in the air and wondered if she was drinking it because of morning sickness.

"Because the two of you are driving me nuts!" Big Viv exploded. "You're an engaged couple, but you don't act like one! Who lets their fiancé run around with another man?"

Vivi rolled her eyes. "We weren't running around."

Big Viv ignored her, glaring at Sebastian. "Well, answer me."

"What man?" Sebastian asked, having no clue what was going on.

Vivi got off the stool, slamming down her teacup. "Listen, Ma, Nico is my friend. A close friend."

Nico. Sebastian bit back a groan. He should have known. If there was one thing that made Big Viv go nuts, it was Nico. What had happened now?

Because judging from Big Viv's meltdown, it wasn't good.

Big Viv shifted her glare to Vivi. "How close? Because you're engaged to marry *him*." She pointed a finger at Sebastian. "You're having *his* baby." Another savage jab in the air toward him. "Whatever existed between you and Nico is long over. Done. *Finito*! So, there's no going down memory lane one last time."

"We weren't doing that! How many times do I gotta tell you, I went with him to that wedding as his friend? He needed a plus one."

"Bah!" Big Viv threw her hands up. "You can say that all you want, but body language says something else."

"Body language?"

"Yes, body language!"

Vivi sighed. "What are you talking about?"

"Body language is another way of talking. Without words. It's the way your body reacts when you're around another person. One that you're attracted to." Big Viv narrowed her eyes. "You may think I'm old, but my memory is still sharp." She tapped the side of her forehead. "I still remember how you get when you're around Nico. Always getting as close as you can. Touching him. Those lingering looks. The way you talk and laugh with him. Body language! It gives it all away. So, don't stand there and make me think there was no body language going on between the two of you at that wedding. Because I'm sure there was. You think people don't see that? You think they don't talk?"

Vivi crossed her arms over her chest. "And what are they talking about?"

"That you're back with that *idiota*! That my daughter and her high school sweetheart are making a cuckold out of her future husband!"

Vivi rolled her eyes. "You've been watching too many soaps, Ma. So what if they are talking? What's the big deal? Nothing is going on between Nico and me. What does it matter?"

"Because you're marrying Sebastian! You want to bring shame to him?"

"Shame?" Vivi laughed hysterically. "Ma, it's 2022. We're not living in some Italian village where I'm a promised virgin." She pointed to her belly. "In case you've forgotten."

"I don't mind that you went out with Nico," Sebastian said, hoping to defuse the situation.

"*Stunad!*" Big Viv exclaimed before turning her attention to her buzzing phone. She opened a text and her face went white. As white as it had the day she'd gotten that phone call from Italy.

"Ma! What is it?" Vivi asked, rushing to her side.

"Great." She slammed her phone down on the counter. "My day just went from bad to worse!"

"What's wrong?" Sebastian asked.

"It's my mother," Big Viv growled. "She's texting me from the airport. And not the one in Italy."

"Nonna Julia is here in New York?" Vivi asked in disbelief.

Big Viv nodded grimly. "She's here!"

"But she wasn't supposed to arrive until the wedding. We haven't even set a date!"

"Looks like we'll be having the wedding even sooner than we planned."

"Uh, how soon?" Sebastian asked.

Big Viv waved her phone in the air. "Based on this? The sooner the better so we can send her back to Italy."

"I'm sure Dom will get right on it," Sebastian said.

"Forget Dom! I'm firing him."

"Firing him?" Sebastian gasped. "But why?"

"He wasn't working fast enough."

"He was! He was jumping through hoops for you."

"Well, I was the one who was paying him and the customer is always right. And this customer wasn't happy with the quality of service she was getting, so I'm cutting him loose. I'll handle everything from this point on. What's that expression? If you want something done right, do it yourself."

No! Dom was just starting his business, and this wedding was a big chunk of change. Would he be able to keep his business afloat without it?

More selfishly, if Dom wasn't their wedding planner, then when would he see him? What possible reason would he have for wanting to spend time with him? Sure, he *could* still see him, but what if Nico saw them together? Or someone else from the neighborhood. Granted, New York City was big, but there was always a chance of running into someone you knew. What then? If word got back to Big Viv, she would instantly be suspicious. It wouldn't be long before she started putting two and two together. And then, watch out! No one made a fool out of Big Viv Confetta.

Although, what was going to happen when the truth about the fake engagement finally came out?

Sebastian didn't even want to think about it, and he pushed it to the back of his mind.

"I'm not done talking with you," Big Viv said to Vivi as she grabbed her Gucci purse and hurried out of the bakery. "We're going to finish this conversation when I get back."

As soon as she was gone, Sebastian whirled on Vivi. "You went to a wedding with Nico? Seriously?"

"Why are you saying it like that? All hostile?"

"Because I can't believe what I'm hearing. You went to a wedding with Nico. What were you thinking? Why would you do that?" he wailed.

"Why not?"

"You know your mother. You know her temper and how she gets when it comes to him. You knew she would have a meltdown if she found out, and now she has. You pissed her off! And when she's pissed off, she lashes out, which is why Dom is no longer our wedding planner!"

"So, now it's my fault Dom is getting fired?"

"Isn't it?"

"Relax, I'll talk to my mother and unfire him. Happy?"

"Why couldn't you have at least run this by me first?"

"I might have to answer to my mother, but I don't answer to you!"

"Oh, really? May I remind you that I'm in this mess because I'm helping you out and you need to keep me in the loop?"

"You were the one who went off for the weekend with his boyfriend and didn't want to be disturbed, remember?" Vivi shot back. "So, I didn't disturb you. I was being nice. And for that, you give me grief?"

Sebastian took a deep breath. "You're right. I'm sorry. Why is your mother so upset? It can't just be because of Nico."

"Why do you think?" Vivi rolled her eyes. "Deena!"

"Deena?"

"Deena blabbed to her that Nico and I had gone to the wedding together. She was all in my mother's face at her book club on Saturday night. I'm sure she couldn't wait to tell her to get back at her for that cake war they had. You know how my mother gets when it comes to her. She goes crazy! She must have left me ten voicemail messages yesterday, wanting to know what was going on. I ignored them all."

"You don't usually ignore your mother."

"Yeah, well, I was dealing with something else."

"What?"

Vivi exhaled. "I have some news."

"What kind of news?"

"About the baby." Vivi looked down at her belly. "It's Nico's."

Sebastian let out a breath. Finally, they had the answer they'd been waiting for. Which meant, maybe, this was all coming to an end. "Did you tell him?"

"I didn't find out until I got home from the wedding. The letter from the lab was waiting in the mail."

"When are you going to tell him?"

"I'm not."

"You're not? But you wanted Nico to be the father, didn't you? Haven't you always loved him? That's what you said the other night. Now you can be with him! Forget about your mother and Deena. Do what you want. Why wouldn't you tell him you're having his baby?"

Vivi brandished her phone in Sebastian's face. "This is why!"

Sebastian skimmed the articles of Nico and Candy on the web. "Oh."

"Is that all you have to say?"

"You can't be mad at him, Vivi. You're not a

couple. You're single. He's single. You did break up with him."

"He says there's nothing going on between them."

"And you don't believe him?"

"Why should I? Pictures don't lie, do they?"

"Pictures can be manipulated. Headlines, too. It's all about click bait."

"Nico said something like that, too."

"You believe it when I say it, but not him?"

"I don't know what to believe," she said, sounding on the verge of tears. "We were having such a nice time at the wedding. I was almost going to tell him the truth, that he might be the baby's father, and then I got this Google alert. Lately, there have been too many pictures of him and Candy together. Where there's smoke, there's fire, right?"

"I know they were involved once, but isn't it over between them?"

Vivi sniffed. "He says it is."

"Then, why don't you believe him?"

"How many times has it been over between me and Nico and we've gotten back together? Who's to say the same thing isn't happening with Candy, huh?"

"But there's a difference," Sebastian softly pointed out. "Nico loves you. He doesn't love her."

CHAPTER
TWENTY-SIX

There was dead silence in the back of the black stretch limo Big Viv had rented.

She and her mother sat next to each other, but neither one spoke. Big Viv tried to make conversation, asking about Italy and assorted relatives, but her mother wasn't interested, giving only one or two-word answers as she looked out the window on their way to Brooklyn. Finally, Big Viv gave up. She was a sixty-three-year-old woman, yet whenever she was with her mother, she was a little girl who could never please her. Fine. Let her give her the silent treatment. She'd give it right back. It was too late to change things. Too many years had gone by with too little communication. She had her life and her mother had hers. Still, who didn't want their mother's love and approval?

Big Viv hated to admit it, but she'd always felt like her mother didn't love her. That's why she had always tried so hard with Vivi. Maybe she was too much of a presence in her daughter's life, maybe she meddled more than she should, maybe she needed to take a step back, but it was only because she loved her daughter so much. She hoped Vivi knew that. She never, ever wanted her to feel the way she did with Julia.

Suddenly, Big Viv had a sobering thought. What if Vivi thought of her the way she thought of her own mother? Big Viv would know, wouldn't she? After all, they worked together. Talked all the time. Saw each other practically every day. But still...

There were things she had done. Like separating Vivi from Nico. But she'd only done that because she loved Vivi. She didn't want her to get hurt, and she hadn't trusted Nico. Because of Deena.

It all came back to Deena leaving Brooklyn. She'd been so upset, but her mother hadn't. If anything, her mother had been ecstatic. Almost gloating. One day, Big Viv made the mistake of telling her mother she hadn't heard from Deena since she'd left. She thought she would at least write to her if she couldn't afford to call. Her mother had wasted no time giving her opinion. *I told you she was no good! Always thinking she was better than the rest of us in the neighborhood. Well, now she's gone and proved it. The only person she ever thought about was herself. She was never your friend, and now you know it.*

Oh, how her mother had hated Deena. Maybe it was because Deena pushed her to do more. Be more. She was always a rebel, breaking the rules and taking Big Viv along for the ride. How many times had she come home a bit tipsy after a night at the movies when Deena had spiked their Cokes with vodka? How many times in high school, her junior and senior year, had she told her mother she was spending the night at Deena's for a slumber party, but had actually gone to the discos, staying out until three in the morning? How many times had she bought clothes that were provocative, daring, sexy and kept them at Deena's because she knew if her mother saw them, she would make her return them?

As the car sped along, Big Viv took another look at her mother and made a promise to herself. She was going to pull back. She wouldn't be so overbearing. She would give Vivi her space.

But she would start after Vivi and Sebastian's wedding.

———

Sebastian was placing a tray of cherry cheesecakes in the bakery's front window when the gruesome twosome made an appearance. "Can this day get any worse?" he muttered out loud.

Vivi, who was helping a customer, followed Sebastian's gaze to the front door of the bakery, where Deena and Nico entered. After finishing up with her customer, Vivi told the other two cashiers to take a fifteen-minute break.

"What do you two want? Haven't you done enough damage, Deena? Come to do some more? You already ruined my Monday thanks to your big mouth."

"That bad, huh? Your mother always had a temper. You never know what's going to set her off."

"You knew exactly what you were doing."

Deena raised a hand, crossing her heart. "I swear, I thought she knew you had gone to that wedding with Nico. Don't you tell her everything?"

Not everything, Sebastian thought to himself as his eyes flitted between Vivi's belly and Nico.

"What do you want? My mother's gone out for a while, but she'll be back soon. I'd rather not have a repeat of the other day."

"I feel so bad about the cake fight with Big Viv that I want to make things up to you."

"How?" Vivi suspiciously asked.

"I'm performing a new cabaret act at a casino in Las Vegas this weekend. I know your wedding is soon, so I'd love to fly you and your girlfriends out for a bachelorette party. The casino is lending me their private jet and they've offered a discount on all the rooms."

Nico turned toward a silent Sebastian. "Don't think you're being left out. While Vivi and her friends are ogling male strippers, we'll be doing our own fair share at your bachelor party."

"Bachelor party?" Sebastian gasped.

Nico eagerly nodded. "I know the best strip joints in Las Vegas."

"I bet you do," Vivi said, her voice dripping with acid.

"What do you say?" Deena asked. "Are you in? Your mother is welcome to come along, too, but I doubt she'll accept the invitation since it's from me."

"Give us a minute," Vivi said, making eye contact

with Sebastian and tilting her head toward the back of the bakery.

"What are they up to?" Sebastian asked Vivi once they were alone.

"I don't know, but it *is* a free trip to Vegas. And I don't know about you, but I could use some time away from my mother. Deena's probably right, she won't come along. She'll give me grief for going, but screw it! Are you in?"

Spending time with Nico was the last thing Sebastian wanted to do, but he was sick of being manipulated by Big Viv. And Vivi was right, Big Viv was definitely going to go through the roof once she found out. A change of scenery was just what he needed.

"I'm in."

With that, they returned to the front of the bakery.

"We'd love to accept your invitation," Vivi announced to Deena while continuing to ignore Nico, who was imploring her with his eyes to look at him. Sebastian almost felt sorry for him. Almost.

"Wonderful!" Deena exclaimed. "Just let me know how many of your girlfriends will be coming along and I'll reach out to the hotel for rooms."

"You do the same," Nico told Sebastian.

Deena happily clapped her hands together. "This is going to be so much fun." Her eyes ping-ponged between Vivi and Sebastian. "Your last chance to be wild before getting married. Remember, what happens in Vegas, stays in Vegas!"

As he watched Deena and Nico leave the bakery, Sebastian wondered why those words sounded so ominous.

———

"That went better than I thought," Aunt Deena told Nico once they were outside the bakery. "Although, you could have opened your mouth a bit more. How do you expect Vivi to forgive you if you don't talk to her?"

"She's still mad at me. She wouldn't even look at me, so I doubt she would have listened to a word I said."

"Like mother, like daughter."

"Explain to me again how this is all going to work."

"You wanted to be alone with her, right?" Aunt Deena asked, rummaging through her oversized Michael Kors shoulder bag. "Away from her mother. This is your opportunity."

Nico threw up his hands in exasperation. "But I don't have a plan."

Aunt Deena pulled out the compact and lipstick she had been searching for. "You'll figure one out."

"If you say so." Nico paused. "Aunt Dee, I've got a question."

"What?" she asked, pursing her lips and staring into her compact while applying a coat of Chanel ruby red lipstick.

"What caused the falling out between you and Vivi's mother? You were best friends, so how did you go from being besties to sworn enemies?"

Aunt Deena snapped her compact shut and capped her lipstick, tossing them back into her bag. "That's all on Big Viv."

"What do you mean?"

"It's her fault," she stated, her voice emotionless as she removed her Versace sunglasses from the top of her head and slid them over her eyes. "All her fault."

Before Nico could ask anything else, a black stretch limo pulled up to the curb in front of the bakery. The limo door opened and out stepped Big Viv, followed by an older woman.

"What are you doing here?" Big Viv exclaimed at the sight of Deena. "Come to start another dessert war? I should send you the bill for all the clean-up Vivi had to do."

Nico noticed the older woman giving his aunt an icy glare. She sort of resembled Estelle Getty's character, Sophia Petrillo, from *The Golden Girls*. Same clothes, same teased blonde bouffant, same dangling straw handbag.

Aunt Deena took off her sunglasses, eyes widening when she saw the woman. "Mrs. Tortoro. Only you could make ninety-three look fabulous." She went to give her a hug, but Mrs. Tortoro pulled away, scowling. Aunt Deena laughed. "You never liked me, did you, Mrs. Tortoro? You always thought I was a bad influence on Viv, didn't you? Well, maybe I was. But we had a hell of a lot of fun together!" Aunt Deena slipped her sunglasses back on, looking every inch the star she was. "What brings you back to Brooklyn?"

"My mother's come for the wedding," Big Viv said.

"So soon?" Deena asked.

"What do you mean?" The words slipped out before Nico could stop himself.

"If I can pull enough strings, Vivi and Sebastian will be getting married next weekend," Big Viv announced.

Nico tried not to panic. Vivi couldn't be marrying Sebastian next weekend. She couldn't. He loved her. And she loved him, if only she would stop being so stubborn and admit it.

Okay, it was time for the gloves to come off. To expose Vivi and Sebastian's sham engagement and get Vivi to admit not only that the baby she was carrying was his, but that she loved him. He would do whatever he had to.

And Las Vegas was where he was going to do it.

Sebastian heard the last of Big Viv's words as he walked out of the bakery and saw Nico and Deena walking away. Big Viv was planning for him and Vivi to be married *next* weekend? It was impossible. This couldn't be happening. But it was. And it was his own fault.

"Nonna Julia!" Vivi exclaimed, rushing past him and giving her grandmother a hug.

Nonna Julia endured it, then pulled away, giving the outside of the bakery a critical look.

"This place still looks the same. You haven't changed anything?" She faced Big Viv. "How do you expect to grow your business if you're stuck in time?"

she asked in her heavily accented English. "You have to make improvements. You have to draw in new customers while keeping the old ones. Otherwise, you lose them to the competition. You always have to be one step ahead! It's simple common sense, but then you never had much of that, did you?"

Ouch. Okay, that was harsh, Sebastian thought, wondering if he should introduce himself or wait for one of the women to do it.

"Ma and I have lots of ideas for improving the bakery," Vivi told her grandmother. "We just haven't gotten around to them yet. We're planning on adding an outdoor seating area for when the weather is nice. And we're going to expand part of the bakery so we can offer cappuccinos, espressos, gelato, and Italian ices."

"That's a start, but you should have done that years ago. Think of all the money you could have made."

"There's more to life than making money," Big Viv said.

Nonna Julia threw a hand up in the air. "Bah! You can never have enough money."

"Viv's is the best bakery in Brooklyn," Sebastian said, coming to Big Viv's defense. "We have loyal customers who visit us every day, and there are always lines out the door during the holidays."

Nonna Julia narrowed her eyes and stared at him. "Who are you?"

Vivi slipped her arm through Sebastian's and introduced him. "This is Sebastian, Nonna. My fiancé, and our baker. He works here."

Nonna Julia inspected him from head to toe. Once, then a second time. "You're marrying him?" She stared at Vivi in disbelief. "You sure?"

Sebastian couldn't help but take offense. She made it sound like there was something wrong with him. Unless...no. She couldn't have gaydar, could she?

"Of course I'm sure! Why wouldn't I be?"

Nonna Julia shrugged. "You're the one marrying him, not me."

"Let's go inside the bakery," Big Viv said, holding open the door.

Nonna Julia walked inside, already starting to complain about the display cases, as Sebastian followed after them. He was already counting down the days until he could escape to Las Vegas.

CHAPTER
TWENTY-SEVEN

It was the dinner from hell.

To celebrate Nonna Julia's return, Big Viv decided to take them out to one of Brooklyn's best Italian restaurants, Gargiulo's, in Coney Island. But instead of a fun family reunion, they were stuck dealing with a pint-sized monster.

There was a problem with everything Nonna Julia ordered, and she sent it all back to the kitchen. Her appetizer—the eggplant parmigiana was too mushy. Her first course—the lentil soup was too salty. Her second course—her filet mignon was overcooked. The bread basket—too many slices of bread with seeds, and she couldn't eat seeds. The wine—too sour. The espresso—too cold. The dessert

—the top of her crème brulee wasn't hard enough. She didn't hear a crack when her spoon hit the caramelized top.

Nothing made her happy. Except maybe complaining. And no matter how hard Sebastian tried to engage her in conversation, she just stared at him blankly, pretending she didn't understand a word of English when he knew she did.

He wasn't the only one she treated shabbily. She was pretty unpleasant to Big Viv, too. He didn't know what she was saying since she kept talking to Big Viv in Italian, but he could tell it wasn't very complimentary because as the evening went on, Big Viv became more and more subdued.

She was always larger than life. Now, it was like the light in her had been snuffed out. She looked exhausted. Defeated. All because of the evil gnome sitting next to her. No wonder they called her *la strega*. She had cast a spell of unpleasantness over the entire evening, and Sebastian had a feeling it was going to linger for her entire visit. And so, Big Viv kept filling her wine glass with merlot and emptying it until it was clear to Sebastian that she had become a bit tipsy.

It was while they were waiting for the check,

when Vivi and Nonna Julia were in the ladies room, that Big Viv leaned over to Sebastian. "So, what do you think of your future grandmother?"

Sebastian chose his words carefully, unsure if Big Viv wanted him to praise or disparage the woman. "She's one of a kind."

Big Viv snorted. "That's one way of putting it. She was never there for me when I was growing up. Always too busy with the grocery store or my older brothers and sister. I was the forgotten child. Sometimes, they would start dinner without me because no one called me to come to the table. Can you believe that? Who forgets to call their kid to the table? That's why I've tried so hard with Vivi. I never wanted her to feel the same way I did. Unwanted. Unloved. I didn't want to make the same mistakes. I wanted Vivi to know I was always there for her. That she could count on me."

Sebastian's heart broke. At that moment, he wanted nothing more than to give Big Viv a huge hug and reassure her that she was loved by Vivi. Instead, he placed his hand over hers and gave it a gentle squeeze. "You are *nothing* like your mother, trust me. I grew up with Vivi, remember? I was always around. You're a great mom with a huge heart. Sure, the two of you have your fights, but you always kiss and make up. She knows how much you love her. But—"

Big Viv pounced, a look of panic on her face. "But what?"

Did Sebastian dare to go there? If he did, maybe it would be a way out of this mess. "I know how much you love Vivi, but you can't always protect her. She's not a little girl anymore. You have to let her grow up. Make her own decisions. Otherwise, how else is she going to learn from her mistakes?"

"Decisions about what?"

"Like getting married. Maybe even marrying a man her mother doesn't approve of."

"Who said I don't approve of you? I'm throwing you this big wedding, aren't I?"

Sebastian took a deep breath. He was nervous, not knowing how his next words would go over. Beads of sweat broke out on his forehead, but he had to say it. "I'm not talking about me."

"Then, who are you talking about?" The truth dawned on Big Viv a second later and she frowned. "You're talking about Nico."

Sebastian knew he had to tread lightly. "What did Nico do that was so wrong, other than being related to Deena DiGrigorio?"

She waved a hand in the air. "I don't wanna talk about Deena."

"But we have to talk about her," Sebastian gently prodded. "This feud that the two of you have is the whole reason why Vivi and Nico couldn't be together. Don't you think it's gone on long enough? She was your best friend, wasn't she?"

Big Viv remained silent. Then, she took a small sip of wine. "It was always hard for me to make friends. You're never going to believe this, but when I was a kid, I was very shy. I think it had to do with English not being my first language. I was always afraid of saying the wrong word or phrase and having people laugh at me."

"How did you and Deena become friends?"

"It was first grade and we were in the cafeteria for lunch. These two snotty little bitches in our class, Marissa Reynolds and Amanda Harmon, came up to me and asked what I was eating for lunch because it smelled so bad. It was a provolone and prosciutto sandwich. You think my mother knew about Fluffernutter sandwiches or peanut butter and jelly? Hell, we were lucky if she bought Nutella. Well, they started holding their noses and waving their hands in front of their faces, chanting, 'Stinky! Stinky! Stinky! You and your sandwich are stinky!'.

Other kids started joining in and I could feel the tears filling my eyes. The last thing I wanted was to cry in front of everyone. I didn't know what to do." Big Viv took another sip of wine and a smile broke out across her face. "And then, I didn't have to do anything because Deena came over, took a big bite of my sandwich, and said it was the most delicious thing she'd ever eaten. She told Marissa and Amanda she felt sorry for them because they weren't Italian and Italians ate the best food. After that, she plopped herself next to me, gave them a death glare, and we were joined at the hip from that day on."

"That's such a sweet story," Sebastian said, choosing his next words carefully. "You must miss her. You were friends for a long time."

Big Viv took a longer sip of wine. "Of course I miss her. She was my best friend. Like a sister."

"So, what happened?"

Big Viv's face turned dark and her anger bubbled over. "How the hell should I know? One day we were friends, and the next day she was gone to Hollywood and I never heard from her again. No phone calls. No letters. Nothing. Obviously, our friendship meant nothing to her. And if it meant nothing to her all those years ago, it means nothing to her now."

"Maybe there was a reason you stopped hearing from her."

"What reason? You think I haven't asked myself that question over the years?"

"Maybe you and Deena should talk," Sebastian gently suggested. "Clear the air and see if you can salvage your friendship."

Big Viv pounded a fist on the table, jiggling her wine glass and causing some merlot to spill onto the white tablecloth. Sebastian jumped back in his chair. "Why should *I* be the one to make the first move? *She's* the one who stopped talking to me. I didn't start this, she did! And since I didn't start it, I'm not gonna be the one to end it. If she wants to be friends again, then she has to make the first move."

Sebastian wasn't sure if he'd heard her correctly. "Are you saying you'd be willing to give Deena another chance?"

Big Viv shrugged. "I don't know. So much time has gone by. What would be the point?"

"Nico and Vivi," Sebastian said. "They could finally be together."

"Be together? How much wine did you drink tonight? *You're* the one marrying Vivi. *You're* the father of her baby."

Oops. Sebastian needed to watch what he said.

He didn't need Big Viv getting suspicious. That would be a disaster.

"Of course," Sebastian assured her. "But let's just pretend. Say Vivi and I weren't engaged and there was no baby."

"No baby?" Big Viv gasped, a horrified expression on her face as she grabbed the salt shaker and tossed some crystals over her shoulder. "Bite your tongue!"

"Let's say Vivi and Nico could be together," Sebastian continued. "I'm not afraid to say it. Nico was always Vivi's first love. I know it, and you know it."

"So?"

"If it was possible for Vivi to be happy with the man she loves, wouldn't you want that? Every parent wants their child to be happy."

Big Viv snorted. "You think I wanna be related to Deena? It would drive me nuts. She's cold and calculating with no feelings."

"But how often would you really see her? She lives in California. And you know Nico loves Vivi. He's never stopped loving her."

Big Viv nodded. "Well, most of the time." Big Viv's face darkened. "He's broken her heart more than once. You don't think I know about all the times they got back together? I have eyes all over the neighborhood and they report back to me. I always know what's going on. No one ever pulls a fast one on me."

Sebastian tried not to visibly gulp, wondering if Big Viv was dropping a hint that she knew his engagement to Vivi was a sham. He chased away the thought. If she knew the truth, she would have come right out with it weeks ago.

"But who caused Nico to break Vivi's heart the first time?" Sebastian pointed out, unable to believe he was coming to Nico's defense. "You and his mother. Would it really be the end of the world if Vivi married Nico?"

"Why are we talking about this? It's too late for that." Suddenly, it was as if Big Viv had sobered up and she stared at Sebastian with sharp eyes. "Way too late. She's marrying you, the father of her baby, *right*?"

There was a tone of steel in her voice that made Sebastian suddenly break out into a nervous sweat. Maybe now wasn't the time to come clean. "Right," he said.

Big Viv poured herself some more merlot. "You've always been a good friend, looking out for Vivi. Wanting what's best for her. You've stuck by her, even when people in the neighborhood have talked about me behind my back. I know it wasn't always easy for her, hearing those Mafia rumors. Being called a Mafia princess." Big Viv leaned closer to Sebastian. "Wanna hear a secret?"

Sebastian leaned in, waiting.

"Everyone has always thought I started the bakery with Mafia money. That I took up with Big Tony Cicero after Vivi's father died and he gave me a loan." Big Viv shook her head. "But I didn't. I started the bakery with money from the life insurance policy Vivi's father had taken out. I just let everyone believe what they wanted to believe," Big Viv whispered. "It's good if people are scared of you, right?"

"Right," Sebastian agreed for the second time, wondering if Big Viv was sending him some sort of coded message.

The waiter brought over the check and Big Viv slapped down her platinum American Express card.

"I always felt like I was a failure to my mother," Big Viv told Sebastian. "That I never measured up. That's why I want this wedding to be perfect for Vivi. I never want her to feel like she's a failure to me. You're going to make my daughter happy, right? That's all I want for her."

Sebastian squirmed uncomfortably in his seat before answering. "Right."

———

The following morning Sebastian was in the shower when Liam knocked on the bathroom door. "What is it?"

"You have a visitor."

"Who?"

"Who do you think? Dom."

Why would Dom show up unannounced? Sebastian's stomach clenched. This couldn't be good. "Tell him I'll be right out."

"If I were you, I would take my time. He looks pissed. What did you do?"

Uh oh. If Dom was pissed, it meant Big Viv had fired him. How did he play this? Admit he knew about it, or play dumb? He really hadn't thought she would go through with it once she cooled off. Obviously, she hadn't. And now he had a mess to clean up. A big mess.

Sebastian quickly rinsed off, toweled himself, and threw on a T-shirt and shorts before finding Dom on the couch in the living room. Before he could say anything, Dom jumped to his feet.

"She fired me!" he exclaimed, his voice filled with shock. "Big Viv fired me!"

Sebastian decided to admit the truth. "I know."

Dom stared at Sebastian in disbelief. "You knew? And you didn't think to give me a head's up?"

Liam stuck his head out of the kitchen. "Not cool, Bash."

"She said she was going to fire you, but I didn't believe her. I thought Vivi would stop her. She told me she would. Yesterday was a crazy day. I meant to call and warn you, but I didn't have time. And I didn't want to do it over a text. Honestly, I really didn't think she was going to do it, and I didn't want to worry you unnecessarily. But we can fix this. We'll get Vivi to undo it. You're not fired. You're still our wedding planner."

Dom's voice was low. Dangerously low, Sebastian noted. "She also told me something else."

"She did?" he asked, his voice cracking. He had an inkling of what Dom's next words were going to be.

"Uh huh. That you're getting married next weekend."

"That's a bit of an exaggeration."

"Is it?" Dom folded his arms across his chest.

"Are you or are you not getting married next weekend?"

"I don't know. Maybe? If Big Viv gets her way."

Dom threw his arms up in the air in exasperation. "What's going on, Sebastian? Tell me the truth. Don't keep me out of the loop. I thought we were in this together."

Liam came out of the kitchen with a bowl of Cheerios, spooning them into his mouth. "Yeah, what's going on? Are we having a wedding next week? Do I get to be in it? I look really good in a tux."

Sebastian ignored his roommate. "It's a long story, but I promise I can explain everything. In Las Vegas."

"Las Vegas?" Dom asked in disbelief. "Did you say Las Vegas?"

Sebastian nodded. He knew he had to put the right spin on this, otherwise Dom would never say yes to the trip. "We're going to Las Vegas. For a bachelor and bachelorette party."

"You're kidding, right?"

"No," Sebastian squeaked out. "Deena DiGregorio is performing a new cabaret act and has the casino's private jet. She offered to fly us all out, but we have to pay for our own rooms. It's her way of apologizing for the cake brawl at the bakery last week."

"Why would I tag along? Why would I even want to?"

"You're our wedding planner, aren't you?"

"I'm your *fired* wedding planner," Dom pointed out. "And wedding planners don't usually go to bachelor and bachelorette parties."

"Then, you're one of my groomsmen."

"That doesn't make sense. We just met."

"We'll come up with something," an exasperated Sebastian exclaimed. "As long as you come to Las Vegas with me. I need you there, Dom. Please. As my friend. I can't do this alone."

"Why do you want me to come so badly? Are you trying to sabotage your engagement?"

"I don't know. Maybe I am. This is a chance for us to be together. Away from Big Viv and all this wedding nonsense."

"But you know that's only a temporary fix. You're still going to have to come back. And if Deena is flying everyone out, then I'm going to assume Nico will be along."

"He's the one throwing me the bachelor party," Sebastian admitted.

Dom stared at Sebastian. "Isn't he already

suspicious of us? What's he going to think when he sees us together? How will you explain it?"

Sebastian ignored the question. "Are you saying you don't want to come to Vegas with me?"

"No, that's not what I'm saying. Don't put words in my mouth. I'm trying to be smart. Nico is no dummy. He wants Vivi back and he'll do anything to prove your engagement is not legit."

Sebastian knew he was right. There had to be a way to outsmart Nico. "Okay, I've got it. You'll come with Liam."

"Liam?"

"As his boyfriend."

"What?"

"He'll cover for us, won't you, Liam?"

Liam looked up from his bowl of Cheerios. "I will?"

"Yes, you will!"

"Now you want me to pretend to be in a fake relationship?" Dom asked, his voice dangerously low again.

"What's the harm in it? Nico already thinks you and Liam are an item. It won't look suspicious if you tag along. Please, Dom. Do this for me. I promise we're not going to have to pretend much longer. Last night, I had a long talk with Big Viv about the Deena situation and I felt like I was making some headway. If I can just get the two of them together to talk, we can put this whole mess behind us. The engagement with Vivi will be over, she'll be with Nico, and we can be together."

Dom shook his head. "I don't know. I have to think about it. Are you sure about Big Viv and Deena?"

"As sure as I can be. Don't worry, I can handle Big Viv."

"I'm not so sure about that. Because if Big Viv has her way, by this time next week you're going to be a married man."

"Please say you'll come," Sebastian pleaded. "I need you to come."

Dom sighed. "Let me give it some thought. I'll get back to you."

And then, he left the apartment.

———

Just when Dominick didn't think this situation could get any crazier, it did.

The first thing he did once he left Sebastian's apartment was call Lolly. Before she could even say hello, he began to fill her in.

"What do I do?" he asked when he was finished and he finally allowed her to talk.

"Don't you want to spend time with him?"

"Yes, but I don't want to pretend."

"Would it help if I tagged along?"

"To Las Vegas?"

"Yep. Vivi called the other day and asked me if I would be a bridesmaid. I guess she's scrambling to find bodies. Since this whole thing is a sham, what does it matter? I said sure. So, now you have to come. Two of your very favorite people are going to be in Las Vegas. You can't stay behind and miss out on all the fun."

"I don't know if fun is the right word. More like disaster."

"Why are you being so stubborn?"

"Stubborn? *I'm* being stubborn," Dominick screeched. "Explain, please."

"It's a free trip to Las Vegas."

"The airplane ride is free," Dominick pointed out. "I would still have to pay for a hotel room."

"We'll share. It'll cost less."

"It's not about the cost of the room."

Lolly sounded exasperated. "What are you so afraid of? You like this guy, right?"

"I more than like him," Dominick slowly admitted. "I'm falling in love with him."

"And that's bad?"

"What happens if this all falls apart?" Dominick asked. "What happens if he goes through with the wedding to Vivi? And what if he decides to stay with her and raise the baby?"

"You really don't think that's going to happen, do you?"

"I don't know. Who would have thought I'd be dealing with all this? I'm supposed to be planning weddings, not planning my own love life. Falling in love is supposed to be fun and spontaneous. It shouldn't be this complicated."

"I get that you're afraid. I'm always that way too at the beginning of a new relationship. And I will admit you and Sebastian have had a rocky start. But you have to take a deep breath and dive in. Either it will lead to something wonderful or it won't. But you'll never know unless you try."

"But this whole situation is so complicated and messy."

"Isn't that what life is? Otherwise, it would be boring. Come on!" Lolly urged. "Tell him you're going. We'll have a great time."

"Promise?"

"Promise."

Dominick didn't want to fight with Lolly anymore. And he didn't want to fight with Sebastian. He just wanted to be with him, put this whole mess behind them, and look forward to the future. If going to Las Vegas was a step in the right direction, if it meant that eventually he and Sebastian could be together, then he had to take that chance.

"I don't know why I'm agreeing to this. I can already smell trouble brewing. But okay, count me in. We're going to Las Vegas."

CHAPTER
TWENTY-EIGHT

"Ever have sex on a plane?"

Dominick stopped buckling his seatbelt and looked at Liam like he had two heads. "Excuse me?"

"You know, the Mile High Club. I've done it four times in a plane," Liam stated matter-of-factly. "Twice with a flight steward, once with a boyfriend, and another time with a guy I met on Grindr seconds before the plane took off."

"If that was an invitation, thanks, but no thanks."

"Uh, I don't think I asked you, did I?" Liam pointed out.

Dominick realized Liam was right. He was just so used to him always hitting on him that he had just assumed.

"Of course, if you wanted to, I'm happy to oblige," Liam offered. "You know, just to keep Nico off balance."

Dominick lowered his voice, not wanting to be overheard. "If there's anyone I'm going to have sex with on a plane, it's Sebastian, not you."

"Obviously. But there's a first time for everything."

Dominick couldn't help himself. He burst out laughing. "You're too much. I've never met anyone as horny as you. You know this isn't real, right? We're not dating. We're pretending."

Liam put a hand on Dominick's knee and gave it a gentle squeeze. "I know, but Nico doesn't. We have to make it look real for him, don't we?" Liam raised his eyebrows suggestively. "Imagine if he went to use the bathroom and we accidentally forgot to lock the door and he found us?"

"That's *not* going to happen," Dominick firmly stated, removing Liam's hand and placing it back in his lap.

Liam shrugged. "I'm just saying. If you and Sebastian want to throw him off the trail, you've got to mislead him. And who better to mislead him with than me?"

"We'll mislead him another way. With our clothes on. Besides, I'm not into open relationships. When I'm with a guy, he's the only guy for me."

"Whatever works for you." Liam gave the passing flight steward a flirty smile.

Dominick jabbed Liam in the side with his elbow. "That goes for you, too! At least for this weekend. No cruising. No Grindr. No hook-up apps. No escorts. You only have eyes for me, got it?"

Liam rubbed his side, giving Dominick a cross look. "But you're not planning to sleep with me! What am I supposed to do all weekend?"

"Gamble? See a show? Go to an all-you-can-eat buffet?"

Sebastian, sitting behind them, stuck his head between their seats. "What are you two whispering about?"

Dominick removed a magazine from the pouch in the seat in front of him and started casually flipping through it. "Liam was telling me how much fun it is to have sex on a plane."

"What?"

"Sex. On a plane," Dominick repeated.

"I heard you the first time." His eyes lit up. "Sounds like fun. What do you say, Dom?"

Dominick abandoned his magazine, turning around in his seat. "Are you out of your mind?"

Sebastian seemed to give it some thought before answering. "I don't think so."

"No." Dominick's voice was firm. "N-O. It's too risky."

"But that's what will make it so much more fun," Sebastian argued. "Come on. You know you want to."

"Do it! Do it! Do it!" Liam began softly chanting.

"No," Dominick repeated, feeling his resolve start to melt. He was determined to remain strong. "We can't."

Sebastian locked eyes with Dominick and then gazed down at his crotch. "I'm up for it if you are."

Dominick bit his lower lip, beginning to become aroused. Sex on a plane with Sebastian. Not only would there be the risk of getting caught, but the chance of being caught by Nico would probably add an extra thrill to the experience. Dominick imagined the two of them together in such a tight, cramped space. Sebastian pressed against a wall, pants down, lubed and ready for Dominick's entry. They'd have to be very quiet. They couldn't risk getting caught. He'd have to cover Sebastian's mouth with his hand to muffle his screams. Because when Sebastian came, he loved to be loud. Or perhaps they'd use a gag, with Sebastian's hands tied behind his back. They could indulge in a little bit of role play. Dominick could be the bounty hunter taking a resistant Sebastian into custody. He'd have to be trussed up to make sure he didn't pull any fast moves, powerless against whatever Dominick had to do to keep him in line.

Or perhaps Sebastian would have to fall to his knees and show Dominick how far he'd be willing to go for his freedom. Yes, that tiny bathroom could be a nice little cell where they could get into all sorts of naughty things. Maybe Sebastian would turn the tables and Dominick would be at his mercy, forced to bend over as Sebastian gave him the cock he'd been eyeing since they first met. And if they were discovered by a male flight attendant, well, who's to say he wouldn't want to join in the fun and be the middle in a Dominick and Sebastian sandwich? He could just see the two of them grinding away with a cute twink between them, kissing roughly as they became members of the Mile High Club.

But would it be worth it in the end? If they got caught—by anyone—it would be game over. Everything would implode, explode, and shatter into pieces. Yes, it would get Sebastian out of his engagement to Vivi, but it might also ruin his friendship with her. He didn't think it was the way Sebastian wanted to untangle himself from his upcoming wedding. And there would still be Big Viv to deal with. Why did he feel like he was in a movie trying to detonate a bomb and he had to choose between cutting a red or blue wire?

"As tempting as the offer is, let's play it safe and save the sex games for another time," he firmly stated.

"Spoilsport," Sebastian grumbled under his breath as he leaned back in his seat, waiting for the plane to take off.

———

"That is one fine looking man," Lolly told Vivi as they walked onto the plane and found their seats. "I can see why you can't take your eyes off him."

"My eyes aren't on him," Vivi said as she stored her Louis Vuitton carry-all in an overhead compartment before taking the window seat and buckling up. At the front of the plane, she could see Nico taking the seat behind his aunt.

Lolly rolled her eyes. "Don't bullshit me. You haven't taken your eyes off him since he arrived at the airport. Who is he? Granted, the guy gives off hardcore sex vibes and he's got a fantastic ass that I'd love to get my hands on, but why are you drooling over him when you have Sebastian? He ain't too shabby."

"It's a long story."

Lolly reached for a flute of champagne from a passing flight attendant. "We're going to be in the air for five and a half hours. I've got all the time in the world."

Vivi gave a deep sigh. Why not? She couldn't confide in any of her other bridesmaids, which wound up being Foxy's three daughters, also coming to Las Vegas, because they would blab whatever she told them to Foxy and then Foxy would blab it all to Big Viv. Maybe talking with someone who was an outsider and not part of the world she grew up in would help.

"As hard as this is to believe, this all started in 1977, the year *Saturday Night Fever* came out. My mother and Deena DiGregorio were best friends. Until they weren't..."

———

Nico couldn't keep his eyes off Vivi. She looked so beautiful, giving off casual glam in a pair of cut-off jeans and a black bustier top covered with an oversized khaki utility jacket to ward off the plane's air conditioning.

Yet, she was blatantly ignoring him. At the airport while they waited to board the plane, whenever he tried to make eye contact with her, she either pretended she didn't see him or looked the other way. When he said hello, she just stared at him from behind her sunglasses, not saying a word, before turning away.

She was cold. Ice cold. That had to mean something, right? That she still cared. Otherwise, why would she be treating him this way? Why not just rip into him again? Was she afraid of what she might do or say? So instead, she said nothing?

He still hadn't figured out a way to win her back, but he was going to. He didn't know how. He didn't know when. But he did know that Sebastian and Dom were going to be the key to whatever plan he came up with. Not for one second did he believe those two weren't involved. Call it his own version of gaydar. He just had to be patient, bide his time and then he'd have the proof he needed to bring this engagement to an end.

Sebastian drained another glass of champagne. Was it his second or third? He couldn't remember. He didn't usually drink. But if anyone had a reason, it was him, wasn't it?

What had he been thinking suggesting to Dom that they have sex on the plane? It was crazy. It had to be the pressure of the whole ridiculous situation.

First, he could feel Nico's eyes on him. Ever since they'd arrived at the airport, he'd felt Nico's eyes following his every move. Sebastian knew he needed to be extra careful whenever he was around Dom. All it would take was one mistake and Nico would go running back to Brooklyn and Big Viv, exposing everything.

Then, there was Liam and Dom. He tried to keep his eyes off them, but it was hard. He hated to admit it, but he was jealous. He wanted to be the one sitting close to Dom, whispering in his ear, laughing with him. Even though Liam was a horndog—a very persuasive horndog— Sebastian knew Liam would never sleep with a man Sebastian had feelings for. While sex was no different than going for a jog or a bike ride for Liam, it wasn't true for Sebastian. If he was going to get naked with a man, it was because he had feelings for him. And he had feelings for Dom. Deep ones that kept growing. He was falling in love with Dom. No, he was wrong. It was more than that. He was already in love with Dom, and he wanted to be with him. All the time, not just when they could find time to sneak off and be together.

Finally, there was the wedding. A date had been set. Next Saturday, he and Vivi would be married. He couldn't even wrap his head around the thought. Was it no wonder he was drinking glass after glass of champagne? His life was a mess.

Thank God his family wasn't around for any of this. His parents were on a six-month cruise in Europe, far, far away from Brooklyn, and his two older brothers lived across the country. So, they were all out of the loop. He didn't know how he would explain it to them. He couldn't even explain it to himself.

After flagging down a passing flight steward for a refill, Sebastian decided to distract himself. And who better to distract himself with than Deena DiGregorio? Plus, it might be a chance to learn more about the feud, only from Deena's point of view. It would be interesting to get her take on it and see how it compared to Big Viv's version.

The seat next to hers was empty, so he slid into

it. "Deena." He clinked his champagne glass against hers. "Thank you again for the trip to Las Vegas."

She waved a hand. "Think nothing of it. The owner of the casino is very close to me."

Sebastian wondered how close, if Deena was allowed to use the casino's private jet. He had to admit she did still ooze sex appeal. Maybe she and the casino owner had something going on. "When you were growing up in Brooklyn in the seventies, did you ever think you'd be where you are today?"

Deena shrugged. "I had big dreams. Who doesn't? You just have to make them come true. You need drive and determination. I had that."

"Ever think of writing a book?"

Deena laughed. "Who would want to read a book about me?"

"You're a celebrity. Celebrities write their memoirs all the time. You have lots of fans. I'm sure they'd be interested in your story. A girl from Brooklyn goes out to Hollywood and makes it big."

"I might have gone out to Hollywood, but I never forgot where I came from. I'm still a Brooklyn girl at heart."

"That's right. You always come back to the old neighborhood. You and Vivi's mother were best friends back then."

"We were," Deena said, all the warmth evaporating from her voice.

"But you're not anymore. What went wrong?"

"Why are you asking *me* that question?" Deena looked offended.

Sebastian scrambled to do damage control, but he'd had too much champagne. "I just assumed—"

Deena cut him off. "Assumed what? That it was all *my* fault? Sure, you work for that woman, so she's probably brainwashed you. If anyone is to blame for our friendship ending, it's Big Viv, not me! She's the one who turned her back on me. I tried to stay in touch with her after I left, but she ignored me. For years."

Through the fog of champagne, Sebastian latched onto the words Deena had just said.

I tried to stay in touch with her after I left but she ignored me. For years!

Something wasn't adding up. Big Viv thought Deena had cut off all ties to her, and Deena thought Big Viv had done the same.

Which was it?

Before Sebastian could ask another question, Deena pulled out a sleep mask. "If you don't mind, I'm going to catch a little beauty sleep. I want to look fresh when we arrive in Las Vegas. Maybe you want to take a nap, too, so you've got energy for later tonight. We want this to be a weekend neither you or Vivi ever forgets. Nico's got lots of plans for you."

I'll bet, Sebastian thought. The only question was what kind?

CHAPTER
TWENTY-NINE

What am I doing in Las Vegas? Vivi wondered as she tipped the bellboy who had carried her bags into her room. Why had she even agreed to this trip? She had thought she could leave Brooklyn and her mother and all the wedding planning behind and have a good time.

Wrong.

She wasn't having a good time. She was miserable. She wanted to be home on her couch, wearing her pajamas, watching Netflix while eating Funyuns and ice cream.

This fake engagement had to come to an end. Soon. Maybe being away from Brooklyn would give her some clarity.

It had helped talking with Lolly, who admitted

she had known most of the story since she was Dom's best friend and he had filled her in, but it still didn't solve her problem. She was engaged to marry a man she wasn't in love with. Who wasn't the father of her baby. Vivi sighed. She had tried to avoid staring at Nico on the plane, but it had been hard. Her eyes automatically kept going to him. More than once, he had caught her staring at him. Each time, he'd given her a smile and each time she'd given him a glare before tearing her eyes away.

She stared at herself in the full-length mirror across the room. The cut-off jeans she wore were too tight. She didn't think she'd be wearing them after tonight. Definitely not until after the baby arrived. The baby. Vivi still couldn't wrap her head around the fact that in nine months she was going to be a mother. She was going to have a little boy or girl. Nico's baby. She sighed again.

They might never be a couple, but he would be a wonderful father. She didn't doubt that. Despite her anger at him, Nico could be gentle, kind, and loving. Hadn't she always seen that side of him? Wasn't that why she had fallen in love with him?

She knew she had to tell him the truth. The only question was when?

———

The elevator was empty when Nico stepped into it. He hoped it would be an express and shoot straight down to the lobby.

It didn't. Instead, it stopped on the next floor, where Vivi was waiting. She had changed outfits and was looking gorgeous in a sleeveless embroidered top with a pink heart, black mini-skirt, and slingback pumps.

At the sight of him, her eyes widened before narrowing into angry slits. Nico gave her a smile. The same kind of smile a wolf might give to the chickens in a henhouse if they could.

"Aren't you getting tired of glaring at me?" he asked.

She turned her head away from him. "I'll wait for the next elevator."

"You sure? I waited ten minutes for this one. Who knows how long the next one will be? Everyone else is probably in the lobby. You don't want to keep them waiting, do you?"

The elevator dinged and the doors began to close. Nico stuck his arm out, and the doors sprung back. "Stop being so stubborn."

Vivi sighed and stepped into the car, making sure she kept enough distance between herself and him.

"I don't bite," he said. "Although, there used to be a time when you liked when I did."

"I used to like a lot of things about you, but not anymore," Vivi said, her tone frosty.

"When are you going to stop being mad at me?"

"I'm not mad," Vivi said. She gave him a forced smile. "See? Truce. Let's just enjoy our weekend."

He leaned against the wall of the elevator. "Explain to me why you and your future husband aren't sharing a room together."

"Excuse me?"

"You're on one floor and Sebastian is on another."

"You're spying on us?" Vivi asked, her voice filled with outrage.

"Call me observant. You had a bellboy take you to one elevator bank while Sebastian was taken to another."

"Not that it's any of your business where we sleep, but it's our last weekend of freedom. Why not have one last hurrah as a single person?"

"What happens in Vegas stays in Vegas?"

"Something like that."

"He's got the room next to your wedding planner."

"You also observed that, did you?"

"Our rooms are on the same floor," Nico stated. "They seem pretty chummy."

"Why wouldn't they be? Dom is planning our wedding and Sebastian is a perfectionist. I'm sure he's breathing down Dom's neck, wanting to make sure every last detail is perfect."

"He's breathing down something but it's not his neck," Nico muttered.

"What did you say?" Vivi demanded.

Nico ignored the question. "I wonder if their rooms have adjoining doors. You know, so you can sneak into one room from the other without going out into the hallway."

"Sneak? Why would you use that word? There's nothing sneaky about Sebastian and Dom."

"Are you sure?"

Vivi closed the distance between them, getting up close in his face. "What are you trying to say?"

"I think you know."

"I think you don't know," Vivi said. "Dom is dating Liam, Sebastian's roommate."

"His gay roommate."

"Yes, his gay roommate. Dom wouldn't be dating Liam if he wasn't gay."

"Sebastian has a lot of gay people in his life. Gay roommate. Gay wedding planner."

"What's your point?"

"Sebastian is gay. You know it, and I know it. He's been gay going all the way back to our high school days. What I don't understand is why you're marrying him. Why you're pretending he's the father of your baby when you know I'm the one who loves you."

"No, I don't," Vivi whispered. "I don't know that."

Nico hit the emergency button of the elevator, causing it to stop abruptly. He pulled Vivi into his arms and kissed her. A long, slow, lingering kiss that he hoped would convey everything he had ever felt for her.

"Sebastian has never kissed you like this, has he?" he whispered, pulling away.

Instead of melting in his arms, instead of returning his kiss, Vivi licked her lips and stepped away from Nico. "What Sebastian and I have is different from what you and I had."

"Your lipstick is smudged. You might want to do

something about that. Or maybe not. I can kiss it all off."

"Don't you dare," Vivi warned.

Nico raised an eyebrow. "You know I love a dare."

But before he could pull Vivi back into his arms, she hit the emergency button and the elevator started moving again. Then, she reached into her purse, pulled out a compact and lipstick, and slowly repainted her lips.

"Vivi, I love you." He didn't know what else to say. How could he get through to her? "You know I do." Nico moved to take her in his arms again, but Vivi held up a hand.

"Stop!"

"Why won't you admit the truth?"

"There's nothing to admit."

"Yes, there is."

The elevator stopped and the doors opened. Vivi recapped her lipstick and returned it to her purse. Then, she walked out into the lobby, but not before turning to sadly look at Nico over her shoulder. "No, there really isn't."

———

Okay, that was a lie, Vivi admitted to herself. A big fat lie. But she couldn't deal with Nico right now.

"What just happened in that elevator?" Lolly asked, rushing to her side, Foxy's eager daughters following behind. They could all sense *something* had happened between Vivi and Nico, but they weren't sure what.

Neither was Vivi. "I'll fill you in later. Right now, we have Deena's show to get to."

Their expectations weren't high, but surprisingly, Deena had a good voice. Yes, the show gave off a throwback vibe from the days when Cher, Tina Turner, and Lola Falana used to perform on the Vegas strip. But Deena's show, with her Bob Mackie-inspired costumes and a medley of hits from the 70s, including a number of songs from *Saturday Night Fever*—of course, no surprise—was entertaining and perfect for the older crowd who wanted to be in bed by nine.

After the show, Foxy's daughters decided to do a little gambling while Nico told them he had a special guys-only evening planned for Sebastian, Liam, and Dom. There was no mistaking the look of panic in Sebastian's eyes, but what could she do? He would need to have his guard up. Hopefully, he wouldn't drink too much. Because if he did, Vivi knew from past experience that his inhibitions would come down and he often did things that were wild and crazy. What might he say or do if she wasn't around to control his drinking?

Vivi closed her eyes. She didn't want to think about it.

Or did she? If Sebastian happened to slip up and the truth came out, the wedding would probably be off. Was that what she wanted?

Deep down, yes. But how would she spin this to her mother? The last thing she wanted to do was make a fool out of her. But they were already in so deep. It would be better to go through with the wedding and then end it. They'd come up with an excuse about why they were divorcing. One that would protect her dignity. Then, Vivi would deal with the baby situation.

"Be good," she mouthed to Sebastian before he was dragged away by Nico and the other guys.

"I don't know about you, but I'm starving!" Lolly exclaimed. "You up for some food? I'm craving a steak."

"With a baked potato loaded with butter and sour cream?" Vivi asked.

"Don't forget the bacon bits, too," Lolly added.

They were walking through the hotel lobby on the way to the restaurant when Vivi stopped in her tracks.

"What's wrong?" Lolly asked. "You look like you've just seen a ghost."

It wasn't a ghost. More like an enemy.

Candy Carlson was walking straight toward her with her girl posse. What was she doing in Las Vegas?

Unless Nico had told her he was going to be here and invited her to come?

No. Nico wouldn't do something like that. He wouldn't be so cruel.

That meant Candy had found out about the trip to Vegas and chased after him. She probably planned on telling Vivi that Nico was her man and to back off. Well, Vivi had had enough. If Candy wanted Nico, she could have him.

But not before getting a piece of her mind.

Realistically, she knew she had no beef with Candy. Vivi and Nico weren't together. He could date whoever he wanted. But Nico would always belong to her. He was her first boyfriend. Her first kiss. Her first everything.

And she'd thrown him away.

She didn't hate Candy. She was jealous of her. She had Nico and Vivi didn't. And that made her want to scratch Candy's eyes out and tear out every hair on her head. She hated to admit it, but Candy looked good. Better than in her videos. Perfect red hair in a pixie cut. Perfect make-up to bring out her huge brown eyes. A killer body dressed head to toe in Prada. Lots of expensive bling around her neck and fingers. All real gold, of course. And the shoes! Christian Louboutin platform heels from his newest collection. They were sold out everywhere.

As the distance closed between them, Candy stopped in her tracks. At the sight of Vivi, she squealed and a huge smile broke out across her face. "I know you!"

"You do, huh?" Vivi grunted, using her Brooklyn tough girl voice.

Candy nodded. "You're Nico's sweetheart!"

Vivi blinked, not sure if she'd heard her correctly. "I am?"

Candy laughed. "Well, it isn't me, that's for sure. That man has been in love with you for I don't know how long. It's one of the reasons things never worked out between us. He just couldn't get over you. He's never stopped loving you."

"He hasn't?" a confused Vivi asked. What was going on? Nothing that Candy was saying made any sense.

"Nope. And who wants to compete with a woman who already owns another man's heart?" Candy continued. She looked to her posse and Lolly. "Am I right?" All the ladies murmured their agreement.

"But aren't you and Nico together?"

"We were, but now we're just friends. With no benefits, I swear! He's my bodyguard."

"That's what he told me."

"And you didn't believe him?'

"The pictures in the newspapers," Vivi began. "All the stuff online..."

Candy waved a hand. "Don't believe any of the crap you read in the papers or on the Net. My publicists are out of control. They make it all up. They're obsessed with my social media numbers and will do or say anything to get me to start trending."

"He was telling me the truth," Vivi whispered.

"Of course he was! Nico is one of the most honest, straight forward guys I know. He would never lie. Don't let him get away," Candy advised. "If you do, you'll regret it. And you'll never get that fabulous engagement ring!"

"What engagement ring?"

"The one he bought for you."

"Nico bought me an engagement ring? When?"

Candy gave it some thought. "A couple of years ago? I found it in his sock drawer when I was putting away some laundry. At first, I thought it was for me. You should have seen the way I threw my arms around him, jumping and squealing and hugging and kissing him. But the entire time, he was dead silent. When I finally calmed down, he explained that the ring wasn't for me. That he had bought it for someone else. For you."

"If he bought it for me, then why didn't he ever give it to me?"

Candy shrugged. "You'd have to ask him. I couldn't really get an answer out of him. He just said he bought it for you."

"What's it look like?" Vivi couldn't help herself.

"Gorgeous! Yellow pear-shaped diamond with a gold band. The sort of rock Richard Burton would have given Elizabeth Taylor. Bling, bling, bling! Honey, put that man out of his misery." Candy gave her a hug. "I don't know what he did to you all those years ago, but don't you think it's time you forgave him?"

"He didn't do anything," whispered Vivi as she

watched Candy walk away. "All he ever did was love me."

———

Sebastian was buzzed. He'd lost count of how many shots he'd had during Deena's show. The tequila had just kept pouring, and he had kept tossing them back. He knew it wasn't such a bright idea to keep drinking, but he was in Las Vegas. Brooklyn was far, far away. He could forget about everything and have a good time.

And where better to have a good time than a gay male strip club, right? Wrong.

"What are we doing here again?" Sebastian asked Nico, confusion in his voice.

"Why should we have all the fun, watching the ladies take it off tomorrow night at your bachelor party?" Nico whispered to Sebastian. "I thought Liam and Dominick would enjoy this. It'll give them something to think about when the ladies are draped all over them."

The last place Sebastian wanted to be was in a gay male strip club! Everywhere he looked, he was confronted by male perfection. Chiseled chests, firm pecs, tight abs, and even tighter asses. Handsome faces with kissable lips. Bulges that demanded to be noticed. He didn't know where to look first. He felt like a kid in a candy store.

And that was the problem. He shouldn't be in this candy store. Not if he wanted to keep Nico believing he was straight. As hard as he tried, he couldn't keep his eyes off all the hot male flesh on display.

"What's the matter, Bash?" Nico asked. "Uncomfortable?"

"Why would I be uncomfortable?"

Nico shrugged. "I dunno. You look like you're about to break out in a sweat. Too hot in here for you?"

"I'm fine." Sebastian snagged them a corner table and waved over a delectable waiter wearing denim booty shorts and nothing else.

"What can I get you, gentlemen?" he asked, putting paper coasters down on the table.

"Your phone number?" Liam asked.

The waiter locked eyes with him and offered a smile.

"Sorry, he's taken," Dom told the waiter, wrapping a possessive arm through Liam's. "He's an outrageous flirt. All talk and no action. Isn't that right, sweetie?"

Liam didn't immediately answer until Sebastian kicked him under the table.

"Ouch!" He glared at his roommate before turning back to the waiter. "I'm taken."

"Too bad," the waiter said. "What will you all have?"

After their drinks were delivered, the show began. And what a show it was. A non-stop parade of one hot guy after another, taking it all off until there was nothing left to the imagination. Liam and Dom were mesmerized and kept waving dollar bills in the air, placing them in the thongs of their appreciative recipients.

Nico held out a wad of singles to Sebastian. "Wanna give it a try?"

Sebastian drained his orange juice and vodka. "I'll pass."

Nico shrugged, waving a dollar bill high above his head. When a blonde stripper resembling Zac Efron came over, Nico asked, "Do you give lap dances?"

"That can be arranged. For a price."

Nico reached into his wallet and pulled out some hundred dollar bills. "How much?"

The stripper removed three of the bills. "Follow me."

"Oh, the dance isn't for me." Nico pointed to Sebastian. "It's for him. The groom."

The stripper's face lit up. "Congratulations. Is he your future husband?"

"No!" Sebastian and Nico answered at the same time, both sounding horrified.

"Thanks, but no thanks," Sebastian told the dancer.

"Well, since Nico has already paid for the dance, I'm happy to take it," Liam told the dancer and followed him to a private room.

"That was supposed to be your lap dance," Nico told Sebastian.

"Why would I want a lap dance from a male stripper?"

Nico shrugged. "Practice for tomorrow night? You've probably never had a lap dance, have you? I thought if I got you one tonight, you'd know what to expect."

"Uh huh," Sebastian answered. "Very thoughtful of you." *You probably have a hidden camera in that room and wanted to catch me with a boner as Zac grinded his crotch against mine.*

"I try to be," Nico said. "We can get another stripper if you want. Pick a guy. Any guy."

The only guy I want is Dom. But I can't have him

because of you. Sebastian waved his empty glass at their passing waiter and ordered a refill. "I'll skip the lap dance. Thanks."

Nico shrugged. "Okay. How about you, Dom? Want a lap dance? My treat."

Dom gazed around at the strippers, nibbling on a finger. "Decisions, decisions. They're all so tasty. It's hard to make up my mind."

"If you want two, pick two." Nico clapped Sebastian on the back. "It's not every day my friend here gets married. I want to give him a bachelor weekend he'll never forget."

Does Nico think I'm stupid? Sebastian wondered, wanting to shake him off. Obviously, he was trying to trip him up by bringing him to this place. Did he think he didn't have any self-control? It would take more than a hot body for him to crack. Unless, of course, that hot body was Dom's. And speaking of Dom, he wasn't really going to take Nico up on his offer, was he? Before Dom could say anything, Liam returned to their table with a satisfied smile on his face.

"Have a good time?" Nico asked.

"No complaints."

Nico turned to Sebastian. "See?"

Liam grabbed Nico by the hand. "Come dance with me."

Nico shrugged at Sebastian and Dom, took a sip of his beer, and followed Liam out onto the dance floor. Much to Sebastian's surprise, Nico seemed fine with all the dirty dancing moves Liam was using, grinding against him.

"Were you really going to have a lap dance?" Sebastian asked Dom.

"Why not? It would have been fun, don't you think?"

"For you, yes. For me, no."

"Jealous much?"

"Always. I hate the idea of you being with another guy." Sebastian finished his drink. "I have an idea."

"What?"

"Let's sneak out."

"Sneak out?"

"Liam is keeping Nico busy. We can go off on our own. Maybe make our own fun."

"Our own fun," Dom repeated. "Are you sure? What if we get caught?"

"Either we'll get caught or we won't. If we don't, think of all the fun we get to have. Besides, I have a little insurance policy."

"You do?"

"Right before we left the hotel, Liam told me he'd keep Nico preoccupied so we could have some alone time. You ready to cash in on that policy?"

Dom's eyes lit up and he threw back the last of his martini. "Let's go."

———

"I thought you were starving," Lolly said as she pointed at Vivi's untouched baked potato. "Remember, you're eating for two."

After running into Candy, Vivi and Lolly had found a steakhouse and ordered dinner. But Vivi was no longer hungry. All she could think about was Nico.

"Nico loves me," she told Lolly. "He loves me, and he wants to marry me."

Lolly cut into her petite filet and took a bite. "You never knew that and you've been involved with this guy for how many years? Since you were fifteen, right?"

"Yes, but we were never really together, if that makes sense. We were always breaking up."

Lolly pointed her fork at Vivi. "Because of your

mother and his aunt. So, what's different this time around?"

Vivi pointed a finger at her belly. "This is what's different."

Lolly put down her cutlery, giving Vivi her full attention. "Then why didn't you say so from the beginning? Why pretend Sebastian was the father? Why go through with this fake engagement?"

"I don't know why!" Vivi wailed. "At first, I panicked. I knew my mother would go through the roof if I told her Nico was the father, and I wanted to avoid that. Then, I thought Nico was involved with Candy, and that hurt me. It hurt me more than I wanted to admit, so I wanted to hurt him back."

Lolly went back to cutting her meat. "Well, now you know the truth. He loves you. You can find him and tell him you love him, too. You can be with him, and Sebastian can be with Dom."

Vivi desperately wanted to believe Lolly's words. Could it really be that easy? For so long, she had been unsure of Nico's love for her. Neither one of them had ever had the strength to stand up for themselves. They had always caved to what her mother and Deena had wanted. Because that was how they were raised. That was the Italian way.

Always. Do what your parents told you to do. Even if they were wrong.

But Nico loved her. He wanted to be with her. He wanted to marry her, even without knowing about the baby. The ring he bought proved it. He had bought it years ago, waiting for the right time to give it to her. Maybe now was finally that time. Because as long as she had Nico's love, as long as she had him by her side, then together they could handle her mother and Deena. For all these years, her life had been in limbo. She had thought she would meet someone else and fall in love, someone her mother liked and approved of and didn't hate because of who his aunt was.

But it had always been Nico. They had lost too many years already. They weren't going to lose anymore.

———

They were gone.

Nico's eyes frantically searched the strip club, but he didn't see Sebastian or Dom anywhere. How the hell had that happened?

"Where did they go?" he asked as Liam joined him back at their table.

"Who?"

"Who do you think? Sebastian and Dom!"

Liam shrugged. "I don't know." He moved closer to Nico. "But now that we're alone…" Liam wrapped his arms around Nico, giving him a tight hug. "Why don't we get to know each other a little bit better?"

Was this guy seriously putting the moves on him? Dancing was one thing, but not this.

` "I'm usually not into straight guys, but what can I say?" Liam whispered into Nico's ear. "You're so hot! Like a cross between Sylvester Stallone and John Travolta circa 1975."

Nico unwound himself from Liam's octopus embrace and stepped away. "Thanks, but no thanks, Handsy McGee. I play for the other team."

"Haven't you ever been curious? Wondered what it's like to play with the same equipment?"

"I have played with my own equipment when I was a horny teenager and couldn't get any pussy. Now, I can, so those days are over."

Liam wrinkled his nose. "Don't mention the P word to me, please." He gazed around the strip club. "Where's our waiter? I'm thirsty."

Nico had a feeling Liam was thirsty for more than just a drink. "I thought you were dating Dom."

"Do you see him around?"

"I guess he snuck off with Sebastian. Any idea why that might be?"

Liam shrugged. "I have no idea."

"Maybe it's because Dom is more into Sebastian than you?"

The sudden look of panic on Liam's face only confirmed what Nico had been thinking all along. He threw a wad of cash on the table to cover their bill and left the strip club. Sebastian and Dom couldn't have gone far. He didn't have any proof, but something was going on between the two of them. He was going to find out what.

———

"We're finally alone," Sebastian said as he and Dom walked down the Vegas strip hand in hand.

Maybe walking wasn't the right word. Staggering? Wobbling?

Sebastian knew if he was asked to walk a straight line, he would probably fail. Who could blame him for having had so much to drink? At least they'd escaped the strip club. Sebastian didn't know how much longer he could have resisted all that temptation. Zac had been mighty tempting, but not as tempting as Dom. No one was as tempting as Dom.

"Why does it feel so strange being alone with you?" Dom asked.

"Because we never are. We'll have to get used to it."

"Will we?" Dom asked. He stopped walking and faced Sebastian. "Will we ever be together?"

Sebastian placed a hand against Dom's cheek, caressing it softly. "Of course we will. Don't give up faith." Maybe it was because of the liquor or the temporary sense of freedom, but Sebastian pulled Dom close and gave him a kiss. "We just have to be a little more patient."

"I don't know. You're getting married next weekend. You're on a runaway train and it's picking up speed. At some point, you're not going to be able to jump off."

"Too bad I wasn't already married when Vivi said I was her baby's father. That would have put an end to this nightmare before it even got started."

Dom's eyes widened. "That's it!" he exclaimed. "Sebastian, that's it!"

"What's it?"

Dom practically shook him. "Don't you see? If

you were already married, you wouldn't be able to marry Vivi."

"Already married?" Sebastian asked. "But who would I be married to?"

"Me!" Dom exclaimed.

It took a moment for the words to sink into Sebastian's booze-soaked mind. At first, he thought Dom was kidding. After one look in his eyes, he realized he wasn't. He was serious.

Maybe it was all the tequila and vodka he'd had. Or maybe it was the look of love in Dom's eyes. But his words made sense. Perfect sense. The solution he'd been searching for was right in front of him if he was willing to take it.

Sebastian didn't even have to think about it. He whispered the three-letter word. "Yes." Then again. "Yes." Then again, only louder. Much louder. "Yes! I'll marry you."

———

Once Sebastian agreed, the next step was finding someplace to get married. In Las Vegas, that wasn't a problem. There were wedding chapels everywhere.

"Let's avoid anything kitschy," Dom said. "Let's find a place that's traditional."

"No Elvis impersonator?"

"Absolutely not!"

They went with a simple, straightforward ceremony with an officiant dressed in a suit and his wife playing background music on an electric organ.

"Is this how you always imagined your wedding day?" Sebastian asked as they waited to get started.

"Well, to be honest, I did want something lavish and over the top. A big wedding with all my family and friends."

Sebastian gazed around the sparsely decorated room. There were white crepe paper wedding bells taped to the walls, some sagging silver balloons, and a banner that read, HAPPY WEDDING DAY! "I'm sorry I can't give you that."

"Why are you sorry? It's all just fancy window dressing. That's what I tell all my brides when they freak out about their wedding day not being perfect. When the day is over, it will all be gone except for the person they've married." Dom fixed the collar of Sebastian's shirt. "You're the most important part of this day. Nothing else matters. Just you. And when this wedding is over, you'll still be here, right by my side. As my husband. And that will be the best part of all." Dom gave Sebastian a quick peck on the lips. "Do you still have the rings?"

Before arriving at the chapel, they had stopped at the first jewelry store they could find and picked out two simple gold bands. Sebastian handed one to Dom.

"Don't lose it," he teased.

Dom formed a fist around the ring. "Never."

Seconds later, the ceremony began. When it was time, they slipped the rings on each other's fingers. And then, they heard those magic words. "I now pronounce you husband and husband. You may now kiss your groom."

Sebastian and Dom wasted no time making it official. They wrapped their arms around each other and brought their lips together. At first, the kiss was sweet and gentle. Then, it became a little heated, and more heated, as if the realization that they were husband and husband was fueling the feelings they had for each other. The kiss was fierce and hungry before they pulled away from each other with identical grins on their faces.

They were married. They were husbands. It was the most wonderful feeling. They kissed again and had confetti thrown at them and posed for wedding pictures they were told they could pick up the next day.

As they left the wedding chapel, they stopped to

look at the pictures of other recently married couples on display outside the front entrance. They all looked so happy. But they weren't as happy as Sebastian and Dom. No one could be as happy as they were.

"Now, it's time for the honeymoon," Sebastian whispered into his husband's ear.

"What are we waiting for?" Dom took Sebastian's hand in his and pulled him in the direction of their hotel. "To the honeymoon suite!"

CHAPTER
THIRTY

Something was wrong. Big Viv could feel it in her bones.

It didn't have to do with Vivi and Sebastian's trip to Las Vegas. She knew what that was—just another attempt of Deena's to get under her skin.

It was something else.

Ever since last Friday night during the book club at Foxy's, Big Viv had been mulling over Carla's words. She couldn't get them out of her mind. What had Carla done? It was driving her crazy enough that finally she decided to take some action, which was why she was on Carla's front porch, ringing her doorbell. When the door finally opened, Carla looked surprised to see her.

Big Viv held up a pastry box. "I thought I'd drop by with some sweets and we could have a little chat."

Carla eyed her suspiciously, keeping the door open slightly, as if at any moment she might slam it shut in Big Viv's face. "About what?"

Big Viv barreled past Carla and into the house. No way was she keeping her out. "The past."

She hadn't been inside Carla's house since the late 1970s and it still looked the same. Gold shag carpeting. Furniture covered in plastic. A big box TV instead of a flat screen. Black velvet drapes decorated with gold tassels. Crucifixes and photos of Mary and an assortment of saints hanging on the walls. From what she could see of the kitchen, it still had the same avocado-colored appliances. It was like time had been frozen.

"I happened to overhear something you said last week at Foxy's," Big Viv said, making herself comfortable on the couch while she opened the box of cookies she had brought. "I don't think it was something you would have said if Deena and I had been around."

Carla blushed. "I had a little too much to drink that night. I don't remember what I said."

"I'll refresh your memory. You said you had put

me and Deena in our places. What did you mean by that? I want to know."

Carla shrugged. "Why would I say something like that?"

Big Viv shrugged back. "I don't know. You said it, not me. I also noticed you sounded angry when you said the words. But also satisfied. Like you were proud of what you had done."

Carla slid into the armchair across from Big Viv, crinkling the plastic as she sat. "What could I have done?" She reached for a seven-layer cookie and bit into it. "I was the girl on the outside. The one no one wanted to make part of the group."

"That's not true," Big Viv said. "Deena and I always made you feel included. We tried our best, but you know how teenage girls can be. There's always got to be someone in charge, and she's the one who calls the shots."

"Is that an apology?" Carla laughed bitterly. "If it is, it's too little, too late."

"I'm not apologizing. I have nothing to apologize for. I was always a good friend to you. Deena, too."

Carla laughed again. "Yeah, right."

"She was!"

"That bitch always thought she was better than

the rest of us. Always making sure the guys noticed her. Always putting the moves on another girl's boyfriend."

"Deena might have been a flirt, but she never stole anyone's boyfriend. That wasn't her style."

"That's not what Patricia told me."

Now, they were getting somewhere. "What did Patricia tell you?"

"During senior year, Deena went after a guy Patricia was interested in. Mario Mastroni."

Big Viv rolled her eyes. "Patricia and Mario never dated! Patricia was always trying to get Mario's attention—or rather, into his pants. But he only had eyes for Deena. If anything, Patricia was the one going after another girl's guy."

"Deena knew Patricia wanted to date Mario. That's why she kept toying with him."

"That's not true."

"Mario wasn't the only guy she stole," Carla triumphantly stated.

Big Viv sighed. "Who else did she steal?"

"Anthony."

"Anthony?" The name didn't ring any bells with Big Viv. "Who was Anthony?"

"The guy who was supposed to take me to the senior prom."

"Who told you that?" Big Viv asked as an uneasy feeling started to spread through her. She was pretty sure she knew whose name Carla was going to say.

"Patricia."

Of course. Now, it was all starting to make sense. The last thing Big Viv wanted to do was hurt Carla, but it looked like there wasn't going to be any way to escape from the truth of what happened all those years ago in high school. The question was, how could she soften the blow? "Really? Well, Patricia lied."

"What do you mean?"Carla asked, her voice heavy with confusion. "Patricia told me."

Big Viv didn't know any other way to say it, so she went with the truth, placing a hand on Carla's shoulder. "You were catfished by Patricia."

"Catfished?" Carla shook off Big Viv's hand. "What does that mean?"

"She placed that ad," Big Viv gently explained. "She answered your letters. There was no Anthony to take you to the senior prom. He never existed. She wanted you to be waiting at home all night. She wanted to humiliate you. She was always a twisted bitch."

Carla stared at Big Viv. Just stared, until finally she found her voice. "How would you know that?"

Big Viv was silent for a second before admitting, "She told us."

"When?"

"At the prom."

"All of you?"

Big Viv nodded. "You can ask Foxy or Chunky. Deena, too. They'll tell you it's true."

Carla looked numb. "Patricia told me Deena had stolen him. That he had come to our high school one afternoon to surprise me and when Deena found out who he was, she went after him. She told him I was dating someone else and to forget all about me. Patricia said Deena told him he needed to teach me a lesson for dating another guy behind his back and he should stand me up the night of the senior prom."

"That's a lie!" Big Viv exclaimed, coming to Deena's defense. "If Deena did that, then why would she and I have come to your house after the prom to see if you were okay?"

"To gloat."

"Deena didn't come to gloat. She was worried about you. She felt bad about what had happened. We both did."

Carla threw the cookie she had been nibbling back in the box. "But not bad enough to say anything about it, huh? To warn me. To give me a head's up. Instead, Patricia let me make a fool of myself, telling all of you about this guy. Sharing his letters! Making me sit here alone all night."

"How could we warn you? We didn't know what Patricia had done until the night of the prom! By then, it was too late. How could we have stopped her? And even if we had known, you know what Patricia was like back then. The last thing anyone ever wanted was to get on her bad side."

"Better me than you. Is that what you're saying?"

Big Viv didn't answer. What could she say? Carla was right.

"Then, you both deserve what I did," Carla stated. "Not just Deena. Consider it payback."

"What did you do, Carla?" Big Viv asked again. "Tell me. I want to know."

"Do you?" Carla sank back into her chair, a smug smile on her face. "Are you sure? You might not like it."

Big Viv slowly nodded. How bad could it be? Especially if it was something Carla had done forty-five years ago.

"Okay, I'll tell you. Remember my job with the post office?"

"Yes."

"Your house was on my route. I delivered your mail every day." Carla paused as her pale lips turned up into a smirk. "Well, I was supposed to."

"Supposed to..." Big Viv repeated.

"Not every letter addressed to you made it into your mailbox."

"What are you talking about?" Big Viv snapped, losing patience. "Spit it out."

"I kept Deena's letters."

"What letters?"

Carla leaned forward, her eyes glistening with malice. "The letters she wrote to you from California."

Big Viv gasped. "Deena wrote to me?"

"Of course she did. Every week. You were her best friend. Why wouldn't she write? That is, until she got tired of sending you letters that went unanswered. I think she gave up after two years of no response."

"But all these years, I thought..."

"Yes, you thought Deena had turned her back on you. That she had ended your friendship. Well, newsflash. She didn't. You did that all by yourself."

"But why would you do something like that?" It

was all Big Viv could do not to lunge out of her chair and throttle Carla.

"Would you believe me if I said I was trying to protect you?"

"Protect me from who?"

"Deena! She was a bad influence. She would have had you follow after her to California. We couldn't let that happen. We knew what a bitch she was."

Big Viv was still trying to process what Carla had revealed, but her head was spinning.

"Do you realize what you've done? For forty-five years, I've been angry at Deena. I thought she had turned her back on our friendship. And she thought the same thing of me! How could she not when I never answered her letters? Deena was my best friend. We were like sisters."

Carla laughed bitterly. "If you were like sisters, why didn't you ever try to make amends with her? I'll tell you why. Because of your pride. Big Viv Confetta is always right and everyone else is always wrong. Well, it wasn't me that cost you forty-five years of friendship with Deena. You did that all by yourself."

Big Viv rose off the couch. She couldn't stand

being around Carla any longer. All she wanted to do was leave. "You're pathetic."

And then Big Viv remembered Carla's earlier words. She had said we. *We* couldn't let that happen. *We* knew what a bitch she was. "Who else knew about those letters?" she demanded. "Who knew you didn't deliver them?"

"It wasn't my idea not to deliver Deena's letters," Carla began. "I can't take credit for that. Someone else suggested it. At first, I didn't want to do it. I could have lost my job if anyone found out. So, I demanded to be paid, and I was. Very nicely, too."

"Who?" Big Viv demanded. "Who was paying you to not deliver Deena's letters?"

"Who do you think? Who else would have hated Deena as much as I did?"

"Patricia?"

"Patricia didn't have the money to pay me off for two years," Carla scoffed. "Guess again."

And then, Big Viv realized who it had been. Only one other person in her life would have had the money to pay off Carla. Only one other person in her life had hated Deena as much as Carla did. And somehow, the two of them had joined forces. But she didn't want to believe it. She couldn't. What kind of person could be so cruel and heartless? For a second, she thought she was going to be sick. She took a deep breath and fought back the nausea.

Carla nodded as she saw Big Viv connect the dots. "That's right," Carla confirmed before Big Viv could ask the question. "It was your mother. She's the one who wanted to put an end to your friendship with Deena. It was all her idea."

CHAPTER
THIRTY-ONE

It was seven o'clock in the morning and Nico was ready for bed. He'd spent most of the night looking for Sebastian and Dom and hadn't found them anywhere. It was like they had disappeared into thin air.

Well, he had one idea where they might be—and what they might be doing!—but when he'd knocked on their hotel room door, there had been no answer. Where could they be?

Then, during his more thorough search of the city that never sleeps, he walked by a 24-hour wedding chapel, and he stopped in his tracks. And blinked.

At first, he thought his eyes were playing tricks

on him. But as he stepped closer to the photographs on display and got a better look, one wedding photo jumped out at him. A photo of two grooms. And the grooms were Sebastian and Dom. There was no mistaking the wedding bands on their fingers, or the banner above them announcing, HAPPILY MARRIED!

Nico whipped out his cellphone and took photos. "I've got you now Bash!"

———

No.

No, no, no. This could not be happening.

Sebastian stared again at the wedding band on his finger, and then down at Dom. They were married. Married! But they couldn't be. He was engaged to Vivi.

Last night was a blur. There had been drinking. Too much drinking. Tequila. Vodka. Champagne. His pounding headache was proof of that. But he seemed to recall a wedding chapel and standing next to Dom. Reciting vows. Saying the words I do.

Dom slowly opened his eyes and smiled at Sebastian. It was a smile of pure happiness. "Good morning, handsome." He caressed his cheek. "Or should I say, Good morning, husband."

Even though his stomach was tied up in knots over what they had done, hearing the word come out of Dom's mouth loosened the knots and made Sebastian feel all warm and happy inside.

He was married. To this sweet, charming, handsome, irresistible man. He had a husband! Could there be anything better than that?

Sebastian leaned forward for a kiss, but stopped himself. Before they could have their own happily ever after, there was still the issue of the Evil Queen to deal with. Otherwise known as Big Viv. She was going to blow a gasket once she found out what he had done. All that planning. All the money that had been spent.

And then there was Vivi! What was her reaction going to be when she found out? Not to mention their families. He and Dom were both Italian; when their mothers found out they'd gotten married without them, there was going to be a tidal wave of maternal guilt coming their way.

"Okay, I see a thousand different expressions flying across your face right now." Dom propped himself up on a pillow. "What's going on? Tell me."

Sebastian said the words softly. "What have we done?"

Dom looked at him in disbelief. "What do you mean? We got married." Dom waved his left hand in front of Sebastian's face. "I asked, you said yes, we said 'I do' to make it official, and now we're going to live happily ever after."

Sebastian captured Dom's hand in his, holding it close to his heart. "Sweetie, that sounds wonderful, but it's not going to be that easy. Remember, I'm engaged to marry Vivi."

"Not anymore you're not." Dom yanked his hand away and waved his wedding band in front of Sebastian again. "See? Married to me!"

Sebastian swatted away Dom's hand, even though he was thrilled by his possessiveness. "Stop doing that." He flopped face first into his pillow.

"Babe, what's wrong?"

"What's wrong? We're due back to Brooklyn for my wedding, and unless I want to be a bigamist with a husband and a wife, I can't say 'I do.'"

"But you never really wanted to."

"That's not the point. God, what was I thinking last night?"

Dom's voice turned hard. "I thought you were thinking you wanted to marry the man you loved."

He threw back the sheets, revealing all his lovely nakedness, and started to leave the bed. "That you wanted to spend the rest of your life with *me*."

"Wait." Sebastian grabbed Dom by the arm and pulled him back into bed. "Of course I wanted to marry you. Of course I'm thrilled that we've made it legal. But don't you see? We've got a couple of hurdles we still need to get through."

"We'll get through them." Dom gave Sebastian a gentle kiss on the lips. "Together."

The gentle kiss soon turned into a heated one. Before things could progress any further, however, they were interrupted by a knock on the door.

"Did you order room service?" Sebastian asked.

Dom shook his head. "How could I order room service? I just woke up. Maybe you arranged it last night when we were upgraded to the honeymoon suite?"

Did I? Sebastian wondered. He had no memory of it. "Who is it?" Sebastian called out.

"Complimentary breakfast for the newlyweds."

Sebastian's sixth sense tingled, warning him that something was amiss. *Danger, Will Robinson! Danger!*

Sebastian turned to Dom. "If I ask you to do

something for me, will you do it? No questions asked."

"What?"

"Hide."

"Hide?" Dom repeated. "But why?"

"I'll explain later. For now, please just hide."

Dom sighed, but he left the bed and threw a robe on, slipping into the bathroom before closing the door. Once Dom was hidden, Sebastian threw on his own robe and answered the door.

Unsurprisingly, he found himself face to face with Nico. He knew he had recognized that voice.

"What do you want?" he asked, blocking Nico's entrance into the room.

Nico gave Sebastian a smile. A huge one, which only made Sebastian more nervous. Then, he held up his phone, sliding his finger across the screen. "Take a good look. What do you see?" Nico waved the phone in front of Sebastian's eyes. "I'll tell you what you see. Two grooms. You and Dom. Recently married. I guess there's not going to be a wedding in Brooklyn."

Sebastian knew there was only one way to deal with a bully. To stand up to him. He'd been doing it since high school, and he wasn't about to stop now. "What is this, blackmail? All along, you knew something was off about my engagement to Vivi, and now you have the proof. Congrats. I'm gay. I always have been and always will be. I guess you'll be flying back to Brooklyn later today to show those photos to Big Viv and blow our wedding out of the water."

Nico shook his head, slipping his phone back into his pocket. "No, Sebastian, I'm not here to blackmail you. I'm not here to cause trouble. I'm here for one thing and one thing only."

"What's that?" Sebastian asked with suspicion.

"Your help," Nico implored.

"With what?"

"Vivi."

"Vivi?" Sebastian stared at him in confusion. "I don't understand." What kind of game was he playing? Nico knew Vivi was his Achilles heel and that he would do anything for her. So, was she in some sort of trouble, or was this a trap? Regardless, Nico had said her name and now Sebastian was required to listen.

"You have to convince Vivi that I love her," Nico insisted. "That I want to marry her."

Those were the last words Sebastian had been expecting to hear. "What about Candy?"

Nico rolled his eyes. "There is no Candy.

Nothing is going on between us. It's Vivi I want. It's always been Vivi."

Sebastian didn't know why, but he opened the door and allowed Nico to enter the room. After closing it, he faced him. "Start talking."

"I know I was pretty lousy to you back in grammar school and high school. And I know I already apologized, but I'm going to do it again. I'm sorry. Really sorry. I can't undo all the things I did and said, but I want you to know, I didn't do it because you're gay. I was jealous. I was always jealous of you, especially of what you had with Vivi. Things were always so easy between the two of you. You were like two halves of the same whole."

"We were friends. Best friends. That's all. There was never anything romantic between us. Ever."

"I know that. Now. But back then, there were so many obstacles keeping us from being together and I couldn't do anything about them. Instead, I took it all out on you."

"And made my life miserable," Sebastian snapped, as all the past hurt resurfaced. "Do you have any idea what it was like for me? Always wondering what you were going to do or say next? Do you know what it's like to be different from everyone else when all you want to do is fit in? Do you know what it's like to be laughed at constantly?"

"I'm sorry," Nico said again. "But you stood up to me, Sebastian. You've always stood up to me and you've always been there for Vivi. After everything I did all those years ago, you don't have to help me, but I need your help. I wouldn't be here if I didn't."

"Isn't that sort of selfish? Apologizing now when you want something? Shouldn't you have apologized to me years ago?"

"Would you have listened? Would you have believed me?"

Sebastian sighed. "Probably not."

"The only reason I've wanted to expose this wedding as a sham is so I can have Vivi. I've lost her so many times over the years. I don't want to lose her again. I can't. I'll admit my aunt's motives for stopping the wedding might be different, but she's always had an issue with Big Viv."

"The feud," Sebastian said, rolling his eyes.

"The feud," Nico agreed. "Maybe, at first, I wanted to get even with Big Viv, too, for taking Vivi away from me all those years ago. But then, I asked myself if it would be worth it. Sure, I might get a small bit of satisfaction, but if I hurt her mother, I might lose Vivi. So, you know what I said to myself?"

"What?"

"Screw the feud. This is about me and Vivi finally being together, and if my aunt and Big Viv don't like it, then too bad."

"I believe you," Sebastian said. "I do."

"Does that mean you'll help me?"

"You know I would do anything for Vivi. And she loves you," Sebastian admitted, watching Nico's face light up as he said the words. "She always has, always will. What do I need to do?"

Before Nico could answer, there was another knock on the door.

"Bash? Are you awake? It's Vivi."

Nico panicked. "She can't find me here! You gotta hide me!"

Dom opened up the bathroom door and stuck his head out. "In here!"

Startled, Nico stared at Dom in disbelief, but he rushed into the bathroom, letting the door click shut as Sebastian opened the other one.

"What are you doing in the honeymoon suite?" Vivi asked as she breezed in. "When I went to your old room and you didn't answer, I called the front desk and they told me you had been upgraded. Why would they do that?"

"I can explain."

"Explain what?"

"This." Sebastian held up his hand with the wedding band on it.

Vivi's eyes widened with shock as she stared at Sebastian's hand. "You got married? To Dom?"

Sebastian slowly nodded his head.

"How could you do this to me?" she wailed, pounding him on the chest with her fists. "How?"

Sebastian knew she would be upset, but he hadn't expected this. "Vivi, calm down," he said as he tried to control her flying fists. "I know I broke my promise to you and I feel awful about it, but in my defense, I had too much to drink last night. When Dom and I decided to get married, in that moment, I went for what I wanted most—him."

"You idiot!" Vivi shrieked. "I will not calm down! How could you get married without me, your best friend, being there?"

Sebastian dropped Vivi's fists. "Wait, you're not upset that I married Dom?"

"Of course not! You love him. You want to be with him. Why would I stand in the way of true love?"

"Well, for weeks we've kind of been pretending we're the ones who are in love. There's a wedding happening in Brooklyn for us next weekend, remember?"

"I'm sorry," Vivi said, sinking down on the unmade bed and scattering rose petals to the floor. "I'm sorry I put you through all that. I know you only did it because I put you on the spot. I was coming here to tell you I can't marry you."

Sebastian wasn't sure he'd heard her correctly. "Why not?"

"Because I realized something last night. I love Nico. I want to marry him."

"But what about your mother? What about Deena?"

"I don't care what they think. If they're unhappy, let them be unhappy. I'm tired of being told what to do. I've always loved Nico and I want to be with him."

Sebastian was just about to tell Vivi she should say those words directly to Nico when there was another knock on the door.

"Expecting anyone?" Vivi asked.

"No," Sebastian said with a worried frown as a new knot formed in his stomach. He'd already had two unexpected visitors this morning. He didn't know who the third could possibly be.

The knocking became more urgent as Sebastian

walked over to the door. He gasped when he opened it. Standing on the other side of the door was Deena. An extremely smug looking Deena.

Uh oh. This wasn't good at all.

"Good morning, Sebastian," Deena purred. "You're looking well this morning. Well, a little hungover, but who wouldn't after their wedding night?"

"Wedding night?" Sebastian repeated. How could she know he and Dom were married?

"And look who else is here," Deena said, as she sauntered into the room. "Vivi! I get to share my news with both of you at the same time."

"What are you talking about, Deena?" Vivi impatiently asked, rising from the bed.

"Did anyone ever tell you that you sound exactly like your mother when you're pissed off?"

"I'll take that as a compliment. Now, get to the point," Vivi urged.

Deena shrugged. "Sure. There isn't going to be any wedding in Brooklyn next weekend," she announced.

"Really?" Vivi asked. "And why is that?"

"Because your groom is already married." Deena held up her phone, showing them a photo of Sebastian and Dom's marriage license. "I was heading back to my hotel last night after my show when I saw you and your new husband coming out of that wedding chapel. Naturally, I was curious. All it took was a few bucks to the minister to find out about his latest wedding. Wasn't it nice of him to let me take this photo when I asked?" She turned to Vivi. "Can you imagine your mother's reaction when she finds out? Not to mention everyone else's. I can't wait to share this. You've made her the biggest fool in Bensonhurst!"

Sebastian was silent. Vivi, too. Neither one of them had wanted to hurt Big Viv. Yes, she could be domineering and controlling, but it always came from a place of love. Love of family. Love of friends. They had just wanted to make her happy. But in trying to do that, they had both made themselves unhappy and the entire situation had spiraled out of control.

Now, Deena was threatening to blow everything up before they could do damage control. They couldn't allow that to happen, but how could they stop her? Sebastian didn't think reasoning would work. There was too much history and animosity between Big Viv and Deena. It was a constant game of one upmanship, and Deena now had the upper hand.

But before Sebastian or Vivi could say anything, Nico stepped out of the bathroom. "Aunt Dee, what do you think you're doing?"

Sebastian watched as Vivi turned her head in the direction of the bathroom, a look of shock on her face. It matched Deena's. But quickly, Deena's shocked expression transformed into one of craftiness.

"Finally putting an end to this sham engagement, that's what!" she gleefully exclaimed. "Your old high school chum got married last night, but not to Vivi. He married his wedding planner."

"I know."

"You do?"

"I do."

"Good. Now, all we have to do is drop the bomb on Big Viv. You can back me up since you obviously know what's going on."

Nico shook his head. "No."

"No?" an outraged Deena exclaimed. "What do you mean no?"

"You heard me. N-O. No. We're not doing that."

"Why not?"

"Because there's still going to be a wedding in Brooklyn. Only instead of Sebastian being the groom, it's going to be me."

"You want to marry me?" Vivi whispered.

"Yes," Nico said, turning to face her. "I've wanted to marry you for such a long time, but I never had the courage to do anything about it. I thought you didn't want me or you wouldn't have me. Because, you know, the feud."

"I've always wanted you. I've always loved you. I fell in love with you the very first day I saw you."

"I heard everything you said to Sebastian."

"Then, why did you keep hiding?"

"I was about to come out when my aunt showed up, and I wanted to hear what she had to say." He gave Deena a stern look. "In case I had to remind her who's calling the shots."

"Why were you hiding in the first place?" Vivi asked.

"I came here this morning to ask for Sebastian's help."

"With what?"

"A question." Nico closed the distance between himself and Vivi, wrapping his arms around her. "Two questions, actually."

"Okay," she said, gazing up at him. "Ask away."

"I want you to be honest with me."

Vivi nodded. "Okay. I will. Promise."

"Am I the father of your baby?"

Vivi softly nibbled on her lower lip, then whispered, "Yes."

Nico let out a whoop of joy, lifting her up in a hug. "We're having a baby!"

"You're happy about it?"

"Of course I am." Nico gave Vivi a long, lingering kiss. "Very happy."

"What's your other question?"

"Will you marry me?"

Vivi didn't hesitate to answer. She threw her arms around Nico and gave him the biggest hug of her life. It was fifteen years' worth of hugs. Hugs that she should have been giving to him every single day, along with kisses and smiles and whispers and knowing looks. And most importantly, along with all the mentions of "I love you" given so many times over the years that it would be impossible to keep track of how many times she uttered the words. She held on to Nico as tightly as she could, inhaling his scent, afraid if she let go, she would find herself suddenly waking up from a dream, all alone in her bed. Because this was what she had always wanted. To be with him. She kissed him. A deep, long, lingering kiss, which he returned with a staggering amount of passion. And in that kiss, Vivi knew she had found happiness. Forever. Because she was finally going to be with the man she had always loved.

"Yes. Yes, yes, yes! Now, show me that ring you've been carrying around in your pocket."

"How do you know about the ring?"

"A friend told me." Vivi waggled her fingers in front of Nico's face. "The ring. I want to see this gorgeous engagement ring."

"Absolutely not!" Deena screeched. "The two of you cannot get married."

Nico glared at his aunt. "Why not?"

"You know what her mother did to me all those years ago."

"That's not my problem. It's yours. Vivi and I are getting married, and there's nothing you can do to stop us."

Deena threw her arms up in the air. "Fine. Marry her. But don't think her mother isn't going to try to put up roadblocks."

"Then help us with those roadblocks. Please? For me, your favorite nephew?"

"You're my only nephew," Deena grudgingly pointed out.

"Don't you see, Aunt Dee? If you made the first move, if you told Big Viv you were sorry, it might fix things between the two of you."

A look of horror washed over Deena's face. "You expect *me* to be the one to say I'm sorry to Big Viv? Never! I wasn't the one who did anything wrong. I never, ever understood why she stopped talking to me. It was like a knife to my heart. She was my very best friend."

"If anyone should be saying I'm sorry, it's me."

At the sound of the unexpected voice, everyone turned around and gasped.

Standing in the doorway, staring at all of them, was Big Viv.

CHAPTER
THIRTY-TWO

Big Viv didn't know where to begin. There was so much to tell.

After she'd left Carla's, she'd gone back to her house and had it out with her mother, who confirmed everything Carla confessed. And not only had her mother paid Carla to withhold her letters, her mother also admitted to deleting every phone message Deena had left on the family answering machine and not passing along messages if she spoke to Deena on the phone. Big Viv was speechless. She hadn't thought Carla was lying, but she still couldn't believe the way she'd been manipulated by her mother all those years ago.

And the old woman showed not one bit of remorse.

"That girl was trash," she said. "Always taking you out of the neighborhood. Always pushing you to do more. Want more! That girl gave you ideas. Crazy ideas! If I hadn't cut her out of your life, you would have been chasing after her to California and God only knows what would have happened to you out there. It's bad enough you stayed here alone when we all went back to Italy."

"Deena didn't do so bad for herself," Big Viv said.

Her mother spat. "She's a *putana*! We all know how she made it in Hollywood. On her back!"

"You don't know anything about Deena. How can you say that?"

Her mother shook her head in disgust. "You were always stupid when it came to that girl. How I raised such a stupid daughter, I'll never know. I can't stand to look at you. I'm going to stay at a hotel until the wedding, and then once it's over, I'll be on the next plane back to Italy."

Big Viv shrugged, trying to hold herself together. She wasn't going to cry or show her mother how upset she was. Foolishly, she had thought maybe, just maybe, Vivi's wedding would help bring her and her mother closer, but she had been wrong. Now, she knew once her mother went back to Italy, she would probably never see her again. "If that's what you want, I'll make some calls for you."

"I can do it myself." Her mother looked at her one last time with disappointment blazing in her eyes before leaving the room. "*Stupida.*"

After finishing with her mother, Big Viv booked the next flight to Las Vegas. She wasn't sure what she was going to do or say once she got out there, but she knew that's where she needed to be. As she was leaving the house for the airport, Carla showed up on her doorstep.

"What do you want?" Big Viv asked.

Carla handed Big Viv a pile of letters. "These belong to you. They're Deena's letters."

Big Viv snatched them out of Carla's hands like they were the most precious thing in the world.

"Don't worry, they're all sealed," she said as Big Viv started flipping through them. "I don't know why I kept them all these years. But they're yours. They belong to you. Deep down, I guess I always knew that."

"You think giving me these letters makes up for what you did?" Big Viv spat as her anger started to bubble again. "It doesn't. We might not have been close friends, but we were friends, and I always tried to be good to you. To your family. But all that time, you were stabbing me in the back. Do you know how much that hurts?"

"I'm sorry," Carla said, eyes brimming with tears. "I thought—"

Big Viv held up a hand. "Stop! I don't want to hear what you thought," she snapped, trying to keep her temper in check, trying not to say vicious, hurtful things. Because all she wanted to do was lash out. It was taking all her self-control not to.

"Can you ever forgive me?" Carla asked, lips trembling.

"I don't know," Big Viv answered honestly. "I just don't know."

Big Viv read the letters on the flight to Las Vegas. Her heart ached. The early letters were fun and upbeat as Deena told her about her new life. The parties she went to. The people she was meeting. But as the weeks and months went by, the reality of life in Hollywood began to sink in for Deena. There were challenges she faced, including producers and directors with grabby hands. It was way before the era of #MeToo, so Deena had no choice but to suck it up. Somehow, she survived. All it took was one role and after that, everything else fell into place.

"Deena didn't do anything wrong," Big Viv announced.

"See!" Deena triumphantly exclaimed. "I told you. All these years, she's been the one holding a grudge."

"That's right, I have. But not for the reason you think. I didn't do anything wrong, either."

"What do you mean? You just said you were holding a grudge."

"I know what I said," Big Viv explained. "But all these years, I thought you turned your back on me. On our friendship. That you thought you were better than me."

"I never—"

"I know! I know *now*. But back then, I didn't. For years, I didn't. I was made to believe that."

"Made to believe that?" Deena repeated. "I don't understand."

"I never knew about the letters."

"Letters?"

Big Viv reached into her oversized Louis Vuitton shoulder bag and pulled out the stack. "These are the letters you sent me from California. Letters I never received."

"How could that be? You're holding them in your hand."

"They were never delivered."

"What?"

"Carla kept them."

"Carla? Why would she do that?"

"My mother," Big Viv said grimly. "My mother paid her to do it. And she did other things, too. All to keep you out of my life."

And in that moment, Deena realized Big Viv was telling her the truth. They could all see it on her face. Deena's guard dropped. Her face softened. All her hostility melted away. It was like the clock had been turned back to 1977.

For the first time in years, Deena wasn't angry at Big Viv.

And Big Viv was no longer angry at her, as evidenced when she walked over to her and gave her a long, long hug.

"I'm sorry," Big Viv said, her eyes brimming with tears. "Please don't keep hating me. I couldn't stand it if you did. I want us to be friends again."

At first, Deena was speechless. Then, she found her voice. "I never hated you. Ever. All these years, I was hurt. All those times I visited the bakery, I kept hoping we could start over. But I could never find the words. Instead, I was always so mean and horrible." Deena shuddered. "The things I said."

"I was just as bad."

"You were," Deena laughed. "But they always say you hurt the ones you love."

"We've lost forty-five years," Big Viv said. "All that time! We'll never be able to get it back."

"No, we won't. But we've got so many years ahead of us. And we'll make up for all that lost time if it's the last thing we do. Whenever I came to the bakery, I wanted to ask you why you never answered my letters or returned my calls, but I was afraid to. I thought you didn't approve of what I had done. I thought you were judging me."

Big Viv gasped. "Judging you? Never! Even though I didn't show it, I was so proud of you."

"You were?" a shocked Deena asked.

"Yes, I was. Why wouldn't I be? You went to California to become an actress and you did!"

Big Viv gave Deena another hug and then stopped when she noticed everyone staring. "What are you all looking at?" she asked. "Haven't you ever seen two friends kiss and make up?"

"Ma, I'm thrilled you and Deena are friends again," Vivi said, taking a tentative step toward her. "It will make what I have to tell you so much easier."

"What do you have to tell me? You look so scared."

Vivi took a deep breath and she plunged in.

"SebastianandIaren'tgettingmarried," she said in a rush of words.

"You're not getting married," Big Viv slowly stated, raising one eyebrow. "Why not?"

"Because I'm gay," Sebastian said. "We didn't mean—"

Vivi cut him off. "No, Bash, let me. I started this whole mess. I need to clean it up. Ma, Sebastian isn't the father of my baby."

Big Viv stared at Vivi, shocked. "Then, who the hell is?"

"Nico," Vivi whispered, standing next to him and taking his hand in hers. "And it's Nico I'm going to marry."

At first, Big Viv was silent. Then, she turned to Nico with a glare. "You knocked up my daughter. Got anything you want to say?"

"Can I call you Ma?" he asked.

Big Viv rolled her eyes, turning her attention back to Vivi and Sebastian. "All this time, the two of you have been lying to me?" she asked, eyes narrowing.

"I wouldn't call it lying exactly," Sebastian started to explain.

"What would you call it?"

"Misleading you?"

"Lying," Big Viv corrected.

"Okay, yes. Lying," Sebastian agreed. "But I did it for a reason."

"You did it for my Vivi," Big Viv answered for him. "But why would you do that? You pretended to be in love with her. You pretended you were the father of her baby. You put up with me and all my crazy wedding plans! Why would you do all that?"

Sebastian shrugged. "You have to ask? It's simple. She's my best friend. She needed me."

"Ma, don't be mad at Sebastian. I put him on the spot. He didn't have a choice. I sweetened the deal by offering to back his own bakery, and we're still going to do that, Ma. We owe it to him. We've both put him through hell, and we stopped him from being who he really wanted to be with."

Big Viv shook her head. "No, he had a choice. Everyone always has a choice."

"He didn't!" Vivi exclaimed. "I just told you."

"Let me finish, Vivi. Please," Big Viv said.

"Fine!" Vivi huffed.

"Sebastian had a choice, and he chose to support you. He stuck by your side. He waited for you to do what you had to do, which was tell me the truth. He was a friend." Big Viv gave Deena a sad look. "A better friend than I ever was."

Big Viv went to Sebastian and hugged him tight. Then, she walked over to Nico and did the same. "I'm sorry I was so unfair to you all these years. You've always loved my daughter and I've stood in your way. I never gave you a chance."

"Does that mean I can marry Vivi?"

"Have you asked me for her hand?"

"Ma!" Vivi wailed.

Big Viv snapped her finger. "I want to see the ring."

"Oh, me too!" Deena exclaimed.

"Me three!" Sebastian chimed in.

Nico reached into his pocket and pulled out a small blue velvet box, flipping open the lid. "Mrs. Confetta, I'd like the honor of marrying your daughter."

Big Viv took a closer look at the ring. "It'll do. For now."

"Ma!" Vivi wailed again.

"What?"

"The ring doesn't matter." But Vivi still took a peek at it. "It's gorgeous!" she shrieked, sticking her hand out in front of Nico. "Put it on my finger!"

"Okay, but we have to do this right." Nico got down on one knee and took Vivi's hand in his.

"Vivianna Louise Confetta," he asked, "will you marry me?"

"Yes!" Vivi happily exclaimed as he slid the ring on her finger. It was a perfect fit.

"You really want to marry him?" Big Viv asked.

"Yes."

"Then, marry him."

"Thank you, Ma," Vivi sniffed, her eyes welling up with tears. "Thank you for everything. I know you did what you did all those years ago because you love me."

"I love you so much." Big Viv hugged her daughter, kissing the top of her head. "I should have trusted you to make your own decision, but I didn't. I was afraid of seeing you get hurt. If Nico makes you happy—and I can see that he does—then nothing would make me happier than to have him as my son-in-law."

———

Dominick stayed hidden in the bathroom. It seemed like the smartest thing to do. There was so much going on out in the suite.

He stepped away from the partially opened door where he'd been eavesdropping and sat on the edge of the bathtub, sorting through everything he'd heard.

It was finally over. No more engagement. No more wedding.

Sebastian was a free man. And being free meant he didn't have to be married.

What had they been thinking last night? Yes, it had been wonderful exchanging vows with Sebastian, but they had been drinking. A lot. Perhaps they hadn't been as clear-headed as they should have been. They'd been spontaneous. Impulsive. Maybe they shouldn't have gotten married so quickly. The love was there, but maybe it needed to be stronger to make sure their marriage lasted. Because he loved Sebastian and wanted to be married to him for the rest of his life. But maybe they needed to wait a bit, just to be sure.

"How long are you going to hide in here?" Sebastian asked, sticking his head in the bathroom. "You're missing all the fun. We're going to go down to the bar and celebrate with mimosas."

"I didn't want to interrupt."

"When you get a bunch of crazy Italians together, the only thing you can do is interrupt!" Sebastian held out his hand, laughing. "Come on. Let's get dressed and go."

Dom held up his ring finger. "Did you know if we can get a quickie marriage in Las Vegas, we can also get a quickie divorce? I Googled it."

"Divorce?" Sebastian gasped. "Why would we want a divorce? Are you saying you want to end this marriage?"

"No!" Dominick exclaimed. "Do you?"

"Why would I?"

"You needed an out. So you wouldn't have to marry Vivi. But now Vivi's with Nico." Dominick shrugged. "I just assumed..."

Sebastian swept Dom into his arms. "That's not why I married you, you adorable man. Okay, we both had way too much to drink last night, but we never wouldn't have gotten married if we didn't have feelings for each other, right? Don't you remember what I told you in bed this morning? I wanted to marry you."

"But we haven't been together that long. Our courtship hasn't exactly been smooth. It's been rocky, if anything."

"What does it matter? Sometimes, when you meet the right person, you just *know*. I knew as soon as I met you, Dom. And we want to be together, don't we?"

"Yes."

"I married you because I love you. Because I want to be with you. Always. I'm committed to you, Dom. To us. I want to make this work. Don't you?"

They were the words Dominick had been waiting for, but hadn't known until he heard them. He slowly nodded. "I want this to work."

"So, let's make this work." Sebastian gave him a kiss on the lips. "It's probably not going to be easy all the time. And I'm sure we'll have challenges. But that's the way it is in any relationship. I'm willing to put in the work if you are. I love you, Dom. And if you give me the chance, I'll tell you every day."

"I love you, too," Dominick whispered. "This summer has been crazy, but a good kind of crazy. Life with you will never be dull, Sebastian."

Sebastian laughed. "That I can guarantee. Now, here's a question. How do you feel about a double wedding in Brooklyn? I know we just said our vows last night, but I'm sure Nico and Vivi wouldn't mind sharing their day with us. After all, you did most of the work planning it."

"Weddings are my life. I say yes! I'd love to marry you again."

EPILOGUE

It was the perfect day for a summer double wedding.

The sun was out, shining bright, but it wasn't humid. The church was packed. The whole neighborhood had turned out.

But it wasn't just for the wedding. Everyone also wanted to see Big Viv and Deena together again.

And they didn't disappoint, arriving together at the church in a white limo and walking down the aisle arm in arm, dressed to the nines. Since Las Vegas, they had been joined at the hip, catching up on each other's lives.

Finally, the feud was over.

Everything at the church went smoothly, and both Big Viv and Deena bawled their eyes out when both couples walked down the aisle.

The last week had been a whirlwind. So much to do, and so little time to do it in. Dom took over the rest of the planning of the wedding. Sebastian made two wedding cakes—a dark chocolate cake with Amaretto, dark chocolate ganache, and chocolate buttercream filling decorated with sugar flowers for Vivi and Nico, while he and Dom went the traditional route with a vanilla cake filled with lemon mousse, strawberries, and raspberries.

The day before the wedding, Big Viv and Vivi gave Sebastian a check to open up his own bakery. He turned it down. As touched as he was that they wanted to help him financially, he told them he was going to put his dream of opening a brick and mortar bakery on hold for now. Instead, he planned to buy a food truck and turn it into a mobile bakery, building word of mouth up as he made his way from one borough to another each week with The Bakequeery!

And while their families couldn't attend the wedding because it was happening so quickly, Sebastian and Dom decided they would have a second wedding in nine months once Nico and Vivi's baby was born. After all, they were going to be the baby's godfathers, so why not have a double celebration?

Liam was Sebastian and Dom's best man. When

they got back from Las Vegas, he confessed to both of them that he'd acted so over-the-top and flirty with Dom because he wanted the two of them to be together. He'd hoped that by igniting Sebastian's jealousy, he would fight harder for Dom.

"I never would have crossed the line with Dom, you know that, right?" Liam had asked.

"You could have just told me that," Sebastian had laughed. "It would have spared you a baking soda bath!"

"I was having too much fun watching you freak out. But I knew you had it in you to get the guy you wanted." Liam had then given Sebastian a hug. "You're like a brother to me. I wanted to see you happy. I hope one day I'm lucky enough to find someone just as special as Dom."

It was during the wedding reception as Sebastian and Dom were taking their first dance that Sebastian noticed one of the guests. He blinked in disbelief.

"Dom, take a look across the room. Are my eyes deceiving me or is that—"

"John Travolta!" Dom gasped. "What's he doing at our wedding?"

The music for their dance ended and they hurried off the dance floor, where they quickly found Nico and Vivi at the hot hors d'oeuvres table.

"Did you know he was going to be here?" Sebastian asked Vivi.

Vivi popped a stuffed mushroom in her mouth. "Who?"

Dom pointed across the room. "Him!"

She followed Dom's finger and gasped. "It's John Travolta!"

Nico choked on his glass of champagne mid sip. "John Travolta is at our wedding? Where? I gotta get a picture!"

"And look!" Sebastian exclaimed. "He's going over to talk to Big Viv."

The foursome watched as John charmed Big Viv, taking her by the arm and whispering in her ear, making her laugh while whisking her out onto the dance floor.

"He's holding her awfully tight," Vivi murmured.

"Oh my God," Dom whispered. "Your mother is getting lucky with John Travolta!"

"What are you four whispering about?" Deena asked, appearing behind them with a glass of champagne.

"Did you know he was going to be here, Aunt Dee?" Nico asked.

"Who?"

"John Travolta!"

Deena gazed at the dance floor, and a smile spread across her face. "He made it!"

"How do you know John Travolta?" Dom asked. "Did he come to Brooklyn for the 45th anniversary of *Saturday Night Fever*?"

"Silly boy!" Deena took a sip from her flute. "That's not John Travolta."

"Are you sure? It looks an awful lot like him."

"Well, of course he does." Deena leaned forward with a conspiratorial smile and whispered, "He's a John Travolta impersonator. But I told him to keep that to himself. I hired him for the *Saturday Night Fever* celebration next weekend. The real John couldn't make it. No one will be the wiser. Anyway, since he was in town early, I slipped him a few extra dollars to give Big Viv some TLC, if you know what I mean." She winked and took another sip of champagne. "I figured why not, right?"

"Aunt Dee!" Nico wailed. "Are you crazy?"

"What's the big deal? He's great in the sack. I speak from first-hand experience. I wouldn't do my girl wrong. It's been way too long since she's had some lovin'."

"But if Big Viv finds out he's not the real John Travolta," Nico began. "And that you knew..."

"Well, she's not going to find out, is she?" Deena

said, giving them all a pointed look. "It's a little white lie between friends." She pointed at each of them with her champagne flute. "One that I expect you all to keep to yourselves. *Capisce?* Now, excuse me. I'm going to go mingle with your guests!"

Deena left, leaving the four of them just staring at each other.

Sebastian spoke first. "We say nothing."

"Nothing," Dom chimed in.

"Nothing," Vivi and Nico said together.

"Because if the truth ever comes out," Sebastian warned, "it will be the start of another feud. And I don't know about the rest of you, but I've had my fill of feuds." He grabbed four champagne flutes from a passing waiter and handed them out to Nico, Vivi, and Dom. "A toast," he said, raising his glass. "To us."

"To us," Nico echoed.

"To happily ever afters," Vivi added.

"To happily ever afters," Sebastian repeated before giving Dom a kiss. "I know I've found mine."

ACKNOWLEDGMENTS

Special thanks to my agent, Evan Marshall, for all his advice, help, and support during the writing of this novel. Special thanks to the team at Harbor Lane Books, especially my editor, Michelle, for her insightful comments and editing. Thanks, too, to all my family and friends, who listened to me talk about this book while I was writing it, and to my girl Astoria, Rosanna Chiofalo Aponte, the Vivi to my Sebastian, who inspired the Funyuns scene.

ABOUT THE AUTHOR

Author photo taken by Kevin Mathis

John Salzone grew up in Bensonhurst, Brooklyn. His father was one of eight and he was lucky enough to have both sets of grandparents living next door, as well as two sets of aunts, uncles and cousins living on the same block. Growing up he had twenty-four cousins and his fondest memories are of family gatherings and vacations when everyone would be together, talking in a combination of English and Italian. Parts of *An Offer He Can't Refuse* comes from the memories of his childhood and growing up Italian. John has worked in publishing as an editor, published a number of *New York Times* bestselling authors and written a variety of adult and young adult novels under the names John Hall (*Homecoming Queen; Killer Christmas; Is He or Isn't He?*), Sabrina James (*Secret Santa; Party Girl*) and Jennifer Hall (*Star Quality*). He's currently working on a new rom-com, *A Christmas He Can't Refuse*. He loves hearing from readers and you can email him at: sjamesauthor@yahoo.com

ABOUT THE PUBLISHER

Harbor Lane Books, LLC is a US-based independent digital publisher of commercial fiction, non-fiction, and poetry.

Connect with Harbor Lane Books on their website (www.harborlanebooks.com) and social media @harborlanebooks.

facebook.com/harborlanebooks

x.com/harborlanebooks

instagram.com/harborlanebooks

bsky.app/profile/harborlanebooks.bsky.social

tiktok.com/@harborlanebooks

threads.com/harborlanebooks

youtube.com/harborlanebooks

pinterest.com/harborlanebooks

* 9 7 8 1 9 6 3 7 0 5 2 9 4 *